"You connected with her, Jess. That's the most important thing."

"Talking football is one thing." He rubbed the back of his neck. "Dad talk is something else."

"Sincerity is half the battle." She settled her hand on his arm and felt the heat of his skin through his sleeve.

He met her gaze, and something dark and intense heated in his eyes. "I could *sincerely* screw up that little girl's life without your input. I need *you,* Libby."

The passion of his focus on her face trapped all the air in her chest and she couldn't breathe.

I need you.

The words were deeply personal and became sexually charged, making the blood pound in her ears. Libby swayed toward him but would never be clear on who moved first. In the blink of an eye or the beat of a heart, his mouth was on hers.

Dear Reader,

It's December!

That's exclamation-point-worthy, since I live in Las Vegas and triple-digit heat is just a bad memory. Last year, ten days before Christmas, we actually had snow. Honest. I took pictures, because it felt like a little miracle.

Now the holidays are here again!

This time of year teases our senses with food, decorations, lights, the fragrance of pine. Some of my favorite movies, books and stories are about Christmas. *It's a Wonderful Life. Miracle on 34th Street.* Like the themes of Silhouette Special Edition, love and family are at the heart of these tales. They leave us smiling and possibly reaching for a tissue—in a good way.

Being part of the Harlequin family and sixty years of wonderful romances is a dream come true for me. Especially since I'm a steadfast supporter of happy endings.

So, with 2009 drawing to a close, I hope all of you have a very happy ending to this year. May your December include mistletoe, magic and miracles.

Happy holidays!

Teresa Southwick

A NANNY UNDER THE MISTLETOE

TERESA SOUTHWICK

Silhouette®

SPECIAL EDITION®

Published by Silhouette Books

America's Publisher of Contemporary Romance

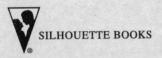

SILHOUETTE BOOKS

ISBN-13: 978-0-373-65496-3

Recycling programs
for this product may
not exist in your area.

A NANNY UNDER THE MISTLETOE

Visit Silhouette Books at www.eHarlequin.com

Printed in U.S.A.

Books by Teresa Southwick

Silhouette Special Edition

The Summer House #1510
  "Courting Cassandra"
Midnight, Moonlight &
  Miracles #1517
It Takes Three #1631
~*The Beauty Queen's Makeover* #1699
At the Millionaire's Request #1769
§§*Paging Dr. Daddy* #1886
‡*The Millionaire and the M.D.* #1894
‡*When a Hero Comes Along* #1905
‡*Expecting the Doctor's Baby* #1924
‡‡*Marrying the Virgin Nanny* #1960
‡*The Doctor's Secret Baby* #1982
‡‡*The Nanny and Me* #2001
‡‡*A Nanny Under the Mistletoe* #2014

Silhouette Books

The Fortunes of Texas:
  Shotgun Vows

Silhouette Romance

Wedding Rings and
  Baby Things #1209
The Bachelor's Baby #1233
**A Vow, a Ring, a Baby Swing* #1349
The Way to a Cowboy's Heart #1383
**And Then He Kissed Me* #1405
**With a Little T.L.C.* #1421
The Acquired Bride #1474
**Secret Ingredient: Love* #1495
**The Last Marchetti Bachelor* #1513
***Crazy for Lovin' You* #1529
**This Kiss #1541
***If You Don't Know by Now* #1560
***What If We Fall in Love?* #1572
Sky Full of Promise #1624
†*To Catch a Sheik* #1674
†*To Kiss a Sheik* #1686
†*To Wed a Sheik* #1696

††*Baby, Oh Baby* #1704
††*Flirting with the Boss* #1708
††*An Heiress on His*
  Doorstep #1712
§*That Touch of Pink* #1799
§*In Good Company* #1807
§*Something's Gotta Give* #1815

*The Marchetti Family
**Destiny, Texas
†Desert Brides
††If Wishes Were…
§Buy-a-Guy
~Most Likely To…
§§The Wilder Family
‡The Men of Mercy Medical
‡‡The Nanny Network

TERESA SOUTHWICK

lives with her husband in Las Vegas, the city that reinvents itself every day. An avid fan of romance novels, she is delighted to be living out her dream of writing for Silhouette Books.

To my friend Mary Karlik,
a talented writer and extraordinarily strong woman.
You're proof that the best things do come in small
packages. I hope 2010 brings you nothing but good things.

Chapter One

Until now, Libby Bradford had never understood how it felt to be so angry you couldn't see straight. At least being this furious kept the grief at bay. Or maybe her fear was so big there was no room for the sadness.

She stared across the utilitarian oak desk in her boss's office. "I really need to talk to someone."

Probably it was the thread of desperation in her voice that made Ginger Davis shut off the computer. "Just a guess, but you didn't come to see me just to discuss the newest show at the Hard Rock Hotel. I'm listening."

Humor normally took the edge off Libby's intensity, but not this time. "Jess Donnelly is going to take Morgan Rose away from me."

"*The* Jess Donnelly?"

"Is there another one?" Libby couldn't imagine the world was big enough for two of him. At least not in his world. "I'm talking about Las Vegas's most eligible and obscenely rich bachelor."

It wasn't often Ginger looked surprised, but she did now. An attractive, brown-eyed brunette somewhere near fifty, she could pass for twenty years younger and it would be pathetically easy for her. Maybe because she loved what she did. As president and CEO of The Nanny Network, she placed thoroughly vetted nannies with famous and wealthy families who cherished competence and confidentiality in equal parts. She had also opened Nooks and Nannies, a preschool that included child care as well as parent and caregiver enrichment classes. Libby was a teacher here.

"Now it makes sense."

Huh?

"What makes sense?" Libby asked her boss. "His attorney called and said that when Jess has child care in place he will take custody of Morgan."

"Mr. Donnelly contacted me about hiring a live-in nanny."

"He did?" Fear balled in Libby's belly.

"Yes. I explained that I recently had two of my employees leave the agency to get married." Ginger removed her glasses. "But you didn't come by my office to hear that I'm shorthanded."

"Not really. It's Morgan I'm concerned about."

"Since Mr. Donnelly didn't share details, I had no idea that he was looking for a nanny for *your* Morgan. I had the impression that your friend Charity left her daughter to you."

Hearing her best friend's name brought a fresh wave of sorrow that hurt Libby's heart. Charity and her husband, Ben, had been in Africa for ten months on a humanitarian mission. They'd been killed by a rebel faction in a raid on the village where they were working.

"No one thought they wouldn't come home." Libby's

voice broke and she stopped, trying to manage the unmanageable emotions.

"Apparently someone thought about it. Otherwise Mr. Donnelly wouldn't be making inquiries about child care," Ginger gently reminded her.

If Libby had been less emotional and more rational she would have commended Morgan's parents for taking care of the details. Except she'd fallen in love with the child she was caring for and giving her up to a man like Jess Donnelly seemed wrong on so many levels.

"Jess *was* named Morgan's guardian in her parents' will," she finally admitted.

"I see."

"I don't," Libby said, squeezing her hands together in her lap. She'd always thought this office a warm place, what with its friendly oak desk and orange and yellow wall prints. But today everything felt cold.

"Why do you question their decision?"

Libby slid forward to the edge of her chair. "Because Charity and Ben trusted *me* with their child when they went halfway around the world."

Ginger's voice was full of gentle sympathy when she asked, "Are you angry because they put a humanitarian effort ahead of their daughter's well-being? Or because they died?"

"Both," Libby said without thinking.

Ginger nodded. "You grew up with Charity and were best friends. You told me that her primary goal in life was to make the world a better place."

"And isn't that ironic? Because the world is so much worse for her not being in it."

Libby had spent more time at Charity's house than with her own messed-up family because there wasn't any tension there and everyone was welcomed with open arms, accepted in a way Libby would never be where she lived. Her friend's folks took the girls to nursing homes, hospitals and women's shelters to give back to their community and make a difference.

"Charity was raised to help people. But now my primary concern has to be raising Morgan the way Charity would want. Her child's welfare is the most important thing."

"It seems to me that she'll be well taken care of."

Not by Jess Donnelly. The man was certainly handsome, wealthy and powerful. From firsthand experience Libby knew he was also arrogant, selfish and shallow. She'd met him the first time when Charity and Ben got married. Her attraction to him was instantaneous. The earth moved. Lightning struck. Cupid's arrow nailed her right smack in the heart.

He'd flirted and fixed his intense blue eyes on her. His thick dark hair and Irish good looks had made quite a lasting impression. She'd have been his for the asking. But he'd never asked.

Actually, he'd left with the other blonde bridesmaid, the buxom one Libby still fondly thought of as the wedding slut. In the nearly six years since Morgan's birth, Libby and Jess had occasionally seen each other, at Morgan's christening, birthday parties, Christmas. Every time their paths crossed, she felt the pull of attraction even though Jess would stick out his hand and say he didn't believe they'd met before, then proceed to introduce himself.

The first time Libby gave him the benefit of the doubt, believing a new hairdo and ten-pound weight loss made her look different. After that it became clear that her breasts just weren't big enough to snag his attention, let alone make her name worthy of remembering.

She pushed the humiliating past from her mind and looked at Ginger. "You think he can really take care of Morgan?"

"Mr. Donnelly certainly has the means to provide for her."

"It takes more than money to raise a child."

"I couldn't agree more," Ginger said. "It's too bad the two of you can't co-parent."

"What do you mean?"

"He has the resources, you have the heart. Seems like a partnership made in child-rearing heaven."

Libby's mind started to hum as an idea began to take shape. "I could be her nanny."

Ginger stared at her. "You already work here at the preschool."

"Which will save you time in the vetting process since I'm already a Nanny Network employee."

Her boss frowned. "Since you have a personal history with the client, I'm not sure this would be an ideal situation."

"I respectfully disagree. Personal history isn't how I'd describe what we have. A handful of get-togethers over the years." And none of them had been the least bit personal, she thought with a mixture of annoyance and yearning that annoyed her even more. "He and I both knew and cared about Morgan's parents. She's a child who needs all the love and support she can get right now. The last thing she needs is to be yanked away from what's familiar and plopped into life with a stern guardian she barely knows."

"You make it sound like a wacky version of *Jane Eyre.*"

"Not my intention," Libby assured her. "Just the opposite. It seems like a win-win situation. You said yourself that with his money and my maternal skills we'd make the perfect parents."

"That was an off-the-cuff comment."

"But it makes sense," Libby said, warming to the role

of persuader. "You said you're short-handed right now. This is the perfect solution. I can do double duty—take care of her for Jess and continue to teach here at the school. I'll bring Morgan with me, just like I have been. Her routine wouldn't change and that's important right now."

Ginger tapped her lip thoughtfully before saying, "There's a certain logic to the idea that I could run by Mr. Donnelly."

"Of course he needs to make the final decision." Libby didn't think that would be a problem. As long as his personal life wasn't inconvenienced, Jess would be happy.

"This could be a short-term answer for everyone," Ginger said cautiously.

Exactly what Libby was thinking. It was impossible for her to imagine loving Morgan any more even if she'd given birth to her. She couldn't simply turn her over to a guy who had the sensitivity of a robot. She especially couldn't hand vulnerable Morgan Rose to him, then walk out of her life.

If Jess approved this arrangement, it would give Libby time to figure out a long-term solution.

Jess Donnelly had agreed to be guardian of his best friend's daughter, but he'd never thought he'd have to. Maybe he'd agreed *because* he never thought he'd have to. People did that all the time, never seriously entertaining the possibility that either parent would die, let alone both of them at the same time.

But the worst-case scenario had come to pass and now he was waiting for Morgan. In a few minutes the child's current caretaker would deliver her. Negotiations between his lawyer and the Nanny Network relayed through his secretary resulted in him expecting the nanny, Elizabeth Bradford, momentarily.

He'd checked the child-care company's references and

called a random selection of current and former clients, all of whom had nothing but high praise for the professionals Ginger Davis had provided. Since he didn't know the first thing about raising a kid, let alone a five-year-old girl, he was more than happy to defer to the kid experts.

It wasn't that Jess didn't like children, so much as he didn't relish the idea of someone depending on him. He knew from firsthand experience how betrayal and disillusionment felt. It was especially unpleasant coming from the one person on the planet you counted on. This was his best friend's kid. The friend he'd vowed to support. Always. A friend who was the brother he'd never had. Jess had promised Ben, given his word, which put the pledge firmly in sacred territory. When you watched a friend's back, you didn't turn your own on a sacred promise.

He blew out a long breath as the pain of loss squeezed his chest. "What the hell were you thinking, Ben? No way am I prepared for this."

The phone rang, jarring him into action. He picked up the extension from the end table by the cream-colored sofa. "Yes?"

"Peter Sexton, Mr. Donnelly. Building security. There's a Miss Morgan Rose Harrison to see you and Libby—"

"They're expected," he said. "Bring them up."

Jess had fervently hoped the newly hired nanny would get here before Morgan so he'd have an on-site expert who could hit the ground running when he took custody of the little girl. If the nanny didn't show up soon, he'd be calling Ms. Davis and make Nanny Network news as the first dissatisfied client putting a big fat black mark on its pristine reputation.

The doorbell sounded and since he was already standing in the two-story foyer, it took only a second to answer. A young woman and small girl stood there—Libby and Morgan.

The taller blonde was slim, blue-eyed and pretty plain. Or maybe plainly pretty. On the few occasions they'd met, he'd never been able to decide. Her shiny hair turned under and barely touched the collar of the white cotton blouse peeking from the neck of her navy sweater. Dark denim jeans did remarkable things to her hips and legs, leaving no mixed feelings about his opinion of her figure, which was firmly in the approval column.

The little, tiny blonde who clutched an old, beat-up doll to her chest had curly hair and brown eyes she'd inherited from her father as well as the hint of an indentation in her determined chin. Both blondes stared expectantly up at him.

"Hi," he held out his hand. "Jess Donnelly."

"We've met."

"Right. How long has it been?"

"Last Christmas. Almost a year ago."

He remembered seeing her under the mistletoe at Ben and Charity's holiday party. It would have been so easy to catch her there and claim the kiss he'd wanted since the first time he'd seen her, but he'd deliberately let the chance slip by. Instinct said she wasn't the sort of woman he could easily walk away from and he didn't get involved with any other kind.

"You look great." An understatement.

Libby glanced at the little girl for a moment. "We missed you at the memorial service."

"Yeah." Pain sliced through him at the reminder that his friend was gone. "I was in Europe on business and there was a snow storm. The airport was closed for two days."

"I see."

He couldn't tell from her carefully neutral tone whether

she did or not. Either way there was nothing he could do about that. And what really mattered was his friend's child.

He looked down at her. "Hello, Morgan. Do you remember me?"

Her blond curls bounced when she shook her head. "Not really."

"That's okay," he said, guilt twisting in his gut. "Welcome to my home."

"Nice place," Libby said. Something flashed quickly through her eyes before she continued in a pleasant voice, "The security gates are pretty cool and a twenty-four hour guard who used his key card to escort us to the penthouse on the top floor of the building, in the private elevator, no less, is a nice touch."

Did he hear sarcasm in her voice? Or was the edge simply a symptom of the awkward situation? Did it matter?

"I'm glad you like it." He looked at the child. "What did you think, Morgan?"

"It's okay," she whispered, looking uncertain as she stepped closer and slid her small fingers into the woman's hand.

"Are you going to invite us in?" Libby asked.

"Of course." Mentally he smacked his forehead as he stepped back and opened the door wider.

"Don't forget your suitcase, Morgan," Libby cautioned.

The little girl nodded, then took the handle of a princess-pink weekend-size bag and rolled it onto the foyer's beige marble floor where no princess suitcase had gone before. The woman did the same with a plain black bag. For the first time he thought about the little girl's things. Surely she had more than would fit into the two pieces of luggage just wheeled in.

Major awkward silence followed that flurry of activity

as the three of them stood there. He wasn't sure what to do next and wished again that the nanny would show up and bail him out. In the meantime he figured that a tour was in order. It's what he normally did with a first-time female guest. Although nothing about this situation could even remotely be described as normal. And this small female would be a permanent resident, a thought that registered pretty high on his uneasiness meter.

"How about I show you around?" he offered.

"We'd like that," Libby answered, then looked down. "What do you say, Morgan? Would you like to see your new home?"

Still clutching Libby's hand, the little girl nodded apprehensively. The solemn look on her pale face said she liked the idea about as much as a double helping of Brussels sprouts.

"Follow me."

He led them into the living room with its floor-to-ceiling windows that showed the extensive outdoor area. Because the penthouse was on the top floor, he had a private pool and patio with barbecue. "If you want a view of the Las Vegas strip, you've come to the right place."

"I'm sure Morgan is thrilled at the idea of looking at the adult entertainment capital of the world," Libby said wryly.

"Good point." Another mental forehead smack.

"Although she'll like looking at the pretty lights. Right, sweetie?" When Libby smiled at the child the tenderness in her expression was almost palpable.

"It's pretty high up," the little girl answered cautiously, keeping her distance from the windows.

Libby looked around the room with its dark wood tables bearing traces of European design. "The couch and chairs are very beautiful, but they look like they'll show every spot."

"I haven't found it to be a problem." He glanced at the cream-colored furniture with the overstuffed brown pillows, then at the child, the first to set foot in his place. Life as he'd known it was about to change.

Jess led them through the kitchen that included a morning room with a door onto the terrace. The spacious formal dining area held a table for eight, matching buffet and china cabinet. They walked through the large family room, past the leather corner group and plasma TV. After showing them the living room and master bedroom, he walked to the other side of the condo and pointed out Morgan's bedroom.

"You'll have a king-size bed and your own bathroom. What do you think?" He glanced at the little girl who was looking back at him as if he'd just beheaded her favorite doll.

"It's awfully big." Her mouth trembled. "What if I get lost?"

Instantly Libby went down on one knee and pulled her into a hug. The gesture was completely natural and struck him as incredibly maternal and reassuring. The way a mother should be. The way his mother had been until everything changed.

Libby tucked the child's hair behind her ears. "It's scary, I know. Change always is. But in time you'll get used to it and hardly remember anything else," she explained.

"What if I wake up and it's dark and I get scared?"

"I'm sure Mr. Donnelly won't mind if you leave lights on." She looked up at him. "Right?"

"Of course."

She gently brushed her palms up and down Morgan's arms. "That's an awfully big bed for a little girl. Probably he'll get you a smaller one, maybe with a trundle. That's a bed that slides underneath and pulls out so if you're afraid at night someone can stay in your room. A new bed means a bedspread and sheets. Maybe the princess ones you like. Then the walls might have to be painted to match. That would be your favorite color and would help you get used to a new place."

"What's your favorite color, Morgan?" Jess asked, struggling to find something to say. With the ladies he had no problem, but little girls were out of his league.

"Pink." She met his gaze and her own was troubled. "Sometimes purple."

"Lavender," Libby clarified.

Neither was an earth tone as far as he knew, but no one would accuse him of being the interior design police. Among other things, he built hotels and exclusive resorts, then hired people to decorate them. Exclusively.

"We can talk about altering things," he said. "But I think it might be best to hold off on any sweeping changes until getting some feedback from a child-care professional."

"I'm a licensed preschool teacher, Mr. Donnelly. I've spent the last few years with kids of all different ages at Nooks and Nannies." Her full lips compressed into a straight line. "And Morgan has been in my care for quite a few months. I think I'm eminently qualified to express an opinion on her new environment and would be happy to consult with you about what will help her adjust to her new and different surroundings."

He studied the twin spots of color on her cheeks and the way her blue eyes darkened to navy with this show of spirit. She was standing up for the kid who wasn't even hers and he wondered suddenly whether or not there was a man in her life. The two thoughts would have been contradictory except for his history.

After his dad died, his mother had elevated him to man-of-the-house status. It was the two of them against the world until she fell in love and remarried, at which time she couldn't get rid of Jess fast enough. So he couldn't help wondering if Libby had a boyfriend. If so, was she relieved to hand off this child so she could put the guy first? And he had no reason to care since she'd be gone in a few minutes. And where was the nanny he *was* paying for her expertise in regard to Morgan's environment?

"I'm getting the distinct impression that you don't like my place," he said.

She stood to look at him, but kept a hand on the little girl's shoulder. "It's spectacular and quite lovely. I've never been in a more beautiful home."

"And yet you're talking redecorating."

"If you don't mind my asking, how big is it?"

"About sixty-five-hundred square feet, including the pool and patio," he answered, unable to completely suppress the note of satisfaction. His mother's main squeeze hadn't been shy about expressing the opinion that Jess was a screwup who wouldn't amount to anything. So sue him for taking pride in his spectacular success.

Libby absently nodded as she glanced around. "It's very big and one doesn't need to look far to realize it's a very adult environment."

"I'm not sure what you're getting at."

"The decor is dark. Strategically lighted artwork hangs in nearly every room. There's expensive glass and pricey figurines on flat surfaces and in cabinets. What if something gets broken because a child is high-spirited and energetic? Sticky hands and art projects aren't compatible with light-colored fabric and expensive wood. How is a five-year-old supposed to feel comfortable here?"

"I'm almost six, Aunt Libby," Morgan piped up.

"Yes, you are, sweetie, right after Halloween, Thanksgiving and Christmas. I forgot that you're almost a grown-up." A smile turned up the corners of her full mouth, then disappeared when she looked at him again.

"Is there a point to the running commentary?" he asked.

"I'd feel more comfortable if you seemed the slightest bit willing to compromise for Morgan's sake."

Jess rested his hands on his hips as he studied her. There was something in her voice and a look skipping across her face that made him think her critique of his habitat was more personal than professional. He hadn't seen her often but their paths had crossed enough for him to know that she was smart, very smart. But he'd never seen this sassy side of her before and wondered if he'd done something to tick her off.

Regardless of her attitude, he would concede that she had a point. "Is it possible to cut me some slack? I wasn't expecting to have a child dropped—" He glanced at Morgan and tempered his words. "This situation is not something I anticipated."

"I understand." For a split second profound sadness stood out in her eyes, reminding him that she'd also lost a friend.

"Look, Libby, let me rephrase. After consulting with Morgan, I will discuss kid-friendly changes to her environment with her nanny." He looked at his watch again. "If she ever gets here."

"If she—" Libby's expression went from sad to surprised. "Did you talk to Ginger Davis?"

"Yes."

"Personally?"

"I made initial contact. Then my representatives were in negotiations with her regarding the particulars," he admitted.

"So you never actually spoke with her about the final arrangement?"

The final arrangement? Just like that he felt the need to defend himself. "I'm deeply involved in a massive resort project. My secretary and lawyer handled all the details." The look in her eyes made him add, "Both are trusted professionals who have been on my payroll for a number of years. I have complete faith in their ability to handle my affairs."

"So you staffed out the responsibility of child care?"

Her tone was neutral, the question more about information gathering to fully understand the situation. But again his defensive instincts kicked in. "I've done my homework regarding The Nanny Network and fulfilled my fiduciary responsibility as Morgan's guardian. Elizabeth Bradford comes highly recommended and will take exemplary care of Morgan."

"Elizabeth Bradford is the nanny?"

"Yes." Something about the way she said it made him brace himself. "Why? Do you know her?"

"I do. And I'm quite sure that she'll take very good care of Morgan."

He detected a definite "gotcha" tone to her voice. "What's going on?"

"You really don't know, do you?"

He couldn't shake the feeling that there was a joke unfolding at his expense. A surprise was coming and in his opinion that was never a good thing. "Know what?"

She tilted her chin up, just a bit defiantly. "Libby is a nickname for Elizabeth. It probably slipped your mind that my last name is Bradford. That makes me Elizabeth Bradford. Apparently you missed the part in the negotiations where Morgan's current and future child-care professional are one and the same person. I'm your new nanny."

Chapter Two

Libby knew she shouldn't be surprised that Jess had introduced himself again and barely remembered the last time he'd seen her. He'd proved over and over that she was about as memorable as a bus bench. Part of her desperately wanted him to notice her. The practical, street-wise part instinctively knew there was as much chance of that as deleting her past and inserting one that included a home where she felt wanted.

More shocking was that he'd been expecting a stranger named Elizabeth Bradford. When Ginger had told her that it was a go for her to be Morgan's nanny, she'd assumed he knew about and had agreed to the arrangement. Obviously she'd assumed wrong. He'd started the ball rolling then turned everything over to his employees, who didn't have a clue about them being acquainted.

"Aunt Libby?" The small hand gripped tighter.

"What is it, sweetie?" With an effort Libby kept her tone even and friendly. Kids didn't miss much going on around them—good and bad. She didn't want the little girl to sense her concern. If anyone was to blame for this misunderstanding, it was Jess. He'd been too busy to take a personal interest, which was exactly the reason she'd felt the need to stay with Morgan in the first place.

"Is it time for SpongeBob yet?" Morgan asked.

"You're right. I forgot." And the distraction would be good, Libby realized. She recognized confusion on Jess's face. "It's a cartoon."

"I knew that. I think. Do you want to watch television?" When the little girl nodded, he pointed into the family room. "Right this way."

He grabbed the remote from a shelf in the entertainment center then turned on the TV. "What channel?"

Libby wasn't surprised that he didn't know off the top of his head. News, sports or movies were probably more his thing. That wasn't his fault. She told him the numbers that were second nature to her and seconds later the big yellow guy with the quirky smile came on the screen followed by the sound of his squeaky voice.

Wow. It was the most awesomely clear, bright, big picture she'd ever seen up close and personal. Probably it was the best, latest and most expensive technology on the market. A far cry from her small, old, economical set.

Libby touched the little girl. "Look, Morgan. SpongeBob has never looked better. What do you think?"

The thin shoulder lifted briefly. "It's fine."

"Why don't you sit on the sofa with your doll?"

Uncertainty glittered in her eyes before she scrambled up onto the big, L-shaped leather corner group. She looked tiny and frightened and Libby hated leaving her by herself, but it was the lesser of two evils. The bigger bad would be this vulnerable child being present for the talk Libby and Jess were obviously going to have.

Ginger was an extraordinarily efficient woman. Because Jess hadn't handled the negotiations personally, obviously something had been lost in translation. Like the fact that he was already acquainted with Elizabeth Bradford.

"We'll just be in the other room, kiddo." She leaned down for a quick hug. "Just a few minutes. Okay?"

Clutching her doll, Morgan stared up with sad brown eyes. "Promise?"

"Cross my heart." She automatically made the gesture over her chest then held up two fingers.

When she glanced at Jess there was an odd expression on his face. Then he angled his head and she followed him into the foyer, where the plain black and princess suitcases still stood, looking very out of place on the marble floor with the fancy crystal chandelier overhead.

Jess, on the other hand, looked right at home. Which he would, since this *was* his home. She'd always wondered what it was like, a part of her curious about the man who couldn't even remember her name. But she remembered everything about him in far too much detail. The flesh-and-blood man was even better than the image she carried around in her head.

Other than the wedding where she'd first seen him in a traditional black tux, the other run-ins had been casual and his clothes reflected that. Formal or informal attire made no difference; he was an extraordinarily handsome man. She thought she'd prepared herself for seeing him face-to-face, but steel girders and cinder blocks wouldn't have been enough to do the job.

It was Saturday and clearly he wasn't dressed for the

office. In his chest-hugging black T-shirt and worn jeans he looked less like the wealthy man she knew he was. His black hair was cut short and the scruff of beard on his cheeks and jaw made his blue eyes look bluer. Her heart hammered, making it hard to think straight, which was darned inconvenient when thinking was important because she had a lot on the line.

He folded his arms over the chest she'd just admired. "So, let me get this straight. You're the nanny?"

"I am." At least she hoped so.

"I don't think so."

"Give me one good reason," she said.

"We know each other—"

"That's not technically true," she interrupted. Best to take the wind out of his sails before he picked up speed with that thought process. "Knowing each other would imply you remember my name. But every time our paths cross you stick out your hand and say 'Hi, I'm Jess Donnelly.'" She slid her own shaking hands into the pockets of her jeans. "That says Teflon brain."

"Excuse me?"

"You know. Teflon. Slippery. Nothing sticks. Like the fact that we've met. In my book, we really don't *know* each other."

"You were Charity's maid of honor. You came to their housewarming barbecue. You're godmother to that child."

"And you're godfather."

"I remember."

"All evidence to the contrary." She bit her tongue but it was too late because the words were already out.

His gaze narrowed on her. "I learned a long time ago not to assume that everyone recalls who I am. I meet a lot of people and always introduce myself." He lifted one broad shoulder in a casual shrug. "It's polite, avoids potential awkwardness and now it's a habit of mine."

"I see." But it wasn't really okay and she didn't know why. "So you're aware that I've been taking care of Morgan for over nine months?"

"Ben mentioned it." A dark look slid into his eyes. "Before he and Charity left—"

"When he asked you to be her legal guardian if anything happened," she finished.

"Yeah."

"Obviously there's been something of a misunderstanding. Just so you know, I'm more than willing to take on the nanny job."

"No."

"Even though I've been caring for her all this time?" She blinked. "Just like that? You don't even want to think about it?"

"There's nothing to think about."

"So you really want to take on a child you hardly know and didn't come to see while her parents were gone? Not even when you found out her mother and father had passed away?"

"I already explained that I was out of the country at the time."

"And I was the one here with her. The one who had to break the news that Ben and Charity weren't coming back."

"I promised my friend that I would raise his child if anything happened to him. I gave my word."

"But they gave Morgan to me," she countered.

"So you want to keep her. I get it." He ran his fingers through his hair. "The thing is they made me her legal guardian."

"Paperwork. It can be changed if you agree."

"I don't."

"Even though you don't really want her?"

"Who said I don't?" he asked sharply.

She raised a hand to indicate his posh penthouse. "There are signs."

"I assured Ben that his daughter would have everything she needed and he shouldn't worry." He looked at her. "So I found the finest child-care service available to provide supervision. Now you're here. How did that happen?"

"Since you were too busy to seal the deal, maybe you should ask your lawyer and secretary."

"I will. And Ginger Davis is on my list, too. Frankly I'm questioning her judgment in sending you."

"She wouldn't have sent me unless you approved," Libby defended. "I'll admit it was my idea—"

"There's a surprise."

She glared at him. "Just think about it and you'll see that this makes sense. Morgan has been with me since her parents left and it could potentially be harmful to leave her in the care of strangers. I'm willing and eager to be her nanny. It's a good plan."

"Define *good*," he said.

"Continuity of care for Morgan at a time when she's especially vulnerable."

"By that you mean yourself." He stared at her. "Why didn't you come to me? Approach me up front and run this scenario by me?"

"I tried."

"Apparently not very hard."

"You're not really like the rest of us, are you? Do you remember what it felt like when the name of gazillionaire Jess Donnelly didn't open doors or grease the wheels in getting you past secretaries, administrative assistants, doormen and security? Right to the top of the food chain?"

"I'll admit there are layers to my organization."

"No kidding." She blew out a breath and struggled for calm. "I didn't set out to campaign for this job. As it happens I already work for Ginger at the preschool. We discussed the arrangement and she decided there was some merit to my suggestion. I assumed that when she said everything had been worked out you'd agreed to it." She folded her arms over her chest. "No one told me negotiations had gone through your minions."

"Look, I've only ever been introduced to you as Libby. I didn't know you and Elizabeth Bradford were one and the same. It seems a conflict of interest since we have a prior relationship."

"What we have isn't a relationship. It's a series of brief encounters, ships passing in the night. Nothing about that is personal enough to prevent me being Morgan's nanny."

He shook his head. "Look, Libby, I don't think this is going to work out—"

"Aunt Libby?"

Jess whirled around and when he moved, Libby saw Morgan behind him. She didn't know how long the little girl had been there. "Hey, sweetie. Is SpongeBob over?"

"No."

"Is something wrong?" Libby asked. Stupid question. Everything was wrong, she realized. But nothing good would come of letting Morgan see her desperation.

"I got scared. You sounded mad."

"I'm sorry. And I'm not mad." Not at you, she wanted to say. She hurried over to the child whose brown eyes were now worried and filling with tears. So much for hiding the highly charged situation from her. "We didn't mean to disturb you."

Morgan brushed a finger beneath her nose and stared uncertainly at Jess. "Is he making you go away?"

"We were just talking about that." She looked at him.

"I don't want you to go. I don't want to stay here by myself. Please, Aunt Libby—"

When Morgan started to cry, Libby gathered her close. "It's going to be okay, baby. It will."

"I d-don't want you to g-go away."

Jess ran his fingers through his hair. "Don't cry, Morgan. Your Aunt Libby isn't going away."

"Really?" Libby said.

Morgan lifted her head and looked at him. "Really?"

"Really. I'm sorry. I didn't handle everything very well. Your Aunt Libby is mad at me." He shrugged when she lifted one eyebrow. Points to him for getting it. "The truth is that you're both going to stay here with me and Aunt Libby is going to be your nanny."

"What changed your mind?"

"You were right," he said. "It wouldn't be a good idea to let a stranger look after her. So I'd appreciate it if you'd stay on. Until she's adjusted to the situation."

"Okay."

"Is that all right with you, Morgan?"

"Yes." She nodded eagerly.

"Then we have a plan for the short term."

That was good enough for Libby. She'd take what she could get and figure out the rest later.

"Seemed like a good idea at the time" was the best way Libby could describe her first week under Jess's roof. Libby had been so sure the living arrangement would take the edge off her attraction, but not so much in the first week. Even when he wasn't there, which was ninety-five percent of the time, the place was all about him.

Pictures of him hiking in Red Rock Canyon. A carelessly discarded expensive silk tie in the family room. The spicy scent of him in *every* room made it feel like having his arms around her. Or was that wishful thinking? Not that it mattered. Or it wouldn't if she could say the idea was unpleasant. Nothing could be further from the truth.

"Aunt Libby?"

"Hmm?" She pulled her thoughts back to tucking Morgan into bed. "Sorry, sweetie. I was thinking about something else."

"That's okay." The little girl pulled the sheet and blanket more securely over her.

"Do you want me to finish the story?"

"No."

Libby studied the serious little face. "Is something on your mind?"

"Yes."

Libby suppressed a smile. When Morgan first came to stay with her this method of communication had taken some getting used to. Instead of blurting out whatever was going through her head, she worked her way to it with a series of questions. It wasn't efficient, but eventually what she needed to discuss got discussed.

"Is everything all right at school? Your kindergarten teacher says you're one of her pet pupils and she's not supposed to have favorites."

Twin dimples flashed on the child's cheeks when she smiled. "Miss Connie is nice."

"She is very nice."

Nooks and Nannies Preschool had a kindergarten class

and Morgan went there while Libby was working with her preschoolers. Charity and Ben had been supposed to come home before first grade to enroll the little girl at the school near their home. Now their child lived in a luxury penthouse condominium, a different home. Fortunately, Jess had agreed with her that changing schools right now wasn't the best plan.

"So if school isn't keeping you up at night, what's bothering you?"

Morgan clutched her doll against her thin chest. "I don't think he likes me."

"Who? A boy at school? Is someone being mean to you?"

"No. That guy."

"Who?" Alarm trickled through Libby.

"My daddy's friend."

"You mean Uncle Jess?"

She nodded. "I don't think he's very happy that we came to live with him."

Libby had hoped Morgan didn't pick up on the signs that he was ignoring them, but no such luck. "Why do you think that, sweetie?"

"He's never here."

"Sure he is," Libby protested. "In the mornings."

Her stomach tightened as she remembered just today he'd come into the kitchen to say goodbye before heading to his office. In his pinstriped navy suit and red tie he'd looked particularly handsome. Freshly shaven, with every hair in place, he'd set her female parts quivering with awareness. Darn him. He'd revved up her hormones, then raced out the door.

"Two times he drank a cup of coffee while I ate cereal. But he doesn't sit down with me. Not like you do, Aunt Libby."

Sometimes a smart and perceptive child could be worrisome and this was one of those times. At least she wasn't perceptive enough to notice Libby's insane crush on Jess, but that probably had more to do with her young age. There was still an ick factor regarding boys.

Libby wished for the good old days because her current plan wasn't coming together very well. Every exposure to Jess was supposed to be like a vaccination and living here should have been the booster. *Should have* being the key words.

"Jess is a busy man, sweetheart. He has lots of people working for him and depending on him."

"Does he eat supper?" Morgan asked.

"I'm sure he does." If he didn't, the impressive muscles that filled out his T-shirt would be fairly nonexistent. And they were definitely existent, positively thriving. In a mouth-watering way. Libby had no ick factor where he was concerned.

"I've never seen him eat supper, Aunt Libby. He doesn't like us."

Libby figured that was true enough for her, but he had no reason to dislike this sweet, innocent child who was right about him not coming home for dinner.

"He doesn't really know us yet," she said. "Give it time. This is new for him. He's not used to us, but that will change. Everything will be all right. You'll see."

"Promise?"

"Cross my heart," she said.

After a big hug and lots of kisses that made Morgan giggle, Libby turned on the world's brightest night light. "Sweet dreams, love bug."

"Okay," Morgan answered sleepily as she rolled to her side.

With a full heart and troubled spirit Libby watched for

several moments, then made up her mind to talk to Jess. It wasn't long before she heard the front door open and close.

Imagine that. We have touchdown right after the kid is in bed. Morgan wasn't the only observant resident of the penthouse. Apparently Jess was aware of her bedtime and how to avoid it and her.

Libby found him in the kitchen, where he was reaching into the refrigerator for a beer and the plate of food saved for him. The angle gave her a chance to admire his excellent butt. That thought was immediately replaced by a mental command for her hormones to back off.

"Hi, Jess."

He straightened and turned to meet her gaze. "Hi."

"How was your day?"

"Fine. Busy." He shrugged. "You?"

"I just put Morgan to bed. You can go in and tell her good-night if you want. I don't think she's asleep yet."

"That's okay. It might upset her routine."

Hers or his? she wondered.

"You must be hungry," she said.

"Why?"

"Besides the plate of food in your hand?"

He glanced at it and a small smile tugged at the corners of his mouth. "I missed dinner."

"We noticed."

"Oh?" He removed the plastic over the meatloaf, mashed potatoes and green beans, then set it in the microwave and pressed the reheat button.

"Yeah, what with your chair at the table being empty and all."

He twisted the top off his beer and took a long swallow, then looked at her. "What's on your mind, Libby?"

"Funny, that's just what I said to Morgan when I tucked

her in bed. I could tell there was something bothering her. She tends to share what's on her mind at bedtime."

"Do I need to know what it is?"

Of course, you nit, she wanted to say. Struggling for patience, she said, "You're her guardian."

"And I pay you to make sure she has everything she needs."

She walked over to the granite-covered island and kept it between them as she met his gaze. "It's also in my job description to make sure you're aware of what's going on with her emotionally. I thought you should know that she's noticed you don't come home for dinner."

"I see."

That's all he could say? Libby rubbed her palms over the black-and-beige granite countertop, but the smooth coolness did little to ease the heat trickling through her. Heat that was part attraction and part annoyance. Just breathing the same air with him raised her pulse when she most needed calm rationality.

In her college speech class there had been discussion of techniques for calming nerves in public speaking. The one about picturing your audience naked came to mind, but with Jess in the same room that only throttled up her quivering nerve endings. Her best bet was to say what she had to and leave.

"Morgan thinks you don't like her."

"That's ridiculous. She's a kid. Of course I like her. How did she get an idea like that?"

"Besides the fact that you work really hard at not being around her?" Libby struggled to keep accusation from her tone.

"I'll cop to the working hard, but it has nothing to do with avoiding her."

"Really?"

"What's this really about?" he asked.

Apparently she'd been unsuccessful in maintaining a neutral expression. She might as well say what had been on her mind.

"Was weather the real reason you couldn't be at Ben and Charity's memorial service? Or was it about dodging the hard stuff? The part where you're Morgan's guardian?"

Stark pain etched itself on his face and looked even darker for the scruff of beard that was three hours past his five o'clock shadow.

"I'll admit to being grateful that weather grounded my plane. But it had nothing to do with the kid and everything to do with the fact that a memorial service meant facing the truth that my friend was gone and he wasn't coming back."

"If anyone knows how you feel, it's me." Missing Charity was still a raw and ragged wound inside her. She was probably the only person on the planet who knew exactly how Jess felt. And she sympathized with him. "I didn't want to go either."

He took another long drink of his beer and pulled the plate out of the microwave. "I'd have been there if weather hadn't shut down the airport."

She believed him and that realization made her feel all gooey inside. Under the circumstances that was the wrong way to feel.

"The fact is," she said, "Ben and Charity made you Morgan's guardian. The designation implies making an effort to be involved with her. Just like Ben would have been if he were here."

A muscle jerked in Jess's jaw as he stared her down. "Define *involved*."

Libby tapped an index finger against her lips as she thought about the question. "Think of her as a resort development. Periodic reports from a project manager. That would be me. Intermittent on-site social interaction with said project. That would be—"

"Dinner?" he guessed.

"Go to the head of the class," she said.

He ran his fingers through his hair, then nodded. "I'll make it a point to be home for dinner tomorrow night."

"Promise?"

"Is that really necessary?"

"I don't want to tell Morgan you'll be here unless it's going to happen," Libby said. Life was full of disappointments and she didn't want more than necessary for a little girl who was dealing with the worst one of all.

"Promise." He made a cross over his heart and held up two fingers.

"Okay, then. It's a date."

Almost instantly she regretted her phrasing. That made it sound too personal, which was so the wrong tone. She wanted him to take an interest in Morgan, not herself. Mostly.

And so she felt the same conflict of smart women throughout time. How could she want him so intensely when she wasn't sure she liked him at all?

Chapter Three

The next night Jess walked into the penthouse and heard Libby's voice, the smoke-and-whiskey huskiness that skipped over his skin and made him hot. Now was no exception. When she stopped talking, a little-girl giggle filled the silence. This was the first time he'd ever heard that sound in his home and it made him smile. Amusement faded fast when he remembered why he was here.

To get involved with Morgan. Libby's words came back to him—like Ben would have been if he'd lived.

"I'm trying, buddy," Jess whispered. "Man, I wish you were here. I'm already screwing this up."

Libby had figured out that he worked late to avoid the situation at home. She'd nailed him and he didn't like it. He also wasn't sure how he felt about her coming up with the idea of being the nanny. On one hand, he was glad to have someone caring for Morgan that she knew and felt comfortable with. Someone who could make her giggle, he thought when the sound came to him again.

On the other hand, Libby had also guessed that he hadn't wanted to go to the memorial service and seemed to share the feeling. She'd gone soft when they discussed it, unlike the harsh way she'd reviewed his home as it related to being kid-friendly. But he could tell that she didn't particularly like him and he didn't particularly care. At least he tried not to because that was a slippery slope straight to hell.

Jess set his briefcase down by the front door, took a deep breath and walked into the kitchen. Every light in the room was on, including the under-the-cabinet fluorescents. Morgan was sitting on one of the six tall, padded wrought-iron stools arranged in a semi-circle around the island. Libby was across from her putting something on a cookie sheet. The glass-topped dinette was set with three woven placemats, plates, eating utensils and glasses. Until the last week, he'd always come home to a dark, silent penthouse. All this light and activity made him feel as if he'd stepped into an alternate universe.

Libby looked up and saw him standing there. "Hi."

"Hi." He lifted a hand when Morgan turned in his direction. "Hey."

"Hi," she said, not quite looking at him.

Until he made his presence known, Libby and Morgan had been talking and laughing. Now it was as if the cone of awkwardness had descended, closing off the giggles. Suddenly the room wasn't quite so bright. Maybe Libby had been wrong about Morgan wanting him there.

He observed Libby, noting how the tailored white cotton blouse and snug jeans set off her curves to perfection. There was uncertainty in her vivid blue eyes. Maybe they took on that extraordinary color because her cheeks were flushed. It didn't matter why, really, because the more he saw her, the more he realized how striking she was.

"So," she said.

"What's for dinner?" He looked at Morgan, who was staring at the beige-and-black design on the granite-covered island.

Libby waited a couple of beats, then answered with ex-aggerated cheerfulness in her tone. "We're having chicken nuggets and french fries."

He moved beside her and studied the mystery chicken pieces arranged in rows on the cookie sheet. He picked one up and examined it. "I have a number of luxury resorts that employ world-renowned chefs and I don't think one of them has this particular entrée in their repertoire."

"It's Morgan's favorite." Libby gave him a look, although her tone was still relatively good-humored. "She chose this for dinner."

He'd meant the words in a teasing way but the little girl looked worried. Clearly she didn't get his sense of humor, but he'd put his foot in his mouth and needed to salvage the situation somehow.

"I can't wait to try this," he said, wondering if his voice had enough enthusiasm or was over-the-top.

"You're going to love it," Libby promised. "Isn't he, Morgan?"

"I guess." She didn't look up.

"And to balance this meal nutritionally, I've made a salad with various kinds of lettuce, veggies, shaved almonds, croutons for crunch and blue cheese crumbles just because."

"Yuck," Morgan commented, wrinkling her nose.

"You know the rule," Libby said.

The little girl heaved a huge sigh. "I don't have to like it, but I have to try it."

"Seems fair," Jess said.

This brought back memories of his own childhood, before his dad died. Before everything went to hell. He knew the signs well enough to know that Morgan was on the dark side now. He wanted to make it better, but he didn't even know how to carry on a conversation without hurting her feelings.

"Why don't you tell Uncle Jess what you did at school today," Libby suggested, as if she could read minds.

His next thought was the realization that the little girl had never addressed him by his given name, let alone said "Uncle Jess." He'd have remembered that. When he'd dropped in on her parents, they'd run interference and the visits had been scattered, infrequent. Not enough for her to remember him.

Now he was the one in charge of running interference, which made him certain that fate had a sadistic sense of humor. It also made him want to put a fist through the wall, but that wasn't an option.

"What did you do in school, Morgan?" he asked, grateful that Libby had thrown him a bone.

Morgan glanced up at him, then down again. "I made a pumpkin."

"It's there on the refrigerator. For Halloween," Libby explained.

He looked behind him and saw the construction paper creation held to the front of the appliance with a magnet. The little girl had colored it green and he was about to say something about pumpkins being orange when he noticed Libby shake her head slightly in a negative motion. Fortunately he wasn't quite as dense as a rock and got her drift.

"Wow, Morgan. I really like your pumpkin," he said. "You did a great job."

"One of the kids said it's the wrong color," she mumbled.

"What do they know? Maybe this is a pumpkin that's not ripe yet," he suggested.

Morgan lifted one slight shoulder in a shrug.

When he met Libby's gaze, her expression was sympathetic. That wasn't something he was used to seeing. If anyone could sense that it was him. When his mother had brought home a guy two years after his dad's death, Jess had known in seconds that he didn't measure up. He'd always gotten the same hostile vibe from Libby.

He was accustomed to her shooting daggers at him when their paths crossed in a party setting with other people around. He'd always noticed her but managed to find someone safe to take his mind off her. That wasn't the case now. Worse, he kind of liked that she was cutting him some slack for his inexperience.

But there was something else about her that was different, too. Her blond hair was tousled around her face, teasing her pink cheeks. The smile she flashed him was bright and beautiful and made his chest feel weird. Intelligence snapped in her eyes and her mouth made him wonder if it would taste as good as he imagined.

From the first moment he met her, he'd been concerned that she could take his mind and libido to a place he'd always managed to avoid going. And he shouldn't be going there now.

"How long until dinner?" he asked. "I'm going to change clothes."

"About fifteen minutes," she answered.

He nodded and headed out of the room. It wasn't nearly enough time, he thought, feeling cornered in his own home. If he hadn't promised to eat dinner with Morgan, he would leave. But he'd crossed his heart and somehow knew that the gesture was tantamount to sacred between Morgan and Libby.

As if that wasn't enough proof of their attachment, the sound of Libby's voice followed by Morgan's giggle sliced into him and rattled around, echoing off the emptiness there.

The female interlopers in his world had a bond—the two of them against the world. He remembered the feeling from long ago and felt a flash of wanting to be a part of it again. But he'd experienced an alliance like they had and found out it wasn't something he could trust. A unit as tight as Libby and Morgan's had no room for him. Even if he wanted to join, which he didn't.

Sooner or later he'd wind up in the cold anyway, so the cold was where he would stay.

Dinner could have been more awkward, but Libby wasn't sure how. Her cheeks and jaw hurt from smiling too much and her brain was tired after thinking so hard to single-handedly keep up a three-way conversation. Jess had stuffed his face full of nuggets and fries, then excused himself—a polite way of saying he couldn't get away fast enough.

Once he'd vacated the table, Morgan released her inner chatterbox and turned back into the child Libby knew and loved. If Ben and Charity had been able to see their daughter's future, would they still have named Jess her guardian? She wasn't so sure. But there was something she needed to discuss with him and finally found him in the morning room.

Libby hadn't thought to look there because it was evening and there were no lights on, which had made her think the room was empty the first time she'd checked. Now she stood in the doorway. The only illumination came from the lights on the Strip that were visible through the floor-to-ceiling windows. As he'd said on her penthouse tour, it was a fabulous sight.

She felt a stab of guilt for pointing out that a five-year-old girl had no frame of reference to appreciate the adult view. It was true that billboards and taxis flaunted advertisements of scantily-clad women that Morgan shouldn't see, but from here the view was classy and breathtaking. And she didn't just mean the lights. Jess looked pretty fabulous, too. But he always did to her.

"Jess?"

The light on a glass-topped table came on instantly. He was sitting in a rattan chair on a plush, cream-colored cushion.

"Is everything okay?"

That depended on what he meant by *everything* and *okay*. But she figured he probably meant was there a crisis for which his presence was required.

"Fine."

"Okay. Good."

"Do you mind if I sit down?"

There was only a slight hesitation before he said no. That could have been her imagination, but she didn't think so because the look in his eyes said she was marginally more welcome than a global financial crisis.

There was an identical chair beside his and she lowered herself into it. The seat was deep and if she slid back, she felt her feet wouldn't touch the floor. Jess, on the other hand, had no problem, what with his long legs.

Before dinner he'd changed out of his suit into a pair of jeans, a cotton shirt and navy pullover sweater. It was a preppy look that he somehow pulled off as rugged. Her stomach did that quivery thing she recognized as acute attraction—unwelcome, but best acknowledged so it could be dealt with.

Libby folded her hands and settled them in her lap, angling her knees toward him. "So, how did you like dinner?"

"Awesome."

"Really?"

"Best I ever had."

"So, you've eaten chicken nuggets before?"

"It's been a while." Something darkened in his eyes. "But, yes, I have."

"The amount you consumed was pretty amazing."

"Did Morgan notice?"

"That you were shoving record-breaking amounts of food in your mouth to redeem yourself for dumping on her favorite meal?"

"Yeah. That."

"No."

"Just so we're clear, I wasn't dumping on her choice. That was humor."

"She's five." Libby gave him a wry look. "She doesn't know *world-renowned, repertoire* or *chef.*"

"I got that." He folded his arms over his chest as he stared out the window.

"Complimenting her artwork was a nice save."

"Oh, please." Now his look was wry. "It was pathetic and you know it."

"What I know," she said, feeling sorry for him in spite of herself, "is that you didn't have a meltdown when you noticed a magnet on the expensive stainless-steel front of your refrigerator."

"Don't think it didn't cross my mind," he answered.

Libby laughed, but it didn't lighten her mood. She wasn't here to worship at the altar of Jess Donnelly and be seduced by his charm and self-deprecating humor.

"But you held back."

"I would have made a joke about it but I was afraid she'd think I wanted her drawn and quartered at dawn."

"You're exaggerating."

"Only a little." He blew out a long breath. "It probably didn't escape your notice that I'm not very good at kid talk."

"No? Really?" she said in mock surprise. "I swear I was planning to get out the duct tape to shut you up."

The corners of his mouth curved up slightly. "In my own defense, it has to be said that I spend my days in meetings about budgets, building materials and stock market shares. Until a week ago I didn't have to know about nightlights, green pumpkins or trying something I don't like."

Libby didn't want to sympathize with what he was going through and worked hard to suppress it. He'd agreed to be Morgan's guardian should anything happen to her parents. The argument that no one expected they wouldn't come home didn't fly with her. For God's sake, they'd gone halfway around the world to a place where bad, life-threatening things happened much more frequently than here in the States.

Jess could have taken the time to get to know Morgan. He could have made the effort to fill his friend's shoes and make the absence of a little girl's father a little easier for her. But he hadn't done that.

He was doing the right thing now and got points for that, but no sympathy for the fact that talking to a little girl, a virtual stranger, wasn't easy. Still, for Morgan's sake, she decided to help him out. Be a bridge.

Libby blew out a breath. "Kid talk takes practice, just like any other language. Ask her questions."

"Like?"

"What's her favorite color?"

"Pink," he answered. "Sometimes purple, better known as lavender."

Would wonders never cease? He'd actually listened that day they'd first arrived. "So ask things you don't know. Such as what she did at school."

"You covered that," he reminded her.

"I found out she made a pumpkin. A good question would be why that, as opposed to a ghost or pirate."

"I just figured it best captured Halloween." He shrugged.

"Of course, but asking shows that you're interested and could get her talking. Which brings to mind an obvious question."

"Obvious to who?"

"Everyone."

"That's where you're wrong, Libby. I have no idea what to say to her next."

"I keep forgetting you don't live in the real world." She sighed. "You do know that Halloween is when kids dress up in costumes and go trick-or-treating for candy?"

It took several moments before the "aha" light came on in his eyes. "So the question is—what does she want to be for Halloween?"

Libby smiled. "Give the man a prize."

"Even though the man doesn't deserve it?"

He sounded sincere. Like he didn't believe getting a clue was anything to be proud of. And she had to agree with him. It wasn't a big deal. But the fact that this being-out-of-his-comfort-zone side to Jess was something that she'd never seen before *did* land squarely in big-deal territory. It could make him sympathy-worthy and she couldn't afford to feel that way. She wasn't here to stroke his ego, but as Morgan's advocate. It was time to bring up the subject she'd come here to discuss with him.

"I just tucked her into bed and we were talking about something—"

Alarm jumped into his eyes. "The fact you're here means she had something on her mind."

"I see you've gone to the bad place where you're expected to eat fish sticks as well as chicken nuggets every night for the rest of your life." She smiled. "Don't worry. It's not about that." His confused male look was so astonishingly cute that there was a definite tug on her heart. "She remembered that you said you would think about making changes to her room."

"Oh." He relaxed. "Okay."

"Letting Morgan put her personality stamp on her own space might help her to niche in with you."

He steepled his fingers and tapped them against his mouth. "I have no objection to that."

"Good. So, let's figure out when you can take her shopping."

He shook his head. "I don't need to approve her taste. Just let her pick out whatever she wants and send the bills to me."

It was like he'd pulled down a shield to hide the vulnerability she'd seen just moments before, when he worried about how to talk to a little girl. What was up with that?

"Shopping with Morgan is a good way to know her and build up a collection of conversational questions," Libby pointed out.

"I'll pass."

"Don't you want to be a part of picking things out?"

"It's not necessary."

"No one said it was. But to continue our discussion of a little while ago, it's a way to break the ice. Which you were just wondering how to do. Because she lives with you now. You're her family."

"No."

"Excuse me, you're her guardian."

"And as such I will make sure she has everything she ever needs, but don't call it family because I don't know how a family is supposed to behave." He met her gaze and there were shadows in his own.

"Ben and Charity believed otherwise or you wouldn't be Morgan's guardian."

"A past like mine makes their judgment questionable."

"What happened to you?" she asked.

"My father died when I was a boy. A little older than Morgan."

"I'm sorry," she said automatically.

"Don't be. It was a long time ago."

"Even so…" She thought for a moment. "It would seem that a loss like that would make you more sympathetic to what Morgan is going through—"

He held up a hand to stop her. "What I know is Ben and Charity meant for me to provide for Morgan's material needs. He was my friend and knew me and my limitations and he still asked me to take her. So I'm prepared to pay the bills." He stood, signaling an end to the discussion. "Is there anything else?"

"I'll let you know."

He nodded. "Then I'll say good night."

When he was gone the chill in the morning room made Libby shiver, a feeling fueled by sympathy she couldn't stop this time. She realized how little she knew about Jess's life. She hadn't been aware that he'd lost his father at such a young age. At a time when he felt the loss destroyed any sense of family for him. What about his mother?

Libby had never known her own. The woman had died before she was old enough to remember her. Her father was still alive, still an opportunist who used people. But she'd grown up watching a family support their own. Even though she'd never felt a part of that family, she understood the dynamic and the love that underscored everything.

Apparently Jess hadn't been as lucky. She'd always thought of him as the golden boy, never touched by tragedy. Obviously there were more layers to him than she'd suspected.

Only time would tell whether that was good or bad.

Chapter Four

Libby pushed the control button and watched the security gates into Jess's luxury condo complex part like the Red Sea. Glancing in the rearview mirror of her practical little compact car, she smiled at Morgan, who was barely awake in her car seat. She'd learned that napping this close to bedtime could vaporize the evening schedule.

"Hey, kiddo. Are you excited about your new princess comforter?"

"Yes," the child answered, then sleepily rubbed her eyes.

"You know, your new bed has to be delivered before you can use the new things."

"When is it coming?" Morgan asked again.

"Saturday." Libby drove into her assigned space next to Jess's. She noted that his car wasn't there yet, which meant he was still working. Or something. She turned off the car's ignition.

"Why can't they bring my bed tomorrow?" Morgan asked.

"Because we're at school all day and no one will be at home to let the delivery men in. They wouldn't know where it goes," she explained.

"What about Uncle Jess?"

Yeah. That was a good question. Libby wanted to warn Morgan not to count on him. The man was unwilling to do the hard work. The answer to what about Jess was as simple as that.

It had to have been hard losing his dad so young, but he was making a deliberate choice to keep this precious little girl at arm's length. No matter what he said about Ben and Charity knowing him, Libby would never believe his passive parenting is what they'd have wanted for their little girl.

But she couldn't say any of that out loud in answer to the question.

"Uncle Jess works, too. Very hard. He can't be here for the delivery." Or anything else, Libby added silently. "So we'll just keep all the bedding stacked in the corner of your room until Saturday."

"Okay." Morgan unhooked herself from the safety seat and opened the rear passenger door.

Libby lifted the twin comforter and the bag with matching sheets and towels from her trunk. The two of them managed to carry the bulky shopping bags to the private elevator, then rode it to the penthouse. She pulled the key from her jeans pocket and turned it in the lock. But when she tried to open the door it didn't budge. After turning the key in the opposite direction, the door opened, which meant she hadn't secured it properly when they'd left earlier.

"That's funny," she said.

"What is, Aunt Libby?" Morgan looked up with big, innocent brown eyes.

"I was sure I locked the door." She always did.

This was a secure building, but leaving an unobstructed way into a luxury penthouse was like an engraved invitation to get ripped off. Her only excuse was that she'd had Jess on her mind a lot. The distraction took a toll and important things like not locking up were the result.

She set the bags down in the foyer and her purse on the circular table.

"I'm thirsty, Aunt Libby."

"How about a gigantic glass of milk?"

The two of them had grabbed a burger at the mall, but before leaving she'd fixed a salad and pasta for Jess, then left it in the fridge.

She smiled down at the little girl. "Soda with your hamburger for dinner was a treat but you still need milk."

"Why?"

"It has calcium to give you shiny hair and strong teeth and bones so you'll grow up big and strong."

Libby walked into the kitchen where the light was already on, which made the hair at her nape prickle with unease. On top of that there was an almost-empty plate of pasta on the counter. One of the bar stools had been pulled out for sitting down on.

"This just keeps getting weirder."

"Uncle Jess ate his dinner," Morgan said.

Libby didn't think so, what with the fact that his car wasn't in its usual space. She didn't think he was home yet. Not only that, there was a half-full wineglass beside the plate. Jess was a beer guy as far as she knew. She picked up the stemware and looked closer.

"Uncle Jess didn't pour this, not unless he's started wearing lipstick."

Libby wondered whether or not she should be afraid.

Should she take Morgan out and call 911? It didn't feel like there was anything bad going on. This had a sensation of familiarity, of being at home and comfortable with the surroundings.

"Aunt Libby—"

"What, sweetie?" she said, preoccupied with what to do.

"It's like that story you read me," Morgan said, excitement humming in her voice. "Remember? The one about the girl and the three bears."

She raced out of the room before Libby could stop her. And she needed to stop her because in that story they found the girl in bed. Hurrying to catch up, Libby went into the family room where she found Morgan standing still, staring down the long hall that led to Jess's bedroom. A beautiful, curvaceous woman was walking toward them wearing a man's black silk robe. Libby was thinking it was probably all she was wearing but couldn't say for sure and didn't really want to confirm. Her next thought was that although she'd never seen him in it, the robe was probably Jess's.

"This is the three bears' story and Goldilocks is a redhead," she mumbled.

The woman tightened the tie at her waist and stopped in front of them. "Who are you?"

"I'm Libby. Who are you?"

"Elena Cavanaugh. I wasn't aware that Jess got married."

"He didn't. How did you get in here?" Libby demanded.

"With the key he gave me. And you?"

Libby settled her hands on Morgan's shoulders. The two of them lived here and shouldn't have to justify their presence. Red, on the other hand, had a lot of explaining to do. "I'm the nanny."

Elena's gaze dropped to Morgan. "I didn't know he had a child."

"A recent development," she explained, giving the small shoulders a reassuring squeeze. "What are you doing here?"

"I'm a flight attendant. Jess gave me a key. We're—" Her gaze dropped to Morgan. "We're *friends*. When my flight schedule brings me to Las Vegas I stop by to say hello."

"Without calling?"

Elena shrugged. "He likes surprises."

"Why are you wearing that robe?" Morgan asked.

"You're a cutie," the woman said with genuine warmth.

"I'm Morgan."

"It's nice to meet you, Morgan. I like your name. And to answer your question, I was just going to take a bath."

"To get ready for bed?" the little girl innocently persisted.

"Something like that." Elena looked at Libby. "But I see that Jess has made some changes around here."

"This all happened recently." Libby glanced down at the child in front of her. "For Morgan. Jess isn't actually her uncle. He's her guardian because…"

Elena nodded slightly, letting her know she didn't have to go into detail in front of the little girl. It was a sensitive thing to do and took the starch out of Libby's indignant outrage over this "arrangement." Though she had no right to it, there was probably a little jealousy stuck between indignance and outrage.

"I think I'll just go and get dressed," Elena said.

Morgan stepped away from Libby. "Are you leaving already?"

"It would be best," the woman answered in the same words Libby was thinking.

"You're not going to sleep over?" Morgan persisted.

"That wouldn't be a good idea." Again her response was exactly what Libby would have said. Elena turned and walked back down the hall.

When they were alone Morgan looked up at her. "I wish she would stay. She's nice, Aunt Libby."

"I can see why you feel that way." The kid meant stunning, Libby thought. What in the world was Jess thinking, giving out keys to his place? Didn't he ever see the movie *Fatal Attraction?* She felt like the queen of snark because Elena seemed nice enough under incredibly awkward circumstances.

The front door opened and closed, and speaking of the devil, he walked into the family room looking like he'd just arrived for a magazine fashion shoot. Charcoal suit, white shirt, red tie. Awesomely appealing. How could he look so good at the end of a long, difficult day? Libby felt as if she'd been run over by heavy equipment and it was his fault.

"Hi," he said, smiling at both of them. "I see you did some shopping."

"My new bed is coming on Saturday," Morgan said. "I got a princess comforter and sheets to match. Want to see?"

He looked from her to Libby. "I think that's the most words she's ever strung together in my presence."

"Mall magic," Libby answered, wondering how to diplomatically bring up Elena in front of a child.

"So you guys had fun?" he asked.

"You could say that."

He must have heard something in her tone because he frowned. "Is something wrong?"

"You could say that, too."

"What's going on?"

"Hi, Jess." The flight attendant stopped just inside the doorway and he whirled around to look at her.

After a couple of beats he said, "Elena." Shock mixed with recognition equaled awkward.

"You look great," she said. The crisp white shirt and

navy pants of her flight uniform made her shapely figure look even more curvy.

"Right back at you." He glanced at Morgan. "I'm sorry I wasn't here when you got in."

"No problem."

"The thing is, this isn't a very good time—"

"Yeah. I kind of figured that out on my own." She smiled with genuine regret as she handed him his key. Then she stood on tiptoe and placed a soft kiss on his lips that clearly said goodbye. Looking first at Libby, then Morgan, she said, "It was nice to meet you both. For what it's worth, I think Jess will be a really good dad."

On what planet? Libby wanted to ask. But Elena was gone before she could say the words even if she dared.

Libby blew out a breath. "I can truthfully say that nothing like that has ever happened to me before."

"I bet she drinks lots of milk," Morgan commented.

"Why?" Jess and Libby asked together.

"Because her hair is shiny. She has nice teeth and is big and strong." Morgan looked wistfully toward the front door. "She's pretty. I want that color hair. And when I grow up, I hope my boobs are like hers."

Jess looked as horrified as Libby felt but she was pretty sure it was for a different reason. Libby was already a woman and there was no chance of her growing into the "assets" necessary to get Jess's attention.

Jess wondered which of the gods he'd pissed off and, more important, what sacrifice it would take to get them off his back. While Libby supervised Morgan's bath and bedtime rituals, he was in the morning room downing his second beer.

When this child fell into his lap, he'd known life would

change, but he hadn't counted on parts of the old one creeping in. Elena looked good, no question about that. She was fun, flirty and fantastic in bed. Part of the fun was her showing up without warning. That was exciting, or at least it used to be. Her goodbye said they were over and he would have understood even if she hadn't returned the key.

The thing was, it didn't bother him, which bothered him more than anything. That was just wrong and he blamed a petite, blue-eyed blonde who didn't seem at all intimidated or impressed by his wealth and power.

He blamed her because she had the damnedest way of creeping into his thoughts at inconvenient times. Board meetings. Business lunches. Phone calls. It was difficult to concentrate when a memory of her tart comments made him smile. Or the way she caught her top lip between her teeth sent his thoughts to kissing first that lip and then the bottom one to see for himself how she tasted.

And suddenly he sensed her behind him. Although she didn't make a sound, he knew she was there. The hair at his nape prickled and his skin felt too tight. That happened when normal blood flow was involuntarily diverted to points south. This was the last thing he wanted or needed.

"Jess? Can I talk to you?"

The last time they'd talked in here was chicken-nugget night. Libby had given him a crash course in child-speak. She'd encouraged him to engage Morgan in conversation and complimented him on what was right with his style. Then he'd seen the light in her eyes dim and extinguish because he'd disappointed her. Libby was a grown-up, but Morgan wasn't. What if he let her down? He was pretty sure conversing with the kid didn't include her sharing that she wanted a big bosom and red hair when she grew up. So he'd already failed her.

Libby didn't understand why family was a hot button for him. How could he explain that love had cost him the only family he had? She wouldn't understand that promises made and broken were what destroyed all he thought he knew about love and loyalty. He wanted to say no to the talking, but knew that wasn't an option.

"Why don't you have a seat?" he suggested, turning to meet her gaze.

"No, thanks. This won't take long."

"Okay. Shoot."

The choice of words was unfortunate because he suspected Libby would very much like to do just that. After Elena left and Morgan said what she said, her nanny had glared at him in a way that could reduce a lesser man to a brown stain on the rug.

"Is Morgan settled?" he asked.

"That's a good question."

Here we go, he thought. "What's wrong?"

The look on her face told him what he already knew—stupid question. "Let's start with the naked woman in your bed."

In his obviously flawed judgment, she sounded jealous, and the idea of that had some merit. "If we're going to discuss this rationally, let's get the facts straight. We don't know if she was naked and I have no independent confirmation that she was in my bed."

"You know what I mean."

"I really don't." It wasn't easy to remember innocence, but he put as much as possible into his voice and expression.

Jess was baiting her, plain and simple. He was deliberately agitating her because, as stupid as it sounded, she was beautiful when she was angry. More beautiful, he amended. Not in the classic, statuesque, turn-a-man's-head way

Elena was. But in a down-to-earth way that was more appealing than he would have ever believed.

"Okay." She put her hands on her hips, drawing his attention to curves that made his palms tingle. "Let me put it like this. Morgan could have walked into a scene featuring a naked woman in your bed. It's not something I want to explain to her. Do you?" She paused thoughtfully and tapped a finger to her lips. "Oh, wait, you're the guy who doesn't do kid talk at all which would make explaining sex to a five-year-old—"

"Almost six," he pointed out.

"Right. Because a couple months would solve the problem entirely."

Definitely beautiful, he thought. "The situation was awkward, I'll admit that. But it wasn't as bad as it could have been. So, I guess I'm wondering what you want me to do."

She blew out a breath. "And I guess I'm wondering how many more keys are out there? How many more of your women are going to show up unexpectedly?"

Elena was the only flight attendant he dated. He'd given her a key because it was convenient for both of them. She'd have a place to stay when she was in Las Vegas and he enjoyed her showing up out of the blue.

He could tell Libby there were no more women, but then they'd have nothing left to talk about. For reasons he couldn't explain, he wasn't quite ready for this conversation to be over. Scratching his head he said, "It's hard to put an exact figure on it."

"*Figure* being the operative word." Sarcasm surrounded every syllable.

"No pun intended." Again he let his expression ooze innocence. "So Morgan had some questions?"

"I managed to do damage control. This time."

"How?"

Her eyes narrowed and the expression was sexy as hell. "She's still young and naïve enough to believe that *people* look past a woman's appearance to find her inner beauty."

Her emphasis on the word *people* told him she really meant men. Truthfully, the kid's comment about growing up had freaked him out big time. "I'm glad you were able to smooth things over."

"Is it necessary for me to point out that boobalicious babes arriving without warning is going to be a problem the older Morgan gets?"

"I will take appropriate action to avoid a repeat of the situation," he assured her.

"How?"

"Excuse me?"

"Do you have a master list of who has access to your home?" she grilled him.

"I've never found it to be necessary."

Her stubborn, pointed little chin lifted slightly. "Now it is."

"Would you feel more secure if I had the locks changed?" Even though it's not necessary, he added to himself.

She nodded. "It's a start."

"I'll take care of it."

"Thank you." She stared at him and caught her top lip with her teeth.

Heat shot straight through him as his mind went to a place where he kissed her until both of them were clinging to each other because neither could catch their breath. The next part of the mental picture had her naked in his bed. Before the vision went any further, he looked closer and noticed there was something else on her mind. And he would bet it had nothing whatsoever to do with his bed.

"What?" he asked.

She shook her head. "It's none of my business."

"Since when has that stopped you?" He shrugged. "Go ahead. Tell me what's on your mind."

"You don't really want to know."

Probably not. But now he was too curious. "Yeah, I do want to know."

"Technically you're my boss. I'm your employee. It's not my place to offer an opinion."

Curiouser and curiouser. Now he really needed to hear what she had to say. "Just pretend I'm the company suggestion box. Or better yet, a comment card. The one that says we're really interested in your feedback. Et cetera. Lay it on me."

"Okay. If you insist." She folded her arms over her chest. "I can't help noticing that you don't seem like the type of guy who embraces parenting. The sort who doesn't do the dance of joy at being tied down."

She was right about that. Ties gave people the power to stab you in the back. If someone was going on the offensive, he preferred to see it coming and take appropriate evasive measures in order to defend himself. Maybe that's why he was so drawn to Libby. She had no problem with telling him what was on her mind, whether or not he wanted to hear it.

Jess met her gaze as the defensive part of him locked and loaded. "My energy has been focused on business for a very long time. I put together some cash and parlayed that stake into something of much greater value. With one enormously successful resort open on the Strip and another one in development, not to mention partnerships in properties all over the world, there's not a lot left over for anything else."

Which is why relationships like Elena worked for him. No demands, just rewards.

"I understand what you're saying," she agreed, in a tone that indicated she didn't see at all. "The problem, as I see it, is that when you're raising a child, being tied down comes with the territory."

Okay. She'd nailed him. Mission accomplished. It was a direct hit on the target. What she meant was that Ben and Charity had picked the wrong guy to take care of their kid. Did she really think he wasn't aware of that?

On the day she'd delivered Morgan, she'd accused him of not really wanting the child. He hadn't confirmed or denied but defended himself with a question. *Who says I don't want her?* Libby was dancing around it again now, but the meaning came through loud and clear. He wasn't the go-to guy and his friend had misplaced his trust.

He was more than ready now to end this conversation.

"Okay, Libby. Point taken. I'm well aware of my short-comings and limitations."

"It's not a flaw," she backpedaled. "Some people just aren't cut out to raise kids. Self-awareness is a good thing."

Jess ran his fingers through his hair. "I don't know why Ben chose me to be Morgan's guardian, but he did."

"And what you're doing is admirable, Jess, but—"

He held up a hand to stop her. "I assured my friend that his child would be taken care of if anything happened to him. It was one of the last conversations we had. You're here in my employ to take care of Morgan. I gave my word and I'm doing my duty."

Disappointment was evident in her eyes again and he hated putting it there. One of the perks of living alone was not having anyone to let down. He would have to learn not to let it bother him the way it was now.

Chapter Five

After her students had gone home for the day, Libby had work to do while Morgan was being supervised in the Nooks and Nannies after-school program. She sat behind the flat oak desk in her brightly decorated classroom. The walls were filled with pumpkins colored by her kids, as well as witches, ghosts and other costumed characters to commemorate the upcoming event. When Halloween was over next week, she wanted to go right into projects for Thanksgiving and Christmas.

As she thumbed through material for ideas, several caught her eye. Paper plates and brown construction-paper feathers to fashion a turkey. If everything was cut out and ready, the kids would have fun pasting it all together. There was another one that used small magazines with the pages folded to form the turkey body, then a pattern to cut out the long neck and head.

It would make a great centerpiece for the dinner table on the big day but would require a lot of supervision, a higher adult-to-child ratio than normal. Mental note: ask for parent volunteers. There were enough involved parents this year to make it a fun exercise for everyone.

Christmas would be next, a time rich in project material from trees and ornaments to Santa and presents, as well as the spiritual side of the season. She wanted this holiday to be special for Morgan, the first without her parents.

The thought made Libby's heart heavy. Her own holiday memories were filled with Charity, and then Ben. Some of them included Jess, because he was their friend, too. A vision of him popped into her mind followed by a familiar yearning that lately had turned into an empty ache. Her seeing-him-every-day plan to crush out her crush didn't seem to be working all that well. Not much had changed from the days when their paths crossed because of mutual friends.

In all fairness, it wasn't Jess's fault that she had the hots for him but left him so cold he couldn't remember her name. She knew that and in spite of it, her longing for him was still an issue even though no one would ever accuse him of being a parent, let alone one she could count on.

The intercom on her phone buzzed and she picked up. "This is Libby."

"Hi, Lib, it's Mary in the office."

"Hey." The receptionist's tone was normally upbeat and cheery. It took Libby a couple of seconds to realize that wasn't the case now. "What's wrong?"

"Morgan is here. She had a little accident—"

"I'll be right there."

Libby ran out of her classroom and to the administration offices, which were in another building. There was a small room just off the reception area where the kids went

with minor scrapes and bumps, where first aid was handled. The door was open and she heard whimpering. The
knot in her chest squeezed against her heart as she braced
herself and walked in.

"Hey kiddo. You have a boo-boo?"

The little girl was sitting on a chair, her right hand
wrapped in a towel. There was blood on her pink sweater,
jeans and white sneakers. It was more shocking because,
for some stupid reason, she hadn't expected to see blood.

She looked at Sophia Green, the Nooks and Nannies
director, who was sitting beside Morgan, an arm around
her shoulders.

"What happened?" Libby asked.

Sophia's gray eyes were serious as she tucked a strand
of reddish-brown hair behind her ear. "She cut her hand."

"How?" Libby knew that question bordered on dense
because it didn't matter. But in that heart-stopping moment,
it was all she could think to say.

"The kids were at outside playtime. Morgan was by
herself near the perimeter fence. She reached through and
picked up a piece of glass."

Libby dropped to her knees beside the little girl. "Oh,
baby—"

"I didn't know it was sharp, Aunt Libby." Tears welled
in her brown eyes.

Words of censure fueled by her own fear were on the
tip of her tongue, but somehow Libby held back. This
wasn't the time for a safety lesson.

"Okay, sweetie. We'll put a Band-Aid on it and fix
you right up."

"About that, Libby—"

If she'd been thinking more clearly, she'd have realized
there would already be a bandage on the boo-boo and

Morgan would be showing it off. Because that wasn't the case she knew it was more serious.

"What?" she asked Sophia.

"It's a little deep," the other woman said gently. "I think she needs stitches."

"Okay."

Libby was doing her best imitation of calm even though her hand shook as she brushed the hair off Morgan's forehead. "I'll call the pediatrician."

"Lib, it will probably be faster to take her to Mercy Medical Center. The emergency room has a pediatric trauma specialist available twenty-four hours a day."

Libby glanced up at the little girl's pale face and frightened eyes. "You don't think that would be scarier?"

Sophia shook her head. "They're specially trained for things like this. Not that I think it's that serious, but the staff knows how to put their littlest patients at ease in these circumstances."

She trusted implicitly her friend's judgment. Sophia had been with the Clark County department of family services before job burnout sent her to Nooks and Nannies. The woman had seen trauma. If anyone knew how to deal with it, Sophia did.

"Okay. We'll go to Mercy Medical Center."

"I'll drive you."

"Thanks."

That way she could call Jess to meet them there, then she could concentrate on keeping Morgan calm.

A couple of hours later Libby was sitting alone with Morgan in one of the emergency room's trauma bays. When they'd been called back she'd insisted Sophia didn't have to stay. That was before she'd known how long they'd be waiting. She still hadn't spoken to Jess. His cell phone went straight to voice mail, which was now full due to all the messages she'd left. Unable to reach him directly, she'd tried his secretary, who'd informed her he was in a meeting and had left strict orders that he wasn't to be disturbed. The problem was that Morgan couldn't be treated until he authorized it.

That wasn't the only problem, just the most pressing. Somewhere deep down inside, Libby knew she wanted him there for herself. She was scared, too, and could really use his support, a strong shoulder to lean on, someone to talk to. Not just anyone. *Him.*

At that moment the privacy curtain moved and she expected to see the nurse who had been checking in on them whenever possible for the last couple of hours. Instead, Jess stood there. She hated how glad she was to see him, how badly she wanted to throw herself in his arms and have him hold her.

"I got here as soon as I could," he said, stopping on the other side of the bed.

Right. Not soon enough, she thought.

Her resentment and anger were out of proportion to the situation and she wasn't sure why. But this wasn't the time to call him on it any more than scolding Morgan after the fact would have been.

"How is she?"

Why do you care? she wanted to ask. But part of her knew that was just taking all her fear and frustration out on him.

She blew out a long breath. "Worn out. We've been here a long time. You got my messages?"

A muscle jerked in his jaw. "Yeah. I need to give permission for treatment."

She nodded. "You could have done it over the phone."

"I've never handled something like this. It seemed better to show up."

"The pediatric trauma specialist—Dr. Tenney—looked at her hand and said no nerves or tendons or anything that would permanently affect her fine motor coordination were compromised."

"That's good," he said.

"It is, but she needs stitches, because of where she cut herself. Movement in her palm will make healing take a lot longer unless he closes the cut."

His mouth thinned to a grim line. "Something like this never crossed my mind. How did you handle stuff while she was with you, after Charity and Ben left?"

Libby met his troubled gaze. "I had power of attorney. I was authorized to approve routine check-ups, visits to the doctor's office and whatever came up. When they died everything changed. You're her legal guardian and I couldn't sign any of the forms. So we've been waiting—"

Her voice cracked and the weakness shamed her, making her more self-conscious.

"Libby, I'm sorry. I had no idea."

"Your secretary said her orders were that you not be disturbed. She's very good at her job."

"Still—" He ran his fingers through his hair. "This should have been an exception."

He looked sincere, she thought. And in all fairness this was a situation she hadn't foreseen. The fact that she'd had a lot on her mind, including him, was no justification for her not to consider what would happen in a medical emergency. But it also made a certain amount of sense that his employees who worked so closely with him knew him better than anyone. Knew his priorities. If a child who needed medical treatment was an exception-worthy event, the woman would have put Libby through to him. She hadn't. And that didn't speak highly of his attitudes toward parenting.

Morgan stretched and opened her eyes. "Hi, Uncle Jess."

"Hey, Morgan. How are you?"

"Not good." She glanced at her hand. "I got a boo-boo."

"I heard. Does it hurt?"

"Not really," she said. "Want to see it?"

His hesitation wasn't all that obvious, but Libby saw. "Sure." He lifted the small surgical drape covering the little hand and winced, turning a little pale. "It looks like it hurts a lot."

"If I hold really still it's okay." Morgan's eyes filled with tears. "But I've been holding still for a long time. I wanna go home."

"Can't blame you," he said. "I'll go do what I have to do to make that happen."

Libby watched him disappear and aloneness surrounded her again. Wasn't she the perverse one? Jess was damned if he did, damned if he didn't. She didn't trust him with this child, but Libby was desperately drawn to his strength and support.

Not more than a few minutes later Jess returned. "Okay. Everything is taken care of. The doctor will be here in a few minutes to fix you up and pretty soon you can go home."

"Thank you, Uncle Jess."

The small, sad voice brought a pained look to his face. "Morgan, I'm very sorry you had to wait so long."

"That's okay."

"No, it isn't," he said. "I didn't get the message and it's my responsibility to let the doctor know he can do what's necessary to make you better. I was in a meeting."

"Was it important?" Morgan asked.

"Yes. It means lots of people will have jobs."

"That's pretty important," the little girl agreed.

Jess shook his head. "My secretary didn't give me the message."

"Why not?"

"Because I told her not to."

"You made a rule?"

"I guess you could say that." He reached out with one finger and brushed a stray strand of hair from her cheek. "I just want you to know that I'm very sorry you had to hang around here so long."

Libby waited for him to say that nothing like this would ever happen again. He didn't. She knew Jess took a promise very seriously and the flip side of that was not to make a vow you couldn't keep. But this was one that he should move heaven and earth to make and not break.

"So," he said, looking down at Morgan. "Other than this trip to the emergency room, how was your day?"

"Okay." The small smile she'd given him disappeared. "But I'm scared about gettin' stitches."

"I can see where you would be," he said seriously. "But I've had them before."

"Really?" Her eyes widened. "Is it gonna hurt?"

"The doctor is going to give you some medicine that will make you not feel anything." He held up his finger. "But here's the thing. The medicine comes through a needle, a really small one and it will feel like a little pinch. Then it might burn for a couple of seconds. After that, you won't feel anything."

"Promise?"

He made the cross over his heart and held up two fingers. "Swear."

He'd told her the truth, Libby realized. It would have

been easy to lie and tell her it wouldn't hurt, but he hadn't done that. Which made his omission about promising to be accessible to Morgan all the more significant. If he couldn't make that promise, Libby would see to it that nothing like this ever happened again. She'd make sure that if Morgan needed anything she wouldn't have to wait. Maybe it was time to do something she'd been considering for a while—consult a lawyer about her alternatives for obtaining legal custody of Morgan.

He'd cited his sense of duty, but in her opinion love should trump obligation.

She didn't ever want this little girl to wait for what she needed until Jess could find time to be available. She didn't ever want this precious child to feel like an unwanted obligation. Libby knew from firsthand experience how painful growing up that way could be.

Twenty-four hours later things were back to normal, whatever that was. Morgan was in the Nooks and Nannies after-school program, where she was being watched over and pampered so Libby had felt confident in resuming her teaching duties. A lot of parents counted on child care and the kids could be thrown off by a substitute. If Morgan needed her, she was right down the hall, as opposed to Jess, who had meetings and left orders not to be disturbed for any reason.

Still, after he'd arrived at the emergency room and expedited the little girl's treatment, he'd been great, making her laugh, distracting her while the doctor stitched her hand. Then he'd taken them home, with a detour to a toy store where he bought what he'd called her brave-little-girl reward. Libby had experienced the E.R. with and without him and definitely preferred him there. Which was a bummer since he couldn't be counted on to show up when needed.

Her classroom door opened and Sophia Green walked in. "Hi, Lib."

Her stomach clenched. "Is Morgan okay?"

"Fine. I just checked on her." The preschool director sighed. "Are you going to the bad place every time you see me now?"

"No." And that was a big fat lie.

"Give it time." She sat in the chair beside the desk. "Morgan says her hand doesn't hurt. I think that very impressive bandage is helping in that regard."

"Good. She does like her Band-Aids."

"Miss Connie is keeping her quiet. Which isn't really all that difficult." Sophia frowned. "How is Morgan coping with losing her parents?"

Libby thought about the question. "Fine. She seemed to take the news okay and was a trouper at the memorial service." Now Libby frowned as she mulled it over. "But she never asked many questions and now she doesn't talk about them at all."

"I see."

But Libby didn't miss the deepening worry lines. "She's had to cope with moving. Jess is practically a stranger to her. That's a lot for a little kid to deal with."

"How's the arrangement working out?" Sophia asked. "I mean you being her nanny."

"You mean what's *he* like. Admit it."

Sophia shrugged. "I think it's perfectly normal to be curious about an above-average-looking wealthy man that my friend is living with."

Wow, that was an understatement in every way. Jess was drop-dead gorgeous and the penthouse lifestyle didn't happen without a couple extra bucks in the bank. But the "living with" part made the arrangement sound way too personal.

"I'm not *living* with him—"

"So you commute there to fulfill nanny duties?" Sophia's expression was all innocence except for the gleam in her gray eyes.

"No. I'm a live-in nanny."

"So, how is that working for you?"

It was Libby's turn to shrug. "Nice place. Morgan doesn't want for anything that money can buy."

"I hear a *but*."

"Let's just say it's a good thing I'm a live-in nanny," Libby hedged. "For Morgan's sake."

"Are you concerned about her welfare?"

"Yes."

"Why?" Sophia persisted.

"For starters, sexy stewardesses show up with their own key and let themselves into the penthouse."

"Why would they do that?"

"Oh, please." Libby rolled her eyes. "You're a grown-up. Do the math."

"They drop by for…" Sophia thoughtfully tapped her lip. "*Benefits* when they're in town."

"Right in one."

"And you're jealous."

Not a question mark anywhere near that statement. How irritating that she was so easy to read. Instead of outright denial, Libby attempted a flanking maneuver. "Why in the world would I be jealous?"

Sophia linked her fingers and settled her hands in her lap. "Because he's a hot guy and you have a crush on him."

"Give me credit for some maturity." Again not a lie.

"Age has nothing to do with it. Secretaries fall in love

with their bosses all the time. And the nanny falling for the guy she lives with is the stuff of romantic fantasies from *Jane Eyre* to *The Sound of Music*."

Libby thought about confessing that her crush wasn't a recent development and had happened years before she'd moved into the penthouse, then decided a lie was easier. "You couldn't be more wrong."

"It wouldn't be the first time," her friend conceded. "So, you're concerned because a sexy stewardess with a key is bad because there's a child in the house."

"A child who subsequently decided when she grows up, she wants to be a redhead with big boobs."

"Oh, my."

"No kidding."

"That's unfortunate, Lib, but give him the benefit of the doubt. This is a major lifestyle change for him."

"I get that." Libby picked up her pen and rolled it between her fingers. "If that was the only thing, I'd shrug it off. But he's a workaholic. His priorities are budgets and business models. What concerns me is that so far he's shown no inclination to change his lifestyle to accommodate Morgan."

Sophia nodded. "That's a concern."

"Yeah. Charity and Ben took care of all the details before they left. They dotted *I*s and crossed *T*s. Their decisions were made with abundant thought. And it begs the question—why did they trust me with Morgan for the short term, but make Jess her long-term legal guardian?"

"I can't answer that." Sophia studied her. "What are you thinking?"

"I'm just wondering who would be the better parent," Libby admitted.

"As in changing the custodial status quo?"

"It's crossed my mind. I have an appointment with an attorney."

Sophia sat forward, her expression shocked. "You're talking about suing for custody?"

"I haven't really thought about it in those terms or that far ahead."

"Have you talked to Mr. Donnelly? Maybe he would be willing, possibly relieved, to step aside. It's possible you'd be doing him a favor. You might be able to work out a mutually agreeable solution."

Libby clicked the top of the pen, sending the point in and out. "Before moving Morgan, I tried to talk to him and couldn't get access. Rich people have a lot of insulation."

"It's probably because they need it," her friend commented. "There are probably a lot of folks who'd like to separate him from a million or two."

That was a good point and something Libby hadn't considered. "I suppose it's not easy to trust when you're in his position. But I tried to talk to him when I brought Morgan, that very first day. He adamantly refused to even consider altering custody. Said he promised his friend."

"Sounds awfully noble to me."

Libby would have thought so, too. Except Jess had put a finer point on it and called Morgan a duty. But then, in the E.R., he'd been so sweet with her. Probably guilt for not being available to authorize her treatment. And yet his interaction with her had seemed to be completely natural. It was so confusing and she didn't know what the right thing was anymore.

"What I know for sure is that I love that little girl like she's my own. For me, walking away isn't an option. I just want to talk to an attorney and find out what my options are—if any."

Sophia nodded thoughtfully. "If he doesn't voluntarily agree to walk away, you could be talking about a legal battle."

"I know."

"It could get expensive," her friend pointed out. "No *could* about it. We're talking lawyers and protracted legal proceedings. All of that can add up fast."

"I get it."

"He's got unlimited funds and you—"

"Don't," Libby finished for her.

But technically she was working two jobs and saving every penny possible. Just in case.

Sophia studied her for several moments. "I hope it doesn't come to that."

"Yeah. Me, too."

But Libby wouldn't run away from it either. If she decided to go that route, it would be because that's what was best for Morgan.

"I have to go. So much paperwork, so little time." Sophia stood and looked down. "I have just one thing to say."

"Do I want to hear this?"

"Doesn't matter. It's not directly about you." She smiled. "Morgan is a lucky little girl."

That surprised Libby, what with losing her parents and all. "Why do you say that?"

"Two good people care enough to be there for her. You and Mr. Donnelly are ready and willing to make sure she's got everything she needs. He's got the money, you've got the emotional thing going on."

"That's what Ginger said. It's how I came up with the idea to be his nanny in the first place."

"There are an awful lot of children that no one wants." Memories turned Sophia's eyes stormy and sad.

Libby wondered, not for the first time, about Sophia's

past, but when she looked like she did now, bringing up the bad stuff just seemed wrong. "Thanks for stopping in. It really helped to talk."

Libby finished up her work, then left the classroom and locked the door before stopping by the day-care center to pick up Morgan. They were on the way to the car before she realized she'd forgotten the folder for a project that she'd wanted to look over for the next day. When they rounded the corner a man was standing there, peeking into her classroom window. She recognized him immediately and her stomach knotted.

Speaking of people who'd like to dip into the bank account of the wealthy, or the not wealthy. Just anyone he could use for his own selfish reasons. Including his own daughter—especially his daughter.

"What are you doing here, Dad?"

Chapter Six

Libby stared at Bill Bradford's charming smile and the crinkly lines around his pale blue eyes. It seemed wrong that her father's dark hair was sprinkled with gray. That should be earned by hard work and worry, neither of which the man had ever done. This was the first time in months that she'd seen him, not since her younger sister Kelly had graduated from high school.

That meant he was up to something.

"What do you want?" she asked, pulling Morgan close to her.

"How are you, Lib?"

"Fine."

"Who's this?" he asked, looking at the little girl.

"Morgan," she answered. "Charity's child."

He nodded. "I heard. Kelly mentioned it. I'm sorry."

Libby didn't answer. This man didn't give a rat's behind about anyone but himself. "What do you want?" she asked again.

"Can't a father say hello to his kid?"

"Of course. But when *you* do, there's an ulterior motive."

The charming smile disappeared and the crinkly lines just made him look old. "Have you talked to your sister?"

"We e-mail all the time. She loves UCLA."

He nodded. "Now that she's away at college, Cathy's parents have suggested I should make other living arrangements."

A nice way to say *get out,* and about darn time, she thought. The man had mooched off Cathy's family for years, ever since Libby was a little girl. There was nothing that tugged on heartstrings more than a motherless child. About the time her folks had his number, Cathy turned up pregnant. She'd lost a child to a debilitating disease and descended into despair and drugs. She'd been on the street when she'd hooked up with Bill Bradford. All Cathy had ever wanted was her own baby to love and her parents would do anything to give her that, even if they also had to take in the baby-to-be's worthless father and his kid.

"What about Cathy?" Libby asked.

"She's staying."

So they were splitting up, which meant Cathy had finally had enough, too. At least the woman had been smart enough not to marry him.

He slid his fingers into the pockets of his jeans. "They didn't give me any warning, so I haven't had a chance to put together a plan. Other living arrangements take money and I haven't had time to save up."

She didn't say it out loud—that he'd had the last eighteen years to put away money, but that took ambition. "I don't have any cash to spare."

"I understand. Just thought I'd check." He looked at Morgan. "I know how expensive it is to have a kid."

Play the guilt card and fishing for information at the same time. Classic manipulation.

"I'm her nanny," Libby explained. "Just a working girl."

"I live with my Uncle Jess," Morgan added. "He has a big, big apartment in a very high building."

Bill forced a smile. "Sounds really nice."

"It is. And he bought me a new bed, with princess sheets." She held up her bandaged hand. "I didn't cry when I got stitches yesterday and he took me to the toy store and got me lots of stuff."

"Your Uncle Jess did that?" Bill Bradford's eyes gleamed with interest.

"Don't even think about it," Libby warned. "Jess Donnelly isn't someone you can—"

"*The* Jess Donnelly, billionaire resort builder?"

Darn. Darn. Darn.

"Look, we have to go." She took Morgan's uninjured hand and led her away.

From behind she heard him say, "Goodbye, Morgan."

"'Bye."

When the little girl slowed to look back, Libby tugged her along.

"See you later, Lib."

Not if she saw him first.

Libby kicked herself for letting anger squeeze out common sense. She was trying so hard to leave her past in the past and didn't want it to spill over into her present. All she wanted was what every woman wanted—a family, someone to love who would love her back. She didn't want to be associated with the man whose DNA she was trying so hard to overcome.

* * *

At dinner around the kitchen table, Jess had Libby on one side and Morgan on the other. She was eating fish sticks and fries, picking them up with her left hand because her right one was wrapped in white gauze. Because of him, her trauma had stretched out far longer than necessary.

He felt like pond scum. Actually worse. Scum was on top of the water. What he was settled lower, deeper, darker and slimier, at the bottom of the water. Because of him, the experience had been worse for Morgan, and remembering the way Libby's voice cracked and her struggle not to cry ripped him up even now. Fear had been starkly etched on her face and bothered him more than he would have believed possible.

When he stopped beating himself up, Jess noticed that the girls were quieter than usual. No small talk tonight to fill the silence. Normally Libby picked up the slack, but tonight she looked different. The sunshine was gone and he wondered why. It was best not to consider why he noticed at all.

He looked at her, then Morgan. "So, how was your day?"

"I didn't have to go to the hop-spital."

"I'm glad about that," he said, trying to keep his voice light. Obviously she remembered his boneheaded attempt to distract her from the upsetting situation with her hand.

"But I didn't get to play outside," the little girl added.

"Why?"

"'Cuz of my hurt hand." She chewed a French fry. "Miss Connie didn't want me to make it worser."

He glanced at Libby, who would normally have corrected the grammar slip, and was surprised when there was no comment. Definitely preoccupied.

"So what did you do inside?" Jess persisted.

"I colored. But not very good."

"How come?"

He directed the question to Morgan, then glanced at Libby, who was passive-aggressively multi-tasking. She was pushing fish stick bites around her plate and brooding at the same time.

"It was hard to hold the crayons in my other hand." She picked up a green bean and popped it in her mouth. "But Miss Connie said it was art stick."

"Is that scholastic terminology? A secret word between students and teachers?" he asked Libby.

"What?" she hadn't been paying attention.

"Her teacher called her coloring 'art stick.'"

"Artistic," she translated.

"Ah. That means it was good," he told Morgan. "Sometimes it's hard to be objective about our own work."

"Huh?"

"It means that we always like what we do so it's not easy to tell whether or not other people will like it, too."

"Oh." But she still looked confused.

"The good news is that while your right hand is getting better, your left got a chance to be a star."

"I guess." Her look was doubtful.

"So you had a quiet day?" He couldn't shake the feeling something had happened.

"Yup." Morgan nodded emphatically. "Then me and Aunt Libby came here."

He noticed she didn't say *home* and on some level it bothered him. "After yesterday, I'm glad everything was peaceful. So, that's all that happened?"

Morgan scrunched her nose thoughtfully. "I forgot. A man came to see Aunt Libby and asked if he could say hello to his kid."

That sent his "uh-oh" radar into on mode. "Who was he? Libby?"

"Hmm?" She glanced at Morgan and the conversation must have registered on some level because she said, "Oh. Just my father."

Jess realized he didn't know anything about her family and suddenly wanted to. "That's nice. Him stopping by, I mean."

"Aunt Libby didn't look happy. She s'plained to him that she's my nanny."

And had been for a while, Jess thought. That meant she wasn't communicating with him regularly.

"I told him I live with you," Morgan continued. "And that you bought me a new bed even before I hurt my hand. But when I didn't cry you took me to the toy store for a 'ward."

"Reward," Libby clarified, tuning in to the conversation now.

"Right," Morgan said. "I told him stuff about you and Aunt Libby said for him not to think about that. But I don't know what that means."

"It was nothing," Libby said. "He just stopped to say hello."

"But you were mad, Aunt Libby."

"I wasn't mad, sweetie." Libby looked startled. "What makes you think I was mad?"

"'Cuz you squeezed my not-hurt hand very, very tight and made me walk away kind of fast. And you didn't even say goodbye to him, which wasn't p'lite."

"I was just in a hurry to get you home," she said. "I'm sorry you thought I was angry."

"That's okay." She slid from her chair. "I hafta go potty."

She raced from the room, the unexpected visitor forgotten. But not to Jess.

When they were alone, he looked at Libby, who wouldn't

make eye contact. "You must have been happy to see your father."

She looked up and there was nothing happy in her expression. "He shows up from time to time."

"You didn't tell him you're working for me?"

"I did today."

Not what he meant and the look on her face told him she knew that. "Does your mother know about this job?"

"She died when I was born."

"I'm sorry," he said automatically.

Before he could ask even one of the million questions that popped into his head, Morgan ran back into the kitchen and Libby was reminding her to slow down and be careful of her hand. After that the routine ritual of table-clearing and bathtime commenced. The fact that it was becoming familiar to him wasn't as disturbing as curiosity about Libby.

He hoped that was because she so obviously didn't want to talk about her father. He figured that was because of a strained relationship, something he understood only too well. He didn't share information about his mother because there was nothing to be gained by telling a story that always managed to piss him off all over again.

He refused to consider that his high curiosity level was due to anything more than Libby's out-of-the-ordinary reserve. Every time their paths had crossed over the years, her smart, sassy sense of humor drew him, among other things that had caught his attention and some that hadn't until she'd moved into his penthouse.

He'd deliberately pretended not to remember her because he couldn't ever completely forget her. He had sensed the moment they met that she could be more to him, which wasn't something he ever wanted. The problem was getting that message where it needed to go. Every day he became more aware that she was bright *and* sexy. Not drop-dead gorgeous, but definitely pretty. And he was damned attracted.

The good news was that Morgan had talked to him more than she ever had and didn't seem to hold the emergency-room fiasco against him. The bad? Every day it was becoming increasingly more difficult to keep himself from kissing the nanny.

And that would be a huge mistake.

Libby expected Jess to work late and miss Halloween, but that hadn't stopped her from hoping she'd be wrong. She wasn't. When he walked into the penthouse, Morgan was already asleep, worn out from trick-or-treating and the excitement of wearing her costume.

He came into the kitchen, where Libby was standing by the island, inspecting the cache of candy the little girl had collected in her plastic pumpkin.

"Sorry I'm late," he said by way of greeting.

"Yeah."

With his jacket slung over his shoulder and held by one finger, he looked every inch a corporate pirate. His tie was loosened and the first button of his white dress shirt undone, with the long sleeves rolled up to mid-forearm. The look was so blatantly male, so incredibly masculine that he quite literally took her breath away. She wasn't prepared for that, but then she never was. There was no way to brace for the overwhelming force of attraction she'd experienced from the moment they'd met.

Jess picked up a chocolate bar and the expression on his face held traces of regret, which was surprising. "Did Morgan have fun?"

"Big time." Libby tossed a small bag of hard candy with

a tear in the package onto the discard pile. "I took her to the District in Green Valley Ranch. The stores surround a big courtyard and were all giving out candy. It had a safe, block-party sort of feel and there were lots of kids. She had a blast."

"I'm sorry I didn't get to see her dressed up."

"It's not too late. She insisted on wearing her princess costume to bed."

One dark eyebrow rose. "You let her?"

"It's a special occasion. Relaxing the rules seemed like a good idea." *Relax* being the operative word since there was something she needed to discuss with him. "You can look in on her if you want."

"I'll do that."

And there was a surprise. Every time she thought she had him figured out he did the unexpected.

He was gone for a while and returned wearing worn jeans and a pale yellow pullover sweater with the neck of his white T-shirt peeking out. Another masculine look that rocked her hormones. She should be used to it by now, but not so much.

"She looks pretty cute," he said. "While I think it's really cool, I have to ask. You don't think the glow-in-the-dark tiara is dangerous?"

Libby laughed. "I tried to talk her out of sleeping in it, but she was willing to take the risk. Then things threatened to get ugly. That wasn't a hill I wanted to die on, since I can take it off when she's sound asleep."

"Sounds like a wise decision." He opened the refrigerator and grabbed a longneck brown beer bottle, then twisted off the metal cap.

"Speaking of wise…"

Libby wasn't anxious to bring up the subject of his father or parental males in general after all the questions he asked about her own. Jess had never shown quite that level of interest in her before and she regretted more than was prudent that it probably wasn't about her at all. For the record, he was smart to be wary of her father.

As much as she didn't want to, she needed to talk—specifically about his feelings after his father died. He might be able to help Morgan more than anyone.

"What?" He took a drink of beer.

"I was hoping you could help with something."

"If I can," he agreed.

"Miss Connie came to see me today."

"Who?"

"Her kindergarten teacher. She was wondering how Morgan's coping with the loss of her parents."

"What do you think?" he asked.

"That's difficult to answer." Absently she twisted the cellophane ends of a candy package. "I had to break the news to her."

Libby remembered that horrible day. Reeling from the news that her best friend wasn't ever coming home. The realization that she'd have to tell Morgan something that no child should have to hear. "She didn't have an immediate reaction except to get very quiet. I figured she was only five and hadn't seen them for months, which is forever to a kid."

"That makes sense." The tone was casual and completely at odds with the hard edges and shadows on his face.

"But the regular phone calls from Charity and Ben stopped. I've sort of been waiting for her to bring up the subject, if she wants to talk about it."

"And?" he prompted.

Libby toed open the stainless-steel trash can, then tossed in the questionable candy before meeting his gaze. "She hasn't mentioned Charity and Ben at all. The thing is, I don't know how a kid would react to something like that."

He leaned a hip on the bar stool beside her. "I'm not sure how I can help."

"You lost your dad when you were just a kid. I was wondering how you handled it."

He'd started to lift the bottle to his mouth and stopped. The expression on his face said he'd rather walk naked in a hail storm than discuss this.

"That was a long time ago. I don't remember anything specific."

Something about his tone made her think he wasn't telling the whole truth about that. For the life of her she couldn't figure out why he wouldn't open up. For all his flaws, shallowness being top of the list, she'd never known him to be deliberately mean. And clearly he was loyal. Maybe she could get him to share.

"Did you talk about how you felt? To a counselor? A teacher? Or some other professional?"

"No." A muscle in his jaw jerked.

"Was there anything your mother did to make it easier?"

He set the beer down with enough force to splash some of the liquid on the counter. "Like I said, it was a long time ago. And I was only a few years older than Morgan."

"Which is why I think you're the best person to consult about how to proceed—"

"That's where you're wrong," he said. "Little girls are way outside my area of expertise."

In essence he was refusing to discuss the issue, which tweaked Libby's temper. "Right. I forgot. Big girls are more your style."

"I like women," he agreed.

Libby remembered. She hadn't meant to say anything

out loud and wasn't sure why she did now. That wasn't exactly true. It was no surprise that he dated, but seeing Elena Cavanaugh had hurt more than she was prepared for. His type was something she would never be, and face-to-face confirmation was tough to reconcile.

"A child is definitely a responsibility," she said, bringing the subject back to the little girl. "Is the obligation cramping your style?"

"Morgan is the daughter of my best friend. He'd have done the same for me."

That wasn't an answer and sounded more like the company line than a reason to raise an orphaned little girl. This time a dash of irritation made her ask, "Did you ever plan to have children?"

"Honestly?"

"Always the best policy," she said.

"Since high school my focus has been on achieving success. I knew business was the best way to do that and concentrated all my energy in college on learning everything I could to get me where I wanted to be. I'm determined to make the name Jess Donnelly as recognizable and synonymous with Las Vegas resorts as Steve Wynn or the Maloof family with their fantasy suites at the Palms Hotel."

"So children aren't now nor have they ever been one of your priorities?"

"No."

"Why doesn't that surprise me?"

His gaze narrowed. "Has anyone ever told you that's quite the talent you've got for lobbing verbal zingers?"

"I'm glad you like it."

"I didn't say that. Just that I noticed."

"That makes two of us." Libby froze, then let out a long breath.

What she noticed reinforced that her recent appointment with the attorney had been the right thing to do. The family law specialist had promised to research the situation and get back to her on options for Morgan's custody—if it became clear that was in the child's best interest. Libby still hadn't made up her mind about that.

Sometimes Jess showed signs of bonding with Morgan, then he pulled back. Like tonight. Missing Halloween.

Or maybe she was painting her perception of him with the rejection brush he used on her. She wasn't proud of the way she yearned for him to become aware of her but couldn't deny the feelings for him that had simmered inside her for so long.

"What did you notice?" he asked.

Like she would actually share her most personal and intimate thoughts with him. "It's not so much that as watching Morgan tonight. She made a couple of comments about kids with the adults around them. Wondering if they were moms and dads."

Jess folded his arms over his chest. "So you're wondering whether or not her teacher is right about a delayed reaction to losing her parents."

"Yeah. It crossed my mind." Among other things, she thought.

"Do you think she needs to see a professional?"

"It's an option," she agreed. "I think it might be best to just observe for a while."

"Okay," he said.

"And I'm thinking it might be a good idea to get out pictures of Charity and Ben. Not only is there a chance she would open up, but we should try and keep their memory alive for their child."

"You're right. Okay."

Okay. There'd been willingness in his voice to do whatever Morgan needed. That was the kind of thing that warmed Libby's heart and fueled her impossible fantasies where Jess was concerned. It's why she wasn't prepared to do anything drastic to uproot Morgan yet again.

As long as Libby was around to keep that little girl from getting hurt, there was no reason things couldn't stay the way they were. And that was the problem. They'd agreed she would stay on as nanny until Morgan adjusted. There was no guarantee he wouldn't decide tomorrow that Morgan was peachy and Libby's services were no longer required.

She didn't think he was there yet. At the moment she was more worried about her secret crush on him. But she'd had a lot of practice in hiding how she felt and would simply keep on not letting Jess see what was in her heart, the feelings that just refused to go away.

Chapter Seven

Libby and Jess had agreed to let the trauma of the E.R. and the sugar rush of Halloween recede before talking to Morgan about her parents. A week after trick-or-treating, the stitches had been removed and the remainder of the candy stash discreetly discarded.

It was Saturday, two weeks before Thanksgiving, a rare cold and rainy day in Las Vegas. Jess had turned on the gas fireplace in the family room where the three of them had watched Morgan's favorite animated movie. A feeling of yearning enveloped Libby just as tangible and encompassing as the cold. She wanted this to be *real*. She wanted a family.

With an effort, she pushed the yearning away even as she dreaded what was coming.

Morgan wiggled on the sofa beside her and looked up. "I'm bored, Aunt Libby."

She met Jess's gaze and gave him a what-do-you-think-about-now? look. He only hesitated a moment before nodding slightly.

Morgan glanced between them and asked, "What did I say?"

Libby fervently wished he would take the lead on this, which was nothing more than classic avoidance. She was the one with a degree in early childhood education, the one with child-care experience. Of the two of them, she could be considered the kid expert, but that was not how she felt in this delicate situation. She loved kids and cared about every single one, but there was a special place in her heart for Morgan. She was emotionally involved, which made knowledge and experience not very useful.

If it was within her power, she would make this child's life perfect and never let anything bad happen. Obviously she was powerless or they wouldn't be here now. And sometimes pain was a necessary therapy to get to a better place. She clung to that with every fiber of her being.

"Aunt Libby? Am I in trouble?"

"No, sweetie." She slid her arm around the child and pulled her close. "Why would you say that? Have you *ever* been in trouble with me?"

"No." She glanced up through her golden lashes to peek at Jess. "But maybe he's mad about somethin'."

Jess studied her, a serious expression on his face. "Did you make the stock prices in my company go down?"

She blinked and shook her head. "I don't know what that means."

"Just tell him no," Libby advised, rolling her eyes at him.

"No," Morgan repeated.

"Then I'm not mad at you," he assured her.

"Morgan, there's something Uncle Jess and I wanted to talk to you about. But if it's not okay with you, we won't."

"What?"

Libby's heart squeezed at the uneasy look on the little girl's face. She'd like nothing better than to blow this off for a rousing session of paper dolls or cutthroat Candyland. Some of it was about Morgan, but another very large part was that it was going to hurt to talk about this. It was another step in the process of realizing that her dearest friend in the world was no longer *in* this world.

Libby took a deep breath and braced herself. "We— Uncle Jess and I—want to talk to you about your mommy and daddy."

Morgan's little body stiffened against her and she looked down at her hands. But not before Libby saw, or maybe it was just a sense, that the little girl had shut down. Pulled an invisible cloak of protection around her. It didn't take a mind reader or kid expert to get that she didn't want to talk about this either. Probably for all the reasons Libby didn't and a whole lot more she couldn't even comprehend.

"What is it, sweetie?" Libby looked at Jess, who was frowning.

"Nothin'."

"Did you know your daddy was my best friend?" he asked.

"Why?" Morgan glanced quickly up at him.

"That's a good question. I'm not sure why he liked me." He thought for a moment. "But I admired him because he was smart. He was funny. And he always had my back."

"Huh?"

Libby could almost see the wheels turning in his mind as he concentrated on finding words to explain an expression that adults generally understood. He really wasn't used to conversing with kids, but he got an A for effort. And major points for looking so darn cute while he did it.

"It means," he finally said, "that he was always there when I needed him."

"Oh."

Libby wondered if Morgan was too young to realize the irony of the fact that she would never experience the quality that Jess had valued so much in her father. And, if she did realize the extent of her loss, was she angry about it? That's part of what this exercise was all about.

She met his gaze, grateful that he'd started the ball rolling, got Morgan talking. Now it was time to follow his lead.

"Morgan," she said, "did you know your mommy was *my* best friend?"

This time the little girl only nodded, giving her nowhere to go conversationally.

"Why?" Jess asked, picking up on that.

She smiled her gratitude. "I respected her because she cared about everyone, including me. She made me laugh. I loved that about her. But one of my favorite things is that she was a girly girl."

Morgan glanced up, the barest spark of interest in her eyes. "Does that mean she liked girl stuff?"

"Not just liked. She *loved* girl stuff more than any girl I know." Libby smiled even though her heart hurt. "She couldn't go into a store without buying lipstick, eyeshadow or blush. Unless the store she was in didn't carry any of those items. She painted my toes the very first time I ever had that done, and spilled nail polish on the rug."

"Did she get in trouble?"

"No. Her parents were cool." More relatives Morgan would never know. Charity's father and mother had died a couple of years ago, within six months of each other. Ben's folks had passed away before the two had met. "She loved earrings and bracelets, too."

"And tiaras?" Morgan asked.

"Probably her favorite—" Libby's voice cracked and she looked up when Jess's fingers touched her shoulder. She appreciated the show of support even though it came with a tingle of awareness. "Your mom would have loved your Halloween costume."

"Really?"

"Really," Jess said. "Your dad, too. He always called you his little princess."

"I'd forgotten that. He said it when you were born." Libby snapped her fingers then reached over to the table beside her and grabbed a stack of photos that she'd gathered together. "Here's a family picture. Your mom's holding you and there's your dad sitting on the hospital bed."

"I remember when they were getting ready to bring you home from the hospital. Your dad and I spent a long time making sure the car seat was hooked up right so you'd be safe." Jess's expression was shadowed with sadness at the memory.

"And on your last birthday you got chalk and drew pictures on the sidewalk outside with your mom and dad. Here's one of the three of you. Remember that, Morgan?"

"No."

Libby felt the force behind the single word, but didn't know whether that was the truth or simply that Morgan was doing her best not to recall.

She tightened her hold on the child. "Why don't you tell Uncle Jess and me something you do remember?"

Morgan was quiet for several moments. "I don't 'member them much."

"What about your dad giving you rides on his shoulders? Or your mom playing boats in the bathtub, with bubbles?" Libby suggested.

"No." Morgan shook her head. "And I don't 'member what they look like anymore."

Libby wasn't surprised. In fact, she'd kind of expected that. As she handed more pictures to the little girl, Jess got up and left the room. She sighed, glad that he'd stayed for the hard part. But she missed his reassuring presence, something else she wished not to feel yet couldn't seem to stop.

"These are pictures of your mom and dad's wedding."

Morgan looked through them, then pointed to one of the maid of honor and best man. "This is you and Uncle Jess."

"That's right." Libby took it from her.

In the photo she was wearing a strapless lavender dress and Jess looked incredibly handsome in a traditional black tuxedo. He had his arm around her and there was a gleam in his eyes as he looked at her. Even now flutters and hormones collided in her belly, sending waves of wanting through her. He'd thoroughly charmed her that day only to profoundly disappoint later, when he left the reception with another bridesmaid.

Jess walked back into the room with his own pile of pictures and Libby's heart pounded as fast and furiously as it had the day she'd met him, during their friends' wedding activities. She hadn't given up on not having a visceral reaction to him. That achievement was still a work in progress.

He sat on the sofa, on Morgan's other side, and handed her a snapshot. "This is your mom and dad in their condo. It was taken at the housewarming party."

"I have some of those, too," Libby said.

Libby found it endearing that in this age of digital photography he'd bothered to have some pictures printed. It was something they had in common. Morgan shuffled through them and pointed out Libby and Jess in every one.

"Here are some taken in the hospital when you were born." Yet again Libby saw herself and Jess.

"These are from her christening." Jess handed them to Libby first.

She was holding Morgan at just a few weeks old and Jess had his arm around both of them. They were her godparents. She met his gaze and saw the sadness she knew was in her own eyes. It was a grief they shared and somehow that made it a little easier to bear.

The last pictures were of Christmas and Morgan's fifth birthday party in January, just before Charity and Ben had left. It was like watching a disaster movie and wanting to beg them not to go because something bad was going to happen, something they couldn't stop. The holidays that were coming up would be Morgan's first without her parents.

She handed the photos back. "Here."

Libby searched for comforting words. Like her parents would always be with her even though she couldn't see them. In the end she was afraid the concept of spirits or ghosts might be more disturbing.

So she only said, "They loved you so much."

Morgan looked up, her big brown eyes sad. "Who's my family now?"

Well, damn, this had backfired. It brought up more questions than comfort and Libby didn't know how to answer. She wanted to say that she and Jess were her family. They were certainly there for her. They were godparents and now the parent figures on the front line of bringing up this child. But family?

The reality was something else.

Libby's path had frequently intersected with Jess's. There had been numerous opportunities to hook up, if he'd been interested in her. Obviously he wasn't. She felt a pain in her heart that had nothing to do with losing her friend and everything to do with big feelings for him that had nowhere to go.

She pulled Morgan into her lap and hugged tight. "Don't worry, sweetie. You're going to be just fine. I'm here. Uncle Jess is here."

Libby swallowed the threatening tears and couldn't look at Jess for fear he'd see. She wanted Morgan's life to be perfect and it never would be. Her best friend wasn't ever coming home again. She squeezed Morgan just a little closer. Charity was gone, but thank goodness a part of her was still here.

Jess sat on the corner group in the family room and tried to concentrate on the football game. It wasn't easy when fragments of yesterday's conversation with Morgan kept popping into his head. He was well aware of his limitations and never planned to have children. Something that Libby had figured out for herself.

Ben had always told him he'd make a great dad and with the right woman Jess would feel differently. This was different, all right, and Libby was the right woman to raise Morgan. But Jess knew he was the weak link, not father material.

Morgan had opened up a little and he hoped she felt better even though he felt like crap. Libby had asked him how he felt when his dad died and he'd felt like crap then, too. He just hadn't known how much worse things could get. His mom had been responsible for the worse part, but at least he'd had her to get him through the first wave of the grief. Morgan didn't have either parent. The poor kid just had him, a bachelor with no idea how to help her. Thank goodness for Libby.

The two of them were doing girly stuff. Stuff that Charity would have done. What would Ben have done? Probably watch football.

On his seventy-inch plasma flatscreen TV, two teams were fighting it out, sweaty and physical. Games were won or lost on a single play. A split-second decision. The Monday-morning quarterbacking didn't come until Monday morning and this was still Sunday night. But Jess was second-guessing his friend. Probably Ben had fully thought out the decision before asking him to be his daughter's guardian. But Jess just couldn't see in himself what Ben had, nothing that would indicate he was capable.

He saw movement from the corner of his eye and looked up to see Morgan standing just inside the entrance to the family room. She was wearing a pink sweater with sneakers to match and jeans.

"Hi," he said.

"Hi," she answered.

They stared at each other for several moments before he asked, "Where's Aunt Libby?"

"Doing stuff."

"I see." And pigs could fly.

"What are you doin'?"

He glanced at the TV, then muted the sound. "I'm watching a football game. The New England Patriots are playing the Seattle Seahawks."

"Oh."

"I'm rooting for the Seahawks," he added.

"'Cuz they're birds?" she asked, moving farther into the room so she could see the screen full-on.

"No, because they're the underdog."

There was confusion in her eyes. "So they're dogs?"

"No." He wanted to laugh at her literal interpretation but she looked so serious he held back. "*Underdog* is just an expression. It means no one thinks they'll win."

"Why do you want them to?"

"Because it would surprise everyone and I like surprises." He looked at her sober little face and in his own mind put a finer point on that statement. He liked *good* surprises, not the kind where friends didn't get to see their kid grow up.

Morgan moved closer, leaning on the end of the corner group. "Are the birds winning?"

"No. But they're only behind by seven points. A touchdown," he explained.

She scratched her nose. "What's that?"

"It's when a team takes the football over the goal line into the end zone to put six points on the scoreboard."

"But you said it was seven."

"It is after they kick the extra point."

"They kick it? Does it hurt?"

"No."

Jess never knew kids took things so literally. He looked at the total confusion on her face and tried to remember a time when he had known absolutely nothing about the game of football. He'd started watching when he was about Morgan's age because he enjoyed spending time with his dad. Because he'd asked questions, his father had patiently explained the basic rules of the game.

After his mother remarried, watching the sport was the only thing he and her husband ever did together without arguing. And every argument was followed by his mom taking a side opposite her own son.

Jess put the remote control on the coffee table. "After a

team scores, they have to kick the ball over the bar between the goal posts for an extra point."

"Six plus one is seven," Morgan said.

"Correct. You're pretty good at math."

"That's what Miss Connie says."

"Your teacher?"

"Uh-huh."

He wasn't sure where to go now. Then Libby's words came back to him. *Kid talk takes practice. Ask things you don't know.*

"Do you like Miss Connie?" It was the next question that popped into his head.

"Uh-huh. She took care of me when I cut my hand."

He tried not to think about how he'd let her down that day. Since then he'd authorized Libby to do whatever might be necessary for Morgan's well-being and instructed his secretary to interrupt him immediately when she called. If that happened, it would be about this child and he wanted to know.

"I'm glad Miss Connie was there for you."

She rubbed a finger on the arm of the furniture. "Aunt Libby told me that my real daddy wishes he could be with me."

"She's right. Your Aunt Libby is a pretty smart lady." And hot. Sharp-witted and sexy. Even when she was calling him on his crap. Maybe he liked her *because* she stood up to him.

Morgan scrambled up onto the sofa and sat with her legs sticking straight out in front of her. "She said that my daddy maked sure I'd be okay with you."

"That's right. He did." And Jess had given a solemn promise to watch over her.

She turned the full force of those big, innocent brown eyes on him. "Does that mean you're my daddy now?"

For a little thing, she carried quite a wallop. The words felt like a sucker punch and he couldn't catch his breath, but the expectant expression on her little face demanded a response.

"I'll make sure you're okay. Your dad asked me to be your guardian and that means I'll take care of you."

"But will you be my daddy?"

Persistence was a good thing, he told himself. He wouldn't be where he was today without it. But right at this particular moment, he wished Morgan had a little bit less.

There was no way he could take Ben's place, but he'd have to be a moron not to see that this little girl needed reassurance. He simply couldn't lie to her.

"I'll always be your Uncle Jess," he assured her.

"But that's different from a daddy," she said.

"How?"

"'Cuz there are things daddies do. I have a list."

"What kind of things?" he asked, feeling dumb as a rock for not instinctively knowing.

She slid off the couch and dug a piece of paper from her jeans pocket. "Stuff like riding a bike."

"Do you have one?"

She shook her head and blond curls danced around her face. "But I'm gonna ask Santa Claus to bring me one."

Note to self, he thought. She was a believer in North Pole lore and wanted a bike for Christmas. He'd have to discuss that with Libby.

"What else is on your list?"

She looked down at the wrinkled paper with uneven printing. "I don't know how to tie my shoes yet. Or swim." Glancing out at the terrace complete with pool, she added, "What if I fall in?"

"If you can't swim that could be a problem. Although your Aunt Libby watches over you pretty carefully." The words were spoken in a calm and reasonable voice. Inside he wasn't quite so Zen. Probably Libby would have brought up the subject of swim lessons when the weather warmed up. Or he might have thought of it himself, but he didn't quite buy that. "Is there anything else?"

"Allowance," she said.

For a couple of beats he didn't have a clue what she meant, then it dawned on him. Weekly earnings for work completed. Chores to be determined by the adult in charge.

"That's a very comprehensive—" He realized the word was too big for her. "A very complete list you've got there. Aunt Libby and I will make sure everything is taken care of."

"Okay." She moved closer and handed the paper to him.

From down the hall Libby called out and Morgan turned her head, indicating she'd heard. "I hafta go."

"Okay. See you later."

"'Bye." She raced out of the room.

When he was alone, Jess let out a long breath. The good news was that their picture presentation featuring Morgan's parents had been successful in bringing up some feelings. The bad news? She wanted Jess to wear the daddy hat. Worse, the look in her big eyes said she trusted him to wear it well, but her belief in him was misplaced.

He'd lived with two sides of the dad thing—the father he'd lost to cancer and the man his widowed mom fell in love with later. His dad had made him promise to be the man of the house. His mom promised that Jess was the most important person in her life. But when she remarried, he'd been caught in the middle and felt like a screwup at everything he touched.

He never wanted to disappoint Morgan the way his mother had him. It's why he never pictured himself with kids. He didn't want to screw up a brand-new life.

Emotional detachment was second nature to him now. It had worked real well because he'd managed to push everyone away except Ben. Now his friend was gone. The good thing about being alone was that there wasn't anyone to let down.

Until now.

Chapter Eight

After putting Morgan to bed, Libby walked into the family room and saw Jess watching TV. But not watching. There was a program on but the sound was muted. He was staring at the big screen with a dark and broody, faraway expression on his face. She'd just come in here to let him know that Morgan was asleep, everything was quiet and to say good-night. She was going to stand in the doorway, not get in close enough for the delicious smell of him to make her hormones dance. It was all about delivering her message, then beat a quick retreat to her room and refuge. It was a plan; it was a *good* plan. Sensible. To the point. In and out before the constant yearning inside her could be whipped into a frenzy of need by prolonged exposure to his potent charm and masculinity.

A closer look at the face that never failed to make her weak in the knees brought out a heavy sigh.

"Jess?"

He looked up. "Hmm?"

"I just wanted to let you know Morgan is asleep."

"Okay."

She cocked her thumb over her shoulder, indicating the area behind her. "I'm going to turn in. Busy day tomorrow."

"Oh?"

"Yeah. The excitement level of the kids really goes up before Thanksgiving. And leading up to Christmas it's a big challenge to keep them under control."

"I bet."

"Right. So I need all the sleep I can get." Or not, as thoughts of him always crept in and disturbed her rest.

"Libby?"

She'd just started to turn away and winced when he said her name. "Hmm?"

He hesitated for a moment. "Speaking of Christmas…could I talk to you for a minute?"

This wasn't part of her plan. It so wasn't what she'd come in here to do and every instinct urged her to come up with an excuse and walk away. But there was something so lost in his expression. Something that tugged at her heart. He didn't look like his usual confident self, which was noteworthy. If she had to guess, she would say he was afraid of something and that wasn't the Jess Donnelly she knew. But, darn, it made him a Jess she wanted very badly to get to know.

She blew out a long breath and moved farther into the room, across the coffee table from him. "What's up?"

Jess hit a button on the remote and light from the TV flickered out behind her. "It's about Morgan."

"I figured." No way would he want to talk about Libby. She wasn't the sort of woman who made a man like Jess look the way he was looking now. "What about her?"

"She talked to me."

Libby wanted to throw her hands in the air and holler *woo-hoo,* but she was pretty sure that wasn't the reaction he was looking for. In fact, his shell-shocked appearance reminded her a lot of the way she'd felt when Morgan asked them yesterday who her family was.

"What did she say?"

He stood and ran his fingers through his dark hair. As usual, her insides liquefied. In his long-sleeved white cotton shirt and jeans worn in all the most interesting places, he was her three-dimensional fantasy guy come to life. The angles of his face were all rugged male and the brooding made him mysterious. The stuff of a romance-novel hero. All she could think about was how it would feel to be in his arms.

"Libby, I am so in over my head."

His words brought her back hard and his unease was contagious. "Oh, my. What did you talk about?"

"I was watching the game. Patriots and Seahawks."

"Okay." That didn't seem relevant, but all right.

"It seemed like there was something on her mind but she didn't come out with anything. I didn't know what to say. The thing is, I'm not into girly girl stuff."

"That's all right." One look at his wide shoulders and the masculine five o'clock shadow darkening his cheeks and jaw would clue anyone in to the fact that he was a manly man who'd recoil in horror at girl stuff.

"So I started talking football," he continued.

"Sticking to your comfort zone is good."

"I explained what a touchdown is. Kicking the extra point and why I root for the underdog."

Libby really liked that about him. "Good for you. But none of that explains why you're upset."

"I'm getting there. Just trying to add context."

"Okay. Didn't mean to interrupt."

"She talked about her teacher a little and I remembered what you said about asking questions."

That was incredibly likable, too. Not only had he listened, but he was trying to apply her advice.

"Then what?" she encouraged.

"She mentioned what you told her, about her dad. That he made sure she'd be okay. With me."

"Right. I did. She needs to feel secure," Libby confirmed.

"That's when she asked if I was her daddy now."

And that explained the brooding look that bordered on panic. "What did you tell her?"

"I explained about being her guardian and taking care of her. But she wanted clarification on the whole daddy thing."

"And?"

He shook his head and stared at a spot over her shoulder. "I can't take Ben's place. I didn't really know what to say so I told her I'd always be her Uncle Jess."

"How did she take that?"

The look on his face said not well, but Libby'd had no indication tucking the little girl in bed that anything was bothering her.

"She gave me a daddy list."

"What?"

He moved closer, until they were nearly touching, and held out his hand with a wrinkled piece of paper. "It's a list of things dads do. Like teaching her how to tie her shoes. Swim. Set an allowance. Ride a bike. By the way, she's going to ask Santa for one for Christmas."

Again, that explained her casual reference to Christmas triggering this confession of the soul. "The good news is that she's opening up."

"The bad news is she's opening up to me. I'm in way over my head," he repeated.

"Don't go to the bad place," she said calmly.

"Give me one good reason why not. I've got no skill set for this. My dad died when I was twelve, and my stepfather—"

"What?"

This was the first time he'd mentioned that. The only time they'd discussed his loss, he'd shut down tighter than a prison during a riot when she mentioned his mother. Libby couldn't help being curious, mostly because this Jess wasn't cocky and confident. This Jess was vulnerable and sensitive. He was someone she could fall for.

"Let's just say he wasn't my idea of a parental role model." Jess set on the coffee table beside him the tattered paper with daddy duties on it, then ran his fingers through his hair. "The point is that nothing in my background has prepared me for this. And I don't want to mess her up."

"That's not going to happen."

"How can you be so sure?"

Good question, but suddenly she needed to reassure him. Putting that into words was tough but his eyes gave away how much he wanted her support.

"I know because you're trying," she said. "You listened to advice and put it to practical use."

"I did?" His clueless expression was so endearing.

"Yes. Granted, your conversation was sports based, but that's irrelevant. You connected with her, Jess. That's the most important thing."

"Talking football is one thing." He rubbed the back of his neck. "Dad talk is something else."

"Sincerity is half the battle." She settled her hand on his arm and felt the heat of his skin through his sleeve.

He met her gaze and something dark and intense heated

in his eyes. "I could *sincerely* screw up that little girl's life without your input. I need *you,* Libby."

The passion of his focus on her face trapped all the air in her chest and she couldn't breathe.

I need you.

The words were deeply personal and became sexually charged, making the blood pound in her ears. Libby swayed toward him but would never be clear on who moved first. In the blink of an eye or the beat of a heart, his mouth was on hers.

One of his arms circled her waist and he pulled her against him. His other hand cupped her cheek and then his fingers tangled in her hair, holding her steady while his lips thoroughly explored hers. He kissed her nose, eyes, cheeks and hair. The contact was so sweet, it felt as if he'd kissed her heart.

They were touching from chest to thigh and his muscular strength in contrast to her feminine curves practically made her hormones weep. Although she'd tried desperately to deny then ignore the yearning for him that had always simmered inside her, she couldn't deny it now. They were so close it was impossible for her not to feel the physical evidence that he wanted her, too.

She could hardly believe that the fantasy she'd harbored from the moment they'd met wasn't a dream. But here he was, holding her and kissing her. She heard his raspy breathing and it was an echo of her own. But doubts crept in. She put her hand on his chest.

"Jess?" Did that wanton, whispery voice really belong to her?

"What?" His lips were on her neck and he stopped kissing her, then blew on the moist place where his mouth had just been.

She shivered and her brain short-circuited, but she managed to say, "This probably isn't a good idea."

"I know."

"There are a lot of reasons why it's not the smartest move," she said, not wanting to leave the shelter of his arms.

"Uh-huh." He cupped her cheek in his palm, then ran his thumb over her kiss-swollen bottom lip. "Can you give me three?"

"Three what?" She couldn't think when he touched her like that.

"Reasons." His gaze lowered to her mouth and heat flared.

"Right this second I can't even name one."

"Then how important are brains and logic?" he asked logically.

For some reason that made perfect sense to her. Probably because the way she felt, she'd implode if she walked away from him now.

"Brains and logic are highly overrated." Her words were almost slurred as the spicy scent of him surrounded and intoxicated her.

He slid his palm down her arm, then let his fingers entwine with hers and led her willingly down the hall, into his bedroom. He picked up a remote control from the nightstand beside the king-size bed and hit a button. Instantly the window covering parted and the glitz of Las Vegas magically lighted the dark room.

She'd been in the master suite before, but never with Jess. The bed was an imposing four-poster oak frame with matching nightstands. An armoire and dresser were arranged around the room's perimeter. A black-and-beige comforter covered the mattress, hiding the sheets beneath.

She looked up and her breath caught at the way outside light caressed the rugged line of Jess's jaw and shadowed the angles of his face. He needed a shave and she knew from minutes ago that the stubble would scrape her face, but she welcomed every tangible experience. It was better than a pinch to make this moment real and scratch it into her consciousness.

"Does that remote control gizmo turn down the bed for you?" she asked.

He shook his head, a sexy, wicked gleam in his eyes. Reaching beside him, he yanked the bedding down, revealing the silky, cream-colored sheets.

"Okay?"

"That works, too."

Jess let his gaze roam over her from head to toe. When it settled on her mouth, heat flared and he groaned. "You are one sexy little schoolteacher."

"Me?"

He nodded. "And just so you know. The innocent thing works for me."

"What innocent thing?"

His only answer was to kiss her, unleashing a sense of urgency. They pulled, tugged and yanked on each other's shirts and jeans, desperate for skin-to-skin contact. With her clothes scattered around her, Libby crawled into the bed and stretched out, the sheets cool to her naked, heated flesh. A moment later, Jess was beside her, kissing, touching, taking her to a level of desire that she'd never known.

He cupped her right breast in his hand, brushing his thumb across the taut nipple. "Beautiful," he breathed.

The approval started a glow deep inside that expanded to every part of her. She settled her palm over his knuckles and heard him suck in a harsh breath. Slipping his hand from beneath hers, he traced a tender touch down over her belly, then slid a finger inside her, teasing her in the most intimate way. Her hips lifted, communicating her sense of need.

He rolled to his side, reached into the nightstand and pulled out a condom. In seconds he opened it and covered himself. Then he was beside her again, kissing, stroking and taunting her with his touch. Her thighs automatically parted in invitation and he settled over her, balancing his weight on his forearms.

He entered her with tender slowness, then sighed with satisfaction, which was quite possibly the sweetest sound she'd ever heard. He stayed still for agonizing seconds before pushing fully into her. His tension was tangible just before he stroked and plunged, again and again.

He took her to the edge and in a blinding flash of light, they both went over. Pleasure poured through her and she held on tight as he shuddered in her arms. They didn't stir for a long time, drenched in satisfaction and too sated to move.

Finally, Jess rolled away. Even with her eyes still closed, some part of her registered that a light went on somewhere. Minutes later it went off, just before she felt the mattress dip beneath his weight.

He gathered her to his side and brushed a kiss on her temple. "Wow."

"Wow, indeed," she murmured.

It was the last thing she remembered before falling asleep in his arms.

Libby felt her bed move and opened one eye, expecting to see Morgan. Instead, the French doors leading to the terrace were a big clue that this wasn't her bed, and she wasn't in her room. She had a very good idea who'd caused the mattress to dip. Glancing behind her, she identified Jess's broad shoulder and muscular back.

"Holy Mother of God—"

She groaned softly as everything came back to her in a rush of heat followed by a dear-Lord-what-have-I-done feeling. If a feeling could be rhetorical this one was because she didn't need an answer spelled out. It was there in every pleasure-saturated muscle in her body. She'd had the best sex of her life with Jess Donnelly, after which she remembered feeling safe and warm and happy.

The dim light peeking through the shutter slats told her that it was morning, but she had no idea of the time. The clock was on the other nightstand and seeing it would require major mattress movement to see over Jess's shoulder. That would risk waking him, the last thing she wanted. Facing him after what they'd done would be awkward enough, but when it happened, she wanted to *not* be stark naked in his bed. Fully clothed, preferably with multiple layers, would be marginally better.

Before sliding out from beneath the protection of the covers, Libby tried to figure out how to cover herself. She had a vague, passion-filled memory of her blouse and sweater flying one way, jeans, panties and bra going another.

What she wouldn't give for that black satin robe, but she had no idea where he kept it. She'd never seen it on him. T-shirts and sweatpants were Jess's early morning ensemble of choice, and were adorably manly at that—other than seeing him without a stitch, of course. The urge to peek under the covers now was almost irresistible, not to mention brash, brazen and downright wanton. She could go through his closet, but that seemed an invasion of privacy. A stupid thought seeing as they'd been as intimate as a man and woman could be just a few hours before.

The indistinct outline of the master-suite bathroom was straight ahead. Maybe she could slip in there and wrap herself in a towel, then make it to her room before Morgan woke up and missed her.

Just then there was a flash of light in the hall and the little girl's voice drifted to her.

"Aunt Libby? Uncle Jess?"

Libby groaned miserably. This was like one of those horrible dreams when for no apparent reason you're in a ladies' restroom naked from the waist up. Do you walk out and suffer the mortification? Or stay put and endure slightly less humiliation? Libby never got the chance to decide.

The little girl walked in and said, "Uncle Jess, I can't find Aunt Libby."

"Morgan, sweetie, I'm here," she whispered, hoping he was an extraordinarily sound sleeper. The bedside light went on, instantly dashing that fantasy.

"Morgan?" His voice was raspy from sleep.

In her pink princess nightgown, she appeared on his side of the bed. "I had a bad dream."

That makes two of us, Libby thought.

"A nightmare?" Jess repeated.

The little girl nodded as her solemn brown eyes assessed the two of them. "How come Aunt Libby is in your bed?"

"That's a very good question. I'm glad you asked." He glanced over at her and arched one dark eyebrow. "I'm thinking you should field this one."

Libby would rather poke herself in the eye with a stick and thought of multiple names to call him, starting with *coward,* then moving on alphabetically. But that wouldn't be helpful.

Stalling for time, she said, "Come over here, Morgan."

While the little girl padded over to the other side of the bed, Libby held the covers tightly to her chest and piled two pillows behind her back, trying to create an illusion of dignity under the least dignified circumstances imaginable. She patted the space beside her, indicating that Morgan should climb up. When she did, Libby pulled the comforter over her and snuggled her close.

"Do you want to tell me about the bad dream?" Maybe a distraction would help.

"I don't 'member. It was just scary."

"I'm sorry you were scared, sweetie." And feeling terribly guilty for not being close when she was. "But you're okay now. That's the most important thing. Right?"

"Yup." She nodded. "And it wasn't dark in my room."

"Good. That high-wattage nightlight is doing the trick." Beside her she felt the bed move as Jess fluffed pillows behind his back.

"There's enough light in there to illuminate the runway at McCarran Airport," he said wryly.

Morgan looked at him. "So why is Aunt Libby sleepin' in your bed, Uncle Jess?"

Libby still didn't have an acceptable G-rated answer fit for a five-year-old's tender ears. All she could come up with was, "I didn't mean to fall asleep."

And that was the honest truth. If she could rewind and have a do-over, she would have walked away before he had a chance to unleash his vulnerability.

"Are you scared of the dark, too?" Morgan asked.

"You could say that," Jess answered.

But it wouldn't be true, Libby thought, aiming a glare in his direction. His fleeting grin indicated her look had been promptly received and instantly ignored.

Was he even the slightest bit bothered by what was happening? The same man who just hours ago was concerned about messing up this child? If there was any silver lining, it was that Morgan was too young to understand.

"Are we gonna have a baby?" the little girl asked.

"What?" Libby and Jess said together.

There was very little satisfaction to be had from the fact that the *B* word had gotten his attention in a big way.

"Why would you think that?" Libby asked, trying desperately to keep her tone calm, cool and in control.

"I heard one of the kids at school."

"Carrie?" Libby asked, and the little girl nodded. "Her mother is pregnant."

"What did you hear Carrie say?" Jess asked.

Morgan rubbed her nose. "Her mommy's tummy is gettin' big because there's a baby inside. She's gettin' a little brother 'cuz her mommy and daddy sleep in the same bed."

"I see." So much for Morgan being too young to understand, Libby thought. Although there was some comfort in that it didn't sound like the mechanics of the birds and bees was being shared. "It's true that Carrie's mom is going to have a baby."

"Can we have one, too?" Morgan asked. "I want a baby brother. Or a sister. Is your tummy gonna get big, Aunt Libby? 'Cuz you slept in Uncle Jess's bed."

Libby winced at the heartbreakingly hopeful tone. Disappointing this already wounded child wasn't something she would knowingly do. But if she and Jess had done anything right in the midst of so much wrong, it had been taking precautions against conceiving a child. And if there was a God in heaven, a merciful God, she amended, He wouldn't punish them for a single weak moment.

She was trying to formulate a generic, nonresponsive response when the alarm on Jess's nightstand went off.

"Saved by the bell," he muttered.

That's for sure.

Now she had to figure out how to resolve this situation

to keep everyone's dignity and sensibilities in one piece. "It's time to get ready for school, Morgan. Do you want to wear your new lavender jumper?"

"But you said I shouldn't wear that 'cuz I might get paint on it," the little girl reminded her.

"How about just this once if you promise to be very careful?"

"I will be," the little girl said sincerely. "I promise not to get it dirty."

"Okay then. Why don't you run along to your room and pick out a long-sleeved blouse to go with it?"

"Okay. I can get dressed all by myself." She pushed off the comforter, scrambled down from the bed, then raced out of the room.

As soon as they were alone, Jess reached down to the floor beside him and grabbed his shirt, then tossed it to her.

"Thanks."

"Don't mention it."

Words to live by.

She shrugged into the too-long sleeves with as much modesty as possible. When she slid from the bed, the shirt-tail hit her mid-thigh, which was all the coverage she needed for her escape. Without a backward glance, she left the master suite and hurried to her own room.

She pulled the collar tightly to her and sniffed. The material smelled like Jess, making her stomach shimmy as always when his fragrance surrounded her. That reaction was fraught with problems.

It meant that sleeping with Jess hadn't neutralized her crush. On top of that, Morgan was delighted at the prospect of adding a baby to the mix. Libby was no shrink, but she would bet part of that reaction was about them being a family, which she'd clearly indicated she wanted.

The reality was that Jess had only agreed to this nanny arrangement for the short term. After last night's slide into the personal, he could have major second thoughts. It was quite possible that he'd decide Morgan had adapted and Libby's temporary employment could be permanently over.

What if he told her to go? That her work there was done?

The thought of leaving Morgan broke her heart. She would be out in the cold without the child she loved as her own.

And without Jess.

Chapter Nine

A kid walking in on Jess the morning after he'd had mind-blowing sex with a beautiful, complicated woman was a sitcom scenario that had nothing to do with his life. At least it hadn't until now.

He needed to man up and make adjustments.

It was weird that sleeping with Libby had brought him to that realization. And even after she had annihilated his willpower, he still couldn't decide if she was that beautiful or was just growing on him. Sitting on the brightly colored plastic bench across from her, Jess watched her watching Morgan climb around the play equipment at the fast-food burger place down the street from the complex where he lived.

Complex was the operative word. Had he suggested this kid-friendly dinner outing because he was manning up? Or to avoid talking about what happened that morning?

Even though she'd been naked in his bed, Libby had handled the situation like a seasoned pro. He still couldn't believe the little girl had connected the dots and gone to wanting a baby sibling. He didn't know what to do with one kid, let alone two.

The real question was why he'd slept with Libby in the first place. He'd been attracted to her for years without acting on it. Granted, having her under his roof made it more of a challenge, but he'd been handling it for weeks. Until last night.

He wanted to believe that his control had slipped because the scope of his responsibility was finally sinking in and he'd reached out to her. Nothing more than a moment of weakness. But that didn't explain why he wanted her again.

She looked at him then and something in his expression made her eyes widen and her lips part. "So," she said, releasing a long breath. "Can you believe Thanksgiving is next week?"

"Time flies." *When you're having fun,* he added to himself. Last night could be filed under the heading "too much fun." It was the reason for the tension arcing between them now. The post-sex conversation that needed to happen was like the elephant in the room. Everyone knew it was there, but avoided bringing up the subject.

"Uncle Jess. Aunt Libby, look at me," Morgan called out to them from the top of the climbing apparatus in the playroom where kids were allowed to expend their energy.

"I see you," Libby said. "Be careful up there."

"I'm going to slide down, Uncle Jess. Watch me," she called.

"I'm watching." And checking out the structure for possible risks.

When the little girl slid through the red tube to the rubberized floor, they both watched her go right back up.

Libby glanced at him. "Last year I spent Thanksgiving with Charity and Ben and Morgan."

He'd gone to Aspen with a cover model. Now he couldn't even remember her face. If he never saw Libby again, he knew that her clear blue eyes, bright smile and determined chin would be unforgettable.

"Do you need the holiday off? To have dinner with relatives?" Maybe the father she didn't want to talk about?

"No." Libby tensed and met his gaze. "What about you? If there are family commitments, I can make myself scarce."

"No."

"No commitments? Or no family?"

"It's just my mom. She does her own thing. We're not close." They had been once, before she threw him under the bus one too many times for the guy who'd replaced his dad.

"I'd be happy to cook dinner," Libby suggested.

"Or I could order from a restaurant."

"You don't trust me?" she asked, challenge in her eyes.

"You have to admit that breaded tubular tenders containing questionable meat products are more your thing."

"That's about getting a finicky five-year-old to eat. I'm actually a pretty good cook."

"Do you enjoy it?" he asked.

"Yes. But I can see you're skeptical. I might surprise you."

She already had. And not just because of how responsive she'd been beneath his hands and mouth.

"So you really want to do the turkey-and-a-big-meal thing?" he asked, getting his mind back into the conversation with an effort. "It's a lot of work and not in your job description."

The gleam in her eyes dimmed, but she recovered quickly. "I think a quiet dinner with Morgan would be just right this year."

"Okay, then."

"Look at me climb up," Morgan called to them. Her voice echoed in the big room.

Jess watched her foot slip and said, "Be careful, Morgan."

"I will." The little girl looked over her shoulder and grinned.

"Are you sure she's okay?" he asked Libby.

"I'd be more worried if there were a lot of kids in there with her. But by herself she's fine."

Having been alone for a long time, he could relate to that. "So, back to Thanksgiving."

She nodded thoughtfully. "With my class I try to emphasize that the holiday is about being thankful for our blessings. We can carry that theme over with Morgan." Her mouth pulled tight for a moment. "It's really sad when you think about it."

"What?" He took a sip from the straw in his cup.

"Neither of us has anyone to be with on the holiday. Morgan had family and now they're gone. How do you spin that into something thankful?"

"Good question."

"If I hadn't agreed to keep her, they wouldn't have gone," she said sadly. "They wanted to do it before she started first grade, before she got caught up in sports and other extracurricular activities."

He wondered whether or not she knew about his part in this, then decided to get it off his chest. "There's plenty of guilt to go around."

"What do you mean?"

"There were costs involved in their humanitarian cause.

I gave them the money to make it happen because they were both determined. A fire in the belly."

Jess waited for her anger and recrimination but it never materialized.

She nodded as if understanding exactly what he meant. "I saw that commitment, too. It was something they talked about and planned to do before having children, but Morgan was an accident. Then they adjusted their time frame and tried to do justice to the compassionate cause so emotional to them and the child they loved so much. But if either of us had just said no—"

"Charity and Ben would be alive," he finished for her.

"Yeah."

"For what it's worth, I'm glad not to bear this guilt alone. I'm thankful to share it with you."

She nodded even as a frown marred the smooth skin of her forehead. "What we don't share equally is custody of Morgan."

For reasons he'd never know, they'd asked him to be the legal guardian and he'd made a promise to her parents. The expression on Libby's face told him she didn't understand. "And that bothers you?"

"I love her very much, Jess."

"It shows."

"And I need to know where I stand," she added.

"You're her nanny."

"But for how long?"

"I'm not following," he said.

"The day I brought Morgan to you, we agreed to this arrangement until Morgan adjusted to the situation."

He remembered. Even then he'd realized that Morgan needed someone familiar. He'd agreed Libby should stay even though there was the potential for a conflict of interest because of a personal connection, one that had become even more personal. Now they were getting closer to the elephant in the room.

"I need you, Lib." He hadn't meant for the words to come out with quite so much hunger and hoped she hadn't noticed.

"Define *need*," she said.

"I'd have to be made of stone not to get how right you've been."

She blinked. "I'm sorry. Did you just say I was right?"

"I deserve that," he said, smiling. "But I'm not too proud to admit when I'm wrong. Putting a roof over Morgan's head isn't the beginning and end of my responsibility. Fatherhood isn't about being a placeholder. A guy needs to be proactive in a kid's life and I have no idea how. That's where you come in."

"Oh?"

"I'm counting on your guidance to effectively interface with Morgan."

Libby's look was wry. "For starters you have to talk to her like a regular person, not a computer geek."

"See? That's exactly what I mean."

"I'm not sure I understand," she said.

This was where the conversation got awkward. He wasn't in the habit of sleeping with a member of his staff. It wasn't a company rule, just his own personal code. When you crossed that line, things got weird and upset the work environment.

In this case that involved Morgan. She'd had enough to deal with already and loved Libby, counted on her. He wouldn't be to blame for her losing someone else that she needed in her life. Jess needed her, too, but he was a grown-up and could put his feelings aside.

"Jess?"

"You're a vital *employee,* Libby."

Surprise was evident on her face. "Meaning?"

"What happened last night was my fault." There, he'd said it. Time to drop-kick the elephant into oblivion.

"I see." Her tone said that was a lie.

"I'm counting on you to help navigate this child-rearing situation with Morgan. She has to take priority over everything." Even wanting Libby again. "We need to put last night behind us and move forward. For Morgan's sake it can't happen again."

"You're right, of course. I couldn't agree more. Consider it forgotten."

The words were politically correct, but her face told the truth. It wasn't like him to read feelings, but he could now. Maybe because this was Libby.

He recognized the hurt in her eyes from all the times he'd pretended not to remember her. But what he saw there now was somehow worse.

With a cup of tea, Libby sat alone in the morning room as the lights of Las Vegas stood out in stark relief against encroaching twilight. This six-thousand-square-foot penthouse was a lot of real estate, but without Morgan it really felt enormous and empty. What made her uneasy was that she was getting a preview of what life would be like without Morgan when Jess decided he could navigate the child-rearing waters by himself.

Take today, for instance.

He'd escorted Morgan to the movies and suggested Libby might like the afternoon off to relax after working so hard on Thanksgiving dinner the day before. They'd had such a nice day and the little girl didn't seem to be comparing the holiday to last year's with her parents. Now it was T-day plus one and so much for him *needing* Libby.

A shiver danced down her spine at memories of the intense expression in his eyes when he'd said that. Her female radar had clicked on and cranked up. But that was before he delivered the stunning blow.

He didn't want her.

That declaration had followed his song and dance about finally getting that a father should be proactive. That he'd been disconnected from the situation. *Jess Donnelly was wrong* should be splashed on a billboard and displayed on the 15 freeway for everyone to see that he'd actually said it out loud. But that had just been to grease her goodwill for the real message.

She wasn't an Elena Cavanaugh, who had a free pass to his bed whenever she wanted. Not only that, he'd had to go and be noble about it. Taking the blame. Saying it was his fault. Again he was wrong. Libby had been a willing and eager participant.

And now she was alone. He'd taken an ecstatic Morgan to an IMAX theater to see the latest animated movie. Libby didn't know what to make of his behavior. Based on her own recent experience, he was too capricious and that made him untrustworthy.

Like her father.

With Jess, Morgan would never have to worry about a place to live and food on the table like Libby had. But emotional starvation could be every bit as harmful. Still, there was no reason to take him on regarding his guardianship as long as she could be Morgan's nanny. Unlike the firm stand he'd taken on their personal detour, he hadn't given her an answer on how long she could expect to be in Morgan's life.

She hadn't heard anything from the attorney, which meant he was still researching the options. Hopefully it was a step she would never have to take, but knowledge was power and...

Libby heard the beep from the deactivated security system that signaled the front door opening. She painted a smile on her face and felt like the world's biggest phony when she went to meet them.

"Hi, guys. How was the movie?"

Jess was standing in the foyer holding Morgan, who had her arms around his neck. "Her tummy doesn't feel good."

That sounded like a direct five-year-old quote and Libby hurried over to them. She brushed her hand over the little girl's quilted pink jacket. There was a nasty stomach flu going around. A lot of kids had missed school because of it.

"What's wrong, sweetie?"

"I might hafta throw up again." Morgan didn't lift her head from Jess's shoulder.

Alarmed, Libby looked at him. "Again?"

"The Lexus can be cleaned," he said, choosing his words carefully.

Libby had to like that response and knew she was being bitchy for not wanting to. She looked at Morgan's pale face and pathetic expression as she felt her forehead. "It doesn't feel like you have a fever. I'm so sorry you don't feel well. Do you think you can handle a quick, warm bath?"

"Will you help me?" the little girl asked.

"Of course. Don't I always?"

"Yes." Morgan nodded, still using Jess's broad shoulder for a pillow.

It was enough to make female hearts go "aww," and Libby was no exception. She looked up at him and couldn't decipher the intense expression on his face. "Will you carry her into the bathroom?"

"Of course."

But he didn't add "don't I always?" because he hadn't yet established a pattern of involvement with this child. So far it was only words to the effect that he'd changed.

But as promised, he carried Morgan into the large, luxurious bathroom and set her down on the fluffy pink accent rug beside the beige tub. Backing away, he said, "I'll be right outside if you need me."

"That's okay. I've got her."

He shook his head. "It's the least I can do. Can I get anything?"

Lately he'd done a lot of talking about needing her. Only once had it been about *her,* the night he'd taken her to bed. Otherwise the need was all about her child care skills. If it weren't for Morgan, she'd quit the nanny gig and just teach. It was too hard being around Jess. Then she thought about not being with this little girl she loved so much and knew leaving voluntarily would never happen.

Libby had removed the jacket and was on her knees releasing the pink Velcro sneaker fasteners. She looked up and saw that he sincerely wanted to help. "Okay. Yeah. Her nightgown is in the top right-hand drawer of her dresser. Panties and socks, too."

"Okay. I'm on it."

That was different. She'd let him off the hook, but he hadn't taken the out. Again she had to admire him.

Libby turned on the tub's gold hot and cold fixtures to start the water. When the temperature was warm enough, she put down the stopper. There was a soft knock on the door and Jess stuck his arm in. In his big hand he held all the requested night wear.

"Anything else?" he said.

She went over and took the things from him. "This is great. Thanks."

"It's the least I can do," he said again.

His participation was beginning to sound like penance. Was that guilt she heard in his voice? There was a story and she was getting awfully curious. She quickly removed the rest of Morgan's soiled clothes and lifted her into the tub's warm water.

"Morgan, what did you have at the movies?" she asked as she soaped up a washcloth.

"I don't 'member, Aunt Libby. I'm too tired." She sat quietly.

Normally she was giggly and active at bathtime, so Libby washed, dried and dressed her as fast as possible. She carried her into her room and tucked her into bed. Her eyes closed as she turned onto her side and she fell asleep almost instantly.

After turning on the nightlight, Libby left and went to find Jess.

She found him in the family room at the wet bar, pouring himself a drink. The front of his powder-blue sweater and worn jeans had stains similar to what was on Morgan's clothes. That probably happened when he'd carried her all the way up here.

"Rough day?" she asked.

"You have no idea." He tossed back the contents of the glass in one swallow, then sucked in a breath. "Is she okay?"

"Sleeping."

"That's good."

"I wonder if she has the stomach virus that's been going around school." Libby waited for him to take that and run with it.

"No. It's all my fault."

That sounded familiar. Was he being noble again? "What did you do?"

"I let her have popcorn, soda, red vines and ice cream," he confessed.

"Ooh." She winced at the sheer volume of junk.

"I know. Go ahead. Take your best shot. You can't call me anything worse than I've already said to myself. I can't believe I was that stupid. She's five—"

"Almost six," Libby reminded him.

"She's a little kid and I fed her like she was the Seattle Seahawks' defensive line. I have no idea what I was thinking."

"I didn't say anything."

"Maybe not, but I can almost hear you thinking it," he accused.

"Actually, I hadn't gone there yet. But now that you mention it…what *were* you thinking?" She moved closer and the recessed lighting illuminated the dark, guilt-ridden expression in his eyes.

He ran his fingers through his hair. "I wanted her to be happy. To have a good day. If she asked for it, she got it. I forked over the money without considering the consequences. I practically got her whatever she looked at."

"That's really pretty sweet." Libby didn't have the heart to help him beat himself up. She was peeved at him for brushing her aside, but this wasn't about her. How could she be mad when he was doing exactly what she'd been urging from the beginning?

"Sweet?" He shot her an annoyed look. "Don't even talk about sweet. And don't be nice to me. I'm an idiot who doesn't deserve the consideration."

"You are," she agreed, just to humor him. "But you're an idiot with a good heart."

"That's not making me feel better."

"Okay. How about this? Why in the world would you let her have all that junk food?" Her voice dripped with mock censure.

He paced in front of the floor-to-ceiling windows for several moments then stopped in front of her. "You're making fun of me."

"Just a little."

One corner of his mouth curved up in a most appealing way. "Am I overreacting?"

"You're being a goof."

"And you're being too kind. I made her sick, Lib."

"Just an accessory to the crime," she corrected. "I'd be willing to bet that you didn't personally shove all that sugar into her mouth."

"The thing is, I remember how empty I felt after my dad died. Maybe this was all about preventing her from feeling that way. Giving her twice as much to compensate for losing both of her parents."

Libby put her hand on his arm, an automatic gesture of comfort, but the warmth seeped into her and surrounded her heart, setting up a siege situation. "You're on the right track, Jess. Spending time with her. Doing fun stuff—"

"Like making her sick?" He shook his head. "A shrink would have a field day with me."

"And me. And probably everyone we know or ever hope to know."

"Okay. Point taken. But I guess what I need to know is how to avoid another incident in the future."

"Really?" She couldn't help smiling.

"Of course really. What do I do?"

She tapped her lip thoughtfully. "What would you say

to an employee who wanted a promotion that they weren't qualified for?"

"I'd say no."

"Exactly. *N-O*. Practice it. Next time you're tempted to go to the dark side, just say no."

"Believe it or not, I actually said that to her today."

"All evidence to the contrary," Libby commented wryly.

"Ha-ha." He folded his arms over his chest. "She wanted to go in the bathroom and I couldn't go with her."

"Good call. A man in the ladies' room might have been a problem." She respected his protective instincts, but added, "It would have been okay to let her go in if you stood outside and waited."

"I did better than that."

"Oh?"

"I found a female security officer and she went into the ladies' room with Morgan." He smiled proudly at his problem-solving brilliance.

Libby just stared and somehow stopped herself from saying "aww." If his goal had been to melt her heart, all she could say was mission accomplished. She felt all gooey inside, which didn't make her one bit happy. And she couldn't even say she hadn't been warned.

At the burger place he'd told her that he was ready to take on the responsibility of parenting Morgan. But Libby hadn't really believed he meant what he said. She'd have been wrong and needed her own billboard to that effect on the 15 freeway.

That brought her to the biggest problem. She'd been able to temper her attraction to Jess with disapproval when he behaved in the usual shallow way. But that was happening less and less and made her wonder if she'd been wrong about him all along.

If that was the case, it would make working for him even more difficult. How was she going to protect herself from falling for the man who needed her, but didn't want her?

Chapter Ten

This was his first parent-teacher conference and Jess wondered if Connie Howard, kindergarten teacher, could tell he was a fraud. The fiftyish, blue-eyed brunette obviously was aware of the circumstances that had landed Morgan in his care. But did she realize that not long ago he'd been a carefree bachelor who gave house keys to hot flight attendants and now the little girl wanted red hair and big boobs when she grew up?

Whoever was in charge of fate had a wacky sense of humor if they thought he could raise this child into adulthood with any chance for normal. Then again, fate had also sent him Libby.

He glanced up from Morgan's file on the kindergarten teacher's desk to look at Lib. With her blond hair pulled back, her slender neck was right out there, tempting him to taste her again. Her full lips compressed with concentration, then curved upward in a smile. She was so smart, so witty, and still managed to be sweet and nurturing. These days he actually looked forward to going home and it wasn't about sex. That couldn't happen again because it could cost him Libby and he'd be lost without her. Correction: Morgan would be lost.

"It's a pleasure to finally meet you, Mr. Donnelly."

"Likewise," he said, wondering if that comment was judgment or simply a statement of fact. He could thank his mother's second husband for his inclination to dissect a conversation and separate out the criticism. With his stepfather, most of it was negative so there was very little guessing involved.

"Morgan is a delightful child," the teacher continued. "So sweet and eager to be of help and do the right thing."

"I couldn't agree more." Libby glanced at him and smiled.

He returned it, then struggled to return his focus to the teacher. "She's a good kid."

Right. And he'd had so much experience with kids that he'd earned the right to have an opinion.

"So how's she doing?" he asked.

"Academically? Just fine. Morgan is solidly at grade level in everything. In fact she's one of my brightest students," Miss Connie said. "But there is something I'm concerned about."

"What?" he asked, before Libby could.

"Socially she's having a difficult time."

"Is someone being mean to her? A bully?" Libby asked. "I wish you'd said something sooner—"

"It's not that," Connie assured them. "Morgan isolates herself. The children were reaching out, but they've stopped. There's only so much rejection a person can take."

Jess glanced at Libby again and wondered if she'd

reached her quota from him. He remembered every rejection, perceived and real, that he'd ever dumped on her. Yet not long ago, he'd kissed her and she'd kissed him back, loving him until he'd thought his head would explode. And he rejected her yet again. He wouldn't blame her if she said adios, but thank goodness she loved Morgan more than she found his behavior objectionable.

"She doesn't have friends?" Libby asked, surprised and obviously upset.

Connie shook her head. "She's quiet and introspective. She keeps to herself and makes no effort to establish friendships."

"But in preschool there was nothing like this," Libby protested.

"She made friends easily," Connie agreed. "But just after she started kindergarten her best friend moved away."

"Oh—" Libby's tone was part whisper, part groan. "I'd forgotten."

"On top of that she lost her parents," Jess added. "It doesn't take a mental giant to figure out a trauma like that would change her. Saying goodbye to her friend is a loss, too."

"That's very true." Connie looked at them. "I think her parents' deaths have affected her more deeply than she lets on. Children react according to their personality. Some become rowdy and act out in order to get attention. Others internalize their feelings and become more quiet. It's my opinion that Morgan falls into the latter category. I believe she's reluctant to form attachments for fear of losing anyone else she cares about."

Jess could relate. He'd been doing that since his own dad had died. His mother had promised to be there for him but it only lasted until she fell in love and remarried. Then she couldn't be bothered with him. His fiancée was no better. When he put the ring on her finger, she'd vowed to love him forever. But when he'd brokered a risky business deal, she'd decided forever was only as long as he could afford the life-style to which she'd like to become accustomed. He still had that ring somewhere as a reminder not to form attachments.

Ben was the only one who'd overrun Jess's defenses, through sheer persistence. It worked because the risk had paled in comparison to the reward. Memories of his friend stirred the stockpile of sadness he'd always carry with him.

"What should we do?" Libby anxiously twisted her fingers in her lap.

"Give her time. I know it's a cliché, but time does heal the wounds," Connie said.

"She said something recently." Besides asking if Jess was her daddy now. Besides giving him the list of respon-sibilities that weighed like a stone on his chest. "When Libby and I broached the subject of her folks being gone, she asked if we're her family now."

"That's right." Libby glanced at him, then back at the teacher.

"Probably she's instinctively reaching out to find where she belongs now." Connie leaned her elbows on the desk and settled her chin on folded hands. "She's dealing with an unimaginable loss, and at the same time wanting to fit into a domestic unit."

No one had ever before accused him of being domestic, Jess thought. It was hard to be a unit all by yourself, even though it was the way he'd always wanted things to be. Now he had to rethink that.

"As far as what to do?" Connie sighed. "Make her feel secure."

"Piece of cake," Libby said wryly.

"I know. Just take things one day at a time and be there for her. Encourage her to talk about what's on her mind."

Check that, he thought, thanks to Libby. She was the one who had encouraged him to discuss things. On his own he would have put a great deal of effort into avoiding any conversation about personal feelings.

"She seems to enjoy hanging out with Jess," Libby said.

He felt two pairs of eyes on him and shrugged. "I just explained the basics of football."

"And you took her to the movies," she revealed.

He so didn't want to talk about something that felt a lot like a failing grade in Fatherhood 101.

"That's good. Keep it up—" There was a knock on the door and Connie called out, "One minute."

Libby glanced behind her. "Your next appointment?"

"Yes, I'm sorry. If you'd like, we can schedule a time to speak more about this when parent conferences are over."

"That would be great." Libby slid the strap of her purse onto her shoulder.

Jess stood, too, and held out his hand. "Thank you, Ms. Howard. I appreciate your insight."

"You're welcome." Her look was sympathetic. "Hang in there."

Jess put his hand to the small of Libby's back as he guided her out of the room and past the mom and dad who were next. His palm tingled with the contact and he wanted to slide his arm around her, pull her closer, make the touch more intimate. With a great deal of effort, he kept his hand right where it was until she stopped in the empty hallway outside the classroom.

Libby looked up at him, her blue eyes filled with concern. "Before we pick her up from Sophia's office we need to talk."

About Morgan. Right. He needed to get his mind off the way Libby's body fit so perfectly to his and back on how to help Ben's little girl cope.

"Okay. You first."

"Me?" She held out her hands in a helpless gesture. "I don't have any answers."

"You're the expert. It was you who realized she was forgetting Charity and Ben and organized operation photo retrospective." He resisted the impulse to tuck a stray blond hair behind her ear. "By the way, thanks for the pat on the back in there."

"What?"

"Telling her teacher that I hang out with her," he explained.

"You do."

"So do you," he pointed out. "You're always there for her, even here at school."

"That's all good," she conceded. "We both do stuff with her."

"But she wants a family." He ran his fingers through his hair. "I'm not sure how to do that."

"At least you had one."

Meaning she hadn't, he realized. She'd tried to get him to talk about his feelings about losing his dad, but he'd gone on the defensive. Maybe that had been a boneheaded move. "Things were great in my family before my dad died. Then my mother found a guy and remarried."

"You don't look happy about it," she said, studying him.

He didn't want to talk about that part. "The point is, I remember a time when Mom, Dad and I did stuff. All of us together."

"You think Morgan wants to do that with you and me?" she asked, surprised.

"I'm shooting in the dark here," he conceded. "But I

don't think Ben would want me to let his daughter grow up socially stunted. I've got baggage from my past, but the bright spot was always Ben. How can I not do everything to make sure Morgan has a shot at the best parts of being a kid? How can I not leave any stone unturned so that she can find a best friend? So she can find her Ben?"

"Or Charity," Libby agreed. "So you're saying we should do family activities?"

"What's the harm?"

He winced even as the words came out of his mouth. That meant spending more time with Libby and struggling to keep his feelings in check. The feelings that could jeopardize his commitment to his best friend's child. But if hanging out with Morgan and Libby would help, then he was in. Keeping his distance from a woman had been instinctive until Libby came to live with him. She'd short-circuited all the barriers he kept in place. But somehow he would find a way to maintain an emotion-free zone and not further complicate this already complicated arrangement.

After all, where was the harm in doing the right thing?

"Do I want to know how you got tickets for a sold-out Christmas show on ice at the last minute?" Libby asked.

They were in a luxury box at the Orleans ice arena waiting for the crowd to thin out before leaving.

"I could tell you my secret, but then I'd have to kill you." Jess's smug look disappeared as he glanced at Morgan, peering down at the oval of ice below. "Just kidding."

"She didn't hear and I knew you were joking."

Libby had thought he was being funny earlier when he'd come home and announced he had tickets for the holiday show. Their conference with the teacher had only been two nights ago and he was already taking on the duty of family outings. No, not family. This was simply the three of them out and about. That's all.

"Seriously," she said, "how does one get the best seats in the house at the last minute?"

"You told me once that I'm not like other people."

"I remember."

She hadn't meant it in a good way, so his point was lost on her. She'd meant that he had layers of people between him and opportunists like her father who would try and take advantage of the man who'd recently landed on the list of the world's billionaires. The Internet was a fertile source of information and she only felt the tiniest bit guilty for Googling him.

It wasn't a question of which business had garnered him a place in affluent company, but more about whether or not a business existed that he didn't own. And that was only a slight exaggeration.

"But you're changing the subject." She glanced out the glass and noted that people were still filing out of the arena. Morgan was engrossed in watching the big machine driving around the ice to smooth it. "Exactly how did you snag these tickets?"

"That wasn't changing the subject. I'm explaining that I really am like everyone else. If you cut me I bleed. If you wrong me I hurt."

"Is that Shakespeare?"

"I have no idea, but it sounds like something he would have written. That's not important. My point is that the only way I'm different from the average person is my tax bracket."

"Because the amount you send the Treasury Department could neutralize the national debt?"

"I wouldn't go that far." He thought for a moment as they watched the people below slowly walking up the aisles toward exit signs. "The difference between me and the average person is that when I say money is no object, it's not lip service."

"Or bragging?"

"Never." There was an angelic expression on his face as phony as your average get-rich-quick scheme. "It's not bragging if it's true. Admittedly, some of the assets that put me in wealthy company are in stocks and bonds. It's not all sitting in a bank, or a hidden safe in the penthouse. Or under my mattress."

"Okay. I get it. So, are you saying you greased some palms to get the tickets?"

"I know people who know people who hooked me up. For the right amount of money."

"As easy as that."

Libby slid the strap of her purse more securely on her shoulder as she studied him. Jess Donnelly was better looking than the average guy, so much so that he would probably get some notice in Hollywood. Visually that was all that set him apart. His penthouse was luxurious and pricey, but not unobtainable. Tonight he was wearing jeans and a cream-colored pullover sweater with the collar of his white shirt peeking up from beneath it. The clothes were expensive and came from well-known designers, but labels weren't visible.

The cars he drove weren't cheap, but also were not one-of-a-kind standouts. And suddenly she wondered what a billionaire did with all those billions.

"So, other than getting tickets, where does all that money go that you're not bragging about?" She met his inquisitive gaze without looking away. "It's no secret you've got it, but I can't see where."

"If you've got it, there's no need to flaunt it."

"Humor me. My imagination is limited and I have no idea how one would spend when money is no object."

"Idle curiosity?" he asked.

When she was thinking about Jess Donnelly it never felt idle, but she was definitely curious. "Pretty much."

He thought for a moment. "I have real estate all over the world. Location. Location. Location. It's always a good investment."

"Where, for instance?" She folded her arms over her chest.

"A house in the Hamptons. Another in Aspen. Condo in Hawaii."

"Yeah," she said wryly. "Me, too. What a coincidence."

He grinned at her sarcasm. "Then there's the Gulfstream."

"Jet?" she asked.

"No, the hang glider." Who knew he would see her sarcasm and raise her a bite or two? "Technically the plane is for business, but it gets me from point A to point B faster than commercial airlines." A shadow darkened his eyes when he added, "Unless there's bad weather and everything is grounded."

"Do you have a boat?"

He shook his head. "But I'm looking into buying one."

She figured he was probably talking yacht classification. For her it would be something in the rowboat family. In all the years she'd known him, she'd never once thought in terms of him being wealthy. But he'd told her that since high school he'd focused on achieving success. He'd concentrated on business in college and learned everything that would get him where he wanted to be. The name Jess Donnelly was definitely right up there with the big boys.

Morgan watched the Zamboni drive off the ice, then joined them. "Uncle Jess, you promised me a souvenir."

"I did. Are you ready to go pick something out?" Her

blond curls danced around her face when she nodded en-thusiastically and he said, "Okay. Let's do it. I think the crowd has pretty much cleared out."

The three of them left the box with Morgan between them, holding their hands. They rode down in the private elevator that let them off where the merchandise was on display. There were T-shirts, character dolls, stuffed animals and an array of snow globes. While Morgan walked around looking at everything, Jess and Libby followed to keep her in sight.

"It was awfully nice of you to grease palms and bring us here," she said.

He slid his hands into the pockets of his jeans as he watched the little girl gingerly touch a doll with pink net tutu and tiara. "Is Miss Connie a good teacher?"

Funny how she'd never noticed him answering questions in a roundabout way. That made her question how well she'd actually known him. Over the years she'd made a lot of general assumptions and formed an opinion that could be flawed.

This time Libby had a pretty good idea where he was going with his response. "Her reputation as an educator is impeccable. Her insight into kids is legendary."

He nodded. "So it wouldn't be especially smart to ignore advice from a legend."

"Not only did you not ignore her, you set a land-speed record for implementing her suggestion."

Libby figured this outing was about the three of them doing something together. It was homework. Literally. Except it had begun to feel real and that was dangerous, in a very personal way.

"Uncle Jess?" Morgan ran over and looked up at him. "I found something."

"Good for you."

She continued to stare upward. "Maybe more than one thing."

"Show me," he encouraged.

She bit her lip. "I can't decide. There's a princess doll and a whole set that has magic markers and a coloring book with Santa Claus and elves and the North Pole."

"Maybe we should get both."

The little girl's eyes got bigger and the look on her eager face was more magic than the markers. "But I saw some dresses and shoes. Costumes. Like the ice skaters wore. For playing dress-up."

He squatted down to her eye level and without hesitation said, "That sounds too good to pass up. I guess we'll have to get all three if you can't make up your mind."

Morgan smiled, then threw her arms around him. "Thank you, Uncle Jess."

He picked her up and met Libby's gaze. "It's not red vines and ice cream. Probably won't make her sick."

"True. You've mastered saying no to junk food. But princess paraphernalia, not so much."

"You can tutor and lecture till the hereafter won't have it, but it's impossible to say no to that face."

"I see what you mean." Libby's heart squeezed at the carefree smile Morgan was wearing. It had been missing for a while. "A little spoiling can buy a whole lot of security."

After purchasing everything, they headed for the valet stand in front of the resort to retrieve the car. Morgan chattered as they walked.

"I want to be an ice skater when I grow up."

Jess glanced at Libby. "I guess that's a better career choice than hair color and body parts."

She laughed. "You'll get no argument from me."

When they got to the lobby decorated for the holidays with ornaments, garland and a tree, Morgan's happy expression slid away. She stopped and stared longingly at the lights and shiny ornaments on the branches.

"Do you have a Christmas tree, Uncle Jess?"

He guided her out of the flow of people walking in and out of the busy lobby, then went down on one knee in front of her. "Do you want a tree, kiddo?"

One small shoulder lifted in a shrug. "I guess."

"We can do that." But her solemn expression didn't budge and he noticed. "What is it, Morgan?"

"I don't know if Santa knows how to find me."

"What do you mean?" he asked.

"I'm not livin' in the same place and he might not know where to leave my presents."

Libby's heart squeezed again, but this time it wasn't a happy thing. Last year this child's life was carefree and normal. Now it had turned upside down.

Jess rubbed a hand over his neck. "What do you think we should do about that?"

Libby put a hand on the little girl's shoulder and pulled her close. "I bet a visit to Santa would take care of that."

"Really?" Morgan looked up.

"Really. We can go see him and you can give him your new address and tell him what you want for Christmas," she suggested.

"That sounds like a pretty good idea to me," Jess agreed.

Morgan didn't look convinced. "Are you sure?"

"Absolutely." Jess pulled the princess doll from the bag he carried and handed it to her. "And we'll get the best tree ever. Maybe one for your room, too."

That put the smile back on her face. "Promise?"

He crossed his heart and held up two fingers. "I swear."

Libby knew she was there because of how seriously he took his vows. She'd been hired as the nanny for the child he'd sworn to care for. They'd agreed she would stay until Morgan adjusted, which was happening before her eyes. Every holiday and occasion without Ben and Charity would set a precedent for the next one when Morgan wouldn't remember what it had been like before Jess.

But Libby wondered how long before she had to see what it was like without Morgan and him.

He was really stepping up for her. That meant Libby had even more face time with him and that was the last thing she needed. Sex hadn't meant any more to him than it did with a surprise visit from the flight attendant, but it meant quite a lot to Libby.

Lust with a generous helping of respect very well could equal love, but he only wanted her as the nanny. Tonight was a sign that it wouldn't take long for him to get the hang of daddyhood. She knew from growing up with a father who'd tossed her aside when he could use his newest kid to put a roof over his head that personal value had a short shelf life.

Libby wondered how much longer Jess would have any use for her.

Chapter Eleven

The Saturday after the ice show, Jess admired the ten-foot tree in the corner of his family room. You had to love twelve-foot ceilings at Christmastime, especially when trying to impress a little girl. He glanced at the little girl in question and noticed that she'd fallen asleep on the sofa.

He opened his mouth to alert Libby, then closed it again, the better to concentrate on her. Just reaching up to adjust an ornament, she flashed a slice of bare flesh when her sweater slid up. The sight of that smooth skin winking in and out tweaked the ache he'd carried inside since making love to her. If he was being honest, he'd carried it around longer than that. But being with her had made it worse.

Of all the mistakes he'd made in his life, and they were legion, that's the one he wanted back.

Not because it wasn't fantastic. That was the problem. It was better than awesome and he wanted her again, a slippery slide into relationship hell. He sighed as he admired Libby's shapely rear end. Compared to her, flight attendants with keys were simple and uncomplicated.

"This is the most beautiful tree I've ever seen." When she glanced over, he was pretty sure she hadn't caught him staring at her butt. "How did you get all this stuff so fast?"

"Again, I remind you, when you say money is no object, you have to mean it."

"Ah. How could I forget?" She nodded knowingly.

"I made some phone calls. Had stuff delivered. The shopping with Morgan for more ornaments you already know about." He shrugged. "Easy."

"It smells heavenly." Libby breathed in the pungent scent of pine. "And it's truly the most spectacular tree."

"It's the first one I've ever had," he said.

Her hands stilled before she slid him a surprised look. "Ever?"

"Since I've been on my own." It felt like he'd been alone most of his life. Until now.

"Wow." Her gaze dropped to the couch. "Morgan's awfully quiet. Is she asleep?"

"Yeah."

Libby peeked over the high back of the sofa, then came around to stand beside him. She smiled down at the blond pixie. "She's worn out from all the excitement. You sure didn't waste any time following through on your promise."

"I didn't get to be a billionaire by standing back and twiddling my thumbs."

He smiled, remembering that conversation. She'd been sincerely curious about how a guy spent his money. His gold-digger radar didn't pick up any signs of ulterior motive. Unlike the visitor he'd had at his office yesterday.

"Libby, there's something I need to talk to you about."

"Okay," she answered without hesitation. "First let me put Morgan to bed."

When she started to lift the child, he said, "Let me."

"I can do it."

"No doubt. But she's almost six, which means she's pretty heavy."

He didn't wait for a response, but scooped up the little girl and carried her to bed. She was so small, so defenseless. A powerful wave of protectiveness washed over him that was less about his promise and more about a hold on his heart.

In her pink bedroom, a small tree with white lights stood on the dresser. Jess smiled, recalling how shocked, surprised, excited and delighted Morgan had been when he'd kept his promise.

Libby slipped off the small sneakers, then pulled the princess sheet and matching comforter over the little girl. "She can sleep in her sweatpants and T-shirt just this once," she whispered.

He nodded, because nanny knew best.

When they were back in the family room, she began to stack empty ornament boxes. "What did you want to talk about?"

Her blond hair shimmered from the glow of the holiday lights and made his hands ache to touch her. And that wasn't all. His body ached, too, in places he'd never known existed. Then he realized she'd said his name.

"Hmm?"

"You said there was something you needed to talk to me about."

"Right." He slid his fingers into his jeans pockets to keep from making another mistake he couldn't take back. "Your father came to see me yesterday at my office."

It wasn't surprise that stilled her hands this time, but shock. Not in a good way. Jess couldn't tell for sure since she was bathed in multicolored lights, but he'd bet all the color had drained from her face.

"He did?"

"Yup."

"And you talked to him?"

"I did."

"Why?"

"It was only polite since he dropped by," Jess said drily.

She shook her head. "I mean you're insulated from regular folks. How did he get past your people?"

"My staff has instructions to make sure I get every message." After what happened when Morgan got hurt, he wasn't taking any chances. "I was told a Bill Bradford wanted to see me. He said he's your father."

"What else did he say?" She stood, her whole body looking rigid enough to shatter.

"He said that you had a pretty sweet deal working as a nanny for a guy like me. And he feels he's entitled to a piece of it because of all the years he took care of you."

"That sounds like my dad." There was nothing warm or especially proud in the confirmation. It was more like disgust and humiliation. "I'm sorry he bothered you, Jess. I'll make sure it doesn't happen again."

"I offered him a job." He knew she was going to ask him why and that would be tough to answer since it had been purely a knee-jerk reaction.

"Doing what?"

He shrugged. "That's up to the Human Resources department. I instructed the director to find something fitting his qualifications."

"I don't think he has any. And he's not your obligation."

"Funny thing about responsibility. It's a hard habit to break."

She tilted her head and her hair was like a silky, golden curtain. "I get the feeling we're not talking about my father anymore."

"Good catch. I was remembering my mother."

"What about her?"

Jess didn't know why he'd admitted that. Maybe to keep Libby from feeling bad, like she had the only dysfunctional parent on the planet. Maybe it was about erasing the guilty, horror-stricken expression from her beautiful blue eyes, so full of holiday hope moments before. Whatever the reason, the cat was out of the bag now and not going back in without a fight.

He blew out a long breath. "After my dad died, I tried to man up like he'd told me. *Take care of your mother,* he'd said. She was only too happy to let me. She promised it was the two of us against the world and let me have a say in decisions. Because she didn't know what she'd have done by herself."

"That must have made you feel pretty good about yourself," Libby commented.

"Yeah. But the self-esteem was like a house of cards."

"I'm guessing by that remark and the hint of bitterness in your voice that things were bumpy when she remarried."

"Good guess." Even he heard the hard edge in his tone and resolved to work on that. "It's not easy for a guy to go from top dog to go-away-kid-you-bother-me."

"The balance of power shifted?"

"Understatement. On a scale of one to ten, my opinion went from the top into negative territory. It was like that promise never happened. She threw me under the bus every time—"

"Every time what?"

"Something happened at school."

She folded her arms over her chest. "Like what?"

He shifted his feet and resisted the urge to look away, at the same time regretting bringing this up. "Fights."

"And?"

"I started hanging out with a different group."

"By 'different' I'm going to take a leap here and guess this group didn't take the path of least resistance."

"You're implying they were looking for trouble?" He almost smiled. "I'd say it was more about pushing the envelope."

"So you got into trouble. Sounds like that was out of character for you."

"It was more of a growth period."

She frowned. "So how did your mother throw you under the bus?"

Jess hadn't meant a casual remark about responsibility to turn into a cheesy, this-is-your-life moment.

He didn't want to talk about the past because there was no way to change it. Done. Over with. What you couldn't fix you ignored. Move on. But genuine concern and empathy shone in her eyes and he couldn't hold back.

"I was accused of cheating on a test."

"In what subject?" she asked.

"Math, I think." Actually, it had been AP Geometry. A trauma that big wasn't something he'd forget.

"For what it's worth, math is not my thing—"

"I didn't cheat," he said, angry that she seemed to believe the worst.

"I didn't say you did. That was commiseration."

"It was a rumor started by a jerk pissed off at me for stealing his girlfriend."

"And your mother didn't believe you were innocent?"

"Give the lady a gold star." He remembered his rage that she listened to his stepfather paint him with the juvenile delinquent brush and believed everyone but her own son. It was a gut-level betrayal and something he couldn't forgive. "On top of that her husband had had enough of 'the punk.' He gave her a choice—him or me."

"Oh, Jess, she didn't—"

"She did. I ended up in boarding school—more of a military academy. His suggestion." That was bad enough, but what bothered Jess most was that his mother had never looked at his father the way she did the new guy. She'd thrown love under the bus, too.

"That's awful." Libby put her hand on his arm. "I'm so sorry that happened to you."

"Not your fault." That was his standard macho reply, but it was strange how her touch, the connection, somehow made him feel better.

"Kids should feel they have someone in their corner. A support system. But—"

"What?" When she pulled her hand away he missed the warmth.

"I hate to play devil's advocate, but I am a teacher."

"And how many of your little angels do you accuse of cheating on arts and crafts?"

"You're not going to distract me." The corners of her mouth curved up. "This is the scenario as I understand it. You were running with kids who had questionable judgment and that tends to make adults form an opinion that may be unfair. Put yourself in your mother's shoes—"

"Do I have to?"

She ignored that. "What if the educational professionals from Morgan's school told you she'd been fighting, cheating on tests, hanging out with kids who smoke and had sex—"

"Stop right there." He covered his ears and started to hum.

Laughing, she pulled his arms down. "Seriously, what would you do?"

His first instinct would be to talk to Libby and get her advice. All he said was, "I wouldn't dump her in boarding school."

"Because she's a duty?"

"I believe in keeping my word," he said. "Unlike people who make empty promises."

She nodded. "I sympathize. You just described every man I ever dated."

"And I sympathize. My dating history is pretty checkered, too."

"It can't be as bad as mine," she said.

"On the contrary. I made the mistake of asking a woman to marry me."

Her eyes widened. "What happened? Something must have, since I know you're not married now."

"It lasted until I made a business deal that public opinion said was going to ruin me. She bailed."

"That's bad. But you had the last laugh, Mr. Billionaire. At least you took a chance. I never did."

"Because of your dad?"

Her gaze jumped to his. "Probably."

After meeting the guy, he could understand. He also felt protective of her and that wasn't like him. He waited for more, but she didn't say anything. Not even in the spirit of he'd bared his soul and she could, too. He'd never thought her mysterious, but he did now. And damned if she didn't wear it well. But he couldn't help wishing mystery was all she wore right now.

"Since you're probably wondering, I offered your father a job because maybe he needed a second chance."

Her lips pressed tightly together for a moment. "Nice of you. And just maybe he won't let *you* down."

What did that mean?

As if he needed one more reason to not be able to get her out of his mind. If only he could figure out a way to get her back in his bed without upsetting the delicate balance of this life they were making for Morgan. He didn't want to jeopardize it. He just wanted her with every fiber of his being.

But he was doing his damnedest to make the best of this second chance, to do the right thing and not act on those feelings.

Las Vegas was chilly at night in December.

Libby pulled the collar of her coat more snugly around her neck and watched as the carousel turned with Morgan riding one of the horses. Jess stood beside her and every time the two of them came around she waved, and tried to hang on to her heart.

It wasn't easy. Since the teacher conference, Jess had been engaged in making Morgan feel secure. Tonight they were touring the Magical Forest at Opportunity Village. It was the biggest fund-raiser of the year for the organization that provided jobs and assistance to adults who experienced disabilities or traumatic brain injury that had left them physically or intellectually challenged.

The grounds of the facility were transformed into a Christmas village, complete with toy shop at the North Pole. Pathways wound through the displays and lights turned the place into—well—a magical forest. And Morgan was laughing when the carousel brought her around again.

The sight made Libby smile. If he didn't take them somewhere, at home he suggested board games and watching TV together. He was there every night for dinner, a complete turnaround from the guy who thought raising a child was only about writing the checks. This felt like a family.

Whoa. Libby stopped herself right there. In her experience family was just an illusion, like this village. Also in her experience, the things men did were selfish, fraught with ulterior motives. How long could he keep up this front? It wasn't real, and she would be an idiot to let herself get sucked in. Morgan's welfare was her priority and always would be.

The carousel slowed and came to a stop. She watched Jess gently lift the little girl down from the horse and trailed behind as she raced ahead. The ride operator smiled as he said something to Morgan. Then the two of them came through the white wooden gate and joined her at the spectator fence.

Libby dropped to one knee. "Did you have fun, Morgan?"

"I guess."

She looked up at Jess. "How about you?"

"I don't think I ever realized how awesome a carousel is."

"It sure looked like you guys were having a blast."

Libby stood and took the little girl's hand in hers while Jess walked on her other side. The three of them strolled along the pathway oohing and aahing at candy canes, lighted sleighs, Christmas trees and reindeer.

"Look." Libby pointed to a display with elves wearing striped leggings, red pointy hats and green curly-toed shoes. "Santa's helpers are getting the toys ready for delivery on Christmas Eve. Isn't that cool, Morgan?"

"Kind of."

Something was up. She'd been happy and smiling on the

ride, and had been responding to all the togetherness. Now the withdrawn little girl was back. Libby looked up at Jess, who shrugged, indicating that he'd noticed and had no idea why the child's mood had changed.

"Are you warm enough, sweetie?"

"Just fine, cuddles," Jess answered, clearly trying to lighten things up.

"I wasn't talking to you, sweet cheeks," Libby said wryly.

"Oh." He looked at Morgan. "Are *you* warm enough?"

"Uh-huh."

"Does your tummy feel okay after going in circles on the carousel?" Libby asked.

"Yup."

"Hey, kiddo, do you want to go to the gift shop and pick out a toy?" Jess suggested.

Morgan shook her head. "Not really."

That was a stunner. What was bugging her that a little retail therapy couldn't cure?

They were coming up on a wooden bench with a black wrought-iron frame. Libby pulled the little girl over and sat her down. Then she and Jess took up positions on either side.

"Maybe we should rest a minute," Libby suggested.

"Great idea. I don't know about you, Morgan, but I'm tired."

No answer. The short little legs stuck straight out in front of her as she stared down and plucked at the denim on her knee. Libby met Jess's gaze and shrugged. Finally she decided to just come straight out and ask.

"What's wrong, Morgan?"

"Nothin'."

"Come on, kiddo." Jess slid his arm across the bench back. "You were laughing on the ride and now you're not so happy. What happened?"

She looked up. "That man."

"What?" His expression went from concerned to furious in a heartbeat.

"The one at the carousel—"

"Go on," Libby encouraged. There was a knot in her stomach. "Did he do something?"

"No." The little girl shifted. "He said Merry Christmas. Have fun with your mom and dad."

Libby bit back a groan and saw the same reaction on Jess's face. The guy had made an honest mistake. They were trying to be a family and should have expected this to happen. It was good they looked like a bonded unit, but it was supposed to make this child feel secure, not sad.

She forced herself to ask the question even though the answer was clear. "How did that make you feel?"

"Not good." She looked up. "My mommy and daddy aren't coming back. Right?"

"Sweetie, we already talked about this," Libby reminded her.

"I know. But I still kept hopin'."

And now it's beginning to sink in that death means you'll never see someone again, Libby thought sadly. It was a lesson she wished this innocent child never had to learn.

Libby took one of the little hands into her own. "Sweetie, is that why you don't play with the other kids? Because you know how hard it is and how much it hurts to lose people you care about?"

She didn't react for several moments, then finally looked up. "I'm scared that you and Uncle Jess are gonna leave."

Jess went still, as if he'd taken a punch to the gut. "I'm not going anywhere, Morgan. I'll be here for you, kiddo. I promise."

He made the cross over his heart and held up his fingers.

Libby understood now why a promise meant so much to him. The person who should have loved him most had broken a solemn vow and hurt him deeply. The fierce expression on his face said he'd never do that to anyone—especially this innocent child. If he gave his word, you could believe he would keep it.

Libby didn't have any legal standing, but if feelings counted for anything she could promise that, too. She pulled the little girl into her lap and held her tight. "I love you so much, Morgan."

The child held herself stiffly for several moments, then curled into the embrace. "I love you, too."

Libby kissed the top of her head and rocked her gently. "Good."

"And you too, Uncle Jess."

He slid over, eliminating the space as he put his arm around both of them. "Back at you, kid."

Morgan looked at both of them. "Does this mean I should call you Mommy and Daddy?"

Wow, way to reach in and squeeze a heart, Libby thought. She looked at Jess and realized this was how he must have felt when Morgan gave him the daddy list. The night they made love. That memory made her lightheaded when she had to focus.

"Is that what you want to call us?" she asked.

Morgan mulled that over for several moments. "I like calling you Aunt Libby and Uncle Jess."

"Okay, then," he said. "That settles it."

"But—" She scratched her nose. "If I do call you that, can you still keep doin' mommy and daddy stuff anyway?"

Libby nodded, which was the only answer she could make, what with the lump in her throat. She blinked back tears as Jess held out his arms and pulled Morgan to him.

"Kiddo, we're there for you even if you call us Fred and Wilma Flintstone."

Morgan giggled. "Okay."

So just like that he'd fixed her five-year-old world. For Libby? Not so much. Fred and Wilma were married and had equal rights to Pebbles. Libby just worked for Jess and couldn't count on this lasting forever. She did love Morgan, so much. As if this child were her own.

And the man?

She was doing her level best not to fall for him and he was making that awfully hard.

"Uncle Jess?" Morgan put her arms around his neck. "It's kinda cold out here."

"It certainly is. What was I thinking?" He stood with her in his arms.

"You were prob'ly thinkin' that it's warm in the gift shop."

He laughed at her sly hint. "When did you get to be a mind reader? That's almost word for word what I was thinking."

He hefted Morgan onto his strong shoulders and started down the sidewalk. Libby trailed after them, heart heavy as she wondered if this was a glimpse of her future.

Being left behind.

Chapter Twelve

"Do you think she'll be all right?"

Libby and Jess had just returned to the penthouse after dropping Morgan off for Nicole Smith's sixth birthday party. He'd fretted all the way. As much as Libby wanted to join in, she figured one of them had to remain calm and rational. Since she was the nanny and a professional, it was her job not to freak out right along with him.

"Morgan really wanted to go," she reminded him for the umpteenth time. "That's a good thing. It means she's ready to risk making friends."

"Okay," he said, pacing back and forth across the family room. "Then maybe I'm not ready for it."

"I would have said something if I thought she wasn't going to be fine. Even though I'm a little nervous, too," she admitted.

In front of the floor-to-ceiling windows he suddenly

stopped walking and looked ready to spring into action. "Maybe we shouldn't have let her go."

"We talked about this, Jess. The group of girls is small. I know all of them and their parents, all good, responsible people. Sophia is there to help supervise. They're going to the Bellagio to see the Christmas decorations in the conservatory. The ratio of kids to adults is two to one—"

"I'd feel better if it was the other way around."

"That's not completely true," she said.

"Oh?"

"You'd feel better if you were there."

"Are you saying I can't delegate?" He folded his arms over his chest. "Because I can delegate just fine. I do it all the time. Every day, in fact. You can't run multiple companies like I do without trusting other people to do the job they were hired for."

"Exactly."

"What does that mean?"

"It means that Morgan is with Sophia, whom *I* trust because she's in charge of kids every day. The mom of the little birthday girl is a teacher's assistant hired by Sophia. She's worked at Nooks and Nannies for a year and a half."

"But what if Morgan wanders off? Or an adult turns her back and someone grabs her? What if she disappears—"

"What if a meteor levels the hotel?"

His eyes narrowed on her. "What if you're making fun of me?"

"No *if* about it," she said, grinning.

This was a very different man from the one who'd played clueless tour guide in this penthouse on that first day with Morgan. Different from the one who'd told her to buy whatever the little girl needed and send the bills to him. For a man to whom money was no object, worrying was a far cry from signing checks.

Libby couldn't resist teasing him because it was either that or kiss him. He was so darn cute and caring. A little less cute didn't make a difference to her one way or the other. It was the caring part that was getting under her skin in a big way.

"Jess, it's a very public place. There are 'eyes in the sky.'" She was referring to the inconspicuous security cameras installed in all the hotels. "And the limo you hired will chauffeur them back to Nicole's for the sleepover."

"Do you think she'll last the night?"

"The important thing is that she knows she doesn't have to. I think we made it pretty clear to her and every adult in the southern Nevada area that if she wants to come home she can call—no matter what time it is. We'll come and get her. Or she can just call if she wants to chat."

He raked his fingers through his hair. "I can't believe I let you talk me out of going."

"So you can shadow her?" Libby shook her head. "She needs just a little space."

"I wish I'd said no, even though you're right that she needs to do this."

The approval burrowed inside and warmed her heart and soul. He didn't like it, but he'd taken her advice and that made her like him even more than she already did. The shallow Jess would have given permission for the outing and never given it another thought. This guy wanted to trail the group to make sure she was safe.

Libby wished with all her heart that she'd never gotten to know this side of him. It was much easier to deal with this man when she disliked him.

"There was no good reason not to let her go."

"You don't think preventing me from turning gray overnight is good enough?"

"First of all I seriously doubt you'll turn gray that fast." Looking at his thick, dark hair made her want to run her fingers through it. That evoked visions of an unforgettable night in his bed with twisted sheets and hot kisses. "Second, the adults assured you that if she so much as stubs her toe we'll know about it." She felt for the cell phone in her jeans pocket just to make sure it was still there.

He didn't miss the movement. "You're nervous, too."

"I admitted that. What's your point?"

"My point is that I don't understand how you can sound so annoyingly rational when you feel the same way I do."

"Because both of us going off the deep end is too ugly to contemplate."

Jess thought about that for several moments, then nodded. "Okay. I can see the wisdom in that."

"Believe me, I'd like nothing better than to wrap her in a cocoon and make sure nothing bad happens to her ever again. But that's about my peace of mind, not what's in her best interest." Libby took a breath when he moved in front of her. "It was clear that she really wanted to do this. And it's such an important step in the healing process. Feeling secure enough to make friends."

"I know." He sighed. "That doesn't mean I have to like it."

"Who are you and what have you done with Jess Donnelly?"

"*Now* why are you making fun of me?"

"A little while ago I was remembering the day I brought Morgan here for the first time. You were, shall we say, not what I would call embracing your new role."

"That was before I realized that this place is too big and too quiet without Morgan." He glanced around the room and there was a sincerely sad expression in his eyes. There was no question that he missed the little girl.

"I didn't cut you any slack, Jess. I'm very sorry about that."

"It's okay."

"No, it's not. But, for what it's worth, I think Charity and Ben knew exactly what they were doing when they made you Morgan's legal guardian."

He smiled. "It's nice of you to say that. I'm just doing the best I can."

"They'd expect nothing more or less," she assured him.

She'd been so wrong about him. He was having separation anxiety issues just like a real dad and the *aha* light went off in Libby's head. She needed to make a call and tell the attorney to stand down. No way would she initiate any action to take Morgan away from him.

"What?" he asked, noting the way she stared.

"This reaction makes it hard for me to believe you never thought about having children. Especially knowing you were engaged at one point. Which means you were thinking about marriage and settling down."

"And you know how well that turned out. Clearly her agenda was very different from mine."

That comment neither confirmed nor denied what she suspected. In spite of his turbulent childhood, he'd been willing to take a chance on having a family and the woman had turned him against it.

Libby felt the hot blast of anger as it rolled through her. The self-centered witch had hurt him and given him one more reason to avoid commitment. Why would he even think about giving a relationship another shot? That would be stupid and a stupid man wouldn't be smart enough to make billions.

"And you?" he asked.

"What about me?" She knew what was coming and was sorry she'd brought the subject up. Talking about herself, especially to him, wasn't easy.

"Don't you want kids of your own?"

"I have children," she answered. "Every one of my students is one of my kids."

"You're evading the question," he accused, one dark eyebrow lifting.

"The God's honest truth is not an evasion. I genuinely care about every child in my care."

"I don't doubt that. But that kind of nurturing instinct makes me think you'd want the whole experience of pregnancy, birth, baby. The whole nine yards."

"You left out romance," she said.

"So tack it on. Can you honestly say you don't want the package?"

It's exactly what she wanted. But real life never worked in her favor. "I don't expect romance."

"Why?" He looked sincerely interested.

If she'd known talking about herself would take his mind off Morgan, she'd have turned the conversation in that direction a long time ago. Then again, maybe not.

A conversation about a father who manipulated and used his children and other people for his own selfish agenda wasn't something she was especially proud of. Then there was the fact that she shared his DNA. Not that she could ever imagine her and Jess together as a couple, but sharing the reality of her dysfunctional early years wouldn't endear her to him. The truth was that she was too cynical about men to ever let one romance her.

Now he was waiting for her to answer his question about why she didn't expect it. Taking a page from his book to change focus, she asked, "Are you looking for romance?"

"We're not talking about me. Thank goodness. I'm much more interested in you."

Rational thought was no match for the hormones unleashed by that comment. It was incredibly seductive. "Don't be. I'm pretty boring."

"Not to me." He stepped so close their bodies nearly touched. Behind him lights from the Christmas tree bathed the room in a magical glow. Her heart started pounding when a hungry expression darkened his face and jumped into his eyes.

"It would be so damn simple if you were dull and unexciting," he whispered.

Libby knew he was going to kiss her. It wasn't about being psychic, but more about how very badly she'd been wanting him to do just that. At this moment she only knew that simplicity was highly overrated. Complications were so very tempting. She was the moth to his flame and all she could think about was how much she wanted him to burn her.

And how wrong that would be.

She was on borrowed time with Morgan—and Jess. The little girl was at a birthday sleepover now, proof that very soon Libby's services would no longer be needed. This felt like a father, mother, child—a family—but she couldn't afford to hope it was real. Every day Jess was doing the right thing, which made her care about him more. It also brought her closer to losing everything she'd ever wanted after glimpsing how wonderful it all could be.

Jess dipped his head, but before he could make contact, she backed away.

Libby turned, not sure where she was going. Anywhere away from him. She made it to the family-room doorway before his words stopped her.

"Don't go."

She wanted to ignore him and run away, but it was like some force prevented her from moving. Slowly she turned toward him. "I have to."

"Why?"

There was no point in lying because surely he could see in her eyes that she was his for the taking. "Because I want so badly to stay."

"Go with that," he advised.

"It's not that easy."

He moved closer but didn't touch her, not with his hands. But the heat from his body and the spicy scent of his skin wrapped around her and she could feel him everywhere.

"You know I want you, Lib." His voice was deep, low, erotic.

"Why?" For years he'd barely remembered her name. All of a sudden he noticed her and the timing couldn't be worse. She wanted things to go on just as they were, even if not having him became more painful every day. "Never mind. I don't really want to know."

"It's a question for the ages, isn't it?" He smiled, but there was no humor in it. "What combination of hair color, facial features and body type makes just the perfect blend of chemistry to generate attraction?"

"Do you have an answer?" She stared up at his unsmiling face and started to tremble. Whatever chemistry had attracted her the very first time had only grown more potent.

"No." He ran his fingers through his hair. "On paper you're completely wrong for me."

Anger pricked her and she snapped, "Well, you're no prize either, buster."

This time when he grinned it was all amusement. "And then you hit me with a zinger and I don't give a damn about anything else. I guess that means I'm pretty messed up."

Just like that, anger evaporated, leaving nowhere to hide. "Join the club." Still, one of them had to be strong. "We agreed this wasn't a good idea."

"I vaguely remember that conversation. But for the life of me, at this moment I can't recall what the heck I was thinking." Slowly, he reached out and trailed his index finger over her cheek.

Libby shivered and whispered in a strangled voice, "It had something to do with me being a vital employee."

"You are that." Cupping her face in his palm, he added in an achingly soft tone, "Vital. Much more than you know."

"I recall exactly what you said." She was struggling for control here. It was getting more difficult by the second to keep in mind exactly why this was a bad idea because the look in his eyes and the sensation of his touch combined to chip away at her best intentions. Although there was that saying about the road to hell being paved with them.

"What exactly did I say?" The words were laced with amusement.

"That you needed my guidance with Morgan. You're counting on me to navigate the strange and wonderful world of child-rearing."

He frowned. "I don't believe I used the words strange or wonderful."

"I embellished." She shrugged in a so-sue-me gesture.

"What's your point, Lib? I'm sure you have one."

"How can you be so sure?"

"Because you're one of the brightest women I've ever known. On top of being too sexy for my own good, you're quick, witty and sassy. You say what you think regardless of whether or not I want to hear it. Do you have any idea how rare that is in my world?"

She shook her head. "And that's my point. We come

from different worlds. I'm here because of Morgan. What happens when she doesn't need me anymore?"

His expression turned gentle and understanding. He nodded slightly, as if knowing where she was coming from. "She'll always need you. Whatever happens, we'll work it out."

Easy for him to say. He had the law on his side. She wanted him with every fiber of her being and had never quite understood that expression until this moment. But she managed to pull together one last-ditch effort to deflect the desire growing rapidly inside her.

"The best way to work it out is for me to walk away. Right now," she said, regret clear in her voice.

He glanced up, then met her gaze. "Are you willing to risk it?"

"Why? What risk?"

"It seems wrong to waste perfectly good mistletoe."

Heart sinking, she looked upward and remembered him explaining to Morgan about what happens when someone catches you beneath the pesky green sprig. He took half a step closer and wrapped his arm around her waist, pulling her snugly against him. It was like her whole being sighed in surrender as she curled into his warmth. Then he dipped his head again and there was no way she could break the sensuous spell.

His lips met hers and it was instant fire sucking the oxygen from her lungs. *In for a penny, in for a pound,* she thought, wrapping her arms around his neck and sliding deeper into the Donnelly magic. He tasted her slowly, a featherlight touch that tangled her senses and knotted her insides—in a very delicious way.

As he kissed her into oblivion, his hands moved up and down her back, over her waist, then stopped when his palms cupped her tush. Pleasure nipped through her and she made a needy little moany noise that earned a seductive guttural sound from him.

Libby instinctively pressed her lower body against him, feeling the ridge of his arousal that proved the truth of his statement that he wanted her. Lust slammed through her and she couldn't seem to get close enough.

Breathing hard, she mumbled against his mouth, "You have too many clothes on."

He smiled with his lips still on hers. "Funny, I was just thinking the same thing about you."

"Kissing under the mistletoe is carved in stone, but—"

"Anything else is just going to be uncomfortable," he finished for her.

"You're a mind reader," she accused.

"It's a gift."

"'Tis the season," she whispered, reveling in what he was giving her. A priceless night to remember.

"I have an idea." He kissed her neck with a thoroughness that stunned her senses.

"Should I be afraid?" Stupid question. It was way too late to worry about that.

"Never."

In one fluid movement, he bent and settled his broad shoulder at her midsection, then straightened and lifted her off her feet.

"Jess—" His name came out half squeal, half scream. "Put me down."

"Not yet." He purposefully walked down the hall to his room.

"What are you doing?" Besides giving her a different perspective on his excellent butt.

"Not giving you time to think or change your mind."

"I can respect that."

He set her on her feet beside his big bed and grinned. Then he turned, fiercely focused. Reaching out with shaking hands, he slowly unbuttoned her blouse, tugged it over her arms and off. Then he unhooked the closure of her jeans and settled his palms on her hips.

He rubbed a thumb over the bulge in her pocket and pulled out her cell phone. "I think this might be safer here," he said, putting it on the nightstand beside the bed.

Libby undid the holster from his belt and set his phone beside hers. "We wouldn't want to miss a call."

"No." He reached around, unhooked her bra and let it slide off. Then he filled his palms with her breasts. "Perfect."

His sigh of satisfaction made her smile when she remembered her annoyance that she wasn't memorable to him in this area. How things had changed. How perfect it felt to have him touch her this way. She could have stayed like this forever except for the overwhelming yearning to touch him back.

After slowly unbuttoning his shirt, she rested her hands on his chest, savoring the way the coarse dusting of hair tickled her fingers. Leaning forward, she trailed kisses over the contour of muscle until he groaned with sexual frustration.

"You're killing me, Lib."

"I have the power."

Challenge glittered in his eyes before he said, "We'll see about that."

In half a minute he had the rest of their clothes on the floor and her in the middle of his bed. He kissed her neck, then slid his mouth to her breast. A surge of pleasure shot through her and turned her insides liquid with heat. Her thighs quivered as she writhed with the need to have him inside her.

"Jess—you're killing me," she echoed.

With his mouth on her belly he laughed. "Sweet revenge."

"Please—"

Without answering he took protection from the night-stand and covered himself. Then he rolled to his back and with his hands on her waist, settled her over his length. He matched the rhythm of his hips to hers and pressure built inside her. In a flash of light, pleasure exploded through her. A moment later he went still and groaned out his own release.

Revenge had nothing to do with it and when he pulled her into his arms it was simply sweet. Again she felt as if she wanted to stay there forever. Maybe that was possible.

Christmas was the season for hope.

Chapter Thirteen

Jess heard a breathy little female groan just before he felt a smooth, soft, shapely leg thrown over his. He smiled, remembering the intriguing female who was attached to all that sex appeal.

Libby.

Elizabeth Bradford.

The nanny he'd finally caught under the mistletoe who had then proceeded to kiss the living daylights out of him.

He opened his eyes and watched her sleep, full mouth relaxed and soft, blond hair wild around her face. Running his hands through the silky golden strands had been as much of a turn-on as getting her naked. It had been even better than the last time because he knew where to touch and what to do to push her over the edge.

For him following her over was as simple as looking at her, and he wasn't sure when she'd become so important.

Somehow this woman had worked her way inside him. He wasn't sure yet, but he might not mind. He wasn't sure yet, but he might just like waking up to find her in his bed.

He raised up on an elbow and rested his head on his palm. With the other hand, he brushed strands of her hair away to better study the curve of her cheek, the determined line of her jaw, the smooth skin on her forehead.

Looking closer he noticed a small scar that disappeared into her hairline. He'd never noticed it before, probably because her hair was hiding it.

What else did she hide?

A wave of what he could only describe as protective curiosity washed over him. She'd revealed very little about herself and what little he knew had been pried from her with a lot of effort. If it didn't cause her pain, chances were she'd have blabbed freely. What did she keep bottled up inside? He wanted to know everything.

He reached over and gently traced the jagged mark near her hair and her eyes blinked open. She looked startled, which he took to mean that waking up in a man's bed didn't ordinarily happen to her. He kind of liked that.

"I didn't mean to wake you."

"It's okay." Her voice was rusty.

Just a few hours ago it had sounded similar, but for a very different reason. The memory of her passionate response made his body grow tight with the need to have her again.

Shyly, she pulled the sheet more securely over her breasts and the gesture made him smile. The movement contrasted so drastically with her bold and breathless reaction last night.

"I have to go," she said.

"Why?" That was the last thing he wanted.

"I shouldn't be here. What if Morgan—" Her eyes grew wide. "She's still at the sleepover."

"Yeah. There was no call, so she made it all night."

Jess couldn't believe he'd forgotten, but so had Libby. Part of him was glad he'd made her forget. Part of him was appalled that he could. But he wasn't used to thinking about anyone besides himself, and apparently the parental muscles needed more of a workout. Yup, *appalling* pretty much described his feeling of not remembering.

The little girl had become very important to him and forgetting for any reason wouldn't happen again. He'd never realized how empty and lonely his life had become before the female invasion. No way did he want to go back to an estrogen-free zone.

"I miss her," he said.

"Me, too."

"Without her here it feels like something's out of whack." He traced a finger down her neck and across her bare shoulder. "On the plus side, she can't walk in on us."

"We need to pick her up by ten," Libby reminded him. "I have to clean up."

Before he could talk her out of that, she was up and on his side of the bed, grabbing his shirt to throw on. After gathering her clothes, she set a land-speed record in escaping. Faintly he heard the bathroom door close.

A shrill ring interrupted his thoughts and he reached over to retrieve the cell from the nightstand beside him. It wasn't his phone, but he answered in case it was about Morgan.

"Hello?"

"Ms. Bradford, please," said a female voice on the other end of the line.

"I'm sorry. She can't come to the phone. Can I take a message?"

"That would be great. I'm a temp. Mr. Erwin has been swamped and apologizes for the length of time it's taken to respond to Ms. Bradford. He hired me to help his secretary make follow-up calls."

"I see." Too chatty, Jess thought. Not a good quality in a business professional. "What's the message?"

"Mr. Erwin would like Ms. Bradford to call his law office for an appointment to discuss her options in her child custody case."

Jess's blood ran cold as an icy anger pushed through him. He couldn't believe he'd been so stupid yet again. When he realized the person on the other end of the phone was trying to get his attention, he said, "Don't worry. I'll give Ms. Bradford the message."

He slapped the phone closed as anger caught fire inside him.

That call was definitely about Morgan, but not in a way he'd ever expected. And he should have. Letting his guard down had been a big mistake. Suddenly he minded very much that Libby had made him care and he hated that it had been so pathetically easy for her.

After quickly cleaning up, Libby found Jess waiting for her in the kitchen. His hair was still damp from his own shower, making him even more devastatingly handsome than when she'd opened her eyes a little while ago to see him staring tenderly down at her in his bed.

But when she looked closer, the intense expression on his face clued her in that something was terribly wrong. This wasn't the easygoing man who'd gently brushed the hair off her face just a little while ago.

"Jess? What is it? Morgan—"

"Yeah. In a way. You had a call." His voice was chilly and sent a shiver through her.

"Was it Sophia? Is Morgan ready to come home?"

He held out her cell phone, careful not to touch her when she took it. "It was from your attorney. He wants to talk to you about a custody issue."

Libby gasped as if he'd sucker punched her. "I can explain—"

"Of course you can." His voice dripped sarcasm. "But I'm pretty sure there's nothing you can say that I want to hear."

"Jess, please listen—"

"I have to pick up Morgan." He left and the penthouse door slammed moments later.

Libby realized that she had as much chance of stopping him as she did of sticking out her foot to halt a runaway train. Stupid. Stupid. Stupid. She'd meant to contact the lawyer and cancel his services, but dealing with Morgan and Jess had made her forget about everything else. Maybe since he hadn't fired her on the spot, there was a chance that when he cooled down, he'd be willing to hear her out.

Hours later, when he still hadn't returned with Morgan, she didn't know what to think. She was wearing a path on the tile and carpet because six thousand square feet wasn't big enough to pace away her tension. The need to do *something* mushroomed inside her until she couldn't stand it.

Sliding her cell phone out of her jeans pocket, she pushed the speed dial. When a familiar female voice answered, she said, "Sophia, it's Libby."

"Hi. Did Morgan talk your ear off about what a wonderful time she had?" Her friend's voice was normal and upbeat. "It was so great, Lib. I wish you'd seen the way she interacted with the girls. She's making friends. There was one little rough patch and she wanted to call home but I managed to calm her down—"

"I wish you'd let her." It might have prevented what could be an even rougher patch.

"Did you talk to Jess? He told you how well Morgan did last night, right?" Concern replaced the cheerful tone in Sophia's voice.

"I haven't seen him yet," Libby admitted.

"But he picked Morgan up a long time ago." Moments passed before Sophia asked, "What's wrong?"

"He found out I consulted an attorney about custody."

"Oh." There was a long pause before she said, "I can hear it in your voice that he didn't take it well."

"He was so angry, Sophia. I should have listened to you and given him the benefit of the doubt. He wouldn't even let me explain."

"For what it's worth, he didn't show any of that when he picked Morgan up. He's so sweet with her."

"I know." Her stomach twisted at the magnitude of the mess she'd made of everything. "He's not the man I believed he was."

"And you thought he was that man because of your father." Sophia had heard Libby's pathetic story. She was one of those people who'd seen it all, heard it all and far worse, so nothing shocked or surprised her.

"Yeah. And when Jess found out about the lawyer, he went to the bad place because of stuff that happened to him as a kid."

"You two make quite a pair."

"What does that mean?"

"If you weren't in the middle of all this you'd get it." Sophia sighed. "You and Jess are hiding from the bad stuff, just like Morgan. Talk to him, Lib. Tell him what you went through growing up."

"I doubt that it will make a difference to him. If you'd seen the way he looked at me…" She closed her eyes, trying and failing to shut out the dark expression in his eyes. "He'll never forgive me."

"Not for you. Do it for Morgan. You and Jess are grown-ups and it's about time for you to deal with the past if you're going to get Morgan through this."

"What makes you think he'll listen to anything I have to say?"

"Because it's clear that he loves that little girl. Don't you see? The two of you together are best to raise Morgan because of what you've been through. All this time you haven't faced up to the past for yourselves, but I believe you'll get it right for a kid who just doesn't need another challenge in her short life."

"From your mouth to God's ear," Libby said fervently.

She thanked her friend for not saying "I told you so," said goodbye, then resumed pacing. What with hindsight being twenty-twenty, she wished she'd given Jess a fair chance. A couple of times she'd tried to talk to him about her standing in Morgan's life and he'd only said she shouldn't worry, it would be all right. Now? Not so much.

And this mess was all because Sophia had been right about something else. What Libby felt for Jess was more than a crush and thinking the worst of him had been the best way to keep from getting hurt.

Boy, that sure backfired. *Fired* being the operative word. Libby was pretty sure she'd fallen in love with him. Unless she could convince him that her motive had been pure, she was also pretty sure he was going to fire her.

Worried? Oh, yeah. She'd never been more scared in her life.

It was after seven that night when Libby finally heard the front door open. She hurried to the foyer and was breathless when she saw Jess with a sleepy Morgan in his arms.

"Hi," she said.

Jess wouldn't look at her, but the little girl gave her a huge smile. She wiggled until he put her down. Once free she ran over for a hug and Libby dropped to one knee to gather her close.

"Aunt Libby, it was so fun. We slept in the living room on mattresses with air in 'em. And we had pizza. And cake. I didn't eat too much and get sick."

"Good for you." Libby chanced a glance at Jess but there was nothing in his expression that gave a clue about what he was thinking. "What did you do all day?"

"Uncle Jess took me to the park. He pushed me on the swings. Then we went to a movie and shopping. We saw all the Christmas decorations at the mall, but I was too hungry to wait in the big line to talk to Santa."

It wasn't necessary to hear it in so many words. Clearly he'd stayed out all day to avoid her. But the activities had all been kid-friendly and family-oriented, yet more evidence piling up that she had misjudged him terribly.

"Are you hungry, sweetie?" She looked up at Jess, but again he wasn't the one who answered.

"Uncle Jess took me to a real restaurant, Aunt Lib." The little girl's brown eyes grew big and round as her tone turned reverent.

"He did?"

Curls bounced when she nodded. "It was in that big place where the water dances."

"Bellagio?"

Morgan shrugged. "I couldn't read the food on that big thing—"

"The menu?"

"Yeah. That. He read me everything but I didn't know what it was and there were no chicken nuggets. So he got them to make me a hamburger and french fries."

"Money is no object," she mumbled, looking up at him.

It was like he was standing guard, as if he expected her to steal the child away. Just that morning she'd awakened in his bed. The look in his eyes had said he wanted her again, a very different expression from the current one that said he wanted her gone. Cold fear coiled in her belly as she realized that Sophia was right. Libby needed to share her past to explain the unexplainable behavior.

"Aunt Libby, the tables had candles with real fire. And the napkins weren't paper—" A big yawn interrupted the narrative.

It was the opening she'd been waiting for. "You look tired, little girl."

She nodded. "Nicole's mom told us a bunch of times to go to sleep 'cuz we were talking a lot."

That was so blessedly normal and the words squeezed her heart. "Okay, then, let's get you cleaned up and to bed."

Rubbing her eyes, Morgan said, "Okay."

Libby stood and took the child's hand to lead her down the hall to the bathroom. Jess finally spoke.

"I'll be in to kiss you good-night, Morgan."

"Okay." She smiled at him. "Thank you for the beautiful dinner, Uncle Jess."

"You're welcome, Princess." His smile was tender as he looked at the little girl.

Libby desperately wanted to rewind her life, to a place where he didn't despise her. She both wanted and dreaded the talk she needed to have with him. She struggled not to hurry Morgan too much but at the same time, she wished to slow down the bath and bedtime reading ritual. In the end, the child took care of it and simply fell asleep.

Libby turned off the bedside lamp, then put on the nightlight. She stood in the doorway for a few heartbreaking moments, watching the sweet child in even sweeter sleep. Somehow she couldn't memorize hard enough the after-bath scent, the blond curls and round cheeks highlighted against the princess-pink pillowcase. Jess had called her Princess, just like her father had, and that brought a lump to Libby's throat.

Libby knew she could wish for a do-over until hell wouldn't have it, but nothing could change what she'd done. It was time to face the music and fix her mistake.

She took a deep breath and went looking for Jess, finding him on the first try in the morning room. His back was to her as he stared out the window at the lights of Las Vegas below. There was a tumbler in his hand.

"She must be exhausted," Libby said. "She fell sound asleep before I was halfway through the story."

He tipped the glass to his mouth and drained the contents. Whiskey. Neat. Unlike this situation. Then he turned and she felt that familiar tickle in her belly when she looked at him. It had always been there but was even more powerful since she'd made love with him. She had a horrible sinking feeling that he was the only man who could do this to her.

She'd hoped the force of his anger had ebbed, but the glare lasering holes through her now made clear how wishful that thinking had been.

"Let me explain, Jess."

"Save your breath. You were scheming to take Morgan away from me. Do I have it right?"

"It's not that simple." She moved farther into the room, leaving a foot of space between them. Maybe proximity would help her get through to him. "I love Morgan as if she were my own child. Her best interests have always been and will always be my first priority."

"Then one would have to presume that you don't think living with me is best for her."

"I didn't at first," she admitted.

"And you came to this conclusion because…" He folded his arms over his chest and fixed the intensity of his gaze on her.

"In my experience, I'd only known you to be self-absorbed."

"I see. And what did I ever do to give you that impression?" The tone was flat, but the dark look grew even darker.

"For starters, at Ben and Charity's wedding you disappeared with one of the bridesmaids."

"And I never remembered your name," he finished. "I should be drawn and quartered in the town square."

Hearing him say the words out loud made *her* feel like the shallow, self-absorbed one. "It goes to environment. Yours didn't seem kid-friendly. I thought she'd be better off with me."

"I gave my word."

"So you said."

"And you manipulated the situation to get the nanny job. Now I see why. To gather information for a custody fight."

"It wasn't like that. I gave my word, too. When they left her in my care I promised to keep her safe. Even from you, if necessary."

Glaring, he set the tumbler down on the table, then met her gaze. "I would never hurt her."

"Not on purpose. But think about it, Jess. Women had keys to your place, let themselves in and got naked. You slept with whoever showed up. Kind of like surprise sex." She blew out a long breath, trying to erase the memory of how sweet sleeping with Jess Donnelly had been. "I'm not saying it was wrong for you. But it is for a child. It seemed obvious to me that being guardian to a little girl would mess up the life you had in place."

"And you didn't believe I was capable of changing?" The words sizzled with resentment.

She hadn't *wanted* to believe it. There was a difference. If she had, there would have been nothing to keep her from falling in love with him. In spite of thinking the worst, she still hadn't prevented that from happening.

"I owe you an explanation for that," she said, neither confirming nor denying. "You wondered about my father and it's about time you knew the truth."

He folded his arms over his chest. "I'm not sure what that has to do with anything now."

Since he didn't refuse to listen, she went on. "My mother died when I was a baby so I have no memory of her, but I do remember living on the streets with Bill. My father. He seemed to be more interested in anything that would take the edge off his reality. Drugs. Liquor."

"And?"

"He found out pretty early on that a little girl, me, would get him the sympathy factor and along with that came help. Either food, or shelter, or both. And he could always use the excuse that he couldn't leave me alone while he worked and couldn't afford child care. There was probably some truth to it at first. I don't remember."

"Go on." There was disapproval in his eyes, but it wasn't clear whether it was directed at her or her father.

"When he was down and out, he met a woman who was in worse shape than him. Cathy." She'd been good to Libby and so had her folks. They'd done their best, but she'd never felt like one of the family. "She'd lost her only child to a degenerative disease and hit bottom, which was where she found my father and hooked up with him. She got pregnant and the baby gave her something to live for. All she ever wanted was a child to love."

"I see."

She shook her head. "The problem was that neither of them was capable of making a living. Her parents wanted to give her a chance at being happy and took her and my father in. Unfortunately it was a package deal and they had to take me, too."

"So you have a sibling?"

"My sister, Kelly. She's in college in California. UCLA."

"Good school."

"Yeah." She tucked a strand of hair behind her ear. "I love her. But I also resented her growing up."

"Why?"

"She was the one everyone wanted. Cathy did—to replace the child she'd lost. Her parents, for the same reason and because a new baby pulled their daughter out of a dark place. They just wanted her to be happy. And my father was thrilled to have another meal ticket."

"Apparently he needs another one," he said. "Because he reached out to me."

"I didn't plan to mention your name when he came to see me. Morgan let it slip," she explained. "I was afraid he'd be a problem because Cathy's parents told him to find another place to live after Kelly went away to school. He was lazy and used all kinds of excuses not to work. He wore out his welcome and their goodwill a long time ago."

"So he came to you," Jess said.

She nodded. It was harder and more humiliating than she'd expected to relate the details of her past and the good-for-nothing man who was her father. But there was a reason, and it was time to get to it.

"The point is that I know how it feels when no one

wants you. You told me Morgan was a duty, just a promise to a friend. I love her so much, Jess. And she'd just lost her parents. I couldn't bear the thought of her feeling unloved and unwanted."

"It was a shock for me." He shifted his weight as the sadness flashed in his eyes. "My best friend was gone."

"And mine."

"You couldn't cut me some slack? You didn't trust that I would come around?"

"My father never did." But Jess had proved he was nothing like her father. "I went to a lawyer just to explore my options. When I saw your heart opening to Morgan, I planned to drop the matter."

"So I guess getting that call was actually a lucky break," he said.

Her heart dropped, not because of what he said, but the cold tone of his voice. "What do you mean?"

"No matter how you slice it, what you did smacks of disloyalty. I've learned loyalty is the most important quality in an employee."

She winced at the emphasis he put on the last word because in his bed that morning she'd felt like so much more. "What are you saying, Jess?"

"I can't trust you, Libby. And that makes working for me impossible."

"You're firing me?"

"Yes."

Chapter Fourteen

"Ow." Morgan put her hands up to hair wet from her bath. "That hurts when you brush it too hard."

"Sorry, Princess." The bathroom mirror revealed the sheen of tears in her brown eyes and he felt like an ax murderer. Although an actual murderer whose weapon of choice was an ax would probably be a sociopath who felt no remorse.

"You forgot to put the conditioner in the bathtub for me to use."

"Yeah."

She'd declared herself a big girl and perfectly capable of bathing herself. If that were true, would Libby have supervised the situation every night? In the end, he'd figured Morgan had been there for the nightly practice and knew more than he did.

"Aunt Libby says conditioner will make my hair not spit."

He frowned, trying to translate the perfectly good English words and make sense of the statement. All day he'd been on his own with Morgan and felt like an equipment-heavy deep-sea diver in the middle of the Mojave Desert. He was not very fluent in five-year-old girl.

He picked up a gadget that looked like a shrimp fork on steroids and braced himself to go at the blond tangles one more time. "So your hair spits when you don't use stuff on it?"

"The ends do." Morgan stood stoic, solemn and brave.

Aha. *Split* ends. "Next time I'll remember to put that stuff in the tub for you."

"Tell me again why Aunt Libby's not here?"

Instead of tears there was fear in her eyes this time and Jess wasn't sure which was worse. He hated both in equal parts.

That morning when he'd told Morgan, he'd known it was a mistake not letting Libby say goodbye face-to-face. Anger was no excuse, but it was the only one he had.

And he'd been angry because she didn't trust him. Furious that she hadn't even given him the chance to screw up first.

Finding out she'd gone to an attorney about custody had released the feelings of not being good enough that he kept carefully locked away. He'd lashed out and it was impossible to make this child understand why Libby was gone.

Not even her explanation had moved him enough to keep him from firing her, though he'd subsequently found out that it was true. He'd made some calls and verified that her father was basically a freeloader who'd used his daughter to manipulate people into feeling sorry for him. How could a man use a child like that?

He was a manipulator; Jess had spotted that instantly. Instead of throwing him out of the office, he'd called the bluff and offered a job—which her father had accepted.

Something in a warehouse. Time would tell whether or not it worked out.

And wasn't that ironic? He employed the father and fired Libby. If he hadn't, she'd be the one using a shrimp fork on Morgan's hair.

"Uncle Jess?"

His head cleared of Libby's image as he met the unnaturally serious childish gaze in the mirror. "Hmm?"

"Why did Aunt Libby go away?"

"She just couldn't stay with us anymore."

It's what happened when you could no longer trust an employee.

Who was he kidding? She was so much more than that. Clearly he was too dysfunctional to claim even a cursory understanding of interpersonal relationships. But the depth of his anger was a big clue. If he didn't care quite a lot, there would have been no reason to be so furious. Annoyed, maybe, at the inconvenience of a child-care interruption, but certainly not this intensity of rage.

Now it was fading and that left him nowhere to hide.

"Why couldn't she stay with us anymore?"

Because he was an ass. How did you translate that into something fit for five-year-old ears?

The worst thing was that Jess recognized something familiar in Morgan's expression. It was the face of a resigned sort of mourning, the way she'd looked when she first came to live with him. Maybe a distraction was in order.

"So what should we do with your hair?" He'd wanted to say WWLD—what would Libby do? But that wasn't exactly changing the subject. "It's kind of wet."

"It's okay like this."

He wasn't especially fond of the martyr tone, either. It was a sign that he was letting her down. "You probably shouldn't go to bed with a wet head. Maybe I should blow it dry."

"That makes more tangles." She didn't add *you bonehead,* but it was implied.

"What about a ponytail?" That should be simple enough, since he'd accomplished one already that day.

She shook her head. "It's all right, Uncle Jess. The pony you did this morning didn't stay in very well. Not like the way Aunt Libby does it."

"Okay." That was a lie. Nothing was okay. "Then how about another cup of cocoa while it dries?"

"No, thank you." She was far too polite and it felt too wrong. "Aunt Libby says it's not a good idea to have drinks too close to bedtime because it'll make me have to go potty."

"I see."

"Besides," she added, "the cup you made at dinner had an awful lot of lumps in it."

So that's why she'd barely touched it.

Intellectually he knew his expertise in cooking cocoa had no direct bearing on what kind of adult she became. But that didn't stop the feeling that he was on the super-highway to father failure.

"Then I guess it's off to bed with damp hair," he said.

She turned and looked up at him. "You could read me a story while it dries."

"An excellent suggestion," he said with way more enthusiasm than he felt.

Mentally he smacked his forehead. Should have thought of that, Donnelly, he told himself. He'd never become involved in the nighttime routine. His bad in a long and ever-growing list of bads.

Jess followed her to her pink bedroom and watched her pile pillows against the white headboard of her trundle bed. Then she climbed onto the princess sheets and pulled the blanket and matching comforter up to her chest. He picked up the new book they'd bought that afternoon and began reading.

"'Twas the night before Christmas and all through the house…"

He said the words out loud and turned the pages without any clue whether or not his performance left anything to be desired. Did Libby add more enthusiasm to her voice? Probably. Everything she did had an eagerness and passion that awed him.

Should he have cut her some slack? How would he have felt in her situation?

When Jess had adjusted his attitude and accepted this little girl into his life, he'd fallen in love with her. He couldn't imagine his life without her in it and would fight anyone who tried to take her from him. Libby had cared for her a lot longer and loved Morgan, too. She'd tried to talk to him about a guarantee of long-term involvement, but he'd blown her off. In Libby's shoes, would he have gone along with that and not consulted a legal professional about his rights?

"Merry Christmas to all and to all a good night," he read.

He closed the book and looked down, hoping Morgan was asleep. Brown eyes stared up at him. "Did you like the story?"

She nodded. "Thank you for getting the book."

"You're welcome." It had seemed like a good idea at their mall outing. Something to take the sting out of the situation. He glanced at her nightstand and the picture of Morgan sitting on Santa's lap. A neutral topic of conversation. Something about her day, which was a technique Libby had taught him. "Did you enjoy talking to Santa Claus?"

She shrugged and tightened her hold on the ragged

doll he'd seen her first day here in the penthouse. "I thought of something I want for Christmas. Even more than a bicycle."

"What?" He'd buy her the moon if it would put the brightness back in her eyes.

"I wish he could bring Aunt Libby back to us."

"I'm not sure that falls into Santa's purview…" When she blinked cluelessly up at him he said, "That's not in the big guy's job description."

"I still wish he could do it."

"It's okay, Princess. Don't worry. I'm here. I'll always take care of you."

She nodded even as tears filled her eyes. "But you don't cut the crust off my sandwich. I'm pretty sure you don't know how to paint fingernails or French-braid hair either. And what if something happens to you?" Her voice caught when she said, "Aunt Libby didn't get to see me sit on Santa's lap. I really miss her—"

His heart cracked in two as she started to cry and gut instinct had him gathering her into his arms. "It's okay, baby."

"No, it's not." Her little body shook from the sobs. "She's never comin' back. Just like my mommy and daddy. I'll never see her again. I miss her so much, Uncle Jess."

He'd seen right from the beginning that Libby and Morgan were a unit. Now he knew there was no win in splitting them up. He hated that he'd been right about ending up in the cold. Outside looking in. Like always.

But if he'd learned anything from his nanny–slash–child-care professional, it was to pay attention. Morgan needed to see for herself that Libby was alive and well.

If he was being honest, he was grateful for the excuse to see her. It hadn't taken long for him to realize he loved her and the feeling wasn't going away just because she had.

"Do you want to visit Libby?" When she nodded against his chest, he said, "Okay."

She sniffled. "Promise?"

"Cross my heart." Instead of actually doing that, he just held her to his heart. "I miss her, too."

"Jess will be here any minute." Libby paced the living room in Sophia's condo. She'd let her own go after accepting the nanny job. Job? "It was more than a job to me," she murmured, as if her friend had been privy to her thoughts.

"You don't have to tell me that." Sophia was sitting on the chocolate-brown sofa.

The night before last, this woman had taken her in when she had no place else to go, and the place was as warm as its owner. In addition to the two bedrooms and baths, there was a dining area adjacent to the kitchen. Reminders of Christmas were everywhere, from the small tree with multicolored lights to the collection of Santas that covered every flat surface.

"I know how much you love Morgan."

"And it bit me in the backside." Libby deciphered the wry expression on the other woman's face. "I know what you're thinking. You told me so. I went to the attorney early on, when I was so worried that he'd make Morgan feel like nothing more than an obligation. But he's changed, Sophia. He's caring and tender. He makes mistakes—"

"Imagine that. The great Jess Donnelly is actually human."

"I know." Just like Libby knew she'd made the mother of all mistakes. "But he learns from what he doesn't get right. He's so not the man I always believed him to be."

"Not shallow and self-centered?"

Libby shook her head. "He's got more layers than a croissant. He's complicated and flawed, but he wouldn't ever deliberately hurt that little girl. He might have agreed to take her in out of duty, but there's no doubt in my mind that he genuinely cares about her now."

"How can you be so sure?" Sophia shifted and tucked her legs up on the sofa cushion.

"The fact that he called me and asked if he could bring Morgan over tonight, for starters."

"How does that prove anything?"

"She had a meltdown because I left. He's bringing her here in spite of the fact that I'm the last person he wants to see."

Libby couldn't blame him, and that was hard to admit since she'd been blaming *him* for stuff almost from the moment they'd met. What she'd done was unforgivable to a man whose own mother hadn't trusted him.

She would never forget the look in his eyes when he'd fired her. Just as she'd never get over the heartbreaking realization that she'd lost everyone she loved. Morgan. And Jess.

Not that he would ever have cared about her the same way she did for him, but at least he'd respected her. And she'd been able to see him every day. It hadn't been clear how much she'd looked forward to that until she couldn't see him every day.

Yesterday she hadn't seen or talked to him and it had been the longest day of her life.

Sophia shook her head. "That little girl has had too much loss. No wonder she had a reaction to losing you, too."

"And that's my point. He's bringing her here in spite of how much he loathes me."

"I'm not so sure loathe is the *L* word I'd use."

"I'm certain enough for both of us. But it didn't have to be this way." Libby wrapped her arms around her waist. "The thing that really makes me kick myself is that I'd already made the decision to call off the attorney."

"So why didn't you?"

"I got busy." To put a finer point on it, she got naked. With Jess. She'd told Sophia all about that and his past, which made her betrayal so personal to him. "What with everything going on, I simply forgot."

Sophia's gray eyes glittered like polished silver. "See, that's the thing. He doesn't strike me as the sort of man who indiscriminately sleeps with someone who works for him."

"He's not."

"It's possible he's falling in love with you," Sophia said.

Libby remembered him taking the blame the first time and knew in her heart he'd sincerely intended that it wouldn't happen again. When he'd taken her to bed a second time, she'd begun to hope that maybe he did care.

Libby shook her head. "He was so angry. So hurt. Even if there's a grain of truth in what you're saying, what I did to him destroyed it."

The death of hope made her life flash before her without a hint of lightness or color and the pain of that stole the breath from her lungs.

"Don't look like that." Sophia swung her legs off the sofa.

"What?"

"Like someone died."

"It feels that way. If I could just go back—"

There was a knock on the door and Libby felt her stomach drop. Her heart pounded painfully in her chest and she struggled for calm. Morgan had already been upset and needed normal in a very big way.

She glanced at Sophia, took a deep breath, then opened the door. "Hi."

"Aunt Libby—" The little girl pulled her hand from Jess's and launched herself forward.

Libby dropped to one knee and gathered the child close. "Love bug—I missed you so much."

"I missed you, too." Small arms squeezed tight around her neck.

Finally, Libby held her at arm's length just to look at her. She took in the child's jeans and pink T-shirt with the matching quilted jacket. Her ponytail was crooked, but other than that she didn't look any the worse for wear.

"How are you, sweetie?"

"Okay. But Uncle Jess makes lumpy cocoa even though he tried real hard. And my hair got all tangled up." Her eyes filled with tragedy. "Why did you leave me and Uncle Jess?"

Libby glanced up but his expression gave nothing away. He apparently hadn't mentioned that he'd terminated her employment. "It's complicated, sweetie."

Confusion swirled in Morgan's eyes. "I was afraid you went away and weren't comin' back forever. Like Mommy and Daddy."

It hadn't been until much later, after the blowup with Jess, that this possibility had occurred to Libby. She glanced up at him again and her heart dropped. Again. In jeans, white shirt and leather jacket he was a sight for sore eyes. Literally. She'd shed quite a few tears since the last time she'd seen him.

She hugged Morgan close one more time. "I'm fine. See? More important, you're fine."

The little girl nodded uncertainly. "But are you comin' home with us?"

"I'd really like to. But that's up to your Uncle Jess." She looked at him and wondered if he could see in her eyes how very much she wanted to.

Morgan turned and said to him, "It's okay with you. Right, Uncle Jess?"

"It's not that easy, Princess."

Sophia walked up behind her. "Morgan, I think your Aunt Libby and Uncle Jess need to talk by themselves."

"Grown-up talk?" the child asked.

"Yes." Sophia held out her hand. "Would you like to help me wrap Christmas presents in the other room?"

"Yeah."

"Some advice, even though it's unsolicited," Sophia said to Jess as she took the little girl's fingers into her own. "Don't punish someone for caring too much just because of people in your past who didn't care enough."

His mouth pulled tight. "I see good news travels fast."

"You're a father now," Sophia said. "That means setting an example to forgive."

Then Libby was alone with him and the words that came out of her mouth were the first that popped into her head. "Morgan wasn't in school today."

"It was best to keep her home. Things were unsettled," he said.

No kidding. Libby had been hoping he would drop her off at kindergarten, but wasn't surprised he hadn't. She'd managed to get through the day, but not being able to see for herself that Morgan was okay had made her anxious and distracted. "I guess you didn't go into the office?"

He nodded, even as accusation darkened his eyes. Defending herself seemed like the best thing to do. Whether he believed her or not.

"I had every intention of discontinuing the lawyer's services," she said.

"Why didn't you?"

She told him the same thing she'd said to Sophia, "I forgot about it." No way would she admit that being with him, thinking about him, had pushed almost everything else from her mind. "I made the original contact before you changed, Jess. I know now that Morgan's in excellent hands."

"Do you expect me to trust you mean that?"

"I understand your skepticism and probably deserve it. But try to understand where I'm coming from." She took a step closer. "I never belonged anywhere. My dad used me to emotionally blackmail people. When he hooked up with Cathy, she wanted him and I was part of the deal. Her parents wanted her and the new baby. But no one wanted me. For me. Not ever. I never really had a family of my own until Morgan." She drew in a breath. "I was so afraid of losing her that I made a mistake."

"Me, too," he said.

That surprised her. "Really?"

"Firing you was a knee-jerk reaction and I never considered what that would do to Morgan. I should have. I didn't think it through."

"That's understandable. And just when she thought it was safe to let people close to her—"

He nodded. "She has to come first."

"I couldn't agree more." She meant that with all her heart, but wasn't sure where he was going. "What does that mean?"

"That I can put aside my feelings. She's a little kid who's just getting her life back together. I won't be responsible for ripping the rug out from under her a second time."

"I can respect that. But I'm still not sure what you're saying."

"If you're willing, I'd like to rehire you as her nanny." He ran his fingers through his hair. "She needs stability and that's what I intend to give her."

Reading between the lines she knew he was telling her he'd do anything for Morgan—including giving Libby back her job, against his better judgment. It was more than she expected and far more than she deserved.

This was so different from their first negotiation about child care for Morgan. She'd been the one preaching stability for this child, which spoke volumes about how far he'd come. There was no mention of a time frame, nothing on the table about the arrangement being in place until Morgan adjusted. He could terminate her in a day, a week, a month or a year. Libby didn't care. She'd take what she could get.

Without hesitation she said, "I'm willing. I'd do anything for that child."

And she meant anything. Including loving Jess and seeing him, even though she could never have him.

His heart was in the right place, but it could never be hers.

Chapter Fifteen

The day before Christmas Eve, Jess drove past the condo complex security gates, waved to the guard on duty, then parked. When he pulled a pile of festively wrapped presents from the tiny trunk of his sporty car, he made a mental note that shopping for a family-friendly vehicle was at the top of his list when the holidays were over.

He was looking forward to Christmas in a way he never had before, thanks to Morgan and Libby. Thank God she'd agreed to come back to him. The short time she'd been gone had given him a grim glimpse of what life without her would be, not unlike the story in *A Christmas Carol*. Just like Scrooge, he'd gotten the message.

He reached into his jacket pocket, making sure the small jewelers box was still there. It was pretty important, since it represented hopes and dreams for happiness that he'd never let himself expect.

Packages filled his arms, making the route to the penthouse more challenging. Second item on his post-holiday list was house shopping. Morgan should grow up in a regular neighborhood and play with regular neighbor kids. He'd pick out a house and surprise Libby, but he needed her input. Everything she'd said that first day she'd brought Morgan to live with him had been right on. This was a grown-up world, and the next environment he purchased would have to be somewhere a child would feel comfortable. Money was no object and he'd make it happen before Morgan's birthday in January.

He remembered what Sophia had said that night a couple weeks ago. *Don't punish Libby for caring too much.* The words resonated with him—so simple, so profound.

After riding the elevator up to the top floor, he managed to get his door opened.

"Libby?" he called.

"In here," she answered.

He followed the sound of her voice into the family room and found her sitting under the Christmas tree with a wineglass in her hand. A bottle of cabernet that looked like it was about three glasses down sat on the counter of the wet bar.

"I'm having wine." Her eyes were a little too bright and her articulation a little too careful.

"I see that." Morgan was at a friend's for a sleepover and he'd given Libby the night off. Probably the first she'd had since becoming his nanny. "It's about time you had an evening to yourself. I'm going to have a long talk with your tyrant boss about that. He's going to get a piece of my mind."

"But you're my boss. And you're not a tyrant." She'd missed the point because of the little wine buzz going on.

The nanny couldn't hold her liquor, something he found

incredibly sweet, charming and endearing. "Any word from Morgan?"

"She called a little while ago to say good-night. Having a great time with Nicole." Her expression turned wistful and a little sad. "I hope she's found her Charity."

She meant a lifelong friend. Jess knew that he'd always miss Ben, but wouldn't trade the grief for not ever having known him. Their friendship had made it possible for him to be a decent father to Morgan. "I know what you mean."

"What's all that?" she asked, eyeing the packages.

"Ho, ho, ho." He put the pile of presents under the tree. "I've been doing some shopping."

"I thought you were working late."

"Nope. Fighting the crowds at the mall. It was great, but I wish you'd been there—"

"I don't blame you for working so much," she continued as if she hadn't heard him. Her eyes were sad. "If I were you, I wouldn't want to come home to me either."

Someone was having the tiniest little pity party. "It's not that I didn't want to come home, just that with Morgan at a friend's this was a good time to pick up some things to surprise her. That reminds me, we have to hide this stuff and put it out Christmas Eve so she'll buy into the whole Santa thing—"

"I saw the picture of her with Santa. It's too cute. And I missed it…." Her eyes filled with tears.

"Libby, we can take her to see Santa again. She wanted you there and shouldn't have to miss out on anything. I want her to have the best Christmas ever."

"Of course you do. Because you're a good man."

"I'm glad you think so."

"I didn't always," she admitted.

"No. Really?" he said wryly.

"It's all right. You have every right to hate me. All I ever wanted was to make sure Morgan was happy." She drew in a shuddering breath. "Ginger said that you and I were two halves of a parenting whole. It's what gave me the idea to be your nanny in the first place. She said you have the means and I have the mothering."

"She was right. I didn't always think so," he said, echoing her words. "But now I'm convinced that Charity and Ben knew exactly what they were doing when they left her in your care."

"And made you guardian," she said, gesturing with the empty wineglass.

He took it from her and set it on the wet bar. "That's the part I thought they got wrong."

"No. It's the part they got right." She shook her head just a little too enthusiastically and put a hand to her forehead.

"Are you dizzy?"

Without waiting for an answer, he sat down beside her. The smell of cinnamon and pine mixed with the intoxicating scent of her skin and made him want to hold her. But when he started to put his arm around her, she shook her head again.

"Don't be nice to me. I messed up so badly. Charity and Ben trusted you. Who did I think I was to question that?"

"Who you are is the child-care expert in charge of making sure I don't screw it up too badly." He slid his arm around her waist and tugged her into his lap. Holding her felt so good, so right.

"I do love her," she said, resting her head on his shoulder. "More than anything except you."

Maybe he was actually going to get what he wished for this Christmas. "Oh?"

She nodded. "I think I fell in love with you the very first time we met. At Charity and Ben's wedding. I was the maid of honor and you were—"

"Best man." Not. He remembered that day and thinking, no, *feeling*, that Libby was someone who could really matter to him. He hadn't wanted that and deliberately pushed her away. He would never forget the hurt in her eyes or what an ass he'd been.

"I was a jerk that day."

"Yeah. But you're obviously a trustworthy jerk or Ben and Charity wouldn't have put you in charge of their child. I was so stupid. Someone as stupid as me doesn't deserve to be happy."

"You're wrong, Lib." He laced his fingers with hers. "I admire the depth of your love, your capacity for caring. Not just anyone would have been willing to take on a man with my considerable resources, but you didn't hesitate to go to the mat on this one. I have no doubt you'd do that for anyone you love."

He prayed that she truly meant what she'd said about loving him and it wasn't the cabernet talking.

"Mmm-hmm," she murmured.

"I have a confession to make." He kissed her hair and breathed in the sweet fragrance that clung to it. "I tried very hard not to fall in love with you. And that was before I found out that you'd been let down over and over by the one person who should have protected you. That really made me take a step back, because I didn't want to make a wrong move and hurt you more than you'd already been hurt. But I can't stand on the sidelines anymore. I hope you can understand—"

"Mmm," she whispered, snuggling closer.

"My life was pretty empty before you and Morgan. This

might shock you, but surprise sex isn't all that great. If you'll give me a chance, I swear that I'll always be the kind of man you can count on. Of all people, you know how sacred I hold a promise."

Jess held his breath, waiting for a response to his heartfelt, sincere declaration. But there was only silence before he heard a soft, ladylike snore. He looked down and realized Libby hadn't heard the good part because she was sound asleep.

He kissed her forehead, hoping that would get through somehow. She wasn't the only one who'd go to the mat for love and he wasn't letting her get away that easily. Lifting her in his arms, he carried her down the hall and gently put her to bed.

His bed.

"Aunt Libby, I'm home. Uncle Jess came and got me. Are you okay? Wake up."

Morgan's voice cut through the pounding in Libby's head and she opened one eye. It took several seconds to register that this wasn't her room. Or her bed. Not Morgan's trundle bed either. Her stomach dropped, which did nothing good for the nausea that threatened dire consequences if she moved.

"I'm fine, Morgan," she lied.

"Why are you sleepin' in Uncle Jess's bed?"

Good question. Libby wished she had an answer. She opened the other eye and tried to remember what happened last night. She'd been feeling sorry for herself. She was pretty sure Jess had come home looking like Santa Claus, with his arms full of presents. They'd talked, although the content of the conversation was fuzzy. After that, everything went as blank as a TV screen with no disk in the DVD player.

"Aunt Libby, are you and Uncle Jess going to give me a baby sister for Christmas?"

Good Lord, she hoped not. Sitting up she held in the groan and said, "No, Morgan."

"Uncle Jess said you probably weren't feeling well and that's why you're still in bed. I had to come and make sure you were okay."

"I'm fine, sweetie."

So not true. She felt crappy. Note to self, she thought, never, ever drink on an empty stomach again. Things were starting to come back. Like the fact that Morgan had been at a sleepover last night.

"How did you get home?"

"I told you. Uncle Jess came and got me. Nicole's mom said she needed some quiet time."

Libby could relate to that. "Did you have fun?"

The little girl nodded. "Me and Nicole played dolls and watched movies and ate popcorn. She's my best friend."

"I'm glad." Charity would have liked the little girl, Libby thought.

"Knock, knock." Jess walked in with a tray and set it on the nightstand.

"I have to get up."

Jess stopped her with a hand on her shoulder when she threw the covers aside. "I don't recommend moving around too much yet."

"Aunt Libby, how come you slept in Uncle Jess's shirt?" Morgan's big brown eyes were bigger than ever and puzzled.

She looked down with something close to horror at the white cotton that covered her to mid-thigh.

"Aunt Libby was too tired to put on her pajamas so I let her borrow it," he said. "Looks better on her than me, anyway. Don't you think so, Princess?"

"Yes." The little girl giggled. "Can I go watch TV?"

"That's a good idea." Jess nodded his approval. "But under no circumstances are you to look at any of those presents under the Christmas tree."

"Okay." The gleam of excitement in her eyes was a pretty good indication that the temptation would be too much for her.

Libby tried to glare. "That wasn't fair. In fact, it bordered on mean. You know she's going to check out everything."

He nodded, clearly unrepentant. "Figured it would keep her busy for a while. And give you a break."

"Diabolical," she said.

"It's a gift. No pun intended."

The only gift she wanted right now was information. She had three pressing questions. Why was she in his bed? How did she get out of her clothes and into his shirt? And what happened in between those two things?

"Speaking of gifts, I brought some for you—in a manner of speaking. I suggest starting with two aspirin and a glass of water." Jess handed them to her.

"Thanks," she said after swallowing the caplets.

"Drink it all up like a good girl."

"I don't think that's such a good idea." She put a hand on her traitorous stomach.

"On the contrary. Hydration is the best remedy for a hangover."

"Yeah, about that…" She circled the rim of the glass with her index finger. "So, I guess what with all the wine, I got kind of turned around on the way to my room last night?"

"That's one way of putting it." The bed dipped when he sat on the mattress. Their thighs brushed and in spite of how awful she felt, heat trickled through her. "But I'm not sure what you mean."

"I meant that must be how I ended up here. It was very nice of you to let me sleep in your bed." There was the tiniest questioning tone in her statement.

"Trust me." The gleam in his eyes said just the opposite. "I'm not that swell a guy. It was a night to remember."

Then why couldn't she remember it? Her stomach lurched. "Should I be packing up my things again?"

"You think I'm firing you? After last night?" He shook his head as a very satisfied expression settled on his handsome face. "Not on your life. It will go down in the history books as an epic event."

Epic? Lasting, ageless, unforgettable? Not so much after a couple glasses of very fine cabernet. "I don't know what to say."

"You were amazing and that gives you a pass on saying anything. Here." He handed her a plate and took the glass from her fingers. "Have some toast. It will settle your stomach."

"It will take more than crusty bread," she grumbled. But after a nibble, she realized he was right and chowed down two pieces.

"One of these days you'll learn not to question everything," he said, taking the plate that was now empty except for a few stray crumbs.

"I guess I'm cynical by nature."

"No, by environment." His deep voice went soft and gentle with sympathy. "In time you'll realize that you don't have to be that way with me."

Libby stared at him. Who was this man and what had he done with Jess Donnelly?

"Okay, I give up." She sighed. "I don't remember what happened last night. I don't recall being amazing. And I especially don't understand why you're being so nice to me."

"Ouch," he said, wincing. "Amnesia after such a memorable experience isn't especially good for a man's fragile ego."

She managed a full-on glare. "You've got an ego for sure, but there's nothing the least bit fragile about it."

"Now that's the Libby I've come to know." He grinned.

"Tell me the truth. Did we… Um…" She tried to figure out how to phrase it diplomatically, then threw in the towel along with any dignity she ever hoped to have. "Where are my clothes? Did we sleep together? I'd appreciate it if you'd tell me the truth."

"I wouldn't lie," he said seriously.

"Just a figure of speech. It never occurred to me that you would." He was probably the most honorable man she'd ever known. If he weren't, she wouldn't care about him so much.

"We slept together in the same bed, but nothing happened. Not because I didn't want it to," he added.

"What?"

"I wanted more than anything to make love with you." He was dead serious. "But in your condition that would have been taking advantage. And I love you too much to do that."

The words took several moments to sink in. "I'm sorry. I think my hearing has a hangover, too. I could have sworn you said that you love me."

"You heard right. And I have every reason to believe that you love me, too."

"Oh?" Her heart started to pound.

"You told me so last night." He reached out and tucked a strand of hair behind her ear, then brushed the back of his hand softly down her cheek. "It was right after your remark about being too stupid to deserve happiness."

She winced. "Apparently I have more to apologize for than I thought."

"Not to me." A darkly intense look slid into his eyes. "If you hadn't said what you did it might have taken me a lot longer to say something that's been on my mind for a while now."

"What? Since when?"

"Since I fired you," he said. "Big mistake, by the way. But it could be the best one I ever made."

"I don't get it."

"Something Sophia said got past my stubborn streak, although you had me with your speech. I understand how bad things were for you growing up. In spite of that, you have more decency and integrity than any woman I've ever met."

"What did Sophia say?"

"That I was taking out my past on you. Punishing you for caring too much. She was right. I cared—care—about you and that scared me because I know how easy it is to mess that up."

"Oh?" Libby stared at him, afraid if she looked away this momentous moment would disappear.

"If I hadn't sent you away, I might never have realized that I can't live without you." He raked his hand through his hair. "It wasn't very long, thank God. But as soon as you walked out the door I missed you like crazy. I love you, Libby."

"Really?"

He reached behind him and picked up something from the tray he'd brought in. In the palm of his hand was a black velvet jewelry box. A very small box. Just about the perfect size for a ring.

She could feel her eyes widen as her gaze jumped to his. "Is that what I think it is?"

"I'd been thinking about doing this in a more romantic way, some grand gesture in front of a roaring fire and the magic of the Christmas tree. Partly because after I fired you, it crossed my mind that you wouldn't believe me. Then, last night, you said what you said and I had reason to hope. I'm not a man who lets opportunity pass by and I'm not willing to risk something this important by waiting for a perfect moment. Life isn't perfect. It's messy and wonderful and—"

"Jess? Focus—" Please, please say it, she thought.

Being a man of action, he reached out and pulled her into his arms. Then he stared into her eyes, looking unsure and serious and too cute for words. "My love is as real as your hangover and far more enduring."

She had to admit he was pretty darn good with words, too. "Funny thing. I'm not feeling the hangover so much."

He smiled and flipped open the box to reveal a big, square-cut diamond ring. "Would you do me the honor of becoming my wife?"

"Yes." She threw her arms around his neck. "Yes. Yes."

"You're sure?" he asked, laughter in his voice. "Take your time."

"The heck with that." She drew back and cupped his much-loved face in her hands. "I've been in love with you for a long time."

"Since we met at Charity and Ben's wedding." It wasn't a question.

"How did you know that?"

"You told me last night," he said.

She sighed. "Some day you're going to have to tell me word for word what went down under the Christmas tree."

"It was all good. Or it is now." He slid his arms around her. "I want to be a family with you, Lib."

"We already are. You. Me. Morgan. Family is where you find it and how you make it."

"I hope you don't mind, but I called my mother."

"Mind?" He was a man of surprises, her fiancé. Making even more family. "Of course I don't mind. That's wonderful news. And?"

"She asked us to stop by on Christmas. If that's okay with you," he added.

"More than okay. She's the only mom you've got. It's time to put the bad stuff behind you."

"Yeah," he said. "This will be the best Christmas ever."

She felt a shiver as something brushed over her skin. "Has it crossed your mind that Charity and Ben might have been matchmaking when they left Morgan to us?"

"How do you mean?"

"It's silly, I guess. But I can't help thinking that we have two guardian angels who brought us together in order to make us admit what they've known all along."

"And that would be?"

"That we're soul mates. Stubborn ones, I'll admit. But we were meant to be together and needed a nudge in that direction."

He shrugged. "You could be right."

She refused to be sad when she said, "I think it's their Christmas gift to us."

"Saving the best for last," he agreed softly.

"Speaking of gifts, we should go check on our daughter and make sure she hasn't opened everything under the tree."

He stood with her in his arms. "If so, we'll start a new Donnelly family tradition."

"But there won't be anything under the tree Christmas morning," she protested.

"We'll just buy more. None of that matters as long as I get my nanny under the mistletoe."

"Who needs mistletoe?" she asked, settling her mouth on his.

She was starting a tradition of her own, one she planned on repeating every day for the rest of their lives.

* * * * *

*Bestselling author Lynne Graham is back
with a fabulous new trilogy!*

PREGNANT BRIDES

Three ordinary girls—naive, but also honest and plucky…

*Three fabulously wealthy, impossibly handsome
and very ruthless men…*

*When opposites attract and passion leads to pregnancy…
it can only mean marriage!*

*Available next month from Harlequin Presents®:
the first installment*

DESERT PRINCE, BRIDE OF INNOCENCE

* * *

'THIS EVENING I'm flying to New York for two weeks,'
Jasim imparted with a casualness that made her heart sink
like a stone. 'That's why I had you brought here. I own this
apartment and you'll be comfortable here while I'm abroad.'

'I can afford my own accommodation although I may not
need it for long. I'll have another job by the time you
get back—'

Jasim released a slightly harsh laugh. 'There's no need for
you to look for another position. How would I ever see you?
Don't you understand what I'm offering you?'

Elinor stood very still. 'No, I must be incredibly thick
because I haven't quite worked out yet what you're offering
me.…'

His charismatic smile slashed his lean dark visage.
'Naturally, I want to take care of you.…'

'No, thanks.' Elinor forced a smile and mentally willed him not to demean her with some sordid proposition. 'The only man who will ever take *care* of me with my agreement will be my husband. I'm willing to wait for you to come back but I'm not willing to be kept by you. I'm a very independent woman and what I give, I give freely.'

Jasim frowned. 'You make it all sound so serious.'

'What happened between us last night left pure chaos in its wake. Right now, I don't know whether I'm on my head or my heels. I'll stay for a while because I have nowhere else to go in the short term. So maybe it's good that you'll be away for a while.'

Jasim pulled out his wallet to extract a card. 'My private number,' he told her, presenting her with it as though it was a precious gift, which indeed it was. Many women would have done just about anything to gain access to that direct hotline to him, but his staff guarded his privacy with scrupulous care.

Before he could close the wallet, his blood ran cold in his veins. How could he have made such a serious oversight? What if he had got her pregnant? He knew that an unplanned pregnancy would engulf his life like an avalanche, crush his freedom and suffocate him. He barely stilled a shudder at the threat of such an outcome and thought how ironic it was that what his older brother had longed and prayed for to secure the line to the throne should strike Jasim as an absolute disaster....

* * *

What will proud Prince Jasim do if Elinor is expecting his royal baby? Perhaps an arranged marriage is the only solution! But will Elinor agree? Find out in DESERT PRINCE, BRIDE OF INNOCENCE by Lynne Graham [#2884], available from Harlequin Presents® in January 2010.

Bestselling Harlequin Presents author

Lynne Graham

brings you an exciting new miniseries:

PREGNANT BRIDES

Inexperienced and expecting, they're forced to marry

Collect them all:

DESERT PRINCE, BRIDE OF INNOCENCE

January 2010

RUTHLESS MAGNATE, CONVENIENT WIFE

February 2010

GREEK TYCOON, INEXPERIENCED MISTRESS

March 2010

www.eHarlequin.com

HP12884

New Year, New Man!

For the perfect New Year's punch,
blend the following:

- *One woman determined to find her inner vixen*
- *A notorious—and notoriously hot!—playboy*
- *A provocative New Year's Eve bash*
- *An impulsive kiss that leads to a night of*
  explosive passion!

When the clock hits midnight Claire Daniels
kisses the guy standing closest to her, but
the kiss doesn't end after the bells stop ringing….

Look for

Moonstruck

by *USA TODAY* bestselling author

JULIE KENNER

Available January

red-hot reads

REQUEST YOUR FREE BOOKS!
2 FREE NOVELS PLUS 2 FREE GIFTS!

SPECIAL EDITION®

Life, Love and Family!

YES! Please send me 2 FREE Silhouette Special Edition® novels and my 2 FREE gifts (gifts are worth about $10). After receiving them, if I don't wish to receive any more books, I can return the shipping statement marked "cancel." If I don't cancel, I will receive 6 brand-new novels every month and be billed just $4.24 per book in the U.S. or $4.99 per book in Canada. That's a savings of at least 15% off the cover price! It's quite a bargain! Shipping and handling is just 50¢ per book.* I understand that accepting the 2 free books and gifts places me under no obligation to buy anything. I can always return a shipment and cancel at any time. Even if I never buy another book from Silhouette, the two free books and gifts are mine to keep forever.

235 SDN EYN4 335 SDN EYPG

Name _____ (PLEASE PRINT)

Address _____ Apt. #

City _____ State/Prov. _____ Zip/Postal Code

Signature (if under 18, a parent or guardian must sign)

Mail to the Silhouette Reader Service:
IN U.S.A.: P.O. Box 1867, Buffalo, NY 14240-1867
IN CANADA: P.O. Box 609, Fort Erie, Ontario L2A 5X3

Not valid to current subscribers of Silhouette Special Edition books.

Want to try two free books from another line?
Call 1-800-873-8635 or visit www.morefreebooks.com.

* Terms and prices subject to change without notice. Prices do not include applicable taxes. Sales tax applicable in N.Y. Canadian residents will be charged applicable provincial taxes and GST. Offer not valid in Quebec. This offer is limited to one order per household. All orders subject to approval. Credit or debit balances in a customer's account(s) may be offset by any other outstanding balance owed by or to the customer. Please allow 4 to 6 weeks for delivery. Offer available while quantities last.

Your Privacy: Silhouette is committed to protecting your privacy. Our Privacy Policy is available online at www.eHarlequin.com or upon request from the Reader Service. From time to time we make our lists of customers available to reputable third parties who may have a product or service of interest to you. If you would prefer we not share your name and address, please check here. ☐

SSE09R

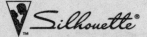

COMING NEXT MONTH
Available December 29, 2009

#2017 PRESCRIPTION FOR ROMANCE—Marie Ferrarella
The Baby Chase
Dr. Paul Armstrong had a funny feeling about Ramona Tate, the beautiful new PR manager for his famous fertility clinic. Was she a spy trying to uncover the institute's secrets…or a well-intentioned ingenue trying to steal his very heart?

#2018 BRANDED WITH HIS BABY—Stella Bagwell
Men of the West
Private nurse Maura Donovan had sworn off men—until she was trapped in close quarters during a freak thunderstorm with her patient's irresistible grandson Quint Cantrell. One thing led to another, and now she was pregnant with the rich rancher's baby!

#2019 LOVE AND THE SINGLE DAD—Susan Crosby
The McCoys of Chance City
On a rare visit to his hometown, photojournalist Donovan McCoy discovered he was the father of a young son. But the newly minted single dad wouldn't be single for long, if family law attorney—and former Chance City beauty queen—Laura Bannister had anything to say about it.

#2020 THE BACHELOR'S NORTHBRIDGE BRIDE—Victoria Pade
Northbridge Nuptials
Prim redhead Kate Perry knew thrill seeker Ry Grayson spelled trouble. It was a case of the unstoppable bachelor colliding with the unmovable bachelorette. But did the undeniable attraction between them suggest there were some Northbridge Nuptials in their near future?

#2021 THE ENGAGEMENT PROJECT—Brenda Harlen
Brides & Babies
Gage Richmond was a love-'em-and-leave-'em type—until his CEO dad demanded he settle down or miss out on a promotion. Now it was time to see if beautiful research scientist Megan Rourke would pose as Gage's fake fiancée…and if their feelings would stay fake for long.

#2022 THE SHERIFF'S SECRET WIFE—Christyne Butler
Bartender Racy Dillon didn't expect to run into her hometown nemesis, Sheriff Gage Steele, in Vegas—let alone marry him in a moment of abandon! Now they were headed back to their small town with a big secret…but was there more to this whiplash wedding than met the eye?

Sharon P

W9-BRP-191

The Author

John Dickson Carr, acknowledged master of the "impossible" crime, invents his tale of kilts and killings with high good humor, delightful characterization, and a fillip of historical scholarship. Other fine Carr mysteries published by Collier Books include:

Arabian Nights Murder (01835)
Blind Barber (01839)
Corpse in the Wax Works (01850)
Crooked Hinge (01851)
Death Watch (01855)
Eight of Swords (01863)
Four False Weapons (01871)
Hag's Nook (01879)
The Mad Hatter Mystery (01881)
Poison in Jest (01880)
To Wake the Dead (01834)

The Case of
the Constant Suicides

JOHN DICKSON CARR

COLLIER BOOKS
A Division of Macmillan Publishing Co., Inc.
New York

The Case of the Constant Suicides

Chapter 1

THE 9:15 TRAIN FOR Glasgow pulled out of Euston half an hour late that night, and forty minutes after the sirens had sounded.

When the sirens went, even the dim blue lights along the platform were extinguished.

A milling, jostling, swearing crowd, mainly in khaki, groped about the platform, its shins and knuckles barked by kit and luggage, its hearing deadened by the iron coughing of engines. Lost in it was a youngish professor of history, who was trying to find his sleeping compartment on the Glasgow train.

Not that anyone had cause for apprehension. It was only the first of September, and the heavy raiding of London had not yet begun. We were very young in those days. An air-raid alert meant merely inconvenience, with perhaps one lone raider droning somewhere, and no barrage.

But the professor of history, Alan Campbell (M.A., Oxon.; Ph.D., Harvard) bumped along with unacademic profanity. The first-class sleepers appeared to be at the head of a long train. He could see a porter, with much luggage, striking matches at the open door of a carriage, where names were posted on a board opposite the numbers of the compartments assigned to them.

Striking a match in his turn, Alan Campbell discovered that the train appeared to be full and that his own compartment was number four.

He climbed in. Dim little lighted numerals over each door in the corridor showed him the way. When he opened the door of his compartment, he felt distinctly better.

This, he thought, was really first-rate in the way of comfort. The compartment was a tiny metal room, green-painted, with a single berth, nickel washbasin, and a long mirror on the door communicating with the next compartment. Its blackout consisted of a sliding shutter which sealed the window. Though it was intensely hot and close, he saw over the berth a metal ventilator which you could twist to let in air.

Pushing his suitcase under the berth, Alan sat down to get his breath. His reading matter, a Penguin novel and a copy of the *Sunday Watchman,* lay beside him. He eyed the newspaper, and his soul grew dark with bile.

"May he perish in the everlasting bonfire!" Alan said aloud, referring to his only enemy in this world. "May he—"

Then he checked himself, remembering that he ought to remain in a good temper. After all, he had a week's leave; and, though no doubt his mission was sad enough in a formal way, still it was in the nature of a holiday.

Alan Campbell was a Scot who had never in his life set foot in Scotland. For that matter, except for his years at the American Cambridge and a few visits to the Continent, he had never been out of England. He was thirty-five: bookish, serious-minded though not without humor, well-enough looking but perhaps already inclined toward stodginess.

His notions of Scotland were drawn from the novels of Sir Walter Scott or, if he felt in a frivolous mood, John Buchan. Added to this was a vague idea of granite and heather and Scottish jokes—which last he rather resented, showing himself no true Scot in spirit. Now he was at last going to see for himself. And if only—

The sleeping-car attendant knocked at the door, and put his head in.

"Mr. Campbell?" he inquired, consulting the little imitation ivory card on the door, on which names could be written with a pencil and rubbed out.

"Dr. Campbell," said Alan, not without stateliness. He was still young enough to get a thrill at the newness and unexpectedness of the title.

"What time would you like to be called in the morning, sir?"

"What time do we get to Glasgow?"

"Well, sir, we're *due* in at six-thirty."

"Better call me at six, then."

The attendant coughed. Alan correctly interpreted this.

"Call me half an hour before we do get in, then."

"Yes, sir. Would you like tea and biscuits in the morning?"

"Can I get a proper breakfast on the train?"

"No, sir. Only tea and biscuits."

Alan's heart sank along with his stomach. He had been in such a hurry to pack that he had eaten no dinner, and his inside now felt squeezed up like a concertina. The attendant understood his look.

"If I was you, sir, I should nip out and get something at the buffet now."

"But the train's due to start in less than five minutes!"

"I shouldn't let that worry you, sir. We'll not be starting as soon as that, to my way of thinking."

Yes: he'd better do it.

Ruffled, he left the train. Ruffled, he groped along a noisy and crowded platform in the dark, back through the barrier. When he stood at the buffet, with a slopped cup of tea and some dry sandwiches containing ham cut so thin as to have achieved a degree of transparency, his eye fell again on the *Sunday Watchman*. And bile rose again in his soul.

It has been stated that Alan Campbell had only one enemy in the world. Indeed, except for a fight in his school days in which he had exchanged black eyes and a bloody nose with the boy who later became his best friend, he could not even remember disliking anyone very much.

The man in question was also named Campbell: though he was not, Alan hoped and believed, any relation. The other Campbell lived in a sinister lair at Harpenden, Herts. Alan had never set eyes on him, and did not even know who he was. Yet he disliked him very cordially indeed.

Mr. Belloc has pointed out that no controversy can grow

more heated, more bitter (or, to a detached observer, more funny) than a controversy between two learned dons over some obscure point that nobody cares twopence about.

We have all, with glee, seen the thing happen. Somebody writes in a dignified newspaper or literary weekly that Hannibal, when crossing the Alps, passed close to the village of Viginum. Some other erudite reader then writes in to say that the name of the village was not Viginum, but Biginium. On the following week, the first writer mildly but acidly deplores your correspondent's ignorance, and begs leave to present the following evidence that it was Viginum. The second writer then says he regrets that an acrimonious note seems to have crept into the discussion, which is no doubt what makes Mr. So-and-So forget his manners; but is under the necessity of pointing out—

And that tears it. The row is sometimes good for two or three months.

Something of a similar nature had dropped with a splosh into Alan Campbell's placid life.

Alan, a kindly soul, had meant no offense. He sometimes reviewed historical works for the *Sunday Watchman,* a newspaper very similar to the *Sunday Times* or the *Observer.*

In the middle of June this paper had sent him a book called, *The Last Days of Charles the Second,* a weighty study of political events between 1680 and 1685, by K. I. Campbell (M.A., Oxon.). Alan's review of this appeared on the following Sunday, and his sin lay in the following words, toward the end of the notice.

"It cannot be said that Mr. Campbell's book throws any fresh light on the subject; and it is not, indeed, free from minor blemishes. Mr. Campbell surely cannot believe that Lord William Russell was ignorant of the Rye House Plot. Barbara Villiers, Lady Castlemaine, was created Duchess of Cleveland in 1670: not, as the printer has it, 1680. And what is the reason for Mr. Campbell's extraordinary notion that this lady was 'small and auburn-haired'?"

Alan sent in his copy on Friday, and forgot the matter. But in the issue nine days later appeared a letter from the author dated at Harpenden, Herts. It concluded:

"May I say that my authority for what your reviewer considers this 'extraordinary' notion is Steinmann, the lady's only biographer. If your reviewer is unfamiliar with this work, I suggest that a visit to the British Museum might repay his trouble."

This riled Alan considerably.

"While I must apologize for drawing attention to so trivial a matter (he wrote), and thank Mr. Campbell for his courtesy in drawing my attention to a book with which I am already familiar, nevertheless, I think a visit to the British Museum would be less profitable than a visit to the National Portrait Gallery. There Mr. Campbell will find a portrait, by Lely, of this handsome termagant. The hair is shown as jet-black, the proportions as ample. It might be thought that a painter would flatter his subject. But it cannot be thought that he would turn a blonde into a brunette, or depict any court lady as fatter than she actually was."

That, Alan thought, was rather neat. And not far from devastating either.

But the snake from Harpenden now began to hit below the belt. After a discussion of known portraits, he concluded:

"Your reviewer, incidentally, is good enough to refer to this lady as a 'termagant.' What are his reasons for this? They appear to be that she had a temper and that she liked to spend money. When any man exhibits astounded horror over these two qualities in a woman, it is permissible to inquire whether he has ever been married."

This sent Alan clear up in the air. It was not the slur on his historical knowledge that he minded: it was the implication that he knew nothing about women—which, as a matter of fact, was true.

K. I. Campbell, he thought, was in the wrong; and knew it; and was now, as usual, trying to cloud the matter with side issues. His reply blistered the paper, the more so as the controversy caught on with other readers.

Letters poured in. A major wrote from Cheltenham that his family had for generations been in possession of a painting, said to be that of the Duchess of Cleveland, which showed the hair as medium brown. A savant from the Athenaeum wanted them to define their terms, saying what proportions they meant by "ample," and in what parts of the body, according to the standards of the present day.

"Bejasus," said the editor of the *Sunday Watchman,* "it's the best thing we've had since Nelson's glass eye. Leave 'em to it."

Throughout July and August the row continued. The unfortunate mistress of Charles the Second came in for almost as much notoriety as she had known in the days of Samuel Pepys. Her anatomy was discussed in some detail. The controversy was entered, though not clarified, by another savant named Dr. Gideon Fell, who seemed to take a malicious delight in confusing the two Campbells, and mixing everybody up.

The editor himself finally called a halt to it. First, because the anatomical detail now verged on the indelicate; and, second, because the parties to the dispute had grown so confused that nobody knew who was calling whom what.

But it left Alan feeling that he would like to boil K. I. Campbell in oil.

For K. I. Campbell appeared every week, dodging like a sharpshooter and always stinging Alan. Alan began to acquire a vague but definite reputation for ungallant conduct, as one who has traduced a dead woman and might traduce any lady of his acquaintance. K. I. Campbell's last letter more than hinted at this.

His fellow members of the faculty joked about it. The undergraduates, he suspected, joked about it. "Rip" was one term; "rounder" another.

He had breathed a prayer of relief when the debate ended. But even now, drinking slopped tea and eating dry sandwiches in a steamy station buffet, Alan stiffened as he turned over the pages of the *Sunday Watchman*. He feared that his eye might light on some reference to the Duchess of Cleveland, and that K. I. Campbell might have sneaked into the columns again.

No. Nothing. Well, at least that was a good omen to start the journey.

The hands of the clock over the buffet stood at twenty minutes to ten.

In sudden agitation Alan remembered his train. Gulping down his tea (when you are in a hurry there always seems to be about a quart of it, boiling hot), he hurried out into the blackout again. For the second time he took some minutes to find his ticket at the barrier, searching through every pocket before he found it in the first one. He wormed through crowds and luggage trucks, spotted the right platform after some difficulty, and arrived back at the door of his carriage just as doors were slamming all along the train, and the whistle blew.

Smoothly gliding, the train moved out.

Off on the great adventure, then. Alan, pleased with life again, stood in the dim corridor and got his breath. Through his mind moved some words out of the letter he had received from Scotland: "The Castle of Shira, at Inveraray, on Loch Fyne." It had a musical, magical sound. He savored it. Then he walked down to his compartment, threw open the door, and stopped short.

An open suitcase, not his own, lay on the berth. It contained female wearing apparel. Bending over it and rummaging in it stood a brown-haired girl of twenty-seven or twenty-eight. She had been almost knocked sprawling by the opening of the door, and she straightened up to stare at him.

"Wow!" said Alan inaudibly.

His first thought was that he must have got the wrong compartment, or the wrong carriage. But a quick glance at the door reassured him. There was his name, Campbell, written in pencil on the imitation ivory strip.

"I beg your pardon," he said. "But haven't you—er—made a mistake?"

"No, I don't think so," replied the girl, rubbing her arm and staring back at him with increasing coolness.

Even then he noticed how attractive she was, though she wore very little powder or lipstick, and there was a look of determined severity about her rounded face. She was five feet two inches tall, and pleasantly shaped. She had blue eyes, spaced rather wide apart, a good forehead, and full lips which she tried to keep firmly compressed. She wore tweeds, a blue jumper, and tan stockings with flat-heeled shoes.

"But this," he pointed out, "is compartment number four."

"Yes. I know that."

"Madam, what I am trying to indicate is that it's my compartment. My name is Campbell. Here it is on the door."

"And my name," retorted the girl, "happens to be Campbell too. And I must insist that it's *my* compartment. Will you be good enough to leave, please?"

She was pointing to the suitcase.

Alan looked, and looked again. The train rattled and clicked over points, swaying and gathering speed. But what he could not assimilate easily was the meaning of the words painted in tiny white letters on the side of the suitcase.

K. I. Campbell. Harpenden.

Chapter 2

IN ALAN'S MIND and emotions, incredulity was gradually giving way to something very different.

He cleared his throat.

"May I ask," he said sternly, "what the initials 'K. I.' stand for?"

"Kathryn Irene, of course. My first names. But will you *please*—?"

"So!" said Alan. He held up the newspaper. "May I further ask whether you have recently taken part in a disgraceful correspondence in the *Sunday Watchman?*"

Miss K. I. Campbell put up a hand to her forehead as though to shade her eyes. She put the other hand behind her to steady herself on the rim of the washbasin. The train rattled and jerked. A sudden suspicion, and then comprehension, began to grow in the blue eyes.

"Yes," said Alan. "I am A. D. Campbell, of University College, Highgate."

By his proud and darkly sinister bearing, he might have been saying, "And, Saxon, I am Roderick Dhu." It occurred to him that there was something vaguely ridiculous in his position as he inclined his head sternly, threw the paper on the berth, and folded his arms. But the girl did not take it like this.

"You beast! You weasel! You worm!" she cried passionately.

"Considering, madam, that I have not had the honor of being formally introduced to you, such terms indicate a degree of intimacy which—"

"Nonsense," said K. I. Campbell. "We're second cousins twice removed. But you haven't got a beard!"

Alan instinctively put a hand to his chin.

"Certainly I have not got a beard. Why should you suppose that I had a beard?"

"We all thought you had. We all thought you had a beard this long," cried the girl, putting her hand at about the level of her waist. "And big double-lensed spectacles. And a nasty, dry, sneering way of talking. You've got that, though. On top of which, you come bursting in here and knock me about—"

Belatedly, she began to rub her arm again.

"Of all the nasty, sneering, patronizing book reviews that were ever written," she went on, "that one of yours—"

"There, madam, you show a want of understanding. It was my duty, as a professional historian, to point out certain errors, glaring errors—"

"Errors!" said the girl. "Glaring errors, eh?"

"Exactly. I do not refer to the trivial and meaningless point about the Duchess of Cleveland's hair. I refer to matters of real moment. Your treatment of the elections of 1680, if you will excuse my plain speaking, would make a cat laugh. Your treatment of Lord William Russell was downright dishonest. I do not say that he was as big a crook as your hero Shaftesbury. Russell was merely a muttonhead: 'of,' as it was put at the trial, 'imperfect understanding'; to be pitied, if you like, but not to be pictured as anything except the traitor he was."

"You're nothing," said K. I. Campbell furiously, "but a beastly *Tory!*"

"In reply, I quote no less an authority than Dr. Johnson. 'Madam, I perceive that you are a vile Whig.' "

Then they stood and looked at each other.

Alan didn't ordinarily talk like this, you understand. But he was so mad and so much on his dignity that he could have given points and a beating to Edmund Burke.

"Who are you, anyway?" he asked in a more normal tone, after a pause.

This had the effect of putting Kathryn Campbell again on her dignity. She compressed her lips. She drew herself up to the full majesty of five feet two.

"Though I consider myself under no obligation to answer that question," she replied, putting on a pair of shell-rimmed glasses which only increased her prettiness, "I don't mind telling you that I am a member of the department of history at the Harpenden College for Women—"

"Oh."

"Yes. And as perfectly capable as any man, more so, of dealing with the period in question. Now will you *please* have the elementary decency to get out of my compartment?"

"No, I'm damned if I do. It's not your compartment!"

"I say it is my compartment."

"And I say it's not your compartment."

"If you don't get out of here, *Dr.* Campbell, I'll ring the bell for the attendant."

"Please do. If you don't, I'll ring it myself."

The attendant, brought running by two peals on the bell each made by a different hand, found two stately but almost gibbering professors attempting to tell their stories.

"I'm sorry, ma'am," said the attendant, worriedly consulting his list, "I'm sorry, sir; but there seems to have been a mistake somewhere. There's only one Campbell down here, without even a 'Miss' or a 'Mr.' I don't know what to say."

Alan drew himself up.

"Never mind. Not for the world," he declared loftily, "would I disturb this lady in possession of her ill-gotten bed. Take me to another compartment."

Kathryn gritted her teeth.

"No, you don't, *Dr.* Campbell. I am not accepting any favors on the grounds of my sex, thank you. Take *me* to another compartment."

The attendant spread out his hands.

"I'm sorry, miss. I'm sorry, sir. But I can't do that. There's not a sleeper to be had on the whole train. Nor a seat either, if it comes to that. They're even standing in third class."

"Never mind," snapped Alan, after a slight pause.

"Just let me get my bag from under there, and I'll stand up in the corridor all night."

"Oh, don't be silly," said the girl in a different voice. "You can't do that."

"I repeat, madam—"

"All the way to Glasgow? You can't do that. Don't be silly."

She sat down on the edge of the berth.

"There's only one thing we can possibly do," she added. "We'll share this compartment, and sit up all night."

A powerful shade of relief went over the attendant.

"Now, miss that's very kind of you! And I know this gentleman appreciates it. Don't you, sir? If you wouldn't mind, I'm sure the company'll make it right with you at the other end. It's very kind of the lady, isn't it, sir?"

"No, it is not. I refuse—"

"What's the matter, Dr. Campbell?" asked Kathryn, with icy sweetness. "Are you afraid of me? Or is it that you just daren't face historical fact when it is presented to you?"

Alan turned to the attendant. Had there been room, he would have pointed to the door with a gesture as dramatic as that of a father turning out his child into the storm in an old-fashioned melodrama. As it was, he merely banged his hand on the ventilator. But the attendant understood.

"Then that's all right, sir. Good night." He smiled. "It shouldn't be so unpleasant, should it?"

"What do you mean by that?" Kathryn demanded sharply.

"Nothing, miss. Good night. Sleep—I mean, good night."

Again they stood and looked at each other. They sat down, with mutual suddenness, at opposite ends of the berth. Though they had been fluent enough before, now that the door was closed they were both covered with pouring self-consciousness.

The train was moving slowly: steadily, yet with a suggestion of a jerk, which probably meant a raider somewhere overhead. It was less hot now that air gushed down the ventilator.

It was Kathryn who broke the tension of self-consciousness. Her expression began as a superior smile, turned into a giggle, and presently dissolved in helpless laughter. Presently Alan joined in.

"Sh-h!" she urged in a whisper. "We'll disturb the person in the next compartment. But we have been rather ridiculous, haven't we?"

"I deny that. At the same time—"

Kathryn removed her spectacles and wrinkled up her smooth forehead.

"Why are you going north, Dr. Campbell? Or should I say Cousin Alan?"

"For the same reason, I suppose, that you are. I got a letter from a man named Duncan, who bears the impressive title of Writer to the Signet."

"In Scotland," said Kathryn, with cutting condescension, "a Writer to the Signet is a lawyer. Really, Dr. Campbell! Such ignorance! Haven't you ever been in Scotland?"

"No. Have you?"

"Well—not since I was a little girl. But I do take the trouble to keep myself informed, especially about my own flesh and blood. Did the letter say anything else?"

"Only that old Angus Campbell had died a week ago; that such few members of the family as could be found were being informed; and could I find it convenient to come up to the Castle of Shira, at Inveraray, for a family conference? He made it clear that there was no question of inheritance, but not quite so clear what he meant by 'family conference.' I used it as a good excuse to get leave for a much-needed holiday."

Kathryn sniffed. "Really, Dr. Campbell! Your own flesh and blood!"

And Alan found his exasperation rising again.

"Oh, look here! I'd never even heard of Angus Campbell. I looked him up, through a very complicated genealogy, and found that he's a cousin of my father. But I never knew him, or anybody near him. Did you?"

"Well . . ."

"In fact, I'd never even heard of the Castle of Shira. How do we get there, by the way?"

"At Glasgow, you take a train to Gourock. At Gourock you get a boat across to Dunoon. At Dunoon you hire a car and drive out round Loch Fyne to Inveraray. You used to be able to go from Dunoon to Inveraray by water, but they've stopped that part of the steamer service since the war."

"And what is that in? The Highlands or the Lowlands?"

This time Kathryn's glance was withering.

Alan would not pursue the matter further. He had a hazy idea that in estimating the Lowlands or the Highlands, you just drew a line across the map of Scotland about the middle; that the upper part would be the Highlands, the lower part the Lowlands: and there you were. But now he felt somehow that it could not be quite as simple as this.

"Really, Dr. Campbell! It's in the Western Highlands, of course."

"This Castle of Shira," he pursued, allowing (though with reluctance) his imagination some play. "It's a moated-grange sort of place, I suppose?"

"In Scotland," said Kathryn, "a castle can be almost anything. No: it's not a big place like the Duke of Argyll's castle. Or at least I shouldn't think so from photographs. It stands at the entrance to Glen Shira, a little way off from Inveraray by the edge of the loch. It's rather a slatternly-looking stone building with a high tower.

"But it's got a history. You, as a historian, of course wouldn't know anything about that. That's what makes it all so interesting: the way Angus Campbell died."

"So? How did he die?"

"He committed suicide," returned Kathryn calmly. "Or he was murdered."

The Penguin novel which Alan had brought along was bound in green for a crime thriller. He did not read such things often, but he considered it his duty, sometimes, in the way of relaxation. He stared from this back to Kathryn's face.

"He was—*what*?" Alan almost yelped.

"Murdered. Of course you hadn't heard about that either? Dear me! Angus Campbell jumped or was thrown from a window at the top of the tower."

Alan searched his wits.

"But wasn't there an inquest?"

"They don't have inquests in Scotland. In the event of a suspicious death, they have what is called a 'public inquiry,' under the direction of a man named the Procurator Fiscal. But if they think it's murder, they don't hold the public inquiry at all. That's why I've been watching the Glasgow *Herald* all week, and there's been no report of an inquiry. It doesn't necessarily mean anything, of course."

The compartment was almost cool. Alan reached out and twisted the mouth of the ventilator, which was hissing beside his ear. He fished in his pocket.

"Cigarette?" he offered, producing a packet.

"Thanks. I didn't know you smoked. I thought you used snuff."

"And why," said Alan with austerity, "should you imagine that I used snuff?"

"It got into your beard," explained Kathryn, making motions of intense disgust. "And dropped all over everywhere. It was horrid.—Big-breasted hussy, anyway!"

"Big-breasted hussy? Who?"

"The Duchess of Cleveland."

He blinked at her. "But I understood, Miss Campbell, that you were the lady's particular champion. For nearly two and a half months you've been vilifying my character because you said I vilified hers."

"Oh, well. You seemed to have a down on her. So I had to take the other side, hadn't I?"

He stared at her.

"And this," he said, whacking his knee, "*this* is intellectual honesty!"

"Do you call it intellectual honesty when you deliberately sneered at and patronized a book because you knew it had been written by a woman?"

"But I didn't know it had been written by a woman. I specifically referred to you as 'Mr. Campbell,' and—"

"That was only to throw people off the track."

"See here," pursued Alan, lighting her cigarette with a somewhat shaky hand, and lighting his own. "Let us get this straight. I have no down on women scholars. Some of the finest scholars I've ever known have been women."

"Listen to the patronizing way he says *that!*"

"The point is, Miss Campbell, that it would have made no difference to my notice whether the writer of the book had been a man or a woman. Errors are errors, whoever writes them."

"Indeed?"

"Yes. And for the sake of truth will you now admit to me, strictly in private and between ourselves, that you were all wrong about the Duchess of Cleveland being small and auburn-haired?"

"I most certainly will not!" cried Kathryn, putting on her spectacles again and setting her face into its severest lines.

"Listen!" he said desperately. "Consider the evidence! Let me quote to you for example, an instance I could hardly have used in the newspaper. I refer to Pepys's story—"

Kathryn looked shocked.

"Oh, come, Dr. Campbell! You, who pretend to be a serious historian, actually give any credit to a story which Pepys received at third hand from his hairdresser?"

"No, no, no, madam. You persist in missing the point. The point is not whether the story is true or apocryphal. The point is that Pepys, who saw the lady so often, could have believed it. Very well! He writes that Charles the Second and the Duchess of Cleveland (who was then Lady Castlemaine) weighed each other; 'and she, being with child, was the heavier.' When we remember that Charles though lean, was six feet tall and on the muscular side, this makes out the lady to be rather a fine figure of a woman.

"Then there is the account of her mock marriage with Frances Stewart, in which she acted the part of the bridegroom. Frances Stewart was herself no flyweight. But is it reasonable to suppose that the part of the bridegroom was enacted by the smaller and lighter woman?"

"Pure inference."

"An inference, I submit, warranted by the facts. Next we have Reresby's statement—"

"Steinmann says—"

"Reresby makes quite clear—"

"*Hey!*" interrupted an exasperated voice from the next compartment, followed by a rapping on the metal door. "*Oi!*"

Both disputants instantly piped down. For a long time there was a guilty silence, broken only by the flying click and rattle of the wheels.

"Let's turn out the light," whispered Kathryn, "and draw the blackout, and see what's going on outside."

"Right."

The click of the light switch appeared to satisfy the disturbed occupant of the next compartment.

Pushing aside Kathryn's suitcase in the dark, Alan pulled back the sliding metal shutter over the window.

They were rushing through a dead world, pitch-black except where, along a purple horizon, moved a maze of searchlights. Jack's beanstalk went no higher than these white beams. The white lines shuttled back and forth, in unison, like dancers. They heard no noise except the click of the wheels: not even the waspish, coughing drone of *war-war, war-war,* which marks the cruising bomber.

"Do you think he's following the train?"

"I don't know."

A sense of intimacy, uneasy and yet exhilarating, went through Alan Campbell. They were both crowded close to the window. The two cigarette ends made glowing red cores, reflected in the glass, pulsing and dimming. He could dimly see Kathryn's face.

The same powerful self-consciousness suddenly overcame them again. They both spoke at the same time, in a whisper.

"The Duchess of Cleveland—"

"Lord William Russell—"

The train sped on.

Chapter 3

AT THREE O'CLOCK on the following afternoon, a mellow day of Scotland's most golden weather, Kathryn and Alan Campbell were walking up the hill comprising the one main street in Dunoon, Argyllshire.

The train, due to reach Glasgow at half past six in the morning, actually got there toward one o'clock in the afternoon. By this time they were ravenously, ragingly hungry, but still they got no lunch.

An amiable porter, whose conversation was all but unintelligible to both Campbells, informed them that the train for Gourock left in five minutes. So they piled into this, and were borne lunchless along Clydeside to the coast.

To Alan Campbell it had been a considerable shock when he woke in the morning, tousled and unshaven, to find himself hunched back against the cushions of a railway carriage, and a good-looking girl asleep with her head on his shoulder.

But, once he had collected his scattered wits, he decided that he loved it. A sense of adventure was winging straight into his stodgy soul, and making him drunk. There is nothing like spending the night with a girl, even platonically, to remove a sense of constraint. Alan was surprised and somewhat disappointed, on looking out of the window, to see that the scenery was still the same as it was in England: no granite cliffs or heather yet. For he wanted an excuse to quote Burns.

They washed and dressed, these two roaring innocents, to the accompaniment of a stern debate—carried on through a closed door and above the splash of running water—about the Earl of Danby's financial reconstruction policy of 1679. They concealed their hunger well, even in the train to Gourock. But when they discovered, aboard the squat tan-funneled steamer which carried them across the bay to Dunoon, that there was food to be had below, they pitched into Scotch broth and roast lamb with silence and voracity.

Dunoon, white and gray and dun-roofed, lay along the steel-gray water in the shelter of low-lying, purple hills. It looked like a good version of all the bad paintings of Scottish scenery which hang in so many houses: except that these usually include a stag, and this did not.

"I now understand," Alan declared, "why there are so many of these daubs. The bad painter cannot resist Scotland. It gives him the opportunity to smear in his purples and yellows, and contrast 'em with water."

Kathryn said that this was nonsense. She also said, as the steamer churned in and butted the pier sideways, that if he did not stop whistling "Loch Lomond" she would go crazy.

Leaving their suitcases at the pier, they crossed the road to a deserted tourist agency and arranged for a car to take them to Shira.

"Shira, eh?" observed the dispirited-looking clerk, who talked like an Englishman. "Getting to be quite a popular place." He gave them a queer look which Alan was afterwards to remember. "There's another party going to Shira this afternoon. If you wouldn't mind sharing the car, it 'ud come less expensive."

"Hang the expense," said Alan, his first words in Dunoon; and it is merely to be recorded that the advertising posters did not drop off the wall. "Still, we don't want to seem uppish. It's another Campbell, I imagine?"

"No," said the clerk, consulting a pad, "this gentleman's name is Swan. Charles E. Swan. He was in here not five minutes ago."

"Never heard of him." Alan looked at Kathryn. "That's not the heir to the estate, by any chance?"

"Nonsense!" said Kathryn. "The heir is Dr. Colin Campbell, Angus's first brother."

The clerk looked still more odd. "Yes. We drove him out there yesterday. Very positive sort of gentleman. Well, sir, will you share Mr. Swan's car, or have one of your own?"

Kathryn intervened.

"We'll share Mr. Swan's car, of course, if he doesn't mind. The idea! Flinging good money about like that! When will it be ready?"

"Half past three. Come back here in about half an hour, and you'll find it waiting. Good day, ma'am. Good day, sir. Thank you."

They wandered out into the mellow sunshine, happily, and up the main street looking into shop windows. These appeared to be mainly souvenir shops, and everywhere the eye was dazzled by the display of tartans. There were tartan ties, tartan mufflers, tartan-bound books, tartan-painted tea sets, tartans on the dolls and tartans on the ash trays— usually the Royal Stewart, as being the brightest.

Alan began to be afflicted with that passion for buying things which overcomes the stoutest traveler. In this he was discouraged by Kathryn, until they reached a haberdasher's some distance up on the right, which displayed in its windows tartan shields (Campbell of Argyll, Macleod, Gordon, MacIntosh, MacQueen) which you hung on the wall. These conquered even Kathryn.

"They're lovely," she admitted. "Let's go in."

The shop bell pinged, but went unheard in the argument which was going on at the counter. Behind the counter stood a stern-looking little woman with her hands folded. In front of the counter stood a tallish, leathery-faced young man in his late thirties, with a soft hat pushed back on his forehead. He was surrounded by a huge assortment of tartan neckties.

"They're very nice," he was saying courteously, "but they're not what I want. I want to see a necktie with the tar-

tan of the Clan MacHolster. Don't you understand? Mac-
Holster. M-a-c, H-o-l-s-t-e-r, MacHolster. Can't you show
me the tartan of the Clan MacHolster?"

"There isna any Clan MacHolster," said the proprietress.

"Now look," said the young man, leaning one elbow on
the counter and holding up a lean forefinger in her face.
"I'm a Canadian; but I've got Scottish blood in my veins
and I'm proud of it. Ever since I was a kid, my father's said
to me, 'Charley, if you ever go to Scotland, if you ever get
to Argyllshire, you look up the Clan MacHolster. We're
descended from the Clan MacHolster, as I've heard your
grandad say many a time.' "

"I keep telling ye: there isna any Clan MacHolster."

"But there's *got* to be a Clan MacHolster!" pleaded the
young man, stretching out his hands. "There could be a
Clan MacHolster, couldn't there? With all the clans and
people in Scotland? There *could* be a Clan MacHolster?"

"There could be a Clan MacHitler. But there isna."

His bewildered dejection was so evident that the proprietress took pity on him.

"What wad your name be, now"

"Swan. Charles E. Swan."

The proprietress cast up her eyes and reflected.

"Swan. That'd be the MacQueens."

Mr. Swan seized eagerly at this. "You mean I'm related
to the clan of the MacQueens?"

"I dinna ken. Ye may be. Ye may not be. Some Swans
are."

"Have you got their tartan here?"

The proprietress showed it to him in a necktie. It was
undoubtedly striking, its predominating color being a rich
scarlet, and took Mr. Swan's fancy at once.

"Now that's what I call something like it!" he announced
fervently, and turned round and appealed to Alan. "Don't
you think so, sir?"

"Admirable. Bit on the loud side for a necktie, though,
isn't it?"

"Yes, I like it myself," agreed Mr. Swan musingly,
holding the tie at arm's length like a painter studying

perspective. "Yes. This is the tie for me. I'll take a dozen of 'em."

The proprietress reeled.

"A dozen?"

"Sure. Why not?"

The proprietress felt compelled to sound a note of warning.

"They're three-and-saxpence each?"

"That's all right. Wrap 'em up. I'll take 'em."

As the proprietress bustled off through a door at the back of the shop, Swan turned round with a confidential air. He removed his hat out of deference to Kathryn, revealing a mop of wiry mahogany-colored hair.

"You know," he confided in a low voice, "I've traveled a lot in my time; but this is the queerest damn country *I* ever got into."

"Yes?"

"Yes. All they seem to do is run around telling each other Scotch jokes. I dropped into the bar of the hotel down there, and the local comedian was bringing the house down with nothing but Scotch jokes. And there's another thing. I've only been in this country a few hours—got in by the London train this morning—but on four different occasions I've been buttonholed with the same joke."

"We haven't had that experience so far."

"But *I* have. They hear me talk, see? Then they say, 'You're an American, eh?' I say, 'No, Canadian.' But that doesn't stop 'em. They say. 'Have you heard about my brother Angus, who wouldn't even give the blood-hounds a cent?' "

He paused expectantly.

The faces of his listeners remained impassive.

"Don't you get it?" demanded Swan. "Wouldn't even give the bloodhounds a cent. C-e-n-t, s-c-e-n-t."

"The point of the story," replied Kathryn, "is fairly obvious; but——"

"Oh, I didn't say it was *funny,*" Swan hastened to assure them. "I'm just telling you how queer it sounds. You don't find mothers-in-law running around telling each other the latest mother-in-law joke. You don't find the English telling each other stories about the Englishman getting the point of the joke wrong."

"Are the English," inquired Alan with interest, "popularly supposed to do that?"

Swan flushed a little.

"Well, they are in the stories told in Canada and the States. No offense. You know the kind of thing. 'You cannot drive a nail with a sponge no matter how hard you soak it,' rendered as, 'You cannot drive a nail with a sponge no matter how wet it is.' Now, wait! I didn't say *that* was funny either. I only ——"

"Never mind," said Alan. "What I really wanted to ask: are you the Mr. Swan who's hired a car to go out to Shira this afternoon?"

A curiously evasive look went over Swan's leathery face, with the fine wrinkles round eyes and mouth. He seemed on the defensive.

"Yes. That's right. Why?"

"We're going out there ourselves, and we were wondering whether you'd mind if we shared the car. My name is Campbell, Dr. Campbell. This is my cousin, Miss Kathryn Campbell."

Swan acknowledged the introductions with a bow. His expression changed, and lit up with good nature.

"Not the least little bit in the world! Only too pleased to have you!" he declared heartily. His light gray eyes quickened and shifted. "Members of the family, eh?"

"Distant ones. And you?"

The evasive look returned.

"Well, since you know what my name is, and that I'm related to the MacHolsters or the MacQueens, I couldn't very well pretend to be a member of the family, could I? Tell me, though." He grew more confidential. "What can you tell me about a Miss or Mrs. Elspat Campbell?"

Alan shook his head, but Kathryn came to the rescue.

"Aunt Elspat, you mean?"

"I'm afraid I don't know anything about her, Miss

Campbell."

"Aunt Elspat," replied Kathryn, "isn't really an aunt, and her name isn't Campbell, though they all call her that. Nobody quite knows who she is or where she came from. She just walked in one day, forty years or so ago, and she's been there ever since. Sort of female head of Shira. She must be nearly ninety, and she's supposed to be rather a terror. I've never met her, though."

"Oh," said Swan, but volunteered no more. The proprietress brought him his parcel of neckties, and he paid for it.

"Which reminds me," he went on, "that we'd better get going, if we want to be in time for that car."

After bidding an elaborate farewell to the proprietress, Swan held open the shop door for them.

"It must be a good way out there, and I want to get back before dark; I'm not staying. I suppose they have the blackout up here too? I want a decent night's rest tonight for once. I sure didn't get one on the train last night."

"Can't you sleep on trains?"

"It wasn't that. There was a married couple in the next compartment, having a hell of a row about some dame from Cleveland, and I hardly closed my eyes all night."

Alan and Kathryn cast a quick, uneasy glance at each other, but Swan was preoccupied with his grievance.

"I've lived in Ohio myself; know it well; that's why I listened. But I couldn't get this thing straight. There was some guy named Russell, and another one called Charles. But whether the dame from Cleveland was running around with Russell, or with Charles, or with this woman's husband, I never did make out. You just heard enough so that you couldn't understand anything. I knocked on the wall, but even after they'd turned out the light ——"

"Dr. Campbell!" cried Kathryn warningly.

But the murder was out.

"I'm afraid," said Alan, "that that must have been us."

"You?" said Swan. He stopped short in the hot, bright, drowsy street. His eyes traveled to Kathryn's ringless left hand. They seemed to be registering something, as though writing it down.

Then he continued, with such a jerking and obvious change of subject that even his smooth voice added to the obviousness of it.

"They certainly don't seem to be feeling any shortage of food up here, anyway. Look in these grocery-store windows! That stuff over there is haggis. It——"

Kathryn's face was scarlet.

"Mr. Swan," she curtly, "may I assure you that you are making a mistake? I am a member of the department of history at the Harpenden College for Women ——"

"It's the first time I ever saw haggis, but I can't say I like the look of it. It can manage to look nakeder than any meat I ever did see. That stuff that looks like slices of boloney is called Ulster fry. It——"

"Mr. Swan, will you *please* give me your attention? This gentleman is Dr. Campbell, of University College, Highgate. We can both assure you ——"

Again Swan stopped short. He peered round as though to make sure they were not overheard, and then spoke in a low, rapid, earnest voice.

"Look, Miss Campbell," he said, "I'm broad-minded. I know how these things are. And I'm sorry I ever brought the subject up."

"But ——!"

"All that business about my losing sleep was a lot of bunk. I went to sleep just as soon as you turned the light out, and didn't hear a thing afterwards. So let's just forget I ever spoke about it, shall we?"

"Perhaps that would be best," agreed Alan.

"Alan Campbell, do you *dare* . . ."

Swan, his manner soothing, pointed ahead. A comfortable blue five-seater car was drawn up before the tourist office, with a chauffeur in cap, uniform, and leggings leaning against it.

"There's the golden chariot," Swan added. "And I've got a guidebook. Come on. Let's enjoy ourselves."

Chapter 4

PAST THE TINY SHIPYARD, past the Holy Loch, under heavy timber-furred hills, up the rise past Heath Jock, and into the long, straight stretch beside deep Loch Eck, the car sped on.

They took to the driver at once.

He was a burly, red-faced, garrulous man with a singularly bright blue eye and a vast fund of secret inner amusement. Swan sat in front with him, while Alan and Kathryn sat in the rear. Swan began by being fascinated with the driver's accent, and ended by trying to imitate it.

Pointing to a trickle of water down the hillside, the driver said that this was a "wee burn." Swan seized on the words as a good thing. Henceforward water in any form, even a mountain torrent which would have carried away a house, became a wee burn: Swan calling attention to it and experimentally giving the letter "r" a sound like a death rattle or a singularly sustained gargle.

He did this to Alan's intense discomfort, but Alan need not have minded. The driver did not mind. It was as though (say) Sir Cedric Hardwicke were to hear the purity of his English commented on with amusement by Mr. Schnozzle Durante.

Those who regarded Scotsmen as dour or uncommunicative, Alan thought, should have listened to this one. It was impossible to stop him talking. He gave details of every place they passed; and, surprisingly, as it turned out from Swan's guidebook later, with accuracy.

His usual work, he said, was driving a hearse. He entertained them with a description of the many fine funerals, to which he referred with modest pride, where he had had the honor of conducting the corpse. And this gave Swan an opportunity.

"You didn't happen to drive the hearse at a funeral about a week ago, did you?"

To their left, Loch Eck lay like an old tarnished mirror among the hills. No splash or ripple stirred it. Nothing moved on the slopes of fir and pine, stretching up to a pate of outcropping rock, which closed it in. What deadened the mind was the quality of utter silence here, of barriers against the world, and yet of awareness behind it: as though these hills still hid the shaggy shields.

The driver was silent for so long a time, his big red hands gripped round the wheel, that they thought he could not have heard or understood. Then he spoke.

"That'd be auld Campbell of Shira," he stated.

"Aye," said Swan, with perfect seriousness. The thing was infectious: Alan had several times been on the point of saying this himself.

"And ye'll be Campbells tu, I'm thinkin'?"

"Those two are," said Swan, jerking his head toward the two in the rear. "I'm a MacHolster, sometimes called MacQueen."

The driver turned round and looked very hard at him. But Swan was perfectly sincere.

"I drove one of 'em yesterday," said the driver grudgingly. "Colin Campbell it was; and as guid a Scot as masel', for a' he talked like an Englishman."

His face darkened.

"Such bletherin' and blusterin' ye niver heard! An atheist forbye, and thocht nae shame tae admit it! Cau'd me ivery name he caud lay his tongue tu," glowered the driver, "for sayin' Shira is no' a canny place. And it isna either."

Again there was a heavy silence, while the tires sang.

"Canny, I suppose," observed Alan, "being the opposite of uncanny?"

"Aye."

"But if Shira isn't a canny place, what's wrong with it? Ghosts?"

The driver whacked the steering wheel with a slow and

dogged hand, as though he were setting a stamp on it.

"I'm no' saying' it's ghaists, I'm no sayin' *wha'* it is. I'm sayin' it isna a canny place, and it isna."

Swan, after whistling between his teeth, opened the guidebook. While the car jolted, and the long afternoon light grew less golden, he turned to the section devoted to Inveraray. He read aloud:

"Before entering the town by the main road, the traveler should look (left) at the *Castle of Shira*.

"This building contains no features of architectural interest. It was built toward the end of the sixteenth century, but has since been added to. It will be recognized by its round tower, with a conical slate roof, at the southeastern corner. This tower, sixty-two feet high, is thought to have been the first effort in an ambitious scheme of building which was later abandoned.

"Tradition has it that in 1692, following the massacre of Glencoe in February of that year ———"

Swan interrupted himself.

"Hold on!" he said, rubbing his jaw. "I've heard about the massacre of Glencoe. I remember, when I was at school in Detroit . . . What the devil's the matter with *him?* Hoy!"

The driver, his good humor now restored, was bending back and forth over the wheel in paroxysms of silent inner amusement, so that tears stood in his eyes.

"What is it, governor?" demanded Swan. "What's wrong?"

The driver choked. His inner mirth seemed like torture.

"I *thocht* ye were an American," he declared. "Tell me, noo. Hae ye heard aboot ma brither Angus, who wadna e'en gie the bluid-hoonds a cent?"

Swan smote his forehead.

"Man, dinna ye see it? Hae ye no sense o' humor? C-e-n-t, cent; s-c-e-n-t, scent."

"Curiously enough," said Swan, "I do see it. And I'm not an American; I'm a Canadian, even if I did go to school in Detroit. If anybody Brother-Anguses me again today, I'll slaughter him. Which reminds me. (Stop chortling, can't you? Preserve a proper Scottish gravity!)

"But about this massacre of Glencoe. We acted it out in a play at school long ago. Somebody massacred somebody. What I can't remember is whether the MacDonalds killed the Campbells, or the Campbells killed the Mac-Donalds."

It was Kathryn who answered him.

"The Campbells killed the MacDonalds, of course," she returned. "I say: they're not still touchy about it in these parts, are they?"

The driver, wiping the tears out of his eyes and becoming stern again, assured her that they weren't.

Swan opened the book again.

"Tradition has it that in 1692, following the massacre of Glencoe in February of that year, Ian Campbell, a soldier in the troop of Campbell of Glenlyon, was so embittered by remorse that he committed suicide by leaping from the topmost window of the tower, dashing out his brains on the pavingstones below."

Swan looked up.

"That isn't what happened to the old man the other day?"

"Aye."

"Another tradition is that this suicide was not caused by remorse, but by the 'presence' of one of his victims, whose mangled body pursued him from room to room, until he had no alternative to keep it from touching him except to ——"

Swan shut up the book with a snap. "I think that's enough," he added. His eyes narrowed, and his voice grew soft. "What happened, by the way? The old man didn't sleep up at the top of the tower, did he?"

But the driver was not to be drawn. Ask no questions, his bearing intimated, and you will be told no lies.

"Ye'll be sein' Loch Fyne i' a moment, and then Shira," he said. "Ah! Luke, now!"

Reaching a crossroads, they turned to the right at Strachar. A glimmer of water spread out before them. And not a person there but uttered an exclamation of sheer appreciation.

The loch seemed long, wide, and southwards, to their left, endless. Southwards it curved in sun-silvered widening, between heavy banks, for miles to join the Firth of Clyde.

But northwards it lay landlocked—narrower, timelessly placid, its glimmering water slate-colored—and ran in the shape of a wedge to its end some three miles away. The smooth-molded hills, black or dark purple except where stray sunlight caught a splashing of pale purple heather or the dark green of pine and fir, closed round it as though patted into shape with a tone of underlying brown.

Far across the loch, along the water's edge, they could dimly see the low-lying white houses of a town, partly screened behind a belt of trees. They saw a church steeple; and, on the dominating hill above, a dot that looked like a watch tower. So clear was the air that even at this distance Alan could have sworn he saw the white houses mirrored in the motionless water.

The driver pointed.

"Inveraray," he said.

Their car swept on. Swan was evidently so fascinated that he even forgot to point out wee burns.

The road—a very good one, like all the roads they had seen so far—ran straight along the bank of the loch parallel with its length toward the north. Thus to reach Inveraray, which was on the opposite bank, they would have to drive to the head of the loch, circle round it, and come back on a parallel course to a point opposite where they were now.

This, at least, was what Alan thought. Inveraray looked very close now, just across the gleaming water at its narrowest. Alan was leaning back expansively, taking comfort from the vast strong hills, when the car stopped with a jerk and the driver climbed out.

"Ge' out," he beamed. "Donald MacLeish'll have a boat here, I'm thinkin'."

They stared at him.

"Did you say boat?" exploded Swan.

"Aye."

"But what in Satan's name do you want a boat for?"

"Tae row ye across."

"But the road goes there, doesn't it? Can't you just drive 'way up there, and come round into Inveraray on the other side?"

"Waste petrol when I've got ma arms?" demanded the driver, not without horror. "No si' a fule! Ge' out. It's five, sax miles by the road."

"Well," smiled Kathryn, who seemed to be preserving her gravity only with considerable effort, "I'm sure *I* don't mind a turn on the water."

"Nor me," conceded Swan, "provided somebody else does the rowing. But, my God, man!" He searched the air with gestures. "What's the big idea? It's not your petrol, is it? It belongs to the company, doesn't it?"

"Aye. But the preenciple's the same. Ge' in."

An almost extravagantly solemn trio, with the driver very cheerful at the oars, was ferried across the loch in the hush of early evening.

Kathryn and Alan, their suitcases at their feet, sat in the stern of the boat facing toward Inveraray. It was that hour when the water seems lighter and more luminous than the sky, and there are shadows.

"Brr!" said Kathryn presently.

"Cold?"

"A little. But it's not that." She looked at the driver, now the ferryman. "That's the place, isn't it? Over there, where there's a little landing stage?"

"That's it," agreed the other, craning round to peer over his shoulder. The rowlocks creaked painfully. "It isna much tae luke at; but they do say, mind, that auld Angus Campbell left mair siller than ye caud shake a stick at."

Silently they watched the Castle of Shira grow up and out at them.

It was some distance away from the town, and faced the loch. Built of ancient stone and brick painted gray, with a steep-pitched slate roof, it straggled along the water side; Kathryn's word "slatternly" occurred to Alan in connection with it.

Most of all you noticed the tower. Round, and of moss-patched gray stone, it reared up to a conical slate roof at the southeastern angle of the house. On the side facing the loch it appeared to have only one window. This was a latticed window, with two lights, set close up near the roof; and from there to the uneven flagstones which paved the ground in front of the house must have been close to sixty feet.

Alan thought of the sickening plunge from that window, and moved uneasily.

"I suppose," Kathryn hesitated, "it's rather—well, primitive?"

"Hoots!" said the driver, with rich scorn. "They hae the electric light."

"Electric light?"

"Aye. And a bathroom tu, though I'm no' sae sure of that." Again he craned over his shoulder, and his face darkened. "D'ye see the man standin' by the wee pier and lukin' at us? That'll be the Dr. Colin Campbell I was tellin' ye aboot. Practices medicine in Manchester, or some sic heathen place."

The figure by the pier partly blended with the gray and brown of the landscape. It was that of a man short in stature, but very broad and burly, with a dogged, truculent lift to the shoulders. He wore an old shooting coat, with corduroy breeches and leggings, and had his hands thrust into his pockets.

It was the first time in many years that Alan had seen a doctor with a beard and mustache. These, though close-cropped, were untidy and gave an impression of shagginess together with the shaggy hair. Its color was an indeterminate brown, touched with what might have been yellow or more probably gray. Colin Campbell, the first of Angus's two younger brothers, was in his middle or late sixties, but looked younger.

He watched them critically as Alan assisted Kathryn out of the boat, and Swan scrambled after them. Though his manner was not unamiable, there was always a suggestion of a bristle about it.

"And who," he said in a heavy bass voice, "might you be?"

Alan performed introductions. Colin took his hands out of his pockets, but did not offer to shake hands.

"Well," he said, "you might as well come in. Why not? They're all here: the Fiscal, and the law agent, and the man from the insurance company, and Uncle Tom Cobleigh and all. This is Alistair Duncan's doing, I suppose?"

"That's the solicitor?"

"Law agent," corrected Colin, with a ferocious grin which Alan rather liked. "Law agent, when you're in Scotland. Yes. That's what I meant."

He turned to Swan, and his shaggy eyebrows drew together over a pair of leonine eyes.

"What did you say *your* name was? Swan? Swan? I don't know any Swans."

"I'm here," said Swan, as though bracing himself, "at the request of Miss Elspat Campbell."

Colin stared at him.

"Elspat sent for you?" he roared. *"Elspat?* God's wounds! I don't believe it!"

"Why not?"

"Because, barring a doctor or a minister, Aunt Elspat never sent for anything or anybody in her life. The only person or thing she ever wanted to see was my brother Angus and the London *Daily Floodlight*. God's wounds! The old girl's more cracked than ever. Reads the *Daily Floodlight* from cover to cover; knows the names of all the contributors; talks about jitterbugs and God knows what."

"The *Daily Floodlight?*" said Kathryn, with virtuous contempt. "That filthy scandal sheet?"

"Here! Oi! Go easy!" protested Swan. "You're talking about my paper."

It was the turn of all of them to stare at him.

"You're not a reporter?" breathed Kathryn.

Swan was soothing. "Now look," he said with great earnestness. "It's all right. I'm not going to use that bit about you and Doc Campbell sleeping in the same compartment on the train: that is, unless I have to. I only——"

Colin interrupted him with a sudden and unexpected deep-throated bellow of laughter. Colin smote his knee, squared himself, and seemed to be addressing the whole universe.

"A reporter? Why not? Come in and welcome! Why not spread the story all over Manchester and London too? Do us good! And what's this about the two scholars of the family being up to hanky-panky on the train?"

"I tell you ——"

"Not another word. I like you for it. God's wounds! I like to see a bit of spirit in the younger generation, the kind *we* used to have. God's wounds!"

He clapped Alan on the back, and put a heavy arm round Alan's shoulders, shaking him. His amiability was as overpowering as his truculence. Then, after roaring all this into the evening air, he lowered his voice conspiratorially.

"We can't put you in the same room here, I'm afraid. Got to keep up some of the proprieties. Let you have adjoining rooms, though. But mind you don't mention this to Aunt Elspat."

"Listen! For the love of ——"

"She's a great stickler for the conventions, in spite of being Angus's mistress for forty years; and anyway, in Scotland, she's now got the status of a common-law wife. Come in! Don't stand there making funny faces! Come in! (Throw up those suitcases, Jock, and look sharp about it!)"

"Ma name's not Jock," said the oarsman, jumping up precariously in the boat.

Colin stuck out his bearded chin.

"It's Jock," he retorted, "if I say it's Jock. Just get that through your head, my lad. Do you want any money?"

"Not from you. Ma name ——"

"Then that's just as well," said Colin, taking a suitcase under each arm as though they were parcels; "because damn me if I know whether I've got any to give you."

He turned to the others.

"That's the situation. If Angus was murdered, by Alec Forbes or anybody else, or if he fell out of that window by accident, then Elspat and I are rich. Elspat and a hardworking, stonybroke G.P. are both rich. But if Angus committed suicide, I tell you straight we haven't got a penny to bless our names."

Chapter 5

"But I understood—" Alan began.

"You understood the old skinflint was rich? Yes! So did everybody else. But it's the same old story." Colin's next remarks were darkly mysterious. "Ice cream!" he said. "Tractors! Drake's gold! Trust a skinflint to be a simpleton when he thinks he can get richer.

"Not that Angus was exactly a skinflint, mind. He was a swine, but a decent sort of swine, if you know what I mean. He helped me when I needed it, and he'd have helped our other brother too, if anybody'd known where to find the bounder after he got into trouble.

"Well, what are we all standing here for? Get on into the house! You—where's *your* suitcase?"

Swan, who had been vainly attempting to get in a word edgeways throughout this, gave it up for the moment as a bad job.

"I'm not staying, thanks very much," Swan replied. He turned to the driver. "You'll wait for me?"

"Aye. I'll wait."

"Then that's settled," roared Colin. "Here—you—Jock. Get round to the kitchen and tell 'em to give you a half. Angus's best whisky, mind. The rest of you, follow me."

Leaving behind them a man passionately announcing to the air that his name was not Jock, they followed Colin to the arched doorway. Swan, who appeared to have something on his mind, touched Colin's arm.

"Look," he said. "It's none of my business, but are you sure you know what you're doing?"

"Know what I'm doing? How?"

"Well," said Swan, pushing his soft gray hat to the back of his head, "I've heard the Scotch were booze-histers, of course; but this beats anything I ever expected. Is half a pint of whisky at one shot your usual tipple in these parts? He won't be able to see the road on the way back, will he?"

"A half, you ruddy Sassenach, is a small whisky. And you!" Colin now got behind Kathryn and Alan, and shooed them ahead of him. "You must have something to eat. Got to keep your strength up."

The hall into which he led them was spacious, but rather musty; and it smelt of old stone. They could make out little in the semi-gloom. Colin opened the door of a room on the left.

"Wait in there, you two," he ordered. "Swan, my lad, you come with me. I'll dig out Elspat. Elspat! *Elspat!* Where the devil are you, Elspat? Oh: and if you hear anybody arguing in the back room, that's only Duncan the law agent, and Walter Chapman from the Hercules Insurance Company."

Alone, Alan and Kathryn found themselves in a long but rather low-ceilinged room with a faintly pervading odor of damp oilcloth. A wood fire had been lighted in the grate against the evening chill. By the light of the fire, and the fainter one which struggled in through the two windows facing the loch, they saw that the furniture was horsehair, the pictures large, numerous, and running to broad gilt frames, and the carpet red but faded.

On a side table lay an immense family Bible. A photograph, draped in black crepe, stood on the red tasseled cloth of the overmantel. The resemblance of the man in the photograph to Colin, despite the fact that he was smooth-shaven and had clear white hair, left no doubt who this was.

No clock ticked. They spoke, instinctively, in whispers.

"Alan Campbell," whispered Kathryn, whose face was as pink as confectionery, "you beast!"

"Why?"

"In heaven's name, don't you realize what they're *thinking* about us? And that dreadful *Daily Floodlight* will print anything. Don't you mind at all?"

Alan considered this.

"Candidly," he startled even himself by replying, "I don't. My only regret is that it isn't true."

Kathryn fell back a little, putting her hand on the table which held the family Bible as though to support herself. He observed, however, that her color was deeper than ever.

"*Dr.* Campbell! What on earth has come over you?"

"I don't know," he was honest enough to admit. "I don't know whether Scotland usually affects people like this——"

"I should hope not!"

"But I feel like taking down a claymore and stalking about with it. Also, I feel no end of an old rip and I am enjoying it. Has anyone ever told you, by the way, that you are an exceedingly attractive wench?"

"Wench! You called me a wench?"

"It is classical seventeenth-century terminology."

"But nothing like your precious Duchess of Cleveland, of course," said Kathryn.

"I acknowledge," said Alan, measuring her with an appraising eye, "a lack of proportions which would have aroused enthusiasm in Rubens. At the same time ——"

"Sh-h!"

At the end of the room opposite the windows there was a partly open door. From the room beyond two voices suddenly spoke together, as though after a long silence. One voice was dry and elderly, the other voice was younger, brisker, and more suave. The voices apologized to each other. It was the younger voice which continued.

"My dear Mr. Duncan," it said, "you don't seem to appreciate my position in this matter. I am merely the representative of the Hercules Insurance Company. It is my duty to investigate this claim ——"

"And investigate it fairly."

"Of course. To investigate, and advise my firm whether to pay or contest the claim. There's nothing personal in it! I would do anything I could to help. I knew the late Mr. Angus Campbell, and liked him."

"You knew him personally?"

"I did."

The elderly voice, which was always preceded by a strong inhalation through the nose, now spoke as with the effect of a pounce.

"Then let me put a question to you, Mr. Chapman."

"Yes?"

"You would have called Mr. Campbell a sane man?"

"Yes, certainly."

"A man sensible, shall we say," the voice sniffed, and became even more dry before it pounced, "to the value of money?"

"Very much so."

"Yes. Good. Very well. Now, Mr. Chapman, besides his life-insurance policies with your company, my client had two policies with other companies."

"I would know nothing of that."

"But I tell you so, sir!" snapped the elderly voice, and there was a little rap as of knuckles on wood. "He held large policies with the Gibraltar Insurance Company and the Planet Insurance Company."

"Well?"

"Well! Life insurance now constitutes the whole of his assets, Mr. Chapman. The *whole* of them, sir. It was the sole one of his possessions which he was sensible enough not to throw into these mad financial ventures of his. Each one of those policies contains a suicide clause . . ."

"Naturally."

"I quite agree. Naturally! But attend to me. Three days before he died, Mr. Campbell took out still another policy, with your company again, for three thousand pounds. I should—ah—imagine that the premiums, at his age, would be enormous?"

"They are naturally high. But our doctor considered Mr. Campbell a first-class risk, good for fifteen years more."

"Very well. Now that," pursued Mr. Alistair Duncan, law agent and Writer to the Signet, "made a grand total of some thirty-five thousand pounds in insurance."

"Indeed?"

"And each policy contained a suicide clause. Now, my good sir! My very good sir! Can you, as a man of the world, for one moment imagine that three days after he has taken out this additional policy, Angus Campbell would deliberately commit suicide and invalidate everything?"

There was a silence.

Alan and Kathryn, listening without scruple, heard someone begin slowly to walk about the floor. They could imagine the lawyer's bleak smile.

"Come, sir! Come! You are English. But I am a Scotsman, and so is the Procurator Fiscal."

"I acknowledge ——"

"You *must* acknowledge it, Mr. Chapman."

"But what do you suggest?"

"Murder," replied the law agent promptly. "And probably by Alec Forbes. You have heard about their quarrel. You have heard about Forbes's calling here on the night of Mr. Campbell's death. You have heard about the mysterious suitcase (or dog carrier, whatever the term is), and the missing diary."

There was another silence. The slow footsteps paced up and down, carrying an atmosphere of worry. Mr. Walter Chapman, of the Hercules Insurance Company, spoke in a different voice.

"But, hang it all, Mr. Duncan! We just can't go on things like that!"

"No?"

"No. It's all very well to say, 'Would he have done this or that?' But, by the evidence, he *did* do it. Would you mind letting me talk for a minute?"

"Not at all."

"Right! Now, Mr. Campbell usually slept in that room at the top of the tower. Correct?"

"Yes."

"On the night of his death, he was seen to retire as usual at ten o'clock, locking and bolting the door on the inside. Admitted?"

"Admitted."

"His body was found early the following morning, at the foot of the tower. He had died of a broken back and multiple injuries caused by the fall."

"Yes."

"He was not," pursued Chapman, "drugged, or overcome in any way, as the post-mortem examination showed. So an accidental fall from the window can be ruled out."

"I rule out nothing, my dear sir. But continue."

"Now as to murder. In the morning, the door was still locked and bolted on the inside. The window (you can't deny this, Mr. Duncan) is absolutely inaccessible. We had a professional steeple jack over from Glasgow to look at it.

"That window is fifty-eight and a quarter feet up from the ground. There are no other windows on that side of the tower. Below is a fall of smooth stone to the pavement. Above is a conical roof of slippery slate.

"The steeple jack is willing to swear that nobody, with whatever ropes or tackle, could get up to that window or down from it again. I'll go into details, if you like ——"

"That won't be necessary, my dear sir."

"But the question of somebody climbing up to that window, pushing Mr. Campbell out, and climbing down again; or even hiding in the room (which nobody was) and climbing down afterwards: both these are out of the question."

He paused.

But Mr. Alistair Duncan was neither impressed nor abashed.

"In that case," the law agent said, "how did that dog carrier get into the room?"

"I beg your pardon?"

The bleak voice rolled on.

"Mr. Chapman, allow *me* to refresh *your* memory. At half past nine that night, there had been a violent quarrel with Alec Forbes, who forced himself into the house and even into Mr. Campbell's bedroom. He was—ah—ejected with difficulty."

"All right!"

"Later, both Miss Elspat Campbell and the maidservant, Kirstie MacTavish, were alarmed for fear Forbes had come back, and might have hidden himself with the intention of doing Mr. Campbell some injury.

"Miss Campbell and Kirstie searched Mr. Campbell's bedroom. They looked in the press, and so on. They even (as I am, ah, told is a woman's habit) looked under the bed. As you say, nobody was hiding there. But mark the fact, sir. Mark it.

"When the door of Mr. Campbell's room was broken open the following morning, there was found under the bed a leather and metal object like a large suitcase, with a wire grating at one end. The sort of case which is used to contain dogs when they are taken on journeys. *Both women swear that this case was not under the bed when they looked there the night before, just before Mr. Campbell locked and bolted the door on the inside.*"

The voice made an elaborate pause.

"I merely ask, Mr. Chapman: how did that case get there?"

The man from the insurance company groaned.

"I repeat, sir: I merely put the question. If you will come with me, and have a word with Mr. MacIntyre, the Fiscal ——"

There were steps on the floor beyond. A figure came into the dim front room, ducking to avoid the rather low door top, and touched a light switch beside the door.

Kathryn and Alan were caught, guiltily, as the light went on. A large, brassy-stemmed chandelier, which could have contained six electric bulbs and did contain one, glowed out over their heads.

Alan's mental picture of Alistair Duncan and Walter Chapman was more or less correct except that the law agent was rather taller and leaner, and the insurance man rather shorter and broader, than he had expected.

The lawyer was stoop-shouldered and somewhat near-sighted, with a large Adam's apple and grizzled hair round a pale bald spot. His collar was too large for him, but his black coat and striped trousers remained impressive.

Chapman, a fresh-faced young-looking man in a fashionably cut double-breasted suit, had a suave but very worried manner. His fair hair, smoothly brushed, shone in the light. He was the sort who, in Angus Campbell's youth, would have grown a beard at twenty-one and lived up to it ever afterwards.

"Oh, ah," said Duncan, blinking vaguely at Alan and Kathryn. "Have you—er—seen Mr. MacIntyre about?"

"No, I don't think so," replied Alan, and began introductions. "Mr. Duncan, we are . . ."

The law agent's eyes wandered over to another door, one facing the door to the hall.

"I should imagine, my dear sir," he continued, addressing Chapman, "that he's gone up into the tower. Will you be good enough to follow me, please?" For the last time Duncan looked back to the two newcomers. "How do you do?" he added courteously. "Good day."

And with no more words he held open the other door for Chapman to precede him. They passed through, and the door closed.

Kathryn stood staring after them.

"Well!" she began explosively. "Well!"

"Yes," admitted Alan, "he does look as though he might be a bit vague, *except* when he's talking business. But that, I submit, is the sort of lawyer you want. I'd back that gentleman any time."

"But, Dr. Campbell ——"

"Will you kindly stop calling me 'Dr. Campbell'?"

"All right, if you insist: Alan." Kathryn's eyes were shining with a light of interest and fascination. "This situation is dreadful, and yet . . . Did you hear what they said?"

"Naturally."

"He wouldn't have committed suicide, and yet he couldn't have been murdered. It ——"

She got no further, for they were interested by the entrance of Charles Swan from the hall. But this was a Swan with his journalistic blood up. Though usually punctilious about his manners, he had still neglected to remove his hat, which clung in some mysterious fashion to the back of his head. He walked as though on eggshells.

"Is this a story?" he demanded: a purely rhetorical question. "Is this a *story?* Holy, jumping . . . look. I didn't think there was anything in it. But my city editor—sorry; you call 'em news editors over here—thought there might be good stuff in it; and was he right?"

"Where have you been?"

"Talking to the maid. Always go for maids first, if you can corner 'em. Now look."

Opening and shutting his hands, Swan peered round the room to make sure they were alone, and lowered his voice.

"Dr. Campbell, Colin I mean, has just dug out the old lady. They're bringing her in here to put me on view."

"You haven't seen her yet?"

"No! But I've got to make a good impression if it's the last thing I ever do in my life. It ought to be a snip, because the old lady has a proper opinion of the *Daily Floodlight,* which other people," here he looked very hard at them—"don't seem to share. But this may be good for a daily story. Cripes, the old dame might even invite me to stay at the house! What do you think?"

"I think she might. But ——"

"So get set, Charley Swan, and do your stuff!" breathed Swan in the nature of a minor prayer. "We've got to keep in with her anyway, because it seems she's the autocrat of the place. So get set, you people. Dr. Campbell's bringing her along here now."

Chapter 6

IT WAS UNNECESSARY FOR SWAN TO POINT THIS OUT, since the voice of Aunt Elspat could already be heard outside the partly open door.

Colin Campbell spoke in a low-voiced bass rumble, of which no words were audible, evidently urging something under his breath. But Aunt Elspat, who had a particularly penetrating voice, took no trouble to lower it.

She said:

"Adjoinin' rooms! Indeed and I'll no' gie 'em adjoinin' rooms!"

The bass rumble grew more blurred, as though in protest or warning. But Aunt Elspat would have none of it.

"This is a decent, God-fearin' hoose, Colin Campbell; and a' yere sinfu' Manchester ways canna mak' it any different! Adjoinin' rooms! *Who's burnin' ma guid electric light at this time o' the day?*"

This last was delivered, in a tone of extraordinary ferocity, the moment Aunt Elspat appeared at the door.

She was a middle-sized, angular woman in a dark dress, who somehow contrived to appear larger than her actual size. Kathryn had suggested her age as "nearly ninety"; but this, Alan knew, was an error. Aunt Elspat was seventy, and a well-preserved seventy at that. She had very sharp, very restless and penetrating black eyes. She carried a copy of the *Daily Floodlight* under her arm, and her dress rustled as she walked.

Swan hastened over to extinguish the light, almost upsetting her as he did so. Aunt Elspat eyed him without favor.

"Swi' on that light again," she said curtly. "It's sae dark a body canna see. Where's Alan Campbell and Kathryn Campbell?"

Colin, now as amiable as a sportive Newfoundland, pointed them out. Aunt Elspat subjected them to a long, silent, and uncomfortable scrutiny, her eyelids hardly moving. Then she nodded.

"Aye," she said. "Ye're Campbells. *Our* Campbells." She went across to the horsehair sofa beside the table which held the family Bible, and sat down. She was wearing, evidently, boots; and not small ones.

"Him that's gone," she continued, her eyes moving to the black-draped photograph, "caud tell a Campbell, our Campbells, i' ten thousand. Aye, if he blacked his face and spoke wi' a strange tongue, Angus wad speir him."

Again she was silent for an interminable time, her eyes never leaving her visitors.

"Alan Campbell," she said abruptly, "what's yere releegion?"

"Well—Church of England, I suppose."

"Ye suppause? Dinna ye ken?"

"All right, then. It *is* Church of England."

"And that'd be your releegion tu?" Aunt Elspat demanded of Kathryn.

"Yes, it is!"

Aunt Elspat nodded as though her darkest suspicions were confirmed.

"Ye dinna gang tae the kirk. I kenned it." She said this in a shivering kind of voice, and suddenly got steam up. "Rags o' Popery!" she said. "Think shame tae yereself, Alan Campbell, think shame and sorrow tae yere ain kith and kin, that wad dally wi' sin and lechery i' the hoose of the Scairlet Woman!"

Swan was shocked at such language.

"Now, ma'am, I'm sure he never goes to places like that," Swan protested, defending Alan. "And, besides, you could hardly call this young lady a ———"

Aunt Elspat turned round.

"Who's yon," she asked, pointing her finger at Swan, "wha' burns ma guid electric light at this time o' the day?"

"Ma'am, I didn't ———"

"Who's yon?"

Taking a deep breath, Swan assumed his most winning smile and stepped in front of her.

"Miss Campbell, I represent the London *Floodlight,* that paper you've got there. My editor was very pleased to get your letter; pleased that we've got appreciative readers all over this broad country. Now, Miss Campbell, you said in your letter that you had some sensational disclosures to make about a crime that was committed here ———"

"Eh?" roared Colin Campbell, turning to stare at her.

"And my editor sent me all the way from London to interview you. I'd be very pleased to hear anything you'd like to tell me, either on or off the record."

Cupping one hand behind her ear, Aunt Elspat listened with the same unwinking, beady stare. At length she spoke.

"So ye're an American, eh?" she said, and her eye began to gleam. "Hae ye heard ———"

This was much to bear, but Swan braced himself and smiled.

"Yes, Miss Campbell," he said patiently. "You don't need to tell me. I know. I've heard all about your brother Angus, who wouldn't even give the bloodhounds a penny."

Swan stopped abruptly.

He seemed to realize, in a vague kind of way, that he had made a slip somewhere and that his version of the anecdote was not quite correct.

"I mean—" he began.

Both Alan and Kathryn were looking at him not without interested curiosity. But the most pronounced effect was on Aunt Elspat. She merely sat and stared at Swan. He must have realized that she was staring fixedly at the hat still on his head, for he snatched it off.

Presently Elspat spoke. Her words, slow and weighty as a judge's summing up, fell with measured consideration.

"Any why should Angus Campbell gie the bluidhoonds a penny?"

"I mean ———"

"It wadna be muckle use tae them, wad it?"

"I mean, *cent*!"

"Sent wha'?"

"C-e-n-t, cent."

"In ma opeenion, young man," said Aunt Elspat, after a long pause, "ye're a bug-hoose. Gie'in' siller tae bluidhoonds!"

"I'm sorry, Miss Campbell! Skip it! It was a joke."

Of all the unfortunate words he could have used in front of Aunt Elspat, this was the worst. Even Colin was now glaring at him.

"Joke, is it?" said Elspat, gradually getting steam up again. "Angus Campbell scarce cauld in his coffin, and ye'd come insultin' a hoose o' mournin' wi' yere godless *jokes*? I'll no' stand it! In ma opeenion, ye skellum, ye didna come fra the *Daily Floodlight* at all. Who's Pip Emma?" She flung at him.

"Pardon?"

"Who's Pip Emma? Ah! Ye dinna ken that either, du ye?" cried Aunt Elspat, flourishing the paper. "Ye dinna ken the lass wha' writes the column i' ye're ain paper! Dinna fash yeresel' tae mak' excuses!—What's yere name?"

"MacHolster."

"Wha'?"

"MacHolster," said the scion of that improbable clan, now so rattled by Aunt Elspat that his usually nimble wits had deserted him. "I mean, MacQueen. What I mean is: it's really Swan, Charles Evans Swan, but I'm descended from the MacHolsters or the MacQueens, and ——"

Aunt Elspat did not even comment on this. She merely pointed to the door.

"But I tell you, Miss Campbell ——"

"Gang your ways," said Aunt Elspat. "I'll no' tell ye twice."

"You heard what she said, young fellow," interposed Colin, putting his thumbs in the armholes of his waistcoat and turning a fierce gaze on the visitor. "God's wounds! I wanted to be hospitable, but there are some things we don't joke about in this house."

"But I swear to you ——"

"Now will you go by the door," inquired Colin, lowering his hands, "or will you go by the window?"

For a second Alan thought Colin was really going to take the visitor by the collar and the slack of the trousers, and run him through the house like a chucker-out at a pub.

Swan, breathing maledictions, reached the door two seconds before Colin. They heard him make a speedy exit. The whole thing was over so quickly that Alan could hardly realize what had happened. But the effect on Kathryn was to reduce her almost to the verge of tears.

"What a family!" she cried, clenching her fists and stamping her foot on the floor. "Oh, good heavens, what a family!"

"And wha' ails you, Kathryn Campbell?"

Kathryn was a fighter.

"Do you want to know what I really think, Aunt Elspat?"

"Weel?"

"I think you're a very silly old woman, that's what I think. Now throw me out too."

To Alan's surprise, Aunt Elspat smiled.

"Maybe no sae daft, ma dear," she said complacently, and smoothed her skirt. "Maybe no' sae daft!"

"What do you think, Alan?"

"I certainly don't think you should have chucked him out like that. At least, without asking to see his press card. The fellow's perfectly genuine. But he's like the man in Shaw's *The Doctor's Dilemma:* congenitally incapable of reporting accurately anything he sees or hears. He may be able to make a lot of trouble."

"Trouble?" demand Colin. "How?"

"I don't know, but I have my suspicions."

Colin's bark was, obviously, very much worse than his bite. He ran a hand through his shaggy mane of hair, glared, and ended by scratching his nose.

"Look here," he growled. "Do you think I ought to go out and fetch the fellow back? Got some eighty-year-old whisky here, that'd make a donkey sing. We'll tap it tonight, Alan my lad. If we fed him that—"

Aunt Elspat put her foot down with a calm, implacable arrogance that was like granite.

"I'll no' hae the skellum in ma hoose."

"I know, old girl; but—"

"I'm tellin' ye: I'll no' hae the skellum in ma hoose. That's all. I'll write tae the editor again—"

Colin glared at her. "Yes, but that's what I wanted to ask you. What's all this tommyrot about mysterious secrets you will tell the newspapers but won't tell us?"

Elspat shut her lips mulishly.

"Come on!" said Colin. "Come clean!"

"Colin Campbell," said Elspat, with slow and measured vindictiveness, "du as I tell ye. Tak' Alan Campbell up tae the tower, and let him see how Angus Campbell met a bad end. Let him think o' Holy Writ. You, Kathryn Campbell, sit by me." She patted the sofa. "Du ye gang tae the godless dance halls o' London, noo?"

"Certainly not!" said Kathryn.

"Then ye hae never seen a jitterbug?"

What might have come of this improving conversation Alan never learned. Colin impelled him toward the door across the room, where Duncan and Chapman had disappeared a while ago.

It opened, Alan saw, directly into the ground floor of the tower. It was a big, round, gloomy room, with stone walls whitewashed on the inside, and an earth floor. You might have suspected that at one time it had been used for stabling. Wooden double doors, with a chain and padlock, opened out into the court on the south side.

These now stood open, letting in what light there was. In the wall was a low-arched door, giving on a spiral stone stair which climbed up inside the tower.

"Somebody's always leaving these doors open," growled Colin. "Padlock on the outside, too, if you can believe that! Anybody who got a duplicate key could . . .

"Look here, my lad. The old girl knows something. God's wounds! She's not daft; you saw that. But she knows something. And yet she keeps her lip buttoned, in spite of the fact that thirty-five thousand pounds in insurance may hang on it."

"Can't she even tell the police?"

Colin snorted.

"Police? Man, she can't even be civil to the Procurator Fiscal, let alone the regular police! She had some row with 'em a long time ago—about a cow, or I don't know what— and she's convinced they're all thieves and villains. That's the reason for this newspaper business, I imagine."

From his pocket Colin fished out a briar pipe and an oilskin pouch. He filled the pipe and lit it. The glow of the match illumined his shaggy beard and mustache, and the fierce eyes which acquired a cross-eyed expression as he stared at the burning tobacco.

"As for me . . . well, that doesn't matter so much. I'm an old war horse. I've got my debts; and Angus knew it;

but I can pull through somehow. Or at least I hope I can. But Elspat! Not a farthing! God's wounds!"

"How is the money divided?"

"Provided we get it, you mean?"

"Yes."

"That's simple. Half to me, and half to Elspat."

"Under her status as his common-law wife?"

"Sh-h!" thundered the quiet Colin, and looked round quickly, and waved the shriveled match end at his companion. "Slip of the tongue. She'll never put in a claim to be his common-law wife: you can bet your boots on that. The old girl's passion for respectability verges on the morbid. I told you that."

"I should have gathered it, somehow."

"She'll never admit she was more than his 'relative,' not in thirty years. Even Angus, who was a free-spoken devil, never alluded to it in public. No, no, no. The money is a straight bequest. Which we're never likely to get."

He flung away the spent match. He squared his shoulders, and nodded toward the staircase.

"Well! Come on. That is, if you feel up to it. There's five floors above this, and a hundred and four steps to the top. But come on. Mind your head."

Alan was too fascinated to bother about the number of steps.

But they seemed interminable, as a winding stair always does. The staircase was lighted at intervals along the west side—that is, the side away from the loch—by windows which had been hacked out to larger size. It had a musty, stably smell, not improved by the savor of Colin's pipe tobacco.

In daylight that was almost gone, making walking difficult on the uneven stone humps, they groped up along the outer face of the wall.

"But your brother didn't always sleep clear up at the top, did he?" Alan inquired.

"Yes, indeed. Every night for years. Liked the view out over the loch. Said the air was purer too, though that's all my eye. God's wounds! I'm out of condition!"

"Does anybody occupy any of these other rooms?"

"No. Just full of junk. Relics of Angus's get-rich-quick-and-be-happy schemes."

Colin paused, puffing, at a window on the last landing but one.

And Alan looked out. Remnants of red sunset lay still ghostly among the trees. Though they could not have been so very high up, yet the height seemed immense.

Below them, westwards, lay the main road to Inveraray. Up the Glen of Shira, and, farther on, the fork where Glen Aray ascended in deep hills toward Dalmally, were tangled stretches where the fallen timber now rotted and turned gray. It marked the track, Colin said, of the great storm which had swept Argyllshire a few years back. It was a wood of the dead, even of dead trees.

Southwards, above spiky pines, you could see far away the great castle of Argyll, with the four great towers whose roofs change color when it rains. Beyond would be the estate office, once the courthouse, where James Stewart, guardian of Alan Breck Stewart, had been tried and condemned for the Appin murder. All the earth was rich and breathing with names, with songs, with tradition, with superstitions—

"Dr. Campbell," said Alan, very quietly, "how did the old man die?"

Sparks flew from Colin's pipe.

"You ask me? *I* don't know. Except that he never committed suicide. Angus kill himself? Hoots!"

More sparks flew from the pipe.

"I don't want to see Alec Forbes hang," he added querulously; "but he's ruddy well got to hang. Alec 'ud have cut Angus's heart out and never thought twice about it."

"Who is this Alec Forbes?"

"Oh, some bloke who came and settled here, and drinks too much, and thinks he's an inventor too, in a small way. He and Angus collaborated on one idea. With the result usual to collaboration: bust-up. He said Angus cheated him. Probably Angus did."

"So Forbes came in here and cut up a row on the night of the—murder?"

"Yes. Came clear up to Angus's bedroom here, and wanted to have it out. Drunk, as like as not."

"But they cleared him out, didn't they?"

"They did. Or rather Angus did. Angus was no soft 'un, for all his years and weight. Then the womenfolk joined in, and *they* had to search the bedroom and even the other rooms to make sure Alec hadn't sneaked back."

"Which, evidently, he hadn't."

"Right. Then Angus locks his door—*and* bolts it. In the night, something happens."

If his fingernails had been longer, Colin would have gnawed at them.

"The police surgeon put the time of death as not earlier than ten o'clock and not later than one. What the hell good is that? Eh? We know he didn't die before ten o'clock anyway, because that's the last time he was seen alive. But the police surgeon wouldn't be more definite. He said Angus's injuries wouldn't have killed him instantly, so he might have been unconscious but alive for some time before death.

"Anyway, we do know that Angus had gone to bed when all this happened."

"How do we know that?"

Colin made a gesture of exasperation.

"Because he was in his nightshirt when they found him. And the bed was rumpled. And he'd put out the light and taken down the blackout from the window."

Alan was brought up with something of a start.

"Do you know," Alan muttered, "I'd almost forgotten there was a war going on, and even the question of the blackout? But look here!" He swept his hand toward the window. "*These* windows aren't blacked out?"

"No. Angus could go up and down here in the dark. He said blackouts for 'em were a waste of money. But a light showing up in that room could have been seen for miles, as even Angus had to admit. God's wounds, don't ask me so many questions! Come and see the room for yourself."

He knocked out his pipe and ran like an ungainly baboon up the remaining stairs.

Chapter 7

ALISTAIR DUNCAN and Walter Chapman were still arguing.

"My dear sir," said the tall, stoop-shouldered lawyer, waving a pince-nez in the air as though he were conducting an orchestra, "surely it is now obvious that this is a case of murder?"

"No."

"But the suitcase, sir! The suitcase, or dog carrier, which was found under the bed after the murder?"

"After the death."

"For the sake of clearness, shall we say murder?"

"All right: without prejudice. But what I want to know, Mr. Duncan, is: what *about* that dog carrier? It was empty. It didn't contain a dog. Microscopic examination by the police showed that it hadn't contained *anything*. What is it supposed to prove anyway?"

Both of them broke off at the entrance of Alan and Colin.

The room at the top of the tower was round and spacious, though somewhat low of ceiling in comparison to its diameter. Its one door, which opened in from a little landing, had its lock torn out from the frame; and the staple of the bolt, still rustily embedded round the bolt, was also wrenched loose.

The one window, opposite the door, exerted over Alan an ugly fascination.

It was larger than in it had seemed from the ground. It consisted of two leaves, opening out like little doors after the fashion of windows in France, and of leaded-glass panes in diamond shapes. It was clearly a modern addition, the original window having been enlarged; and was, Alan thought, dangerously low.

Seen thus in the gloaming, a luminous shape in a cluttered room, it took the eye with a kind of hypnosis. But it was the only modern thing here, except for the electric bulb over the desk and the electric heater beside the desk.

A huge uncompromising oak bedstead, with a double feather bed and a crazy-quilt cover, stood against one rounded wall. There was an oak press nearly as high as the room. Some effort had been made toward cheerfulness by plastering the walls and papering them with blue cabbages in yellow joinings.

There were pictures, mainly family photographs going back as far as the fifties or sixties. The stone floor was covered with straw matting. A marble-topped dressing table, with a gaunt mirror, had been crowded in beside a big roll-top desk bristling with papers. More correspondence, bales of it, lined the walls and set the rocking chairs at odd angles. Though there were many trade magazines, you saw no books except a Bible and a post-card album.

It was an old man's room. A pair of Angus's button boots, out of shape from bunions, still stood under the bed.

And Colin seemed to feel the reminder.

"Evening," he said, half bristling again. "This is Alan Campbell, from London. Where's the Fiscal?"

Alistair Duncan put on his pince-nez.

"Gone, I fear, home," he replied. "I suspect him of avoiding Aunt Elspat. Our young friend here,"—smiling bleakly, he reached out and tapped Chapman on the shoulder—"avoids her like the plague and won't go near her."

"Well, you never know where you are with her. I deeply sympathize with her, and all that; but hang it all!"

The law agent drew together his stooped shoulders, and gloomed down on Alan.

"Haven't we met before, sir?"

"Yes. A little while ago."

"Ah! Yes. Did we—exchange words?"

"Yes. You said, 'How do you do?' and, 'Good-by.' "

"Would," said the law agent, shaking his head, "would that all our social relations were so uncomplicated! How do you do?" He shook hands, with a bony palm and a limp grasp.

"Of course," he went on. "I remember now. I wrote to you. It was very good of you to come."

"May I ask, Mr. Duncan, why you wrote to me?"

"Pardon?"

"I'm very glad to be here. I know I should have made my acquaintance with our branch of the family long before this. But neither Kathryn Campbell nor I seem to serve any very useful purpose. What did you mean, precisely, by a 'family conference'?"

"I will tell you," Duncan spoke promptly, and (for him) almost cheerfully. "Let me first present Mr. Chapman, of the Hercules Life Insurance Company. A stubborn fellow."

"Mr. Duncan's a bit stubborn himself," smiled Chapman.

"We have here a clear case of accident or murder," pursued the lawyer. "Have you heard the details of your unfortunate relative's death?"

"Some of them," Alan answered. "But—"

He walked forward to the window.

The two leaves were partly open. There was no upright bar or support between them: making, when the leaves were pushed open, an open space some three feet wide by four feet high. A magnificent view stretched out over the darkling water and the purple-brown hills, but Alan did not look at it.

"May I ask a question?" he said.

Chapman cast up his eyes with the expression of one who says, "Another one!" But Chapman made a courteous gesture.

"By all means."

Beside the window on the floor stood its blackout: a sheet of oilcloth nailed to a light wooden frame, which fitted flat against the window.

"Well," continued Alan, indicating this, "could he have

fallen out accidentally while he was taking down the black-out?

"You know what we all do. Before climbing into bed, we turn out the light, and then grope across to take down the blackout and open the window.

"If you accidentally leaned too hard on this window while you were opening the catch, you might pitch straight forward out of it. There's no bar between."

To his surprise Duncan looked annoyed and Chapman smiled.

"Look at the thickness of the wall," suggested the man from the insurance company. "It's three feet thick: good old feudal wall. No. He couldn't possibly have done that unless he were staggering drunk or drugged or overcome in some way; and the post-mortem examination proved, as even Mr. Duncan will admit—"

He glanced inquiringly at the lawyer, who grunted.

"—proved that he was none of these things. He was a sharp-eyed, sure-footed old man in full possession of his senses."

Chapman paused.

"Now, gentlemen, while we're all here, I may as well make clear to all of you why I don't see how this can be anything but suicide. I should like to ask Mr. Campbell's brother a question."

"Well?" said Colin sharply.

"It's true, isn't it, that Mr. Angus Campbell was what we'll call a gentleman of the old school? That is, he always slept with the windows closed?"

"Yes, that's true," admitted Colin, and shoved his hands into the pockets of his shooting coat.

"I can't understand it myself," said the man from the insurance company, puffing out his lips. "I should have a head like a balloon if I ever did that. But my grandfather always did; wouldn't let in a breath of night air.

"And Mr. Campbell did too. The only reason he ever took the blackout down at night was so that he should know when it was morning.

"Gentlemen, I ask you now! When Mr. Campbell went

to bed that night, this window was closed and its catch locked as usual. Miss Campbell and Kirstie MacTavish admit that. Later the police found Mr. Campbell's fingerprints, *and only Mr. Campbell's fingerprints, on the catch of that window*.

"What he did is pretty clear. At some time after ten he undressed, put on his nightshirt, took down the blackout, and went to bed as usual." Chapman pointed to the bed. "The bed is made now, but it was rumpled then."

Alistair Duncan sniffed.

"That," he said, "is Aunt Elspat's doing. She said she thought it was only decent to redd up the room."

Chapman's gesture called for silence.

"At some time between then and one o'clock in the morning he got up, walked to the window, opened it, and deliberately threw himself out.

"Hang it all, I appeal to Mr. Campbell's brother! My firm wants to do the right thing. *I* want to do the right thing. As I was telling Mr. Duncan, I knew the late Mr. Campbell personally. He came in to see me at our Glasgow office, and took out his last policy. After all, you know, it's not *my* money. I'm not paying it out. If I could see my way clear to advise my firm to honor this claim, I'd do it like a shot. But can you honestly say the evidence warrants that?"

There was a silence.

Chapman finished almost on a note of eloquence. Then he picked up his brief case and bowler hat from the desk.

"The dog carrier—" began Duncan.

Chapman's color went up.

"Oh, damn the dog carrier!" he said, with unprofessional impatience. "Can you, sir—can any of you—suggest any reason for the dog carrier to figure in this business at all?"

Colin Campbell, bristling, went across to the bed. He reached underneath and fished out the object in question, which he regarded as though he were about to give it a swift kick.

It was about the size of a large suitcase, though somewhat wider in box shape. Made of dark-brown leather, it had a handle like a suitcase, but two metal clasps on the upper side. An oblong grating of wire at one end had been inset for the purpose of giving air to whatever pet might be carried.

To whatever pet might be carried. . . .

In the mind of Alan Campbell there stirred a fancy so grotesque and ugly, even if unformed, as to come with a flavor of definite evil in the old tower room.

"You don't suppose," Alan heard himself saying, "he might have been frightened into doing what he did?"

His three companions whirled round.

"Frightened?" repeated the lawyer.

Alan stared at the leather box.

"I don't know anything about this man Alec Forbes," he went on, "but he seems to be a pretty ugly customer."

"Well, my dear sir?"

"Suppose Alec Forbes brought that box along with him when he came here. It'd look like an ordinary suitcase. Suppose he came here deliberately, pretending to want to 'have it out' with Angus, but really to leave the box behind. He distracts Angus's attention, and shoves the box under the bed. In the row Angus doesn't remember the suitcase afterwards. But in the middle of the night something gets out of the box . . ."

Even Alistair Duncan had begun to look a trifle uncomfortable.

And Chapman was eyeing Alan with an interest which all his skeptical and smiling incredulity could not conceal.

"Oh, see here!" he protested. "What are you suggesting, exactly?"

Alan stuck it out.

"I don't want you to laugh. But what I was actually thinking about was—well, a big spider, or a poisonous snake of some kind. It would have been bright moonlight that night, remember."

Again the silence stretched out interminably. It was now so dark that they could barely see.

"It is an extraordinary thing," murmured the lawyer in in his thin, dry voice. "Just one moment."

He felt in the inside breast pocket of his coat. From this he took a worn leather notebook. Carrying it to the window, and adjusting his pince-nez, he cocked his head at an angle to examine one page of the notebook.

" 'Extracts from the statement of Kirstie MacTavish, maidservant,' " he read, and cleared his throat. "Translated from the Doric and rendered into English, listen to this:

" 'Mr. Campbell said to me and Miss Campbell, "Go to bed and let's have no more nonsense. I have got rid of the blellum. Did you see that suitcase he had with him, though?" We said we had not, as we did not arrive until Mr. Campbell had put Mr. Forbes out of the house. Mr. Campbell said: "I will bet you he is leaving the country to get away from his creditors. But I wonder what he did with the suitcase? He was using two hands to try to hit me when he left." ' "

Duncan peered over his pince-nez.

"Any comments on that, my dear sir?" he inquired.

The insurance agent was not amused.

"Aren't you forgetting what you pointed out to me yourself? When Miss Campbell and the maid searched this room just before Mr. Campbell retired, they saw no suitcase under the bed."

Duncan rubbed his jaw. In that light he had a corpselike, cadaverous pallor, and his grizzled hair looked like wire.

"True," he admitted. "True. At the same time—"

He shook his head.

"Snakes!" snorted the insurance agent. "Spiders! Dr. Fu Manchu! Look here! Do you know of any snake or spider that would climb out of its box, and then carefully close the clasps of the box afterwards? Both clasps on that thing were found fastened on the following morning."

"That would certainly appear to be a stumbling block," conceded Duncan. "At the same time—"

"And what happened to the thing afterwards?"

"It wouldn't be very pleasant," grinned Colin Campbell, "if the thing were still here in the room somewhere."

Mr. Walter Chapman hurriedly put on his bowler hat.

"I must go," he said. "Sorry, gentlemen, but I'm very late as it is and I've got to get back to Dunoon. Can I give you a lift, Mr. Duncan?"

"Nonsense" roared Colin. "You're staying to tea. Both of you."

Chapman blinked at him.

"Tea? Great Scott, what time do you have your dinner?"

"You'll get no dinner, my lad. But the tea will be bigger than most dinners you ever ate. And I've got some very potent whisky I've been aching to try out on somebody, beginning with a ruddy Englishman. What do you say?"

"Sorry. Decent of you, but I must go." Chapman slapped at the sleeves of his coat. Exasperation radiated from him. "What with snakes and spiders—*and* the supernatural on top of it—"

If the scion of the MacHolsters could have chosen no more unfortunate word than "joke" in addressing Elspat Campbell, Chapman himself in addressing Colin could have chosen no more unfortunate word than "supernatural."

Colin's big head hunched down into his big shoulders.

"And who says this was supernatural?" he inquired in a soft voice.

Chapman laughed.

"I don't, naturally. That's a bit outside my firm's line. But the people hereabouts seem to have an idea that this place is haunted; or at least that there's something not quite right about it."

"Oh?"

"And, if I may say so without offense,"—the insurance agent's eye twinkled—"they seem not to have a very high opinion of you people here. They mutter, 'a bad lot,' or something of the sort."

"We are a bad lot. God's wounds!" cried the atheistical doctor, not without pride. "Who's ever denied it? Not me. But haunted! Of all the . . . look here. You don't think Alec Forbes went about carrying a bogle in a dog box?"

"I don't think, frankly," retorted Chapman, "that anybody carried anything in any box." His worried look returned. "All the same, I should feel better if we could have a word with this Mr. Forbes."

"Where is he, by the way?" asked Alan.

The law agent, who had shut up his notebook and was listening with a dry, quiet smile, struck in again.

"That, too, is an extraordinary thing. Even Mr. Chapman would admit something suspicious—something just a trifle suspicious—about Alec Forbes's conduct. For, you see, Alec Forbes can't be found."

Chapter 8

"YOU MEAN," ASKED ALAN, "he did go away to escape his creditors?"

Duncan waved the pince-nez.

"Slander. No: I merely state the fact. Or he may be on a spree, which is possible. All the same, it is curious. Eh, my dear Chapman? It is *curious*."

The insurance agent drew a deep breath.

"Gentlemen," he said, "I'm afraid I can't argue the matter any further now. I'm going to get out of here before I break my neck on those stairs in the dark.

"Here is all I am able to tell you now. I'll have a word with the Fiscal tomorrow. He must have decided by now whether he thinks this is suicide, accident, or murder. On what he does must necessarily depend what *we* do. Can I say any fairer than that?"

"Thank you. No, that will suit us. All we ask is a little time."

"But if you're sure this is murder," interposed Alan, "why doesn't your Fiscal take some real steps about it? For instance, why doesn't he call in Scotland Yard?"

Duncan regarded him with real horror.

"Summon Scotland Yard to Scotland?" he expostulated. "My dear sir!"

"I should have thought this would have been the very place for 'em," said Alan. "Why not?"

"My dear sir, it is never done! Scots law has a procedure all its own."

"By George, it has!" declared Chapman, slapping his brief case against his leg. "I've only been up here a couple of months, but I've found that out already."

"Then what are you going to do?"

"While all the rest of you," observed Colin, throwing out his barrel chest, "have been doing nothing but fiddle-faddling about and talking, other people haven't been idle. I won't tell you what I'm going to do. I'll tell you what I *have* done." His eye dared them to say it wasn't a good idea. "I've sent for Gideon Fell."

Duncan clucked his tongue thoughtfully.

"That's the man who—?"

"It is. And a good friend of mine."

"Have you thought of the—ah—expense?"

"God's wounds, can't you stop thinking about money for five seconds? Just five seconds? Anyway, it won't cost you a penny. He's coming up here as my guest, that's all. You offer him money and there'll be trouble."

The lawyer spoke stiffly.

"We all know, my dear Colin, that your own contempt for the monetary side has not failed to prove embarrassing to you at times." His glance was charged with meaning. "You must allow *me,* however, to think of the pounds, shillings and pence. A while ago this gentleman,"—he nodded toward Alan—"asked why this 'family conference' had been summoned. I'll tell you. If the insurance companies refuse to pay up, proceedings must be instituted. Those proceedings may be expensive."

"Do you mean to say," said Colin, his eyes starting out of their sockets, "that you brought those two kids clear up from London just in the hope they'd contribute to the basket? God's wounds, do you want your ruddy neck wrung?"

Duncan was very white.

"I am not in the habit of being talked to like that, Colin Campbell."

"Well, you're *being* talked to like that, Alister Duncan. What do you think of it?"

For the first time a personal note crept into the law agent's voice.

"Colin Campbell, for forty-two years I've been at the beck and call of your family—"

"Ha ha ha!"

"Colin Campbell—"

"Here! I say!" protested Chapman, so uncomfortable that he shifted from one foot to the other.

Alan also intervened by putting his hand on Colin's shivering shoulder. In another moment, he was afraid, Colin might be running a second person out of the house by the collar and the slack of the trousers.

"Excuse me," Alan said, "but my father left me pretty well off, and if there *is* anything I can do . . ."

"So? Your father left you pretty well off," said Colin. "And well you knew it, didn't you, Alistair Duncan?"

The lawyer sputtered. What he attempted to say, so far as Alan could gather, was 'Do you wish me to wash my hands of this matter?' What he actually said was something like, 'Do you wash me to wish my hands of this matter?' But both he and Colin were so angry that neither noticed it.

"Yes, I do," said Colin. "That's just what I smacking well do. Now shall we go downstairs?"

In silence, with aching dignity, the quartet stumbled and blundered and groped down some very treacherous stairs. Chapman attempted to lighten matters by asking Duncan if he would care for a lift in the former's car, an offer which was accepted, and a few observations about the weather.

These fell flat.

Still in silence, they went through into the sitting room on the ground floor, now deserted, and to the front door. As Colin and the law agent said good night, they could not

have been more on their dignity had they been going to fight
a duel in the morning. The door closed.

"Elspat and little Kate," said Colin, moodily smoldering,
"will be having their tea. Come on."

Alan liked the dining room, and would have liked it still
more, if he had not felt so ruffled.

Under a low-hanging lamp which threw bright light on
the white tablecloth, with a roaring fire in the chimney,
Aunt Elspat and Kathryn sat at a meal composed of saus-
ages, Ulster fry, eggs, potatoes, tea, and enormous quantities of buttered toast.

"Elspat," said Colin, moodily drawing out a chair, "Alistair Duncan's given notice again."

Aunt Elspat helped herself to butter.

"A'weel," she said philosophically, "it's no' the fairst
time, and it'll no' be the last. He gie'd me notice tu, a week
syne."

Alan's intense discomfort began to lighten.

"Do you mean to say," Alan demanded, "that that business wasn't—wasn't serious?"

"Oh, no. He'll be all right in the morning," said Colin.
Stirring uncomfortably, he glowered at the well-filled table.
"You know, Elspat, I've got a bloody temper. I wish I
could control it."

Aunt Elspat then flew out at him.

She said she would not have such profane language used
in her house, and especially in front of the child: by which
she presumably meant Kathryn. She further rated them for
being late for tea, in terms which would have been violent
had they missed two meals in a row and emptied the soup
over her at the fourth.

Alan only half listened. He was beginning to understand
Aunt Elspat a little better now, and to realize that her out-
bursts were almost perfunctory. Long ago Aunt Elspat had
been compelled to fight and fight to get her own way in all
things; and continued it, as a matter of habit, long after it
had ceased to be necessary. It was not even bad temper: it
was automatic.

The walls of the dining room were ornamented with

withered stags' heads, and there were two crossed clay-mores over the chimneypiece. They attracted Alan. A sense of well-being stole into him as he devoured his food, washing it down with strong black tea.

"Ah!" said Colin, with an expiring sigh. He pushed back his chair, stretched, and patted his stomach. His face glowed out of the beard and shaggy hair. "Now that's better. That's very much better. Rot me if I don't feel like ringing up the old weasel and apologizing to him!"

"Did you," said Kathryn hesitantly, "did you find out anything? Up there in the tower? Or decide on anything?"

Colin inserted a toothpick into his beard.

"No, Kitty-kat, we didn't."

"And please don't call me Kitty-kat! You all treat me as though I weren't grown up!"

"Hoots!" said Aunt Elspat, giving her a withering look. "Ye're *not* grown up."

"We didn't decide on anything," pursued Colin, continuing to pat his stomach. "But then we didn't need to. Gideon Fell'll be here tomorrow. In fact, I thought it was Fell coming when I saw your boat tonight. And when *he* gets here—"

"Did you say Fell" cried Kathryn. "Not Dr. Fell?"

"That's the chap."

"Not that horrible man who writes letters to the newspapers? *You* know, Alan."

'He's a very distinguished scholar, Kitty-kat," said Colin, "and as such you ought to take off your wee bonnet to him. But his main claims to notoriety lie along the line of detecting crime."

Aunt Elspat wanted to know what his religion was.

Colin said he didn't know, but that it didn't matter a damn *what* his religion was.

Aunt Elspat intimated, on the contrary, that is mattered very much indeed, adding remarks which left her listeners in no doubt about her views touching Colin's destination in the afterlife. This, to Alan, was the hardest part of Elspat's discourse to put up with. Her notions of theology were childish. Her knowledge of Church history would have been considered inaccurate even by the late Bishop Burnet. But good manners kept him silent, until he could get in a relevant question.

"The only part I haven't got quite clear," he said "is about the diary."

Aunt Elspat stopped hurling damnation right and left, and applied herself to her tea.

"Diary?" repeated Colin.

"Yes. I'm not even sure, if I heard properly; it might refer to something else. But, when Mr. Duncan and the insurance fellow were talking in the next room, we heard Mr. Duncan say something about a 'missing diary.' At least, that's how I understood it."

"And so did I," agreed Kathryn.

Colin scowled.

"As far as I can gather,"—he put a finger on his napkin ring, sending it spinning out on the table to roll back to him —"somebody pinched it, that's all."

"What diary?"

"*Angus's* diary, dammit! He carefully kept one every year, and at the end of the year burned it so that nobody should ever find it and know what he was really thinking."

"Prudent habit."

"Yes. Well, he wrote it up every night just before he went to bed. Never knew him to miss. It should have been on the desk next morning. But—at least, so they tell me— it wasn't. Eh, Elspat?"

"Drink your tea and dinna be sae daft."

Colin sat up.

"What the devil's daft about that? The diary wasn't there, was it?"

Carefully, with ladylike daintiness which showed she knew her manners, Elspat poured tea into the saucer, blew on it, and drank.

"The trouble is," Colin continued, "that nobody even noticed the absence of the diary until a good many hours afterwards. So anybody who saw it lying there could have pinched it in the meantime. I mean, there's no proof that the phantom murderer got it. It might have been anybody. Eh, Elspat?"

Aunt Elspat regarded the empty saucer for a moment, and then sighed.

"I suppause," she said resignedly, "you'll be wantin' the whisky, noo?"

Colin's face lit up.

"Now there," he boomed, with fervency, "there, in the midst of this mess, is the idea that the world's been waiting for!" He turned to Alan. "Lad, would you like to taste some mountain dew that'll take the top of your head off? Would you?"

The dining room was snug and warm, though the wind rose outside. As always in the presence of Kathryn, Alan felt expansive and on his mettle.

"It would be very interesting," he replied, settling back, "to find any whisky that could take the top of my head off."

"Oho? You think so, do you?"

"You must remember," said Alan, not without reason on his side, "that I spent three years in the United States during prohibition days. Anybody who can survive *that* experience has nothing to fear from any liquor that ever came out of a still—or didn't."

"You think so, eh?" mused Colin. "Do you now? Well, well, well! Elspat, this calls for heroic measures. Bring out the Doom of the Campbells."

Elspat rose without protest.

"A'weel," she said, "I've seen it happen befair. It'll happen again when I'm gone. I caud du wi' a wee nip masel', the nicht bein' cauld."

She creaked out of the room, and returned bearing a decanter nearly full of a darkish brown liquid filled with gold where the light struck it. Colin placed it tenderly on the table. For Elspat and Kathryn he poured out an infinitesimal amount. For himself and Alan he poured out about a quarter of a tumblerful.

"How will you have it, lad?"

"American style. Neat, with water on the side."

"Good! Damn good!" roared Colin. "You don't want to

spoil it. Now drink up. Go on. Drink it."

They—or at least Colin and Elspat—were regarding him with intense interest. Kathryn sniffed suspiciously at the liquid in her glass, but evidently decided that she liked it. Colin's face was red and of a violent eagerness, his eyes wide open and mirth lurking in his soul.

"To happier days," said Alan.

He lifted the glass, drained it, and almost literally reeled.

It did not take the top of his head off; but for a second he thought it was going to. The stuff was strong enough to make a battleship alter its course. The veins of his temples felt bursting; his eyesight dimmed; and he decided that he must be strangling to death. Then, after innumerable seconds, he opened swimming eyes to find Colin regarding him with proud glee.

Next, something else happened.

Once that spiritous bomb had exploded, and he could recover breath and eyesight, a fey sense of exhilaration and well-being crawled along his veins. The original buzzing in the head was succeeded by a sense of crystal clearness, the feeling which Newton or Einstein must have felt at the approaching solution of a complex mathematical problem.

He had kept himself from coughing, and the moment passed.

"Well?" demanded Colin.

"Aaah!" said his guest.

"Here's to happier days too!" thundered Colin, and drained his own glass. The effects here were marked as well, though Colin recovered himself a shade more quickly.

Then Colin beamed on him. "Like it?"

"I do!"

"Not too strong for you?"

"No."

"Care for another?"

"Thanks. I don't mind if I do."

"A'weel!" said Elspat resignedly. "A 'weel!"

Chapter 9

ALAN CAMPBELL OPENED ONE EYE.

From somewhere in remote distances, muffled beyond sight or sound, his soul crawled back painfully, through subterranean corridors, up into his body again. Toward the last it moved to a cacophony of hammers and lights.

Then he was awake.

The first eye was bad enough. But, when he opened the second eye, such a rush of anguish flowed through his brain that he hastily closed them again.

He observed—at first without curiosity—that he was lying in bed in a room he had never seen before; that he wore pajamas; and that there was sunlight in the room.

But his original concerns were purely physical. His head felt as though it were rising toward the ceiling with long, spiraling motions; his stomach was an inferno, his voice a croak out of a dry throat, his whole being composed of fine wriggling wires. Thus Alan Campbell, waking at twelve midday with the king of all hangovers, for the moment merely lay and suffered.

Presently he tried to climb out of bed. But dizziness overcame him, and he lay down again. It was here that his wits began to work, however. Feverishly he tried to remember what had happened last night.

And he could not remember a single thing.

Alan was galvanized.

Possible enormities stretched out behind him, whole vistas of enormities which he might have said or done, but which he could not remember now. There is perhaps not in the world any anguish to compare to this. He knew, or presumed, that he was still at the Castle of Shira; and that he had been lured into quaffing the Doom of the Campbells with Colin; but this was all he knew.

The door of the room opened, and Kathryn came in.

On a tray she carried a cup of black coffee and a revolting-looking mixture in a glass eggcup. She was fully dressed. But the wan expression of her face and eyes strangely comforted him.

Kathryn came over and put down the tray on the bedside table.

"Well, Dr. Campbell," were her first unencouraging words, "don't you feel ashamed of yourself?"

All Alan's emotion found vent in one lingering passionate groan.

"Heaven knows *I've* no right to blame you," said Kathryn, putting her hands to her head. "I was almost as bad as you were. Oh, God, I feel *awful!*" she breathed, and tottered on her feet. "But at least I didn't—"

"Didn't what?" croaked Alan.

"Don't you remember?"

He waited for enormity to sweep him like the sea.

"At the moment—no. Nothing."

She pointed to the tray. "Drink that prairie oyster. I know it looks foul; but it'll do you good."

"No: tell me. What did I do? Was I very bad?"

Kathryn eyed him wanly.

"Not as bad as Colin, of course. But when *I* tried to leave the party, you and Colin were fencing with claymores."

"Were what?"

"Fencing with real swords. All over the dining room and out in the hall and up the stairs. You had kitchen tablecloths slung on for plaids. Colin was talking in Gaelic, and you were quoting *Marmion,* and *The Lady of the Lake.* Only you couldn't seem to decide whether you were Roderick Dhu or Douglas Fairbanks."

Alan shut his eyes tightly.

He breathed a prayer himself. Faint glimmers, like chinks of light in a blind, touched old-world scenes which swam at him and then receded in hopeless confusion. All lights splintered; all voices dimmed.

"Stop a bit!" he said, pressing his hands to his forehead. "There's nothing about Elspat in this, is there? I didn't insult Elspat, did I? I seem to remember . . ."

Again he shut his eyes.

"My dear Alan, that's the one good feature of the whole night. You're Aunt Elspat's white-haired boy. She thinks that you, next to the late Angus, are the finest member of the whole family."

"*What?*"

"Don't you remember giving her a lecture, at least half an hour long, about the Solemn League and Covenant and the history of the Church of Scotland?"

"Wait! I do seem vaguely to—"

"She didn't understand it; but you had her spellbound. She said that anybody who knew the names of so many ministers couldn't be as godless as she'd thought. Then you insisted on her having half a tumbler of that wretched stuff, and she walked off to bed like Lady Macbeth. This was before the fencing episode, of course. And then—don't you remember what Colin did to the poor man Swan?"

"Swan? Not the MacHolster Swan?"

"Yes."

"But what was *he* doing here?"

"Well, it was something like this: though it's rather dim in my own mind. After you'd fenced all over the place, Colin wanted to go out. He said, 'Alan Oig, there is dirty work to be done this night. Let us hence and look for Stewarts.' You thought that would be a perfectly splendid idea.

"We went out the back, on the road. The first thing we saw, in the bright moonlight, was Mr. Swan standing and looking at the house. Don't ask me what he was doing there! Colin whooped out, 'There's a bluidy Stewart!' and went for him with the claymore.

"Mr. Swan took one look at him, and shot off down the road harder than I've ever seen any man run before. Colin went tearing after him, and you after Colin. I didn't interfere: I'd reached the stage where all I could do was stand and giggle. Colin couldn't quite manage to overtake Mr.

Swan, but he did manage to stick him several times in the —in the—"

"Yes."

"—before Colin fell flat and Mr. Swan got away. Then you two came back singing."

There was obviously something on Kathryn's mind. She kept her eyes on the floor.

"I suppose you don't remember," she added, "that I spent the night in here?"

"You spent the night in here?"

"Yes. Colin wouldn't hear of anything else. He locked us in."

"But we didn't . . . I mean . . . ?"

"Didn't what?"

"You know what I mean."

Kathryn evidently did, to judge by her color.

"Well—no. We were both too far gone anyway. I was so dizzy and weak that I didn't even protest. You recited something about,

" 'Here dies in my bosom
The secret of heather ale.'

"Then you courteously said, 'Excuse me,' and lay down on the floor and went to sleep."

He became conscious of his pajamas. "But how did I get into these?"

"I don't know. You must have waked up in the night and put them on. I woke up about six o'clock, feeling like death, and managed to push the key in the door out, so it fell on the outside and I dragged it under the sill on a piece of paper. I got off to my own room, and I don't think Elspat knows anything about it. But when I woke up and found you there . . ."

Her voice rose almost to a wail.

"Alan Campbell, what on earth has come over us? Both of us? Don't you think we'd better get out of Scotland before it corrupts us altogether?"

Alan reached out for the prairie oyster. How he managed to swallow it he does not now remember; but he did, and felt better. The hot black coffee helped.

"So help me," he declared, "I will never touch another drop as long as I live! And Colin. I hope he's suffering the tortures of the inferno. I hope he's got such a hangover as will—"

"Well, he hasn't."

"No?"

"He's as bright as a cricket. He says good whisky never gave any man a headache. That dreadful Dr. Fell has arrived, too. Can you come downstairs and get some breakfast?"

Alan gritted his teeth.

"I'll have a try," he said, "if you can overcome your lack of decency and get out of here while I dress."

Half an hour later, after shaving and bathing in the somewhat primitive bathroom, he was on his way downstairs feeling much better. From the partly open door of the sitting room came the sound of two powerful voices, those of Colin and Dr. Fell, which sent sharp pains through his skull. Toast was all he could manage in the way of breakfast. Afterwards he and Kathryn crept guiltily into the sitting room.

Dr. Fell, his hands folded over his crutch-handled stick, sat on the sofa. The broad black ribbon of his eyeglasses blew out as he chuckled. His big mop of gray-streaked hair lay over one eye, and many more chins appeared as his amusement increased. He seemed to fill the room: at first Alan could hardly believe him.

"Good morning!" he thundered.

"Good morning!" thundered Colin.

"Good morning," murmured Alan. "Must you shout like that?"

"Nonsense. We weren't shouting," said Colin. "How are you feeling this morning?"

"Terrible."

Colin stared at him. "You haven't got a head?"

"No?"

"Nonsense!" snorted Colin, fiercely and dogmatically. "Good whisky never gave any man a head."

This fallacy, by the way, is held almost as a gospel in the North. Alan did not attempt to dispute it. Dr. Fell hoisted himself ponderously to his feet and made something in the nature of a bow.

"Your servant, sir," said Dr. Fell. He bowed to Kathryn. "And yours, madam." A twinkle appeared in his eye. "I trust that you have now managed to settle between you the vexed question of the Duchess of Cleveland's hair? Or may I infer that at the moment you are more interested in the hair of the dog?"

"That's not a bad idea, you know," said Colin.

"No!" roared Alan, and made his own head ache. "I will never touch that damned stuff again under any circumstances. That is final."

"That's what you think now," Colin grinned comfortably. "I'm going to give Fell here a nip of it tonight. I say, my boy: would you like to taste some mountain dew that'll take the top of your head off?"

Dr. Fell chuckled.

"It would be very interesting," he replied, "to find any whisky that could take the top of my head off."

"Don't say that," warned Alan. "Let me urge you in advance: don't say it. *I* said it. It's fatal."

"And must we talk about this, anyway?" inquired Kathryn, who had been eyeing Dr. Fell with a deep suspicion which he returned by beaming like the Ghost of Christmas Present.

Rather to their surprise, Dr. Fell grew grave.

"Oddly enough, I think it would be advisable to talk of it. Archons of Athens! It's quite possible the matter may have some bearing on—"

He hesitated.

"On what?"

"On Angus Campbell's murder," said Dr. Fell.

Colin whistled, and then there was a silence. Muttering to himself, Dr. Fell appeared to be trying to chew at the end of his bandit's mustache.

"Perhaps," he went on, "I had better explain. I was very happy to get my friend Colin Campbell's invitation. I was much intrigued by the full details of the case as he wrote them. Putting in my pocket my Boswell and my toothbrush, I took a train for the North. I beguiled my time rereading the great Doctor Johnson's views on this country. You are no doubt familiar with his stern reply when told that he should not be so hard on Scotland since, after all, God had made Scotland? 'Sir, comparisons are invidious; but God made hell.' "

Colin gestured impatiently. "Never mind that. What were you saying?"

"I arrived in Dunoon," said Dr. Fell, "early yesterday evening. I tried to get a car at the tourist agency—"

"We know it," said Kathryn.

"But was informed that the only car then available had already taken a batch of people to Shira. I asked when the car would be back. The clerk said it would not be back. He said he had just that moment received a telephone call from Inveraray from the driver, a man named Fleming—"

"Jock," Colin explained to the others.

"The driver said that one of his passengers, a gentleman called Swan, had decided to stay the night in Inveraray, and wanted to keep car and driver to take him back to Dunoon in the morning. This, with suitable costs, was arranged."

"Infernal snooper," roared Colin.

"One moment. The clerk said, however, that if I would come to the agency at half past nine in the morning—this morning—the car would be back and would take me to Shira.

"I spent the night at the hotel, and was there on time. I then observed the somewhat unusual spectacle of a motorcar coming along the main street with its one passenger, a man in a gray hat and a very violent tartan necktie, standing up in the back seat."

Colin Campbell glowered at the floor.

A vast, dreamy expression of pleasure went over Dr. Fell's face. His eye was on a corner of the ceiling. He cleared his throat.

"Intrigued as to why this man should be standing up, I

made inquiries. He replied (somewhat curtly) that he found the sitting position painful. It required little subtlety to get the story out of him. Indeed, he was boiling with it. Harrumph."

Alan groaned.

Dr. Fell peered over his eyeglasses, first at Alan and then at Kathryn. He wheezed. His expression was one of gargantuan delicacy.

"May I inquire," he said, "whether you two are engaged to be married?"

"Certainly not!" cried Kathryn.

"Then," Dr. Fell urged warmly, "in heaven's name *get* married. Do it in a hurry. You both hold responsible positions. But what you are likely to read about yourselves in today's *Daily Floodlight,* at risk of libel or no, is not likely to find favor with either Highgate University or the Harpenden College for Women. That thrilling story of the moonlight chase with claymores, with the lady shouting encouragement while the two cutthroats pursued him, really did put the tin hat on it."

"I never shouted encouragement!" said Kathryn.

Dr. Fell blinked at her.

"Are you sure you didn't, ma'am?"

"Well . . ."

"I'm afraid you did, Kitty-kat," observed Colin, glaring at the floor. "But it was my fault. I—"

Dr. Fell made a gesture.

"No matter," he said. "That was not what I wanted to tell you. Intrigued and inspired by this revival of old Highland customs, I spoke with the driver, Mr. Fleming."

"Yes?"

"Now here is what I most seriously want to ask. Did any of you, last night, at any time go up into the tower? *Any of you, at any time?*"

There was a silence. The windows facing the loch were open to a clear, cool, pleasant day. They all looked at each other.

"No," returned Kathryn.

"No," stated Colin.

"You're quite sure of that, now?"

"Definitely."

"Mr. Swan," Dr. Fell went on, with a curious insistence which Alan found disturbing, "says that the two men were 'dressed up' in some way."

"Oh, it's silly and horrible!" said Kathryn. "And it's all Alan's fault. They weren't exactly 'dressed up.' They had checkered tablecloths draped over their shoulders for plaids, that's all."

"Nothing else?"

"No."

Dr. Fell drew in his breath. His expression remained so grave, his color so high, that nobody spoke.

"I repeat," Dr. Fell continued, "that I questioned the driver. Getting information out of him was rather more difficult than drawing teeth. But on one point he did give some information. He says that this place is not 'canny'—"

Colin interrupted with a fierce grunt of impatience, but Dr. Fell silenced him.

"And now he says he's in a position to swear to it."

"How?"

"Last night, after they had put up at Inveraray, Swan asked him to drive back here. Swan was going to have another try at getting in to see Miss Elspat Campbell. Now let's see if I've got the geography straight. The road to Inveraray runs along the back of the house, doesn't it?"

"Yes."

"And the front door faces the loch, as we see. Swan asked the driver to walk round and knock at the front door, as a sort of messenger, while Swan remained at the back. The driver did so. It was bright moonlight, remember."

"Well?"

"He was just about to knock at the door, when he happened to look up at the window of the tower room. And he saw somebody or something at that window."

"But that's impossible!" cried Kathryn. "We were—"

Dr. Fell examined his hands, which were folded on the handle of his stick.

Then Dr. Fell looked up.

"Fleming," he went on, "swears he saw something in Highland costume, with half its face shot away, looking down at him."

Chapter 10

IT IS ALL VERY WELL to be hardheaded. Most of us are, even with headaches and shaky nerves. But to find a breath of superstitious terror is far from difficult here.

"Were you thinking," asked Kathryn, "of that story of what happened after the massacre of Glencoe? That the ghost of one of the victims pursued a man called Ian Campbell, who—"

Despairing of words, she made a gesture as of one who jumps.

Colin's face was fiery.

"Ghosts!" he said. "Ghosts! Look here. In the first place, there never was any such tradition as that. It was put into a lying guidebook because it sounded pretty. Professional soldiers in those days weren't so thin-skinned about executing orders.

"In the second place, that room's not haunted. Angus slept there every night for years, and *he* never saw a bogle. You don't believe such rubbish, do you, Fell?"

Dr. Fell remained unruffled.

"I am merely," he answered mildly, "stating what the driver told me."

"Rubbish. Jock was pulling your leg."

"And yet, d'ye know,"—Dr. Fell screwed up his face— "he hardly struck me as a man addicted to that form of gammon. I have usually found that Gaels will joke about anything except ghosts. Besides, I think you miss the real point of the story."

He was silent for a moment.

"But when did this happen?" asked Alan.

"Ah, yes. It was just before the two cutthroats with their lady came out of the back door and set on Swan. Fleming didn't knock at the front door after all. Hearing the shouts, he went to the back. He started up his car and eventually picked up Swan on the road. But he says he wasn't feeling too well. He says he stood in the moonlight for several minutes after he'd seen the thing at the window, and didn't feel too well at all. I can't say I blame him."

Kathryn hesitated. "What did it look like?"

"Bonnet and plaid and face caved in. That's all he could tell with any distinctness."

"Not a kilt too?"

"He wouldn't have been able to see a kilt. He only saw the upper half of the figure. He says it looked decayed, as though the moths had got at it, and it had only one eye." Again the doctor cleared his throat, rumblingly. "The point, however, is this. Who, besides you three, was in the house last night?"

"Nobody," replied Kathryn, "except Aunt Elspat and Kirstie, the maid. And they'd gone to bed."

"I tell you it's rubbish!" snarled Colin.

"Well, you can speak to Jock himself, if you like. He's out in the kitchen now."

Colin rose to find Jock and end this nonsense; but he did not do so. Alistair Duncan, followed by a patient but weary-looking Walter Chapman, was ushered in by the maid Kirstie—a scared-eyed, soft-voiced girl whose self-effacing habits rendered her almost invisible.

The lawyer made no reference to last night's rumpus with Colin. He stood very stiffly.

"Colin Campbell—" he began.

"Look here," grumbled Colin, shoving his hands into his pockets, lowering his neck into his collar, and looking like a Newfoundland dog which has been at the larder. "I owe you an apology, dammit. I apologize. I was wrong. There."

Duncan expelled his breath.

"I am glad, sir, that you have the decency to acknowledge it. Only my long friendship with your family enables me to overlook a piece of ill manners so uncalled-for and so flagrant."

"Hoy! Now wait a bit! Wait a bit! I didn't say—"

"So let us think no more about it," concluded the lawyer, as Colin's eye began to gleam again. Duncan coughed, indicating that he had left personal matters and now dealt with business.

"I thought I had better inform you," he went on, "that they think they may have found Alec Forbes."

"Wow! Where?"

"He's been reported to have been seen at a crofter's cottage near Glencoe."

Chapman intervened.

"Can't we settle it?" the insurance man suggested. "Glencoe's no great distance from here, as I understand it. You could drive there and back easily in an afternoon. Why not hop in my car and run up and see him?"

The lawyer's manner had a sort of corpselike benevolence.

"Patience, my dear fellow. Patience, patience, patience! First let the police find out if it *is* Alec. He has been reported before, you remember. Once in Edinburgh and once in Ayr."

"Alec Forbes," struck in Dr. Fell, "being the sinister figure who called on Mr. Campbell the night the latter died?"

They all swung round. Colin hastily performed an introduction.

"I have heard of you, Doctor," said Duncan, scrutinizing Dr. Fell through his pince-nez. "In fact, I—ah—confess I came here partly in the hope of seeing you. We have here, of course," he smiled, "a clear case of murder. But we are still rather confused about it. Can you unriddle it for us?"

For a moment Dr. Fell did not reply.

He frowned at the floor drawing a design on the carpet with the end of his stick.

"H'mf," he said, and gave the ferrule of the stick a rap

on the floor. "I sincerely trust it is murder. If it is not, I have no interest in it. But—Alec Forbes! Alec Forbes! Alec Forbes!"

"What about him?"

"Well, who is Alec Forbes? What is he? I could bear to know much more of him. For instance: what was the cause of his quarrel with Mr. Campbell?"

"Ice cream," replied Colin.

"What?"

"Ice cream. They were going to make it by a new process, in great quantity. And it was to be colored in different tartan patterns. No, I'm perfectly serious! That's the sort of idea Angus was always getting. They built a laboratory, and used artificial ice—that chemical stuff that's so expensive—and ran up bills and raised merry blazes. Another of Angus's ideas was a new kind of tractor that would both sow and reap. And he also financed those people who were going to find Drake's gold and make all the subscribers millionaires."

"What sort of person is Forbes? Laboring man? Something of that sort?"

"Oh, no. Bloke of some education. But scatty in the money line, like Angus. Lean, dark-faced chap. Moody. Fond of the bottle. Great cyclist."

"H'mf. I see." Dr. Fell pointed with his stick. "That's Angus Campbell's photograph on the mantelpiece there, I take it?"

"Yes."

Dr. Fell got up from the sofa and lumbered across. He carried the crepe-draped picture to the light, adjusted his eyeglasses, and puffed gently as he studied it.

"Not the face, you know," he said, "of a man who commits suicide."

"Definitely not," smiled the lawyer.

"But we can't—" Chapman began.

"Which Campbell are you, sir?" Dr. Fell asked politely.

Chapman threw up his arms in despair.

"I'm not a Campbell at all. I represent the Hercules Insurance Company and I've got to get back to my office

in Glasgow or business will go to blazes. See here, Dr. Fell.
I've heard of you too. They say you're fair-minded. And
I put it to you: how can we go by what a person 'would' or
'wouldn't' have done, when the evidence shows he *did* do
it."

"All evidence," said Dr. Fell, "points two ways. Like
the ends of a stick. That is the trouble with it."

Absent-mindedly he stumped back to the mantelpiece,
and put the photograph down. He seemed very much disturbed. While his eyeglasses came askew on his nose, he
made what was (for him) the great exertion of feeling
through all his pockets. He produced a sheet of paper
scrawled with notes.

"From the admirably clear letter written by Colin Campbell," he went on, "and from facts he has given me this
morning, I have been trying to construct a précis of what
we know, or think we know."

"Well?" prompted the lawyer.

"With your permission,"—Dr. Fell scowled hideously
—"I should like to read out these points. One or two
things may appear a little clearer, or at least more suggestive, if they are heard in skeleton form. Correct me if I am
wrong in any of them.

"1. Angus Campbell always went to bed at ten
o'clock.

"2. It was his habit to lock and bolt the door on the
inside.

"3. It was his habit to sleep with the window shut.

"4. It was his habit to write up his diary each night
before going to bed."

Dr. Fell blinked up.
"No misstatement there, I trust?"
"No," admitted Colin.
"Then we pass on to the simple circumstances surround-
ing the crime.

"5. Alec Forbes called on A. Campbell at nine-thirty
on the night of the crime.

"6. He forced his way into the house, and went up to Angus's bedroom.

"7. Neither of the two women saw him at this time."

Dr. Fell rubbed his nose.

"Query," he added, "how did Forbes get in, then? Presumably he didn't just break down the front door?"

"If you'd like to step out of that door there," responded Colin, pointing, "you can see. It leads to the ground-floor of the tower. In the ground-floor room there are wooden double-doors leading out to the court. They're supposed to be padlocked, but half the time they're not. That's how Forbes came—without disturbing anybody else."

Dr. Fell made a note.

"That seems to be clear enough. Very well. We now take arms against a sea of troubles.

"8. At this time Forbes was carrying an object like a 'suitcase.'

"9. He had a row with Angus, who evicted him.

"10. Forbes was empty-handed when he left.

"11. Elspat Campbell and Kirstie MacTavish arrived in time to see the eviction.

"12. They were afraid Forbes might have come back. This becomes more understandable when we learn of the isolated tower with its outside entrance and its five empty floors.

"13. They searched the empty room, and also Angus's room.

"14. There was nothing under the bed in Angus's bedroom at this time.

"Still correct?" inquired Dr. Fell, raising his head.

"No, it isna," announced a high, sharp, positive voice which made them all jump.

Nobody had seen Aunt Elspat come in. She stood sternly on her dignity, her hands folded.

Dr. Fell blinked at her. "What isn't true, ma'am?"

"It isna true tae say the box tae carry the dog wasna under the bed when Kirstie and I luked. It was."

Her six auditors regarded her with consternation. Most of them began to speak at once, a frantic babble which was only stilled by Duncan's stern assertion of legal authority.

"Elspat Campbell, listen to me. You said there was nothing there."

"I said there was nae *suitcase* there. I didna say aboot the ither thing."

"Are you telling us that the dog carrier was under the bed before Angus locked and bolted his door?"

"Aye."

"Elspat," said Colin, with a sudden gleam of certainty in his eye, " you're lying. God's wounds, you're lying! You said there was *nothing* under that bed. I heard you myself."

"I'm tellin' ye the gospel truth, and Kirstie will tu." She favored them all with an equally malignant look. "Dinner's on its way, and I'm no' settin' places for the parcel o' ye."

Inflexible, making this very clear, she walked out of the room and closed the door.

The question is, thought Alan, does this alter matters or doesn't it? He shared Colin Campbell's evident conviction that Elspat was lying. But she had one of those faces so used to household deceit, so experienced in lying for what she believed a good purpose, that it was difficult to distinguish between truth and falsehood in anything.

This time it was Dr. Fell who stilled the babble of argument.

"We will query the point," he said, "and continue. The next points define our problem squarely and simply.

"15. Angus locked and bolted his door on the inside.

"16. His dead body was found by the milkman at six o'clock on the following morning, at the foot of the tower.

"17. He had died of multiple injuries caused by the fall.

"18. Death took place between ten p.m. and one a.m.

"19. He had not been drugged or overcome in any way.

"20. The door was still locked and bolted on the

inside. Since the bolt was rusty, difficult to draw and firmly shot in its socket, this rules out any possibility of tampering with it."

In Alan's mind rose the image of the shattered door as he had seen it last night.

He remembered the rustiness of the bolt, and the stubborn lock torn from its frame. Jiggery-pokery with string or any similar device must clearly be put aside. The image faded as Dr. Fell continued.

"21. The window was inaccessible. We have this from a steeple jack.

"22. There was no person hiding in the room.

"23. The bed had been occupied."

Dr. Fell puffed out his cheeks, frowned, and tapped a pencil on the notes.

"Which," he said, "brings us to a point where I must interpose another query. Your letter didn't say. When his body was found in the morning, was he wearing slippers or a dressing gown?"

"No," said Colin. "Just his wool nightshirt."

Dr. Fell made another note.

"24. His diary was missing. This, however, might have been taken at some subsequent time.

"25. Angus's fingerprints, and only his, were found on the catch of the window.

"26. Under the bed was a case of the sort used to carry dogs. It did not belong in the house; had presumably been brought by Forbes; but was in any case not there the night before.

"27. This box was empty.

"We are therefore forced to the conclusion—"

Dr. Fell paused.

"Go on!" Alistair Duncan prompted in a sharp voice. "To what conclusion?"

Dr. Fell sniffed.

"Gentlemen, we can't escape it. It's inevitable. We are

forced to the conclusion that either (a) Angus Campbell deliberately committed suicide, or (b) there was in that box something which made him run for his life to escape it, and crash through the window to his death in doing so."

Kathryn shivered a little. But Chapman was not impressed.

"I know," he said. "Snakes. Spiders. Fu Manchu. We were all over that last night. And it gets us nowhere."

"Can you dispute my facts?" inquired Dr. Fell, tapping the notes.

"No. But can you dispute *mine*? Snakes! Spiders—"

"And now," grinned Colin, "ghosts."

"Eh?"

"A rattlebrain by the name of Jock Fleming," explained Colin, "claims to have seen somebody in Highland dress, with no face, gibbering at the window last night."

Chapman's face lost some of its color.

"I don't know anything about that," he said. "But I could almost as soon believe in a ghost as in a dexterous spider or snake that could close up the clasps of a suitcase afterwards. I'm English. I'm practical. But this is a funny country and a funny house; and I tell you *I* shouldn't care to spend a night up in that room."

Colin got up from his chair and did a little dance round the room.

"That's done it," he roared, when he could get his breath. *"That's torn it!"*

Dr. Fell blinked at him with mild expostulation. Colin's face was suffused and the veins stood out on his thick neck.

"Listen," he went on, swallowing with powerful restraint. "Ever since I got here, everybody has been ghosting me. And I'm sick of it. This tomfoolery has got to be blown sky-high and I'm the jasper to do it. I'll tell you what I'm going to do. I'm going to move my things into that tower this very afternoon, and I'm going to sleep there henceforward. If so much as a ghost of a ghost shows its ugly head there, if anybody tries to make *me* jump out of a window . . ."

His eye fell on the family Bible. The atheistical Colin

ran across to it and put his hand on it.

"Then I hereby swear that I'll go to the kirk every Sunday for the next twelve months. Yes, and prayer meeting too!"

He darted across to the door to the hall, which he set open.

"Do you hear that, Elspat?" he roared, coming back and putting his hand on the Bible again. "Every Sunday, and prayer meeting on Wednesdays. Ghosts! Bogles! Warlocks! Isn't there a sane person left in this world?"

His voice reverberated through the house. You might have imagined that it drew back echoes. But Kathryn's attempt to shush him was unneccessary. Colin already felt better. It was Kirstie MacTavish who supplied the distraction, by thrusting her head in at the doorway and speaking in a tone not far removed from real awe.

"That reporter's back again," she said.

Chapter 11

COLIN OPENED HIS EYES. "Not the chap from the *Daily Floodlight?*"

"It's him."

"Tell him I'll see him," said Colin, straightening his collar and drawing a deep breath.

"No!" said Alan. "In your present state of mind you'd probably cut his heart out and eat it. Let *me* see him."

"Yes, please!" cried Kathryn. She turned a fervent face. "If he's dared to come back here, he can't have said anything very awful about us in the paper. Don't you see: this is our chance to apologize and put everything right again? Please let Alan see him!"

"All right," Colin agreed. "After all, you didn't stick him in the seat of his pants with a claymore. You may be able to smooth him down."

Alan hurried out into the hall. Just outside the front door, clearly of two minds on how to approach this interview, stood Swan. Alan went outside, and carefully closed the front door.

"Look here," he began, "I honestly am terribly sorry about last night. I can't think what came over us. We'd had one over the eight . . ."

"You're telling *me*?" inquired Swan. He looked at Alan, and anger seemed less predominant than real curiosity. "What were you drinking, for God's sake? T.N.T. and monkey glands? I used to be a track man myself, but I never saw anybody cover ground like that thick-set old buster since Nurmi retired to Finland."

"Something like that."

Swan's expression, as he saw that he was dealing with a chastened man, grew increasingly more stern.

"Now look," he said impressively. "You know, don't you, that I could sue you all for heavy damages?"

"Yes, but—"

"And that I've got enough on you to make your name mud in the press, if I was the sort of a fellow who bears malice?"

"Yes; but—"

"You can just thank your lucky stars, Dr. Campbell, that I'm *not* the sort of fellow who bears malice: that's all *I* say." Swan gave a significant nod. He was wearing a new light-gray suit and tartan tie. Again his gloomy sternness was moved by curiosity. "What kind of a professor are you anyway? Running around with women professors from other colleges—always going to houses of ill fame—"

"Here! For the love of—"

"Now don't deny it," said Swan, pointing a lean finger in his face. "I heard Miss Campbell herself say, in front of witnesses, that that's exactly what you were always doing."

"She was talking about the Roman Catholic Church! That's what the old-timers called it."

"It's not what the old-timers called it where *I* come from. On top of that, you get all ginned up and chase respectable people along a public road with broadswords. Do you carry on like that at Highgate, Doc? Or just in vacations? I really want to know."

"I swear to you, it's all a mistake! And here's the point. I don't care what you say about me. But will you promise not to say anything about Miss Campbell?"

Swan considered this.

"Well, I don't know," he said, with another darkly significant shake of his head, and a suggestion that, if he did this, it would be only from the kindness of his heart. "I've got a duty to the public, you know."

"Rubbish."

"But I tell you what I'll do," Swan suggested, as though suddenly coming to a decision. "Just to show you I'm a sport, I'll make a deal with you."

"Deal?"

The other lowered his voice.

"That fellow in there, the great big fat fellow, is Dr. Gideon Fell: isn't it?"

"Yes."

"I only discovered it when he'd slipped away from me. And, when I phoned my paper, they were pretty wild. They say that wherever *he* goes, a story breaks with a wallop. They say to stick to him. Look, Doc. I've *got* to get a story! I've incurred a lot of expense over this thing; I've got another car that's eating its head off. If I fall down on this story I won't get the expenses O.K'd, and I may even get the air."

"So?"

"So here's what I want you to do. Just keep me posted, that's all. Let me know everything that goes on. In return for that—"

He paused, shying back a little, as Colin Campbell came out of the front door. But Colin was trying to be affable: too affable, massively affable, with a guilty grin.

"In return for that, just keeping me posted," resumed Swan, "I'll agree to forget all I know about you and Miss Campbell, and,"—he looked at Colin—"what you did as well, which might have caused me a serious injury. I'll do that just to be a sport and show there are no hard feelings. What do you say?"

Colin's face had lightened with relief.

"I say it's fair enough," Colin returned, with a bellow of pleasure. "Now that's damned decent of you, young fellow! Damned decent! I was tight and I apologize. What do you say, Alan Oig?"

Alan's voice was fervent.

"I say it's fair enough too. You keep to that bargain, Mr. Swan, and you'll have nothing to complain about. If there are any stories going, you shall have them."

He could almost forget that he had a hangover. A beautiful sense of well-being, a sense of the world set right again, crept into Alan Campbell and glowed in his veins.

Swan raised his eyebrows.

"Then it's a deal?"

"It is," said Colin.

"It is," agreed the other miscreant.

"All right, then!" said Swan, drawing a deep breath but still speaking darkly. "Only just remember that I'm straining my duty to my public to oblige you. So remember where we all stand and don't try any—"

Above their heads, a window creaked open. The contents of a large bucket of water, aimed with deadly and scientific accuracy, descended in a solid, glistening sheet over Swan's head. In fact, Swan might be said momentarily to have disappeared.

At the window appeared the malignant face of Aunt Elspat.

"Can ye no' tak' a hint?" she inquired. "I tauld ye to gang your ways, and I'll no' tell ye again. Here's for guid measure."

With the same accuracy, but almost with leisureliness, she lifted a second bucket and emptied it over Swan's head. Then the window closed with a bang.

Swan did not say anything. He stood motionless, and merely looked. His new suit was slowly turning black. His hat resembled a piece of sodden blotting paper from beneath whose down-turned brim there looked out the eyes of a man gradually being bereft of his reason.

"My dear chap!" bellowed Colin in real consternation. "The old witch! I'll wring her neck; so help me, I will! My dear chap, you're not hurt, are you?"

Colin bounded down the steps. Swan began slowly, but with increasing haste, to back away from him.

"My dear chap, wait! Stop! You must have some dry clothes!"

Swan continued to back way.

"Come into the house, my dear fellow. Come—"

Then Swan found his voice.

"Come into the house," he shrilled, backing away still farther, "so you can steal my clothes and turn me out again? No, you don't! Keep away from me!"

"Look out!" screamed Colin. "One more step and you'll be in the loch! Look—"

Alan glanced round wildly. At the windows of the sitting room observed an interested group of watchers composed of Duncan, Chapman, and Dr. Fell. But most of all he was conscious of Kathryn's horror-stricken countenance.

Swan saved himself by some miracle on the edge of the pier.

"Think I'll go into that booby hatch, do you?" Swan was raving. "You're a bunch of criminal lunatics, that's what you are, and I'm going to expose you. I'm going to—"

"Man, you can't walk about like that! You'll catch your death of cold! Come on in. Besides," argued Colin, "you'll be on the scene of it, won't you? Smack in the middle of things alongside Dr. Fell?"

This appeared to make Swan pause. He hesitated. Still streaming like an enthusiastic fountain, he wiped the water from his eyes with a shaky hand, and looked back at Colin with real entreaty.

"Can I depend on that?"

"I swear you can! The old hag has got it in for you, but I'll take care of her. Come on."

Swan seemed to be debating courses. At length he allowed himself to be taken by the arm and urged toward the door. He ducked quickly when he passed the window, as though wondering whether to expect boiling lead.

A scene of some embarrassment ensued inside. The lawyer and the insurance man took a hasty leave. Colin, clucking to his charge, escorted him upstairs to change his clothes. In the sitting room a dejected Alan found Kathryn and Dr. Fell.

"I trust, sir," observed Dr. Fell, with stately courtesy, "you know your own business best. But, candidly, do you really think it's wise to antagonize the press quite so much at that? What did you do to the fellow this time? Duck him in the water butt?"

"We didn't do anything. It was Elspat. She poured two buckets of water on him from the window."

"But is he going to—" cried Kathryn.

"He promises that if we keep him posted about what's going on here, he won't say a word. At least, that's what he *did* promise. I can't say how he's feeling now."

"Keep him posted?" asked Dr. Fell sharply.

"Presumably about what's going on here, and whether this is suicide or murder, and what you think of it." Alan paused. "What do you think, by the way?"

Dr. Fell's gaze moved to the door to the hall, making sure it was firmly closed. He puffed out his cheeks, shook his head, and finally sat down on the sofa again.

"If only the facts," he growled, "weren't so infernally simple! I distrust their simplicity. I have a feeling that there's a trap in them. I should also like to know why Miss Elspat Campbell now wants to change her testimony, and swears that the dog carrier *was* under the bed before the room was locked up."

"Do you think the second version is true?"

"No, by thunder, I don't!" said Dr. Fell, rapping his stick on the floor. "I think the first is true. But that only makes our locked-room problem the worse. Unless—"

"Unless what?"

Dr. Fell disregarded this.

"It apparently does no good merely to repeat those twenty-seven points over and over. I repeat: it's too simple. A man double locks his door. He goes to bed. He gets up in the middle of the night without his slippers (mark that), and jumps from the window to instant death. He—"

"That's not quite accurate, by the way."

Dr. Fell lifted his head, his underlip outthrust.

"Hey? What isn't?"

"Well, if you insist on a shade of accuracy, Angus didn't meet an instant death. At least, so Colin told me. The police surgeon wouldn't be definite about the time of death. He said Angus hadn't died instantly, but had probably been alive though unconscious for a little while before he died."

Dr. Fell's little eyes narrowed. The wheezing breaths, which ran down over the ridges of his waistcoat, were almost stilled. He seemed about to say something, but checked himself.

"I further," he said, "don't like Colin's insistence on spending the night in that tower room."

"You don't think there's any more danger?" Kathryn asked.

"My dear child! Of course there's danger!" said Dr. Fell. "There's always danger when some agency we don't understand killed a man. Pry the secret out of it, and you're all right. But so long as you don't understand it . . ."

He brooded.

"You have probably observed that the very things we try hardest to avoid happening are always the things that do happen. *Vide* the saga of Swan. But here, in an uglier way, we have the same wheel revolving and the same danger returning. Archons of Athens! What COULD have been in that dog carrier? Something that left *no* trace, nothing whatever? And why the open end? Obviously so that something could breathe through the wire and get air. But what?"

Distorted pictures, all without form, floated in Alan's mind.

"You don't think the box may be a red herring?"

"It may be. But, unless it does mean something, the whole case collapses and we may as well go home to bed. It has got to mean something."

"Some kind of animal?" suggested Kathryn.

"Which closed the clasps of the box after it got out?" inquired Dr. Fell.

"That may not be so difficult," Alan pointed out, "if it were thin enough to get out through the wire. No, hang it, that won't do!" He remembered the box itself, and the mesh. "That wire is so close-meshed that the smallest snake in existence could hardly wriggle out through it."

"Then," pursued Dr. Fell," "there is the episode of the Highlander with the caved-in face."

"You don't believe that story?"

"I believe that Jock Fleming saw what he says he saw. I do not necessarily believe in a ghost. After all, such a piece of trickery, in the moonlight and from a distance of sixty feet up in a tower, wouldn't be very difficult. An old bonnet and a plaid, a little make-up—"

"But why?"

Dr. Fell's eyes opened wide. His breath labored with ghoulish eagerness as he seemed to seize on the point.

"Exactly. That's it. Why? We mustn't miss the importance of the tale: which is not whether it was supernatural, but why it was done at all. That is, if it had any reason at all in the way we mean." He became very thoughtful. "Find the contents of that box, and we're on the view halloo. That's our problem. Some parts of the business, of course, are easy. You will already have guessed who stole the missing diary?"

"Of course," replied Kathryn instantly. "*Elspat* stole it, of course."

Alan stared at her.

Dr. Fell, with a vast and gratified beam, regarded her as though she were a more refreshing person than even he had expected, and nodded.

"Admirable!" he chuckled. "The talent for deduction developed by judicious historical research can just as well be applied to detective work. Never forget that, my dear. *I* learned it at an early age. Bull's-eye. It was Elspat for a fiver."

"But why?" demanded Alan.

Kathryn set her face into its severest lines, as though they had again returned to the debate of two nights ago. Her tone was withering.

"My *dear* Dr. Campbell!" she said. "Consider what we know. For many, many years she was rather more than a housekeeper to Angus Campbell?"

"Well?"

"But she's horribly, morbidly respectable, and doesn't even believe anybody's guessed her real thoughts?"

(Alan was tempted to say, "Something like you," but he restrained himself.)

"Yes."

"Angus Campbell was a free-spoken person who kept a diary where he could record his intimate—well, you know!"

"Yes?"

"All right. Three days before his death, Angus takes out still another insurance policy, to take care of his old-time love in the event of his death. It's almost certain, isn't it, that in writing down that he did take out an insurance policy he'll make some reference to *why* he did it?"

She paused, raising her eyebrows.

So, of course, Elspat stole the diary out of some horrid fear of having people learn what she did years and years ago.

"Don't you remember what happened last night, Alan? How she acted when you and Colin began talking about the diary? When you did begin to discuss it, she first said everybody was daft and finally headed you off by suggesting that wretched whisky? And, of course, it did head you off. That's all."

Alan whistled.

"By gad, I believe you're right!"

"Thank you so much, dear. If you were to apply a little of that brain of yours," remarked Kathryn, wrinkling up her pretty nose, "to observing and drawing the inferences you're always telling everyone else to draw—"

Alan treated this with cold scorn. He had half a mind to make some reference to the Duchess of Cleveland, and the paucity of inference K. I. Campbell had been able to draw there, but he decided to give that unfortunate court lady a rest.

"Then the diary hasn't really anything to do with the case?"

"I wonder," said Dr. Fell.

"Obviously," Kathryn pointed out," "Aunt Elspat knows *something*. And probably from the diary. Otherwise why all this business of writing to the *Daily Floodlight*?"

"Yes."

"And since she did write to them, it seems fairly clear that there wasn't anything in the diary to compromise her reputation. Then why on earth doesn't she speak out? What's the matter with her? If the diary gives some indication that Angus was murdered, why doesn't she say so?"

"Unless, of course," said Alan, "the diary says that he meant to commit suicide."

"Alan, Alan, Alan! To say nothing of all the other policies, Angus takes out a last policy, pays the premium, and then writes down that he's going to kill himself? It's just—against nature, that's all!"

Alan gloomily admitted this.

"Thirty-five thousand pounds in the balance," breathed Kathryn, "and she won't claim it. Why doesn't somebody tackle her about it? Why don't you tackle her, Dr. Fell? Everybody else seems to be afraid of her."

"I shall be most happy," beamed Dr. Fell.

Ponderously, like a man-o'-war easing into a dock, he turned round on the sofa. He adjusted his eyeglasses, and blinked at Elspat Campbell, who was standing in the doorway with an expression between wrath, pain, uncertainty, and the fear of damnation. They caught only the tail of this expression, which was gone in a flash, to be replaced by a tightening of the jaws and a determination of granite inflexibility.

Dr. Fell was not impressed.

"Well, ma'am?" he inquired offhandedly. "You really did pinch that diary, didn't you?"

Chapter 12

TWILIGHT WAS DEEPENING over Loch Fyne as they descended through the gray ghostly wood of fallen trees, and turned northwards along the main road to Shira.

Alan felt healthily and pleasantly tired after an afternoon in the open. Kathryn, in tweeds and flat-heeled shoes, had color in her cheeks and her blue eyes glowed. She had not once put on her spectacles for argument, even when she had been clucked at for being unfamiliar with the murder of the Red Fox, Colin Campbell of 1752, who had been shot by nobody knows whose hand, but for which James Stewart was tried at Inveraray courthouse.

"The trouble is," Alan was declaring, as they tramped down the hill, "Stevenson has so cast the glamour over us that we tend to forget what this 'hero,' this famous Alan Breck—one 'l,' please—was actually like. I've often wished somebody would take the side of the Campbells, for a change."

"Intellectual honesty again?"

"No. Just for fun. But the weirdest version of the incident was in the film version of *Kidnapped*. Alan Breck, and David Balfour, and a totally unnecessary female, are fleeing from the redcoats. Disguised up to the ears, they are driving in a cart along a troop-infested road, singing 'Loch Lomond'; and Alan Breck hisses, 'They'll never suspect us now.'

"I felt like arising and addressing the screen, saying: 'They damn well will if you insist on singing a Jacobite song.' That's about as sensible as though a group of British secret service agents, disguised as Gestapo, were to swagger down Unter den Linden singing, *There'll Always be an England*."

Kathryn seized on the essential part of this.

"So the female was totally unnecessary, eh?"

"What's that?"

"The female, says he in all his majesty, was totally unnecessary. Of course!"

"I only mean that she wasn't in the original version, and she spoiled what little story was left. Can't you forget this sex war for five minutes?"

"It's you who are always dragging it in."

"Me?"

"Yes, you. I don't know what to make of you. You—you *can* be rather nice, you know, when you try." She kicked the fallen leaves out of her path, and suddenly began to giggle. 'I was thinking about last night."

"Don't remind me!"

"But that's when you were nicest, really. Don't you remember what you said to me?"

He had thought the incident buried in merciful oblivion It was not.

"What did I say?"

"Never mind. We're terribly late for tea again, and Aunt Elspat will carry on again, just as she did last night."

"Aunt Elspat," he said sternly, "Aunt Elspat, as you very well know, won't be down to tea. She's confined to her room with a violent and hysterical fit of the sulks."

Kathryn stopped and made a hopeless gesture.

"You know, I can't decide whether I like that old woman or whether I'd like to murder her. Dr. Fell tackles her about the diary, and all she does is go clear up in the air, and scream that it's her house, and she won't be bullied, and the dog carrier *was* under the bed—"

"Yes; but—"

"I think she just wants her own way. I think she won't tell anybody anything just because they want her to, and she's determined to be the boss. Just as she finished off in real sulks because Colin insisted on having that poor inoffensive Swan man in the house."

"Young lady, don't evade the question. What was it I said to you last night?"

The little vixen, he thought, was deliberately doing this. He wanted not to give her the satisfaction of showing curiosity. But he could not help it. They had come out into the main road only half a dozen yards from the Castle of Shira. Kathryn turned a demure but wicked-looking countenance in the twilight.

"If you can't remember," she told him innocently, "I can't repeat it to you. But I can tell you what my answer would have been, if I had made any answer."

"Well?"

"Oh, I should probably have said something like, 'In that case, why don't you?' "

Then she ran from him.

He caught up with her only in the hall, and there was no time to say anything more. The thunder of voices from the dining room would have warned them of what was in progress, even had they not caught sight of Colin through the partly open door.

The bright light shone over a snug table. Colin, Dr. Fell, and Charles Swan had finished a very large meal. Their plates were pushed to one side, and in the center of the table stood a decanter bearing a rich brown liquid. On the faces of Dr Fell and Swan, before whom stood empty glasses, was the expression of men who have just passed through a great spiritual experience. Colin twinkled at them.

"Come in!" he cried to Kathryn and Alan. "Sit down. Eat before it gets cold. I've just been giving our friends their first taste of the Doom of the Campbells."

Swan's expression, preternaturally solemn, was now marred by a slight hiccup. But he remained solemn, and seemed to be meditating a profound experience.

His costume, too, was curious. He had been fitted out with one of Colin's shirts, which was too big in the shoulders and body, but much too short in the sleeves. Below this since no pair of trousers in the house would fit him, he wore a kilt. It was the very dark green and blue of the Campbells, with thin transversing stripes of yellow and crossed white.

"Cripes!" Swan muttered, contemplating the empty glass. "Cripes!"

"The observation," said Dr. Fell, passing his hand across a pink forehead, "is not unwarranted."

"Like it?"

"Well—" said Swan.

"Have another? What about you, Alan? And you, Kitty-kat?"

"No." Alan was very firm about this "I want some food. Maybe a little of that alcoholic tabasco sauce later, but a very little and not now."

Colin rubbed his hands.

"Oh, you will! They all do. What do you think of our friend Swan's getup? Neat, eh? I fished it out of a chest in the best bedroom. The original tartan of the Clan Mac-Holster."

Swan's face darkened.

"Are you kidding me?"

"As I believe in heaven," swore Colin, lifting his hand, "that's the MacHolster tartan as sure as I believe in heaven."

Swan was mollified. In fact, he seemed to be enjoying himself.

"It's a funny feeling," he said, eyeing the kilt. "Like walking around in public without your pants. Cripes, though! To think that I, Charley Swan of Toronto, should be wearing a real kilt in a real Scotch castle, and drinking old dew of the mountain like a clansman! I must write to my father about this. It's decent of you to let me stay all night."

"Nonsense! Your clothes won't be ready until morning, anyway. Have another?"

"Thanks. I don't mind if I do."

"You, Fell?"

"Harrumph," said Dr. Fell. "That is an offer (or, in this

case, challenge) I very seldom refuse. Thank'ee. But—"

"But what?"

"I was just wondering," said Dr. Fell, crossing his knees with considerable effort, "whether the *nunc bibendum est* is to be followed by a reasonable *sat prata hiberunt*. In more elegant language, you're not thinking of another binge? Or have you given up the idea of sleeping in the tower tonight?"

Colin stiffened.

A vague qualm of uneasiness brushed the old room.

"And why should I give up the idea of sleeping in the tower?"

"It's just because I don't know why you shouldn't," returned Dr. Fell frankly, "that I wish you wouldn't."

"Rubbish! I've spent half the afternoon repairing the lock and bolt of that door. I've carried my duds up there. You don't think *I'm* going to commit suicide?"

"Well," said Dr. Fell, "suppose you did?"

The sense of uneasiness had grown greater. Even Swan seemed to feel it. Colin was about to break out into hollow incredulity, but Dr. Fell stopped him.

"One moment. Merely suppose that. Or, to be more exact, suppose that tomorrow morning we find you dead at the foot of the tower under just such circumstances as Angus. Er—do you mind if I smoke while you're eating, Miss Campbell?"

"No, of course not," said Kathryn.

Dr. Fell took out a large meerschaum pipe with a curved stem, which he filled from an obese pouch, and lighted. He sat back in his chair, argumentatively. With a somewhat cross-eyed expression behind his eyeglasses, he watched the smoke curl up into the bright bowl of the lamp.

"You believe," he went on, "you believe that your brother's death was murder: don't you?"

"I do! And I thundering well hope it was! If it was, and we can prove it, I inherit seventeen thousand five hundred pounds."

"Yes. But if Angus's death *was* murder, then the same

force which killed Angus can kill you. Had you thought of that?"

"I'd like to see the force that could do it: God's wounds, I would!" snapped Colin.

But the calmness of Dr. Fell's voice had its effect. Colin's tone was considerably more subdued.

"Now, if anything should by any chance happen to you," pursued Dr. Fell, while Colin stirred, "what becomes of your share of the thirty-five thousand pounds? Does it revert to Elspat Campbell, for instance?"

"No, certainly not. It's kept in the family. It goes to Robert. Or to Robert's heirs if he's not alive."

"Robert?"

"Our third brother. He got into trouble and skipped the country years ago. We don't even know where he is, though Angus was always trying to find him. We do know he married and had children, the only one of us three who did marry. Robert would be—about sixty-four now. A year younger than I am."

Dr. Fell continued to smoke meditatively, his eye on the lamp.

"You see," he wheezed, "assuming this to be murder, we have got to look for a motive. And a motive, on the financial side at least, is very difficult to find. Suppose Angus was murdered for his life-insurance money. By you. (Tut, now, don't jump down my throat!) Or by Elspat. Or by Robert or his heirs. Yet no murderer in his senses, under those circumstances, is going to plan a crime which will be taken for suicide. Thereby depriving himself of the money which was the whole motive for the crime.

"So we come back to the personal. This man Alec Forbes now. I suppose he was capable of killing Angus?"

"Oh, Lord, yes!"

"H'm. Tell me. Has he got any grudge against you?"

Colin swelled with a kind of obscure satisfaction.

"Alec Forbes," Colin replied, "hates my guts almost as much as he hated Angus's. I ridiculed his schemes. And if there's one thing one of these moody chaps can't stand, it's ridicule. I never disliked the fellow myself, though."

"Yet you admit that the thing which killed Angus could kill you?"

Colin's neck hunched down into his shoulders. He stretched out his hand for the decanter of whisky. He poured out very large portions of it for Dr. Fell, for Swan for Alan, and for himself.

"If you're trying to persuade me not to sleep in the tower—"

"I am."

"Then be hanged to you. Because I'm going to." Colin scanned the faces round him with fiery eyes. "What's the matter with all of you?" he roared. "Are you all dead tonight? We had things better last night. Drink up! I'm not going to commit suicide; I promise you that. So drink up, and let's have no more of this tomfoolery now."

When they separated to go to bed at shortly past ten o'clock, not a man in that room was cold sober.

In gradations of sobriety they ranged from Swan, who had taken the stuff indiscreetly and could barely stand, to Dr. Fell, whom nothing seemed to shake. Colin Campbell was definitely drunk, though his footstep was firm and only his reddish eyes betrayed him. But he was not drunk with the grinning, whooping abandon of the night before.

Nobody was. It had become one of those evenings when even the tobacco smoke turns stale and sour; and men, perversely, keep taking the final one which they don't need. When Kathryn slipped away before ten, no one attempted to stop her.

On Alan the liquor was having a wrong effect. Counteracting the weariness of his relaxed muscles, it stung him to tired but intense wakefulness. Thoughts scratched in his mind like pencils on slate; they would not go away or be still.

His bedroom was up on the first floor, overlooking the loch. His legs felt light as he ascended the stairs, saying good night to Dr. Fell, who went to his own room (surprisingly) with magazines under his arm.

A lightness in the legs, a buzzing head, an intense discomfort, are no tonics for sleep. Alan groped into his room. Either out of economy or because of the sketchiness of the blackout, the chandelier contained no electric bulbs and only a candle could be used for illumination.

Alan lit the candle on the bureau. The meager little flame intensified the surrounding darkness, and made his face in the mirror look white. It seemed to him that he was tottering; that he was a fool to have touched that stuff again, since this time it brought neither exhilaration nor surcease.

Round and round whirled his thoughts, jumping from one point to another like clumsy mountain goats. People used to study by candlelight. It was a wonder they hadn't all gone blind. Maybe most of them had. He thought of Mr. Pickwick in the Great White Horse at Ipswich. He thought of Scott ruining his eyesight by working under "a broad star of gas." He thought of . . .

It was no good. He *couldn't* sleep.

He undressed, stumbling, in the dark. He put on slippers and a dressing gown.

His watch ticked on. Ten-thirty. A quarter to eleven. The hour itself. Eleven-fifteen . . .

Alan sat down in a chair, put his head in his hands, and wished passionately for something to read. He had noticed very few books at Shira. Dr. Fell, the doctor had informed him that day, had brought a Boswell along.

What a solace, what a soothing and comfort, Boswell would be now! To turn over those pages, to talk with Doctor Johnson until you drifted into a doze, must be the acme of all pleasure on this night. The more he thought of it, the more he wished he had it. Would Dr. Fell lend it to him, for instance?

He got up, opened the door, and padded down a chilly hall to the doctor's room. He could have shouted for joy when he saw a thin line of light under the sill of the door. He knocked, and was told to come in in a voice which he hardly recognized as that of Dr. Fell.

Alan, strung to a fey state of awareness, felt his scalp stir with terror as he saw the expression on Dr. Fell's face.

Dr. Fell sat by the chest of drawers, on top of which a

candle was burning in its holder. He wore an old purple dressing gown as big as a tent. The meerschaum pipe hung from one corner of his mouth. Round him was scattered a heap of magazines, letters, and what looked like bills. Through a mist of tobacco smoke in the airless room, Alan saw the startled, faraway expression of Dr. Fell's eyes, the open mouth which barely supported the pipe.

"Thank God you're here!" rumbled Dr. Fell, suddenly coming to life. "I was just going to fetch you."

"Why?"

"I know what was in that box," said Dr. Fell. "I know how the trick was worked. I know what set on Angus Campbell."

The candle flame wavered slightly among shadows. Dr. Fell reached out for his crutch-handled stick, and groped wildly before he found it.

"We've got to get Colin out of that room," he added. "There may not be any danger; there probably isn't; but, by thunder, we can't afford to take any chances! I can show him now what did it, and he's got to listen to reason. See here."

Puffing and wheezing, he impelled himself to his feet.

"I underwent the martyrdom of climbing up those tower stairs once before today, but I can't do it again. Will you go up there and rout Colin out?"

"Of course."

"We needn't rouse anybody else. Just bang on the door until he lets you in; don't take no for an answer. Here. I've got a small torch. Keep it shielded when you go up the stairs, or you'll have the wardens after us. Hurry!"

"But what——"

"I haven't time to explain now. Hurry!"

Alan took the torch. Its thin, pale beam explored ahead of him. He went out in the hall, which smelt of old umbrellas, and down the stairs. A chilly draught touched his ankles. He crossed the lower hall, and went into the living room.

Across the room, on the mantelpiece, the face of Angus Campbell looked back at him as the beam of his torch rested on the photograph. Angus's white, fleshy-jowled countenance seemed to stare back with the knowledge of a secret.

The door leading to the ground floor of the tower was locked on the inside. When Alan turned the squeaky key and opened the door, his fingers were shaking.

Now the earthen floor under him felt icy. A very faint mist had crept in from the loch. The arch leading to the tower stairs, a gloomy hole, repelled and somewhat unnerved him. Though he started to take the stairs at a run, both the dangerous footing and the exertion of the climb forced him to slow down.

First floor. Second floor, more of a pull. Third floor, and he was breathing hard. Fourth floor, and the distance up seemed endless. The little pencil of light intensified the coldness and close claustrophobia brought on by that enclosed space. It would not be pleasant to meet suddenly, on the stairs, a man in Highland costume with half his face shot away.

Or have the thing come out of one of the tower rooms, for instance, and touch him on the shoulder from behind.

You could not get away from anything that close to pursue you here.

Alan reached the airless, windowless landing on which was the door to the topmost room. The oak door, its wood rather rotted by damp, was closed. Alan tried the knob, and found that it was locked and bolted on the inside.

He lifted his fist and pounded heavily on the door.

"Colin!" he shouted. "Colin!"

There was no reply.

The thunder of the knocking, the noise of his own voice, rebounded with infernal and intolerable racket in that confined space. He felt it must wake everybody in the house; everybody in Inveraray, for that matter. But he continued to knock and shout, still with no reply.

He set his shoulder to the door, and pushed. He got down on his knees, and tried to peer under the sill of the door, but he could see nothing except an edge of moonlight.

As he got to his feet again, feeling lightheaded after that exertion, the suspicion which had already struck him grew and grew with ugly effect. Colin *might* be only heavily asleep, of course, after all that whisky. On the other hand ——

Alan turned round, and plunged down the treacherous stairs. The breath in his lungs felt like a rasping saw, and several times he had to pull up. He had even forgotten the Highlander. It seemed half an hour, and was actually two or three minutes, before he again reached the bottom of the stairs.

The double doors leading out into the court were closed, but the padlock was not caught. Alan threw them open—creaking, quivering frames of wood which bent like bow shafts as they scraped the flagstones.

He ran out into the court, and circled round the tower to the side facing the loch. There he stopped short. He knew what he would find, and he found it.

The sickening plunge had been taken again.

Colin Campbell—or a bundle or red-and-white striped pajamas which might once have been Colin—lay face downwards on the flagstones. Sixty feet above his head the leaves of the window stood open, and glinted by the light of the waning moon. A thin white mist, which seemed to hang above the water rather than rise from it, had made beads of dew settle on Colin's shaggy hair.

Chapter 13

DAWN—warm gold and white kindling from smoky purple, yet of a soap-bubble luminousness which tinged the whole sky—dawn was clothing the valley when Alan again climbed the tower stairs. You could almost taste the early autumn air.

But Alan was in no mood to enjoy it.

He carried a chisel, an auger, and a saw. Behind him strode a nervous, wiry-looking Swan in a now-dry gray suit which had once been fashionable but which at present resembled sackcloth.

"But are you sure you want to go in there?" insisted Swan. "I'm not keen on it myself."

"Why not?" said Alan. "It's daylight. The Occupant of the box can't hurt us now."

"What occupant?"

Alan did not reply. He thought of saying that Dr. Fell now knew the truth, though he had not divulged it yet; and that Dr. Fell said there was no danger. But he decided such matters were best kept from the papers as yet.

"Hold the torch," he requested. "I can't see why they didn't put a window on this landing. Colin repaired this door yesterday afternoon, you remember. We're now going to arrange matters so that it can't be repaired again in a hurry."

While Swan held the light, he set to work. It was slow work, boring a line of holes touching each other in a square round the lock, and Alan's hands were clumsy on the auger.

When he had finished them, and splintered the result with a chisel, he got purchase for the saw and slowly sawed along the line of the holes.

"Colin Campbell," observed Swan, suddenly and tensely, "was a good guy. A real good guy."

"What do you mean, 'was'?"

"Now that he's dead ———"

"But he's not dead."

There was an appreciable silence.

"Not dead?"

The saw rasped and bumped. All the violence of Alan's relief, all the sick reaction after what he had seen, went into his attack on the door. He hoped Swan would shut up. He had liked Colin Campbell immensely, too much to want to hear any sickly sentimentalities.

"Colin," he went on, without looking round to see Swan's expression, "has got two broken legs and a broken hipbone. And, for a man of his age, that's no joke. Also, there's something else Dr. Grant is very much excited about. But he's not dead and he's unlikely to die."

"A fall like that ——"

"It happens sometimes. You've probably heard of people falling from heights greater than that and sometimes not even being hurt at all. And if they're tight, as Colin was, that helps too."

"Yet he deliberately jumped from the window?"

"Yes."

In a fine powdering of sawdust, the last tendon of wood fell free. Alan pushed the square panel inwards, and it fell on the floor. He reached through, finding the key still securely turned and the rusty bolt shot home immovably in its socket. He turned the key, pulled back the bolt; and, not without a qualm of apprehension, opened the door.

In the clear, fresh light of dawn, the room appeared tousled and faintly sinister. Colin's clothes, as he had untidily undressed, lay flung over the chairs and over the floor. His watch ticked on the chest of drawers. The bed had been slept in; its clothes were now flung back, and the pillows punched into a heap which still held the impression of a head.

The wide-open leaves of the window creaked gently as an air touched them.

"What are you going to do?" asked Swan, putting his head round the edge of the door and at last deciding to come in.

"What Dr. Fell asked me to do."

Though he spoke easily enough, he had to get a grip on himself before he knelt down and felt under the bed. He drew out the leather dog carrier which had contained the Occupant.

"You're not going to fool around with the thing?" asked Swan.

"Dr. Fell said to open it. He said there wouldn't be any fingerprints, so not to bother about them."

"You're taking a lot for granted on that old boy's word. But if you know what you're doing—open it."

This part was the hardest. Alan flicked back the catches with his thumbs, and lifted the lid.

As he had expected, the box was empty. Yet his imagination could have pictured, and was picturing, all sorts of unpleasant things he might have seen.

"What did the old boy tell you to do?" inquired Swan.

"Just open it, and make sure it was empty."

"But what *could* have been in it?" roared Swan. "I tell you, I'm going nuts trying to figure this thing out! I—" Swan paused. His eyes widened, and then narrowed. He extended a finger to point to the rolltop desk.

On the edge of the desk, half hidden by papers but in a place where it certainly had not been the day before, lay a small leather book of pocket size, on whose cover was stamped, in gilt letters, *Diary, 1940.*

"That wouldn't be what you've been looking for, would it?"

Both of them made a dart for the diary, but Alan got there first.

The name Angus Campbell was written on the flyleaf in a small but stiff and schoolboyish kind of hand which made Alan suspect arthritis in the fingers. Angus had carefully filled out the chart for all the miscellaneous information, such as the size of his collar and the size of his shoes (why the makers of these diaries think we are likely to forget the size of our collars remains a mystery); and after "motorcar license number" he had written "none."

But Alan did not bother with this. The diary was full of entries all crammed together and crammed downhill. The last entry was made on the night of Angus's death, Saturday the twenty-fourth of August. Alan Campbell became conscious of tightened throat muscles, and a heavy thumping in his chest, as his eye encountered the item.

"*Saturday.* Check cleared by bank. O.K. Elspat poorly again. Memo: syrup of figs. Wrote to Colin. A. Forbes here tonight. Claims I cheated him. Ha ha ha. Said not to come back. He said he wouldn't, wasn't necessary. Funny musty smell in room tonight. Memo: write to War Office about tractor. Use for army. Do this tomorrow.

Then there was the blank which indicated the end of the writer's span of life.

Alan flicked back over the pages. He did not read any more, though he noticed that at one point a whole leaf had been torn out. He was thinking of the short, heavy, bulbous-nosed old man with the white hair, writing these words while something waited for him.

"H'm," said Swan. "That isn't much help, is it?"

"I don't know."

"Well," said Swan, "if you've seen what you came to see, or rather what you didn't see, let's get downstairs again, shall we? There may be nothing wrong with this place, but it gives me the willies."

Slipping the diary into his pocket, Alan gathered up the tools and followed. In the sitting room downstairs they found Dr. Fell, fully dressed in an old black alpaca suit and string tie. Alan noticed with surprise that his box-pleated cape and shovel hat lay across the sofa, whereas last night they had hung in the hall.

But Dr. Fell appeared to be violently interested in a very bad landscape hung above the piano. He turned round a guileless face at their entrance, and addressed Swan.

"I say. Would you mind nipping up to—harrumph— what we'll call the sickroom, and finding out how the patient is? Don't let Dr. Grant bully you. I want to find out whether Colin's conscious yet, and whether he's said anything."

"So do I," agreed Swan with some vehemence, and was off with such celerity as to make the pictures rattle.

Dr. Fell hastily picked up his box-pleated cape, swung it round his shoulders with evident effort, and fastened the little chain at the neck.

"Get your hat, my lad," he said. "We're off on a little expedition. The presence of the press is no doubt stimulating; but there are times when it is definitely an encumbrance. We may be able to sneak out without our friend Swan seeing us."

"Where are we going?"

"Glencoe."

Alan stared at him.

"Glencoe! At seven o'clock in the morning?"

"I regret," sighed Dr. Fell, sniffing the odor of frying bacon and eggs which had begun to seep through the house, "that we shall not be able to wait for breakfast. But better miss breakfast than spoil the whole broth."

"Yes, but how in blazes are we going to get to Glencoe at this hour?"

"I've phoned through to Inveraray for a car. They haven't your slothful habits in this part of the country, my lad. Do you remember Duncan telling us yesterday that Alec Forbes had been found, or they thought he had been found, at a cottage near Glencoe?"

"Yes?"

Dr. Fell made a face and flourished his crutch-handled stick.

"It may not be true. And we may not even be able to find the cottage: though I got a description of its location from Duncan, and habitations out there are few and far between. But, by thunder, we've got to take the chance! If I'm to be any good to Colin Campbell at all, I've GOT to reach Alec Forbes before anybody else—even the police— can get to him. Get your hat."

Kathryn Campbell, pulling on her tweed jacket, moved swiftly into the room.

"Oh, no, you don't!" she said.

"Don't what?"

"You don't go without me," Kathryn informed them. "I heard you ringing up for that car. Aunt Elspat is bossy enough anywhere, but Aunt Elspat in a sickroom is simply bossy past all endurance. Eee!" She clenched her hands. "There's nothing more I can do anyhow. *Please* let me come!"

Dr. Fell waved a gallant assent. Tiptoeing like conspirators, they moved out to the back of the house. A brightly polished four-seater car was waiting beyond the hedge which screened Shira from the main road.

Alan did not want a loquacious chauffeur that morning, and he did not get one. The driver was a gnarled little man, dressed like a garage mechanic, who grudgingly held open the door for them. They were past Dalmally before they discovered that he was, in fact, an English cockney.

But Alan was too full of his latest discovery to mind the presence of a witness. He produced Angus's diary, and handed it to Dr. Fell.

Even on an empty stomach, Dr. Fell had filled and lighted his meerschaum. It was an open car, and, as it climbed the mighty hill under a somewhat damp-looking sky, the breeze gave Dr. Fell considerable trouble in its attentions to his hat and the tobacco smoke. But he read carefully through the diary, giving at least a glance at every page of it.

"H'mf, yes," he said, and scowled. "It fits. Everything fits! Your deductions, Miss Campbell, were to the point. It *was* Elspat who stole this."

"But ——"

"Look here." He pointed to the place where a page had been torn out. "The entry before that, at the foot of the preceding page, reads, 'Elspat says Janet G.'—whoever she may be—'godless and lecherous. In Elspat's younger days—' There it breaks off.

"It probably went on to recount gleefully an anecdote of Elspat's younger and less moral days. So the evidence was removed from the record. Elspat found nothing more in the diary to reflect on her. After giving it a careful reading, probably several readings to make sure, she returned the diary to a place where it could easily be found."

Alan was not impressed.

"Still, what about these sensational revelations? Why get in touch with the press, as Elspat did? The last entry in the diary may be suggestive, but it certainly doesn't tell us very much."

"No?"

"Well, does it?"

Dr. Fell eyed him curiously.

"I should say, on the contrary, that it tells us a good deal. But you hardly expected the sensational revelation (if any) to be in the last entry, did you? After all, Angus had gone happily and thoughtlessly to bed. Whatever attacked him, it attacked him after he had finished writing and put out his light. Why, therefore, should we expect anything of great interest in the last entry?"

Alan was brought up with something of a bump.

"That," he admitted, "is true enough. All the same——"

"No, my boy. The real meat of the thing is *here*." Dr. Fell made the pages riffle like a pack of cards. "In the body of the diary. In the account of his activities for the past year."

He frowned at the book, and slipped it into his pocket. His expression of gargantuan distress had grown along with his fever of certainty.

"Hang it all!" he said, and smote his hand on his knee. "The thing is inescapable! Elspat steals the diary. She reads it. Being no fool, she guesses ——"

"Guesses what?"

"How Angus Campbell really died. She hates and distrusts the police to the very depths of her soul. So she writes to her favorite newspaper and plans to explode a bomb. And suddenly, when it is too late, she realizes with horror ——"

Again Dr. Fell paused. The expression on his face smoothed itself out. He sat back with a gusty sigh against the upholstery of the tonneau, and shook his head.

"You know, that tears it," he added blankly. "That really does tear it."

"I personally," Kathryn said through her teeth, "will be in a condition to tear something if this mystification goes on."

Dr. Fell appeared still more distressed.

"Allow me," he suggested, "to counter your very natural curiosity with just one more question." He looked at Alan. "A moment ago you said that you thought the last entry in Angus's diary was 'suggestive.' What did you mean by that?"

"I meant that it certainly wasn't a passage which could have been written by anyone who meant to kill himself."

Dr. Fell nodded.

"Yes," he agreed. "Then what would you say if I were to tell you that Angus Campbell really committed suicide after all?"

Chapter 14

"I SHOULD REPLY," said Kathryn, "that I felt absolutely cheated! Oh, I know I shouldn't say that; but it's true. You've got us looking so hard for a murderer that we can't concentrate on anything else."

Dr. Fell nodded as though he saw the aesthetic validity of the point.

"And yet," he went on, "for the sake of argument, I ask you to consider this explanation. I ask you to observe how it is borne out by every one of our facts."

He was silent for a moment, puffing at the meerschaum.

"Let us first consider Angus Campbell. Here is a shrewd, embittered, worn-out old man with a tinkering brain and an intense love of family. He is now broke, stony broke. His great dreams will never come true. He knows it. His brother Colin, of whom he is very fond, is overwhelmed with debts. His ex-mistress Elspat, of whom he is fonder still, is penniless and will remain penniless.

"Angus might well consider himself, in the hardheaded Northern fashion, a useless encumbrance. Good to nobody—except dead. But he is a hale old body to whom the insurance company's doctor gives fifteen more years of life. And in the meantime how (in God's name, how) are they to live?

"Of course, if he were to die now . . ."

Dr. Fell made a slight gesture.

"But, if he dies now, it must be established as certain, absolutely *certain,* that his death is not a suicide. And that will take a bit of doing. The sum involved is huge: thirty-five thousand pounds, distributed among intelligent insurance companies with nasty suspicious minds.

"Mere accident won't do. He can't go out and stumble off a cliff, hoping it will be read as accident. They might think that; but it is too chancy, and nothing must be left to chance. His death must be murder, cold-blooded murder, proved beyond any shadow of a doubt."

Again Dr. Fell paused. Alan improved the occasion to utter a derisive laugh which was not very convincing.

"In that case, sir," Alan said, "I turn your own guns on you."

"So? How?"

"You asked last night why any person intending to commit a murder for the insurance money should commit a murder which looked exactly like suicide. Well, for the same reason, why should Angus (of all people) plan a suicide which looked exactly like suicide?"

"He didn't," answered Dr. Fell.

"Pardon?"

Dr. Fell leaned forward to tap Alan, who occupied the front seat, very decisively on the shoulder. The doctor's manner was compounded of eagerness and absent-mindedness.

"That's the whole point. He didn't. You see, you haven't yet realized what was in that dog carrier. You haven't yet realized what Angus deliberately put there.

"And I say to you,"—Dr. Fell lifted his hand solemnly —"I say to you that but for one little unforeseeable accident, a misfortune so unlikely that the mathematical chances were a million to one against it, there would never have been the least doubt that Angus was murdered! I say to you that Alec Forbes would be in jail at this moment, and that the insurance companies would have been compelled to pay up."

They were approaching Loch Awe, a gem of beauty in a deep, mountainous valley. But none of them looked at it.

"Are you saying," breathed Kathryn, "that Angus was going to kill himself, and deliberately frame Alec Forbes for the job?"

"I am. Do you consider it unlikely?"

After a silence Dr. Fell went on.

"In the light of this theory, consider our evidence.

"Here is Forbes, a man with a genuine, bitter grudge. Ideal for the purposes of a scapegoat.

"Forbes calls—for which we may read, 'is summoned'— to see Angus that night. He goes upstairs to the tower room. There is a row, which Angus can arrange to make audible all over the place. Now, was Forbes at this time carrying a 'suitcase'?

"The women, we observe, don't know. They didn't see him until he was ejected. Who is the only witness to the suitcase? Angus himself. He carefully calls their attention to the fact that Forbes was supposed to have one, *and* says pointedly that Forbes must have left it behind.

"You follow that? The picture Angus intended to present was that Forbes had distracted his attention and shoved the suitcase under the bed, where Angus never noticed it, but where the thing inside it could later do its deadly work."

Alan reflected.

"It's a curious thing," Alan said, "that the day before yesterday I myself suggested just that explanation, with Forbes as the murderer. But nobody would listen to it."

"Yet I repeat," asserted Dr. Fell, "that except for a totally unpredictable accident, Forbes would have been nailed as the murderer straightaway."

Kathryn put her hands to her temples.

"You mean," she cried, "that Elspat looked under the bed before the door was locked, and saw there was no box there?"

But to their surprise Dr. Fell shook his head.

"No, no, no, no! That was another point, of course. But it wasn't serious. Angus probably never even thought her glance under the bed noticed anything one way or the other. No, no, no! I refer to the contents of the box."

Alan closed his eyes.

"I suppose," he said in a restrained voice, "it would be asking too much if we were to ask you just to *tell* us what was in the box?"

Dr. Fell grew still more solemn, even dogged.

"In a very short time we are (I hope) going to see Alec Forbes. I am going to put the question to him. In the meantime, I ask you to think about it; think about the facts we know; think about the trade magazines in Angus's room; think about his activities of the past year; and see if you can't reach the solution for yourselves.

"For the moment let us return to the great scheme. Alec Forbes, of course, had carried no suitcase or anything else. The box (already prepared by Angus himself) was downstairs in one of the lower rooms. Angus got rid of the women at ten o'clock, slipped downstairs, procured the box, and put it under the bed, after which he re-locked and re-bolted his door. This, I submit, is the only possible explanation of how that box got into a hermetically sealed room.

"Finally, Angus wrote up his diary. He put in those significant words that he had told Forbes not to come back, and Forbes said it wouldn't be necessary. Other significant words too: so many more nails in Forbes's coffin. Then Angus undressed, turned out the light, climbed into bed, and with real grim fortitude prepared for what had to come.

"Now follow what happens next day. Angus has left his diary in plain sight, for the police to find. Elspat finds it herself, and appropriates it.

"She thinks Alec Forbes killed Angus. On reading through the bulk of the diary, she realizes—as Angus meant everybody to realize—exactly what killed Angus. She has got Alec Forbes, the murderer. She will hang the sinful higher than Haman. She sits down and writes to the *Daily Floodlight*.

"Only after the letter is posted does she suddenly see the flaw. If Forbes did that, he must have pushed the box under the bed before he was kicked out. But Forbes can't have done that! For she herself looked under the bed, and saw no box; and, most horrifying of all, she has already told the police so."

Dr. Fell made a gesture.

"This woman has lived with Angus Campbell for forty years. She knows him inside out. She sees through him with that almost morbid clarity our womenfolk exhibit in dealing with our vagaries and our stupidities. It doesn't take her long to understand where the hanky-panky lies. It wasn't Alec Forbes; it was Angus himself who did this. And so ——

"Do I have to explain further? Think over her behavior. Think of her sudden change of mind about the box. Think of her searching for excuses to fly into a tantrum and throw out of the house the newspaperman she has summoned herself. Think, above all, of her position. If she speaks out with the truth, she loses every penny. If she denounces Alec Forbes, on the other hand, she condemns her soul to hell-fire and eternal burning. Think of that, my children; and don't be too hard on Elspat Campbell when her temper seems to wear thin."

The figure of one whom Kathryn had called a silly old woman was undergoing, in their minds, a curious transformation.

Thinking back to eyes and words and gestures, thinking of the core under that black taffeta, Alan experienced a revulsion of feeling as well as a revulsion of ideas.

"And so—?" he prompted.

"Well! She won't make the decision," replied Dr. Fell. "She returns the diary to the tower room, and lets us decide what we like."

The car had climbed to higher, bleaker regions. Uplands of waste, spiked with ugly posts against possible invasion by air, showed brown against the granite ribs of the mountains. The day was clouding over, and a damp breeze blew in their faces.

"May I submit," Dr. Fell added after a pause, "that this is the only explanation which fits all the facts?"

"Then if we're not looking for a murderer—"

"Oh, my dear sir!" expostulated Dr. Fell. "We *are* looking for a murderer!"

They whirled round on him.

"Ask yourselves other questions," said Dr. Fell. "Who impersonated the ghostly Highlander, and why? Who sought the death of Colin Campbell, and why? For remember: except for lucky chance, Colin would be dead at this minute."

He brooded, chewing the stem of a pipe that had gone out, and making a gesture as though he were pursuing something which just eluded him.

"Pictures," he added, "sometimes give extraordinary ideas."

Then he seemed to realize for the first time that he was talking in front of an outsider. He caught, in the driving mirror, the eye of the gnarled little chauffeur who for miles had not spoken or moved. Dr. Fell rumbled and snorted, brushing fallen ash off his cape. He woke up out of a mazy dream, and blinked round.

"H'mf. Hah. Yes. So. I say, when do we get to Glencoe?"

The driver spoke out of the side of his mouth.

"This *is* Glen Coe," he answered.

All of them woke up.

And here, Alan thought, were the wild mountains as he had always imagined them. The only adjective which occurred in connection with the place was Godforsaken: not as an idle word, but as a literal fact.

The glen of Coe was immensely long and immensely wide, whereas Alan had always pictured it as a cramped, narrow place. Through it the black road ran arrow-straight. On either side rose the lines of mountain ridges, granite-gray and dull purple, looking as smooth as stone. No edge of kindliness touched them: it was as though nature had dried up, and even sullenness had long petrified to hostility.

Burns twisting down the mountainside were so far off that you could not even be sure if the water moved, and only were sure when you saw it gleam. Utter silence emphasized the bleakness and desolation of the glen. Sometimes you saw a tiny whitewashed cottage, which appeared empty.

Dr. Fell pointed to one of them.

"We are looking," he said, "for a cottage on the left-hand side of the road, down a slope among some fir trees, just past the Falls of Coe. You don't happen to know it?"

The driver was silent for a time, and then said he thought he knew it.

"Not far off now," he added. "Be at the Falls in a minute or two."

The road rose, and, after its interminable straightness, curved round the slaty shoulder of a hill. The hollow, tumbling roar of a waterfall shook the damp air as they turned into a narrow road, shut in on the right by a cliff.

Driving them some distance down this road, the chauffeur stopped the car, sat back, and pointed without a word.

They climbed out on the breezy road, under a darkening sky. The tumult of the waterfall still splashed in their ears. Dr. Fell was assisted down a slope on which they all slithered. He was assisted, with more effort, across a stream; and in the bed of the stream the stones were polished black, as though they had met the very heart of the soil.

The cottage, of dirty whitewashed stone with a thatched roof, stood beyond. It was tiny, appearing to consist of only one room. The door stood closed. No smoke went up from the chimney. Far beyond it the mountains rose up light purple and curiously pink.

Nothing moved—except a mongrel dog.

The dog saw them, and began to run round in circles. It darted to the cottage, and scratched with its paws on the closed door. The scratching sound rose thinly, above the distant mutter of the falls. It set a seal on the heart, of loneliness and depression in the evil loneliness of Glencoe.

The dog sat back on its haunches, and began to howl.

"All right, old boy!" said Dr. Fell.

That reassuring voice seemed to have some effect on the animal. It scratched frantically at the door again, after which it ran to Dr. Fell and capered round him, leaping up to scrape at his cloak. What frightened Alan was the fright in the eyes of the dog.

Dr. Fell knocked at the door, without response. He tried the latch, but something held the door on the inside. There was no window in the front of the cottage.

"Mr. Forbes!" he called thunderously. "Mr. Forbes!"

Their footsteps scraped amidst little flinty stones. The shape of the cottage was roughly square. Muttering to himself, Dr. Fell lumbered round to the side of the house, and Alan followed him.

Here they found a smallish window. A rusty metal grating, like a mesh of heavy wire, had been nailed up over the window on the inside. Beyond this its grimy window-pane, set on hinges to swing open and shut like a door, stood partly open.

Cupping their hands round their eyes, they pressed against the grating and tried to peer inside. A frowsty smell, compounded of stale air, stale whisky, paraffin oil, and sardines out of a tin, crept out of the room. Gradually, as their eyes grew accustomed to the gloom, outlines emerged.

The table, with its greasy mess of dishes, had been pushed to one side. In the center of the ceiling was set a stout iron hook, presumably for a lamp. Alan saw what was hanging from that hook now, and swaying gently each time the dog pawed at the door.

He dropped his hands. He turned away from the window, putting one hand against the wall to steady himself. He walked round the side of the cottage to the front, where Kathryn was standing.

"What is it?" He heard her voice distantly, though it was almost a scream. "What's wrong?"

"You'd better come away from here," he said.

"What is it?"

Dr. Fell, much less ruddy of face, followed Alan round to the front door.

The doctor breathed heavily and wheezily for a moment before he spoke.

"That's rather a flimsy door," he said, pointing with his stick. "You could kick it in. And I think you better had."

On the inside was a small, new, tight bolt. Alan tore the staple loose from the wood with three vicious kicks into which he put his whole muscle and the whole state of his mind.

Though he was not anxious to go inside, the face of the dead man was now turned away from them, and it was not so bad as the first look through the window. The smell of food and whisky and paraffin grew overpowering.

The dead man wore a long, grimy dressing gown. The rope, which had formed the plaited cord of his dressing gown, had been shaped at one end into a running noose, and the other tied tightly round the hook in the ceiling. His heels swung some two feet off the floor as he hung there. An empty keg, evidently of whisky, had rolled away from under him.

Whining frenziedly, the mongrel dog shot past them, whirled round the dead man, and set him swinging again in frantic attempts to spring up.

Dr. Fell inspected the broken bolt. He glanced across at the grated window. His voice sounded heavy in the evil-smelling room.

"Oh, yes," he said. "Another suicide."

Chapter 15

"I SUPPOSE," ALAN MUTTERED, "it *is* Alec Forbes?"

Dr. Fell pointed with his stick to the camp bed pushed against one wall. On it an open suitcase full of soiled linen bore the painted initials, "A.G.F." Then he walked round to the front of the hanging figure where he could examine the face. Alan did not follow him.

"And the description fits, too. A week's growth of beard on his face. And, in all probability, ten years' growth of depression in his heart."

Dr. Fell went to the door, barring it against Kathryn, who stood white-faced under the overcast sky a few feet away.

"There must be a telephone somewhere. If I remember my map, there's a village with a hotel a mile or two beyond here. Get through to Inspector Donaldson at Dunoon police station, and tell him Mr. Forbes has hanged himself. Can you do that?"

Kathryn gave a quick, unsteady nod.

"He did kill himself, did he?" she asked in a voice barely above a whisper. "It isn't—anything else?"

Dr. Fell did not reply to this. Kathryn, after another quick nod, turned and made her way back.

The hut was some dozen feet square, thick-walled, with a primitive fireplace and a stone floor. It was no crofter's cottage, but had evidently been used by Forbes as a sort of retreat. Its furniture consisted of the camp bed, the table, two kitchen chairs, a washstand with bowl and pitcher, and a stand of mildewed books.

The mongrel had now ceased its frantic whimpering, for which Alan felt grateful. The dog lay down close to the silent figure, where he could raise adoring eyes to the altered face; and, from time to time, he shivered.

"I ask what Kathryn asked," said Alan. "Is this suicide, or not?"

Dr. Fell walked forward and touched Forbes' arm. The dog stiffened. A menacing growl began in its throat and quivered through its whole body.

"Easy, boy!" said Dr. Fell. "Easy!"

He stood back. He took out his watch and studied it. Grunting and muttering, he lumbered over to the table, on whose edge stood a hurricane lantern with a hook and chain by which it could be slung from the roof. With the tips of his fingers Dr. Fell picked up the lantern and shook it. A tin of oil stood beside it.

"Empty," he said. "Burnt out, but obviously used." He pointed to the body. "Rigor is not complete. This undoubtedly happened during the early hours of the morning: two or three o'clock, perhaps. The hour of suicides. And look there."

He was now pointing to the plaited dressing-gown cord around the dead man's neck.

"It's a curious thing," he went on, scowling. "The genuine suicide invariably takes the most elaborate pains to guard himself against the least discomfort. If he hangs himself, for instance, he will never use a wire or chain: something that is likely to cut or chafe his neck. If he uses a rope, he will often pad it against chafing. Look there! Alec Forbes has used a soft rope, and padded that with handkerchiefs. The authentic touch of suicide, or—"

"Or what?"

"Real genius in murder," said Dr. Fell.

He bent down to inspect the empty whisky keg. He went across to the one window. Thrusting one finger through the mesh of the grating, he shook it and found it solidly nailed up on the inside. Back he went, with fussed and fussy gestures, to the bolt of the door, which he examined carefully without touching it.

Then he peered round the room, stamping his foot on

the floor. His voice had taken on a hollow sound like wind along an underground tunnel.

"Hang it all!" he said. "This *is* suicide. It's got to be suicide. The keg is just the right height for him to have stepped off, and just the right distance away. Nobody could have got in or out through that nailed window or that solidly bolted door."

He regarded Alan with some anxiety.

"You see, for my sins I know something about hocusing doors or windows. I have been—ahem—haunted and pursued by such matters."

"So I've heard."

"But I can't," pursued Dr. Fell, pushing back his shovel hat, "I can't tell you any way of hocusing a bolt when there's no keyhole and when the door is so close-fitting that its sill scrapes the floor. Like that one."

He pointed.

"And I can't tell you any way of hocusing a window when it is covered with a steel meshwork nailed up on the inside. Again, like that one there. If Alec Forbes—hullo!"

The bookstand was placed cater-cornered in the angle of the fireplace. Dr. Fell discovered it as he went to inspect the fireplace, finding to his disgust that the flue was too narrow and soot-choked to admit any person. Dusting his fingers, he turned to the bookstand.

On the top row of books stood a portable typewriter, its cover missing and a sheet of paper projecting from the carriage. On it a few words were typed in pale blue ink.

To any jackal who finds this:

I killed Angus and Colin Campbell with the same thing they used to swindle me. What are you going to do about it now?

"Even, you see," Dr. Fell said fiercely, "the suicide note. The final touch. The brush stroke of the master. I repeat, sir: this must be suicide. And yet—well, if it is, I mean to retire to Bedlam."

The smell of the room, the black-faced occupant, the yearning dog, all these things were commencing to turn

Alan Campbell's stomach. He felt he could not stand the air of the place much longer. Yet he fought back.

"I don't see why you say that," he declared. "After all, Doctor, can't you admit you may be wrong?"

"Wrong?"

"About Angus's death being suicide." Certainty, dead certainty, took root in Alan Campbell's brain. "Forbes *did* kill Angus and tried to kill Colin. Everything goes to show it. Nobody could have got in or out of this room, as you yourself admit; and there's Forbe's confession to clinch matters.

"He brooded out here until his brain cracked, as I know mine would in these parts unless I took to religion. He disposed of both brothers, or thought he had. When his work was finished, he killed himself. Here's the evidence. What more do you want?"

"The truth," insisted Dr. Fell stubbornly. "I am old fashioned. I want the truth."

Alan hesitated.

"I'm old fashioned too. And I seem to remember," Alan told him, "that you came North with the express purpose of helping Colin. Is it going to help Colin, or Aunt Elspat either, if the detective they brought in to show Angus was murdered goes about shouting that it was suicide—even after we've got Alec Forbes's confession?"

Dr. Fell blinked at him.

"My dear sir," he said in pained astonishment, and adjusted his eyeglasses and blinked at Alan through them, "you surely don't imagine that I mean to confide any of my beliefs to the police?"

"Isn't that the idea?"

Dr. Fell peered about to make sure they were not overhead.

"My record," he confided, "is an extremely black one. Harrumph. I have on several occasions flummoxed the evidence so that a murderer should go free. Not many years ago I outdid myself by setting a house on fire. My present purpose (between ourselves) is to swindle the insurance companies so that Colin Campbell can bask in good cigars and fire water for the rest of his life . . ."

"*What?*"

Dr. Fell regarded him anxiously.

"That shocks you? Tut, tut! All this (I say) I mean to do. But, dammit, man!" He spread out his hands. "For my own private information, I like to know the truth."

He turned back to the bookstand. Still without touching it, he examined the typewriter. On top of the row of books below it stood an angler's creel and some salmon flies. On top of the third row of books lay a bicycle spanner, a bicycle lamp, and a screwdriver.

Dr. Fell next ran a professional eye over the books. There were works on physics and chemistry, on Diesel engines, on practical building, and on astronomy. There were catalogues and trade journals. There was a dictionary, a six-volume encyclopedia, and (surprisingly) two or three boys' books by G. A. Henty. Dr. Fell eyed these last with some interest.

"Wow!" he said. "Does anybody read Henty nowadays, I wonder? If they knew what they were missing, they would run back to him. I am proud to say that I still read him with delight. Who would suspect Alec Forbes of having a romantic soul?" He scratched his nose. "Still—"

"Look here," Alan persisted. "What makes you so sure this isn't suicide?"

"My theory. My mule-headedness, if you prefer it."

"And your theory still holds that Angus committed suicide?"

"Yes."

"But that Forbes here was murdered?"

"Exactly."

Dr. Fell wandered back to the center of the room. He eyed the untidy camp bed with the suitcase on it. He eyed a pair of gum boots under the bed.

"My lad, I don't trust that suicide note. I don't trust it one little bit. And there are solid reasons why I don't trust it. Come out here. Let's get some clean air."

Alan was glad enough to go. The dog raised its head from its paws, and gave them a wild, dazed sort of look; then it lowered its head again, growling, and settled down with ineffable patience under the dead.

Distantly, they could hear the rushing of the waterfall. Alan breathed the cool, damp air, and felt a shudder go over him. Dr. Fell, a huge bandit shape in his cloak, leaned his hands on his stick.

"Whoever wrote that note," he went on, "whether Alec Forbes or another, knew the trick that had been employed in Angus Campbell's death. That's the first fact to freeze to. Well! Have you guessed yet what the trick was?"

"No, I have not."

"Not even after seeing the alleged suicide note? Oh, man! Think!"

"You can ask me to think all you like. I may be dense; but if you can credit it, I still don't know what makes people jump up out of bed in the middle of the night and fall out of windows to their death."

"Let us begin," pursued Dr. Fell, "with the fact that Angus's diary records his activities for the past year, as diaries sometimes do. Well, what in Satan's name *have* been Angus's principal activities for the past year?"

"Mixing himself up in various wildcat schemes to try to make money."

"True. But only one scheme in which Alec Forbes was concerned, I think?"

"Yes."

"Good. What was that scheme?"

"An idea to manufacture some kind of ice cream with tartan patterns on it. At least, so Colin said."

"And in making their ice cream," said Dr. Fell, "what kind of freezing agent did they employ in large quantities? Colin told us that too."

"He said they used artificial ice, which he described as 'that chemical stuff that's so expen—' "

Alan paused abruptly.

Half-forgotten memories flowed back into his mind.

With a shock he recalled a laboratory of his school days, and words being spoken from a platform. The faint echo of them came back now.

"And do you know," inquired Dr. Fell, "what this artificial ice, or 'dry' ice, really is?"

"It's whitish stuff to look at; something like real ice, only opaque. It—"

"To be exact," said Dr. Fell, "it is nothing more or less than liquefied gas. And do you know the name of the gas which is turned into a solid 'snow' block and can be cut and handled and moved about? What is the name of that gas?"

"Carbon dioxide," said Alan.

Though the spell remained on his wits, it was suddenly as though a blind had flown up with a snap, and he saw.

"Now suppose," argued Dr. Fell, "you removed a block of that stuff from its own airtight cylinders. A big block say one big enough to fit into a large suitcase—or, better still, some box with an open end, so that the air can reach it better. What would happen?"

"It would slowly melt."

"And in melting, of course, it would release into the room . . . what would it release?"

Alan found himself almost shouting.

"Carbonic acid gas. One of the deadliest and quickest-acting gases there is."

"Suppose you placed your artificial ice, in its container, under the bed in a room where the window is always kept closed at night. What would happen?

"With your permission, I will now drop the Socratic method and tell you. You have planted one of the surest murder traps ever devised. One of two things will happen. Either the victim, asleep or drowsy, will breathe in that concentrated gas as it is released into the room; and he will die in his bed.

"Or else the victim will notice the faint, acrid odor as it gets into his lungs. He will not breathe it long, mind you. Once the stuff takes hold, it will make the strongest man totter and fall like a fly. He will want air—air at any cost. As he is overcome, he will get out of bed and try to make for the window.

"He may not make it at all. If he does make it, he will be so weak on the legs that he can't hold up. And if this window is a low window, catching him just above the knees; if it consists of two leaves, opening outwards, so that he falls against it—"

Dr. Fell pushed his hands outwards, a rapid gesture.

Alan could almost see the limp, unwieldy body in the nightshirt plunge outwards and downwards.

"Of course, the artificial ice will melt away and leave no trace in the box. With the window now open, the gas will presently clear away.

"You now perceive, I hope, why Angus's suicide scheme was so foolproof. Who but Alec Forbes would have used artificial ice to kill his partner in the venture?

"Angus, as I read it, never once intended to jump or fall from the window. No, no, no! He intended to be found dead in bed, of poisoning by carbonic acid gas. There would be a post-mortem. The 'band' of this gas would be found in his blood as plain as print. The diary would be read and interpreted. All the circumstances against Alec Forbes would be recalled, as I outlined them to you a while ago. And the insurance money would be collected as certainly as the sun will rise tomorrow."

Alan, staring at the stream, nodded.

"But at the last moment, I suppose—?"

"At the last moment," agreed Dr. Fell, "like many suicides, Angus couldn't face it. He had to have *air*. He felt himself going under. And in a panic he leaped for the window.

"Therein, my boy, lies the million-to-one chance I spoke of. It was a million to one that either (a) the gas would kill him, or (b) the fall would kill him instantly as he plunged out face forwards. But neither of these things happened. He was mortally injured; yet he did not immediately die. Remember?"

Again Alan nodded.

"Yes. We've come across that point several times."

"Before he died, his lungs and blood were freed of the gas. Hence no trace remained for the post-mortem. Had he died instantly or even quickly, those traces would have been there. But they were not. So we had only the meaningless spectacle of an old gentleman who leaps from his bed in order to throw himself out of the window."

Dr. Fell's big voice grew fiery. He struck the ferrule of his stick on the ground.

"I say to you—" he began.

"Stop a bit!" said Alan, with sudden recollection.

"Yes?"

"Last night, when I went up to the tower room to rout out Colin, I bent down and tried to look under the sill of the door. When I straightened up, I remember feeling lightheaded. In fact, I staggered when I went down the stairs. Did *I* get a whiff of the stuff?"

"Of course. The room was full of it. Only a very faint whiff, fortunately for yourself.

"Which brings us to the final point. Angus carefully wrote in his diary that there was a 'faint musty smell in the room.' Now, that's rubbish on the face of it. If he had already begun to notice the presence of the gas, he could never have completed his diary and gone to bed. No: that was only another artistic touch designed to hang Alec Forbes."

"And misinterpreted by me," growled Alan. "I was thinking about some kind of animal."

"But you see where all this leads us?"

"No, I don't. Into the soup, of course; but aside from that—"

"The only possible explanation of the foregoing facts," insisted Dr. Fell, "is that Angus killed himself. If Angus killed himself, then Alec Forbes didn't kill him. And if Alec Forbes didn't kill him, Alec had no reason to say he did. Therefore the suicide note is a fake.

"Up to this time, d'ye see, we have had a suicide which everybody thought was murder. Now we have a murder which everybody is going to take for suicide. We are going places and seeing things. All roads lead to the lunatic asylum. Can you by any chance oblige me with an idea?"

Chapter 16

ALAN SHOOK HIS HEAD.

"No ideas. I presume that the 'extra' thing which ailed Colin, and exercised Dr. Grant so much was carbon-dioxide poisoning?"

Dr. Fell grunted assent. Fishing out the meerschaum pipe again, he filled and lighted it.

"Which," he assented, speaking between puffs like the Spirit of the Volcano, "leads us at full tide into our troubles. We can't blame Angus for that. The death box didn't load itself again with artificial ice.

"Somebody—who knew Colin was going to sleep there —set the trap again in a box already conveniently left under the bed. Somebody, who knew Colin's every movement, could nip up there ahead of him. He was drunk and wouldn't bother to investigate the box. All that saved his life was the fact that he slept with the window open, and roused himself in time. Query: who did that, and why?

"Final query: who killed Alec Forbes, and how, and why?"

Alan continued to shake his head doubtfully.

"You're still not convinced that Forbes's death was murder, my lad?"

"Frankly, I'm not. I still don't see why Forbes couldn't have killed both the others, or thought he had, and then killed himself."

"Logic? Or wishful thinking?"

Alan was honest. "A little of both, maybe. Aside from

the money question, I should hate to think that Angus was such an old swine as to try to get an innocent man hanged."

"Angus," returned Dr. Fell, "was neither an old swine nor an honest Christian gentleman. He was a realist who saw only one way to provide for those he was fond of. I do not defend it. But can you dare say you don't understand it?"

"It isn't that. I can't understand, either, why he took the blackout down from the window if he wanted to be sure of smothering himself with the . . ."

Alan paused, for the sudden expression which had come over Dr. Fell's face was remarkable for its sheer idiocy. Dr. Fell stared, and his eyes rolled. The pipe almost dropped from his mouth.

"O Lord! O Bacchus! O my ancient hat!" he breathed. "Blackout!"

"What is it?"

"The murderer's first mistake," said Dr. Fell. "Come with me."

Hurriedly he swung round and blundered back into the hut again. Alan followed him, not without an effort. Dr. Fell began a hurried search of the room. With an exclamation of triumph he found on the floor near the bed a piece of tar paper nailed to a light wooden frame. He held this up to the window, and it fitted.

"We ourselves can testify," he went on, with extraordinary intensity, "that when we arrived here there was no blackout on this window. Hey?"

"That's right."

"Yet the lamp,"—he pointed—"had obviously been burning for a long time, far into the night. We can smell the odor of burned paraffin oil strongly even yet?"

"Yes."

Dr. Fell stared into vacancy.

"Every inch of this neighborhood is patrolled all night by the Home Guard. A hurricane lantern gives a strong light. There wasn't even so much as a curtain, let alone a blackout, on this window when we arrived. How is it that nobody noticed that light?"

There was a pause.

"Maybe they just didn't see it."

"My dear chap! So much as a chink of light in these hills would draw down the Home Guard for miles round. No, no, no! That won't do."

"Well, maybe Forbes—before he hanged himself—blew out the lantern and took down the blackout. The window's open, we notice. Though I don't see why he should have done that."

Again Dr. Fell shook his head with vehemence.

"I quote you again the habits of suicides. A suicide will never take his own life in darkness if there is any means of providing light. I do not analyze the psychology: I merely state the fact. Besides, Forbes wouldn't have been able to see to make all his preparations in the dark. No, no, no! It's fantastic!"

"What do you suggest, then?"

Dr. Fell put his hands to his forehead. For a time he remained motionless, wheezing gently.

"I suggest," he replied, lowering his hands after an interval, "that, after Forbes had been murdered and strung up, the murderer himself extinguished the lantern. He poured out the oil remaining in it so that it should later seem to have burned itself out. Then he took down the blackout."

"But why in blazes bother to do that? Why not leave the blackout where it was, and go away, and leave the lantern to burn itself out?"

"Obviously because he had to make use of the window in making his escape."

This was the last straw.

"Look here," Alan said, with a sort of wild patience. He strode across. "Look at the damned window! It's covered by a steel grating nailed up solidly on the inside! Can you suggest any way, any way at all, by which a murderer could slide out through that?"

"Well—no. Not at the moment. And yet it was done."

They looked at each other.

From some distance away they heard the sound of a

man's voice earnestly hallooing, and scraps of distant talk. They hurried to the door.

Charles Swan and Alistair Duncan were striding toward them. The lawyer, in a raincoat and bowler hat, appeared more cadaverous than ever; but his whole personality was suffused with a kind of dry triumph.

"I think you're a good deal of a cheapskate," Swan accused Alan, "to run away like that after you'd promised me all the news there was. If I hadn't had my car I'd have been stranded."

Duncan silenced him. Duncan's mouth had a grim, pleased curve. He bowed slightly to Dr. Fell.

"Gentlemen," he said, taking up a position like a schoolmaster, "we have just learned from Dr. Grant that Colin Campbell is suffering from the effects of carbonic acid gas."

"True," agreed Dr. Fell.

"Administered probably from artificial ice taken from Angus Campbell's laboratory."

Again Dr. Fell nodded.

"Can we therefore," pursued Duncan, putting his hands together and rubbing them softly, "have any doubt of how Angus died? Or of who administered the gas to him?"

"We cannot. If you'd care to glance in that cottage there," said Dr. Fell, nodding toward it, "you will see the final proof which completes your case."

Duncan stepped quickly to the door, and just as quickly stepped back again. Swan, more determined or more callous, uttered an exclamation and went in.

There was a long silence while the lawyer seemed to be screwing up his courage. His Adam's apple worked in his long throat above the too-large collar. He removed his bowler hat and wiped his forehead with a handkerchief. Then, replacing the hat and straightening his shoulders, he forced himself to follow Swan into the cottage.

Both of them reappeared, hastily and without dignity, pursued by a series of savage growls which rose to a yelping snarl. The dog, red-eyed, watched them from the doorway.

"Nice doggie!" crooned Duncan, with a leer of such patent hypocrisy that the dog snarled again.

"You shouldn't have touched him," said Swan. "The pooch naturally got sore. I want a telephone. Cripes, what a scoop!"

Duncan readjusted his ruffled dignity.

"So it *was* Alec Forbes," he said.

Dr. Fell inclined his head.

"My dear sir," continued the lawyer, coming over to wring Dr. Fell's hand with some animation, "I—we—can't thank you too much! I daresay you guessed, from the trade magazines and bills you borrowed from Angus's room, what had been used to kill him?"

"Yes."

"I cannot imagine," said Duncan, "why it was not apparent to all of us from the first. Though, of course, the effects of the gas had cleared away when Angus was found. No wonder the clasps of the dog carrier were closed! When I think how we imagined snakes and spiders and heaven knows what, I am almost amused. The whole thing is so extraordinarily simple, once you have grasped the design behind it."

"I agree," said Dr. Fell "By thunder, but I agree!"

"You—ah—observed the suicide note?"

"I did."

Duncan nodded with satisfaction.

"The insurance companies will have to eat their words now. There can be no question as to their paying in full."

Yet Duncan hesitated. Honesty evidently compelled him to worry at another point.

"There is just one thing, however, that I cannot quite understand. If Forbes placed the dog carrier under the bed before being ejected, as this gentleman,"—he looked at Alan—"so intelligently suggested on Monday, how is it that Elspat and Kirstie did not observe it when they looked there?"

"Haven't you forgotten?" asked Dr. Fell. "She *did* see it, as she has since told us. Miss Elspat Campbell's mind is as literal as a German's. You asked her whether there was a suitcase there, and she said no. That is all."

It would not be true to say that the worry cleared away altogether from Duncan's face. But he cheered up, although he gave Dr. Fell a very curious look.

"You think the insurance companies will accept that correction?"

"I know the police will accept it. So the insurance companies will have to, whether they like it or not."

"A plain case?"

"A plain case."

"So it seems to me." Duncan cheered up still more. "Well, we must finish up this sad business as soon as we can. Have you informed the police about—this?"

"Miss Kathryn Campbell has gone to do so. She should be back at any minute. We had to break the door in, as you see, but we haven't touched anything else. After all, we don't want to be held as accessories after the fact."

Duncan laughed.

"You could hardly be held for that in any case. In Scots law, there is no such thing as an accessory after the fact."

"Is that so, now?" mused Dr. Fell. He took the pipe out of his mouth and added abruptly: "Mr. Duncan, were you ever acquainted with Robert Campbell?"

There was something in his words so arresting, even if so inexplicable, that everyone turned to look at him. The faint thunder of the Falls of Coe appeared loud in the hush that followed.

"Robert?" repeated Duncan. "The third of the brothers?"

"Yes."

An expression of fastidious distaste crossed the lawyer's face.

"Really, sir, to rake up old scandals—"

"Did you know him?" insisted Dr. Fell.

"I did."

"What can you tell me about him? All I've learned so far is that he got into trouble and had to leave the country.

What did he do? Where did he go? Above all, what was he like?"

Duncan grudgingly considered this.

"I knew him as a young man." He shot Dr. Fell a quick glance. "Robert, if I may say so, was by far the cleverest and brainiest of his family. But he had a streak of bad blood: which, fortunately, missed both Angus and Colin. He had trouble at the bank where he worked. Then there was a shooting affray over a barmaid.

"As to where he is now, I can't say. He went abroad— the colonies, America—I don't know where, because he slipped aboard a ship at Glasgow. You surely cannot consider that the matter is of any importance now?"

"No. I daresay not."

His attention was diverted. Kathryn Campbell scrambled down the bank, crossed the stream, and came toward them.

"I've got in touch with the police," she reported breathlessly, after a sharp glance at Duncan and Swan. "There's a hotel, the Glencoe Hotel, at the village of Glencoe about two miles farther on. The telephone number is Ballachulish —pronounced Ballahoolish—four-five."

"Did you talk to Inspector Donaldson?"

"Yes. He says he's always known Alec Forbes would do something like this. He says we needn't wait here, if we don't want to."

Her eyes strayed toward the cottage, and moved away uneasily.

"Please. *Must* you stay here? Couldn't we go on to the hotel and have something to eat? I ask because the proprietress knew Mr. Forbes very well."

Dr. Fell stirred with interest.

"So?"

"Yes. She says he was a famous cyclist. She says he could cover incredible distances at incredible speeds, in spite of the amount he drank."

Duncan uttered a soft exclamation. With a significant gesture to the others, he went round the side of the cottage, and they instinctively followed him. Behind the cottage

was an outhouse, against which leaned a racing bicycle
fitted out with a luggage grid at the back. Duncan pointed
to it.

"The last link, gentlemen. It explains how Forbes could
have got from here to Inveraray and back whenever he
liked. Did your informant add anything else, Miss Campbell?"

"Not much. She said he came up here to drink and fish
and work out schemes for perpetual motion, and things of
that sort. She said the last time she saw him was yesterday,
in the bar of the hotel. They practically had to throw him
out at closing time in the afternoon. She says he was a bad
man, who hated everything and everybody but animals."

Dr. Fell slowly walked forward and put his hand on the
handle bar of the bicycle. Alan saw, with uneasiness, there
was again on his face the startled expression, the wander-
ing blankness of idiocy, which he had seen there once before. This time it was deeper and more explosive.

"O Lord!" thundered Dr. Fell, whirling round as though
galvanized. "What a turnip I've been! What a remarkable
donkey! What a thundering dunce!"

"Without," observed Duncan, "without sharing the
views you express, may I ask why you express them?"

Dr. Fell turned to Kathryn.

"You're quite right," he said seriously, after reflecting
for a time. "We must get on to that hotel. Not only to refresh the inner man; though I, to be candid, am ravenous.
But I want to use a telephone. I want to use a telephone
like billy-o. There's a million-to-one chance against it, of
course; but the million-to-one chance came off before and
it may happen again."

"What million-to-one chance?" asked Duncan, not
without exasperation. "To whom do you want to telephone?"

"To the local commandant of the Home Guard," answered Dr. Fell, and lumbered round the side of the
cottage with his cloak flying out behind him.

Chapter 17

"ALAN," KATHRYN ASKED, "Alec Forbes didn't really kill himself, did he?"

It was late at night, and raining. They had drawn up their chairs before a brightly burning wood fire in the sitting room at Shira.

Alan was turning over the pages of a family album, with thick padded covers and gilt-topped leaves. For some time Kathryn had been silent, her elbows on the arm of the chair and her chin in her hand, staring into the fire. She dropped the question out of nowhere: flatly, as her habit was.

He did not raise his eyes.

"Why is it," he said, "that photographs taken some years ago are always so hilariously funny? You can take down anybody's family album and split your sides. If it happens to contain pictures of somebody you know, the effect is even more pronounced. Why? Is it the clothes, or the expression, or what? We weren't really as funny as that, were we?"

Disregarding her, he turned over a page or two.

"The women, as a rule, come out better than the men. Here is one of Colin as a young man, which looks as though he'd drunk about a quart of the Doom of the Campbells before leering at the photographer. Aunt Elspat, on the other hand, was a really fine-looking woman. Bold-eyed brunette; Mrs. Siddons touch. Here she is in a man's Highland costume: bonnet, feather, plaid, and all."

"Alan Campbell!"

"Angus, on the other hand, always tried to look so dignified and pensive that—"

"Alan darling."

He sat up with a snap. The rain pattered against the windows.

"What did you say?" he demanded.

"It was only a manner of speaking." She elevated her chin. "Or at least—well, anyway, I *had* to get your attention somehow. Alec Forbes didn't really kill himself, did he?"

"What makes you think that?"

"I can see it in the way you look," returned Kathryn; and he had an uncomfortable feeling that she would always be able to do this, which would provide some critical moments in the future.

"Besides," she went on peering round to make sure they were not overheard, and lowering her voice, "why should he? He certainly couldn't have been the one who tried to kill poor Colin."

Reluctantly Alan closed the album.

The memory of the day stretched out behind him: the meal at the Glencoe Hotel, the endless repetitions by Alistair Duncan of how Alec Forbes had committed his crimes and then hanged himself, all the while that Dr. Fell said nothing, and Kathryn brooded, and Swan sent off to the *Daily Floodlight* a story which he described as a honey.

"And why," he asked, "couldn't Forbes have tried to kill Colin?"

"Because he couldn't have known Colin was sleeping in the tower room."

(Damn! So she's spotted that!)

"Didn't you hear what the proprietress of the hotel said?" Kathryn insisted. "Forbes was in the bar of the hotel until closing time yesterday afternoon. Well, it was early in the afternoon here that Colin swore his great oath to sleep in the tower. How on earth could Forbes have known that? It was a snap decision which Colin made on the spur of the moment, and couldn't have been known outside the house."

Alan hesitated.

Kathryn lowered her voice still further.

"Oh, I'm not going to broadcast it! Alan, I know what Dr. Fell thinks. As he told us going out to the car, he thinks Angus committed suicide. Which is horrible, and yet I believe it. I believe it still more now that we've heard about the artificial ice."

She shivered.

"At least, we do know it isn't—supernatural. When we were thinking about snakes and spiders and ghosts and whatnots, I tell you I was frightened out of my wits. And all the while it was nothing but a lump of dry ice!"

"Most terrors are like that."

"Are they? Who played ghost, then? And who killed Forbes?"

Alan brooded. "*If* Forbes was murdered," he said, half-conceding this for the first time, "the motive for it is clear. It was to prove Angus's death was murder after all, like the attempt on Colin; to saddle Forbes with both crimes; and to clean up the whole business."

"To get the insurance money?"

"That's what it looks like."

The rain pattered steadily. Kathryn gave a quick glance at the door to the hall.

"But, Alan! In that case . . . ?"

"Yes. I know what you're thinking."

"And, in any case, how *could* Forbes have been murdered?"

"Your guess is as good as mine. Dr. Fell thinks the murderer got out by way of the window. Yes, I know the window was covered with an untouched grating! But so was the end of the dog carrier, if you remember. Twenty-four hours ago I would have sworn nothing could have got out of the dog carrier grating, either. And yet something did."

He broke off, with an air of elaborate casualness and a warning glance to Kathryn, as they heard footsteps in the hall. He was again turning over the pages of the album when Swan came into the sitting room.

Swan was almost as wet as he had been after Elspat's two pails of water. He stamped up to the fire, and let his hands drip into it.

"If I don't catch pneumonia one way or the other, before this thing is over," he announced, shifting from one foot to the other, "the reason won't be for want of bad luck. I've been obeying orders and trying to stick to Dr. Fell. You'd think that would be easy, wouldn't you?"

"Yes."

Swan's face was bitter.

"Well, it isn't. He's ditched me twice today. He's doing something with the Home Guard. Or at least he was before this rain started in. But what it is I can't find out and Sherlock Holmes himself couldn't guess. Anything up?"

"No. We were just looking at family portraits." Alan turned over pages. He passed one photograph, started to turn the page, and then, with sudden interest, went back to it. "Hullo," he said. "I've seen *that* face somewhere!"

It was a full-face view of a light-haired man with a heavy down-curved mustache, *circa* 1906, a handsome face with washed-out eyes. This impression, however, may have come from the faded brown color of the photograph. Across the lower right-hand corner was written in faded ink, with curlicues, "Best of luck!"

"Of course you've seen it," said Kathryn. "It's a Campbell. There's a resemblance, more or less, in every one of our particular crowd."

"No, no. I mean—"

He detached the photograph from the four slits in the cardboard, and turned it over. Across the back was written, in the same handwriting, "Robert Campbell, July, '05."

"So that's the brainy Robert!"

Swan, who had been peering over his shoulder, was clearly interested in something else.

"Wait a minute!" Swan urged, fitting back the photograph again and turning back a page quickly. "Cripes, what a beauty! Who's the good-looking woman?"

"That's Aunt Elspat."

"Who?"

"Elspat Campbell."

Swan winked his eyes. "Not the old hag who—who—" Wordlessly, his hands went to his new suit, and his face became distorted.

"Yes. The same one who baptized you. Look at this other of her in Highland costume, where she shows her legs. If I may mention the subject, they are very fine legs; though maybe on the heavy and muscular side for popular taste nowadays."

Kathryn could not restrain herself.

"But nothing, of course," she sneered, "to compare to the legs of your precious Duchess of Cleveland."

Swan begged their attention.

"Look," he said impressively, "I don't want to seem inquisitive. But—" his voice acquired a note of passion— "who *is* this dame from Cleveland, anyhow? Who is Charles? Who is Russell? And how did you get tangled up with her? I know I oughtn't to ask; but I can't sleep nights for thinking about it."

"The Duchess of Cleveland," said Alan, "was Charles's mistress."

"Yes, I gathered that. But is she your mistress too?"

"No. And she didn't come from Cleveland, Ohio, because she's been dead for more than two hundred years."

Swan stared at him.

"You're kidding me."

"I am not. We were having a historical argument, and—"

"I tell you, you're kidding me!" repeated Swan, with something like incredulous horror in his voice. "There's *got* to be a real Cleveland woman in it! As I said about you in my first story to the *Floodlight*—"

He paused. He opened his mouth, and shut it again. He seemed to feel that he had made a slip; as, in fact, he had. Two pairs of eyes fastened on him during an ominous silence.

"What," Kathryn asked very clearly, "what did you say about us in your first story to the *Floodlight*?"

"Nothing at all. Word of honor, I didn't! Just a little joke, nothing libelous in it at all—"

"Alan," murmured Kathryn, with her eye on a corner of the ceiling, "don't you think you'd better get down the claymores again?"

Swan had instinctively moved away until his back was shielded against the wall. He spoke in deep earnest.

"After all, you're going to get married! I overheard Dr. Fell himself say you had to get married. So what's wrong? I didn't mean any harm." (And clearly, thought Alan, he hadn't.) "I only said—"

"What a pity," continued Kathryn, still with her eye on the ceiling, "what a pity Colin hasn't got the use of his legs. But I hear he's a rare hand with a shotgun. And, since his bedroom windows face the main road—"

She paused, significantly musing, as Kirstie MacTavish flung open the door.

"Colin Campbell wants tae see you," she announced in her soft, sweet voice.

Swan changed color.

"He wants to see who?"

"He wants tae see all o' you."

"But he isn't allowed visitors, is he?" cried Kathryn.

"I dinna ken. He's drinkin' whusky in bed, annahoo."

"Well, Mr. Swan," said Kathryn, folding her arms, "after giving us a solemn promise, which you promptly broke and intended to break; after accepting hospitality here under false pretenses; after being handed on a plate probably the only good story you ever got in your life; and hoping to get some more—have you the courage to go up and face Colin now?"

"But you've got to look at my side of it, Miss Campbell!"

"Oh?"

"Colin Campbell'll understand! He's a good egg! He . . ." As an idea evidently occurred to him, Swan turned to the maid. "Look. He's not pickled, is he?"

"Wha'?"

"Pickled. Soused," said Swan apprehensively, "cock-eyed. Plastered. Full."

Kirstie was enlightened. She assured him that Colin was not full. Though the effectiveness of this assurance was somewhat modified by Kirstie's experienced belief that no man is full until he can fall down two successive flights of stairs without injury, Swan did not know this and it served its purpose.

"I'll put it up to him," Swan argued with great earnestness. "And in the meantime I'll put it up to both of you. I come up here; and what happens to me?"

"Not a patch," said Kathryn, "on what's going to happen. But go on."

Swan did not hear her.

"I get chased along a road," he continued, "and get a serious injury that might have given me blood poisoning. All right. I come round the next day, in a brand-new suit that cost ten guineas at Austin Reed's, and that mad woman empties two buckets of water over me. Not *one* bucket, mind you. *Two.*"

"Alan Campbell," said Kathryn fiercely, "do you find anything so very funny in this?"

Alan could not help himself. He was leaning back and roaring.

"Alan Campbell!"

"I can't help it," protested Alan, wiping the tears out of his eyes. "It just occurs to me that you'll have to marry me after all."

"Can I announce that?" asked Swan instantly.

"Alan Campbell, what on earth do you mean? I'll do no such thing! The idea!"

"You can't help yourself, my wench. It's the only solution to our difficulties. I have not yet read the *Daily Floodlight,* but I have my suspicions as to the nature of the hints that will have appeared there."

Swan seized on this.

"I knew you wouldn't be sore," he said, his face lighting up. "There's nothing anybody could object to, I swear! I never said a word about your always going to bawdy houses. That's really libelous anyway—"

"What's this," inquired Kathryn, breaking off with some quickness, "about you going to bawdy houses?"

"I'm sorry I said that," interposed Swan, with equal quickness. "I wouldn't have said it for the world in front of you, Miss Campbell, only it slipped out. It probably isn't true anyway, so just forget it. All I wanted to say was that I've got to play the game straight both with you and the public."

"Are ye comin'?" asked Kirstie, stil waiting patiently in the doorway.

Swan straightened his tie.

"Yes, we are. And I know Colin Campbell, who's as good an egg as ever walked, will understand my position."

"I hope he does," breathed Kathryn. "Oh, good heavens, I hope he does! You did say he'd got some whisky up there, didn't you Kirstie?"

It was, in a sense, unnecessary to answer this question. As the three of them followed Kirstie up the stairs, and along the hall to the back of the house, it was answered by Colin himself. The doors at Shira were good thick doors, and very little in the nature of noise could penetrate far through them. The voice they heard, therefore, was not very loud. But it carried distinctly to the head of the stairs.

> *"I love a lassie, a boh-ny, boh-ny lassie;*
>   *She's as puir as the li-ly in the dell!*
>   *She's as sweet as the heather, the boh-ny pur-ple*
>   *heath-er—"*

The singing stopped abruptly as Kirstie opened the door. In a spacious back bedroom with oak furniture, Colin Campbell lay on what should have been, and undoubtedly was, a bed of pain. But you would never have guessed this from the demeanor of the tough old sinner.

His body was bandaged from the waist down, one leg supported a little above the level of the bed by a portable iron framework and supports. But his back was hunched into pillows in such a way that he could just raise his head.

Though his hair, beard, and mustache had been trimmed, he managed to look shaggier than ever. Out of this, fiercely affable eyes peered from a flushed face. The airless room smelt like a distillery.

Colin had insisted, as an invalid, on having plenty of light, and the chandelier glowed with bulbs. They illuminated his truculent grin, his gaudy pajama tops, and the untidy litter of articles on the bedside table. His bed was drawn up by one blacked-out window.

"Come in!" he shouted. "Come in, and keep the old crock company. Filthy position to be in. Kirstie, go and fetch three more glasses and another decanter. You! The rest of you! Pull up your chairs. Here, where I can see you. I've got nothing to do but this."

He was dividing his attention between the decanter, somewhat depleted, and a very light 20-bore shotgun, which he was attempting to clean and oil.

Chapter 18

"KITTY-KAT MY DEAR, it's a pleasure to see your face," he continued, holding up the gun so that he could look at her through one of the barrels. "What have you been up to now? I say. Would you like to point out something to me, so that I could have a shot at it?"

Swan took one look at him, turned round, and made a beeline for the door.

Kathryn instantly turned the key in the lock, and held tightly to it as she backed away.

"Indeed I would, Uncle Colin," said Kathryn sweetly.

"That's my Kitty-kat. And how are you, Alan? And you, Horace Greeley: how are *you*? I'm filthy, I don't mind telling you. Swaddled up like a blooming Chinese woman, though they've got more of me than just my feet. God's wounds! If they'd only give me a *chair,* I could at least move about."

He reflected.

Snapping shut the breech of the shotgun, he lowered it to stand against the side of the bed.

"I'm happy," he added abruptly. "Maybe I shouldn't be, but I am. You've heard, haven't you, about what happened to me? Artificial ice. Same as Angus. It was murder, after all. It's a pity about poor old Alec Forbes, though. I never did dislike the fellow. Stop a bit. Where's Fell? Why isn't Fell here? What have you done with Fell?"

Katheryn was grimly determined.

"He's out with the Home Guard, Uncle Colin. Listen. There's something we've got to tell you. This wretch of a reporter, after promising—"

"What the devil does he want to go joining the Home Guard for, at *his* age and weight? They may not pot him for a parachutist; but if they see him against the sky line they'll ruddy well pot him for a parachute. It's crazy. It's worse than that: it's downright dangerous."

"Uncle Colin, *will* you listen to me, please?"

"Yes, my dear, of course. Joining the Home Guard! Never heard such nonsense in my life!"

"This reporter—"

"He didn't say anything about it when he was in here a while ago. All he wanted to do was ask a lot of questions about poor old Rabbie; and what we'd all been saying up in the tower room on Monday. Besides, how could he get into the Home Guard in Scotland? Are you pulling my leg?"

Kathryn's expression was by this time so desperate that even Colin noticed it. He broke off, peering shaggily at her.

"Nothing wrong, is there, Kitty-kat?"

"Yes, there is. That is, if you'd just listen to me for a moment! Do you remember that Mr. Swan promised not to say a word about anything that happened here, if we let him get what stories he wanted?"

Colin's eyebrows drew together.

"God's wounds! You didn't print in that rag of yours that we stuck you in the seat of the pants with a claymore?"

"No, so help me I didn't!" returned Swan, instantly and with patent truth. "I didn't say a word about it. I've got the paper, and I can prove it."

"Then what's biting you, Kitty-kat?"

"He's said, or intimated, dreadful things about Alan and me. I don't know exactly what; and Alan doesn't even seem to care; but it's something about Alan and me being immoral together—"

Colin stared at her. Then he leaned back and bellowed with laughter. The mirth brought tears into his eyes.

"Well, aren't you?"

"No! Just because of a dreadful accident, just because we *had* to spend the night in the same compartment on the train from London—"

"You didn't have to spend the night in the same room here on Monday," Colin pointed out. "But you ruddy well did. Eh?"

"They spent the night in the same room here?" Swan demanded quickly.

"Of course they did," roared Colin. "Come on, Kitty-kat! Be a man! I mean, be a woman! Admit it! Have the courage of your convictions. What were you doing, then, if you weren't improving your time? Nonsense!"

"You see, Miss Campbell," pleaded Swan, "I had to get the sex angle into the story somehow, and that was the only way to do it. *He* understands. Your boy friend understands. There's nothing at all to worry about, not the least little thing."

Kathryn looked from one to the other of them. An expression of hopeless despair went over her pink face. Tears came into her eyes, and she sat down in a chair and put her face in her hands.

"Here! Easy!" said Alan. "I've just been pointing out to her, Colin, that her reputation is hopelessly compromised unless she marries me now. I asked her to marry me—"

"You never did."

"Well, I do so now, in front of witnesses. Miss Campbell: will you do me the honor of becoming my wife."

Kathryn raised a tear-stained face of exasperation.

"Of course I will, you idiot!" she stormed at him. "But why couldn't you do it decently, as I've given you a hundred opportunities to, instead of blackmailing me into it? Or saying I blackmailed you into it?"

Colin's eyes opened wide.

"Do you mean," he bellowed delightedly, "there's going to be a wedding?"

"Can I print that?"

"Yes to both questions," replied Alan.

"My dear Kitty-kat! My dear fellow! By George!" said Colin, rubbing his hands. "This calls for such a celebration as these walls haven't seen since the night Elspat's virtue fell in 1900. Where's Kirstie with that decanter? God's wounds! I wonder if there are any bagpipes in the house? I haven't tried 'em for years, but what I could do once would warm the cockles of your heart."

"You're not mad at *me*?" asked Swan anxiously.

"At you? Great Scott, no! Why should I be? Come over here, old chap, and sit down!"

"Then what," persisted Swan, "did you want that toy shotgun for?"

" 'Toy' shotgun, is it? 'Toy' shotgun?" Colin snatched up the 20-bore. "Do you know it takes a devil of a lot more skill and accuracy to use this than it does a 12-bore? Don't believe that, eh? Like me to show you?"

"No, no, no. I'll take your word for it!"

"That's better. Come and have a drink. No, we haven't got any glasses. Where's Kirstie? And Elspat! We've got to have Elspat here. Elspat!"

Kathryn was compelled to unlock the door. Swan, with an expiring sigh of relief, sat down and stretched his legs like one completely at home. He sprang up again with deep suspicion when Elspat appeared.

Elspat, however, ignored him with such icy pointedness

that he backed away. Elspat gave them each in turn, except Swan, an unfathomable glance. Her eyelids were puffed and reddish, and her mouth was a straight line. Alan tried to see in her some resemblance to the handsome woman of the old photograph; but it was gone, all gone.

"Look here, old girl," said Colin. He stretched out his hand to her. "I've got great news. Glorious news. These two,"—he pointed—"are going to get married."

Elspat did not say anything. Her eyes rested on Alan, studying him. Then they moved to Kathryn, studying her for a long time. She went over to Kathryn, and quickly kissed her on the cheek. Two tears, amazing tears, over-flowed Elspat's eyes.

"Here, I say!" Colin stirred uncomfortably. Then he glared. "It's the same old family custom," he complained in a querulous voice. "Always turn on the waterworks when there's going to be a wedding. This is a *happy* occasion, hang it! Stop that!"

Elspat still remained motionless. Her face worked.

"If you don't stop that, I'm going to throw something," yelled Colin. "Can't you say, 'Congratulations,' or any-thing like that? Have we got any pipes in the house, by the way?"

"Ye'll hae no godless merriment here, Colin Campbell," snapped Elspat, choking out the words despite her working face. She fought back by instinct, while Alan's discomfort increased.

"Aye, I'll gie ye ma blessing," she said, looking first at Kathryn and then at Alan. "If the blessin' of an auld snaggletooth body's worth a groat tae ye."

"Well, then," said Colin sulkily, "we can at least have the whisky. You'll drink their health, I hope?"

"Aye. I caud du wi' that tonight. The de'il's walkin' on ma grave." She shivered.

"I never saw such a lot of killjoys in all my born days," grumbled Colin. But he brightened as Kirstie brought in the glasses and a decanter. "One more glass, my wench. Stop a bit. Maybe we'd better have a third decanter, eh?"

"Just a moment!" said Alan. He looked round at them and, in some uneasiness, at the shotgun. "You're not proposing another binge tonight, are you?"

"Binge! Nonsense!" said Colin, pouring himself a short one evidently to give him strength to pour for the others, and gulping it down. "Who said anything about a binge? We're drinking health and happiness to the bride, that's all. You can't object to that, can you?"

"*I* can't," smiled Kathryn.

"Nor me," observed Swan. "I feel grand!" Swan added. "I forgive everybody. I even forgive madam,"—he hesitated, for he was clearly frightened of Elspat—"for ruining a suit that cost me ten guineas."

Colin spoke persuasively.

"See here, Elspat. I'm sorry about Angus. But there it is. And it's turned out for the best. If he had to die, I don't mind admitting it's got me out of a bad financial hole.

"Do you know what I'm going to do? No more doctoring in Manchester, for the moment. I'm going to get a ketch and go for a cruise in the South Seas. And you, Elspat. You can get a dozen big pictures painted of Angus, and look at 'em all day. Or you can go to London and see the jitterbugs. You're safe, old girl."

Elspat's face was white.

"Aye," she blazed at him. *"And d'ye ken why we're safe?"*

"Steady!" cried Alan.

Even in his mist of good will and exhilaration, he knew what was coming. Kathryn knew too. They both made a move toward Elspat, but she paid no attention.

"I'll hae ma conscience nae mair damned wi' lees. D'ye ken why we're safe?"

She whirled round to Swan. Addressing him for the first time, she announced calmly that Angus had killed himself; she poured out the entire story, with her reasons for believing it. And every word of it was true.

"Now that's very interesting, ma'am," said Swan, who had taken one glass of whisky and was holding out his tumbler for a second. He appeared flattered by her attention. "Then you're not mad at me any longer either?"

Elspat stared at him.

"Mad at ye? Hoots! D'ye hear what I'm saying?"

"Yes, of course, ma'am," Swan replied soothingly. "And of course I understand how this thing has upset you ——"

"Mon, dinna ye believe me?"

Swan threw back his head and laughed.

"I hate to contradict a lady, ma'am. But if you'll just have a word with the police, or with Dr. Fell, or with these people here, you'll see that either somebody has been kidding you or you've been kidding yourself. I ought to know, oughtn't I? Hasn't anybody told you that Alec Forbes killed himself, and left a note admitting he killed Mr. Campbell?"

Elspat drew in her breath. Her face wrinkled up. She turned and looked at Colin, who nodded.

"It's true, Elspat. Come abreast of the times! Where have you been all day?"

It stabbed Alan to the heart to see her. She groped over to a chair and sat down. A human being, a sentient, living, hurt human being, emerged from behind the angry clay in which Elspat set her face to the world.

"Ye're no' deceivin' me?" she insisted. "Ye swear to the Guid Man ——!"

Then she began to swing back and forth in the rocking chair. She began to laugh, showing that she had fine teeth; and it kindled and illumined her face. Her whole being seemed to breathe a prayer.

Angus had not died in the sin of suicide. He had not gone to the bad place. And Elspat, this Elspat whose real surname nobody knew, rocked back and forth and laughed and was happy.

Colin Campbell, serenely missing all this, was still acting as barman.

"You understand," he beamed, "neither Fell nor I ever for a minute thought it *was* suicide. Still, it's just as well to get the whole thing tidied up. I never for a second thought you didn't know, or I'd have crawled off this bed to tell you. Now be a good sport. I know this is still officially a house of mourning. But, under the circumstances, what about getting me those pipes?"

Elspat got to her feet and went out of the room.

"By Jupiter," breathed Colin, "she's gone to get 'em! . . . What ails you, Kitty-kat?"

Kathryn regarded the door with uncertain, curiously shining eyes. She bit her lip. Her eyes moved over toward Alan.

"I don't know," she answered. "I'm happy,"—here she glared at Alan—"and yet I feel all sort of funny and mixed up."

"Your English grammar," said Alan, "is abominable. But your sentiments are correct. That's what she believes now; and that's what Elspat has got to go on believing. Because, of course, it's true."

"Of course," agreed Kathryn quickly. "I wonder, Uncle Colin, whether you would do me a big favor?"

"Anything in the world, my dear."

"Well," said Kathryn, hesitantly extending the tumbler, "it isn't very much, perhaps; but would you mind making my drink just a *little* stronger?"

"Now that's my Kitty-kat!" roared Colin. "Here you are . . . Enough?"

"A little more, please."

"A little *more*?"

"Yes, please."

"Cripes," muttered Swan, on whom the first smashing, shuddering effect of the Doom of the Campbells had now passed to a quickened speech and excitement, "you two professors are teamed up right. I don't understand how you do it. Does anybody (maybe, now?) feel like a song?"

Beatific with his head among the pillows, as though enthroned in state, Colin lifted the shotgun and waved it in the air as though conducting an orchestra. His bass voice beat against the windows.

"I love a lassie, a boh-ny, boh-ny las-sie—"

Swan, drawing his chin far into his collar, assumed an air of solemn portentousness. Finding the right pitch after a preliminary cough, he moved his glass gently in time and joined in.

"She's as pure as the li-ly in the dell—!"

To Alan, lifting his glass in a toast to Kathryn, there came a feeling that all things happened for the best; and that tomorrow could take care of itself. The exhilaration of being in love, the exhilaration of merely watching Kathryn, joined with the exhilaration of the potent brew in his hand. He smiled at Kathryn; she smiled back; and they both joined in.

"She's as sweet as the heath-er, the boh-ny pur-ple heather—"

He had a good loud baritone, and Kathryn a fairly audible soprano. Their quartet made the room ring. To Aunt Elspat, returning with a set of bagpipes—which she grimly handed to Colin, and which he eagerly seized without breaking off the song—it must have seemed that old days had returned.

"A'weel," said Aunt Elspat resignedly. "A'weel!"

Chapter 19

ALAN CAMPBELL OPENED ONE EYE.

From somewhere in remote distances, muffled beyond sight or sound, his soul crawled back painfully, through subterranean corridors, up into his body again. Toward the last it moved to the conviction that he was looking at a family photograph album, from which there stared back at him a face he had seen, somewhere, only today . . .

Then he was awake.

The first eye was bad enough. But, when he opened the second eye, such a rush of anguish flowed through his brain that he knew what was wrong with him, and realized fairly that he had done it again.

He lay back and stared at the cracks on the ceiling. There was sunlight in the room.

He had a violent headache, and his throat was dry. But it occurred to him in a startled sort of way that he did not feel nearly as bad as he had felt the first time. This prompted an uneasy flash of doubt. Did the infernal stuff take hold of you? Was it (as the temperance tracts said) an insidious poison whose effects seemed to grow less day by day?

Then another feeling, heartening or disheartening according to how you viewed the stuff, took possession of him.

When he searched his memory he could recall nothing except blurred scenes which seemed to be dominated by the noise of bagpipes, and a vision of Elspat swinging back and forth beatifically in a rocking chair amidst it.

Yet no sense of sin oppressed him, no sense of guilt or enormity. He *knew* that his conduct had been such as becomes a gentleman, even *en pantoufles*. It was a strange conviction, but a real one. He did not even quail when Kathryn opened the door.

On the contrary, this morning it was Kathryn who appeared guilty and hunted. On the tray she carried not one cup of black coffee, but two. She put the tray on the bedside table, and looked at him.

"It ought to be you," she said, after clearing her throat, "who brought this to me this morning. But I knew you'd be disgusting and sleep past noon. I suppose you don't remember anything about last night either?"

He tried to sit up, easing the throb in his head.

"Well, no. Er—I wasn't ——?"

"No, you were not. Alan Campbell, there never was such a stuffed shirt as you who ever lived. You just sat and beamed as though you owned the earth. But you *will* quote poetry. When you began on Tennyson, I feared the worst. You recited the whole of 'The Princess,' and nearly all of 'Maud.' When you actually had the face to quote that bit about 'Put thy sweet hand in mine and trust in me,' and patted my hand as you did it—well, really!"

Averting his eyes, he reached after the coffee.

"I wasn't aware I knew so much Tennyson."

"You didn't, really. But when you couldn't remember, you just thought for a moment, and then said, 'Umble-bumble, umble-bumble,' and went on."

"Never mind. At least, we were all right?"

Kathryn lowered the cup she had raised to her lips. The cup rattled and clicked on its saucer.

"All right?" she repeated with widening eyes. "When that wretch Swan is probably in a hospital now?"

Alan's head gave a violent throb.

"We didn't ——?"

"No, not you. Uncle Colin."

"My God, he didn't assault Swan again? But they're great pals! He couldn't have assaulted Swan again! What happened?"

"Well, it was all right until Colin had about his fifteenth Doom; and Swan, who was also what he called 'canned' and a little too cocksure, brought out the newspaper article he wrote yesterday. He'd smuggled the paper in in case we didn't like it."

"Yes?"

"It wasn't so bad, really. I admit that. Everything was all right until Swan described how Colin had decided to sleep in the tower room."

"Yes?"

"Swan's version of the incident ran something like this. You remember, he was hanging about outside the sitting-room windows? His story said: 'Dr. Colin Campbell, a deeply religious man, placed his hand on the Bible and swore an oath that he would not enter the church again until the family ghost had ceased to walk in the melancholy Castle of Shira.' For about ten seconds Colin just looked at him. Then he pointed to the door and said, 'Out.' Swan didn't understand until Colin turned completely purple and said, 'Out of this house and stay out.' Colin grabbed his shotgun, and ——"

"He didn't ——?"

"Not just then. But when Swan leaped downstairs, Colin said, 'Turn out the light and take down the blackout. I want to get him from the window as he goes up the road.' His bed is by the window, you remember."

"You don't mean to say Colin shot Swan in the seat of the pants as he ran for Inveraray?"

"No," answered Kathryn. "Colin didn't. *I* did."

Her voice became a wail.

"Alan darling, we've *got* to get out of this insidious country. First you, and now me. I don't know what's come over me; I honestly don't!"

Alan's head was aching still harder.

"But wait a minute! Where was I? Didn't I interfere?"

"You didn't even notice. You were reciting 'Sir Galahad' to Elspat. The rain had cleared off—it was four o'clock in the morning—and the moon was up. I was boiling angry with Swan, you see. And there he was in the road.

"He must have heard the window go up, and seen the moonlight on the shotgun. Because he gave one look, and never ran so fast even on the Monday night. I said, 'Uncle Colin, let *me* have a go.' He said, 'All right; but let him get a sporting distance away; we don't want to hurt him.' Ordinarily I'm frightened of guns, and I couldn't have hit the side of a barn door. But that wretched stuff made everything different. I loosed off blindly, and got a bull's-eye with the second barrel.

"Alan, do you think he'll have me arrested? And don't you *dare* laugh, either!"

" 'Pompilia, will you let them murder me?' " murmured Alan. He finished his coffee, propped himself upright, and steadied a swimming world. "Never mind," he said. "I'll go and smooth him down."

"But suppose I ——?"

Alan studied the forlorn figure.

"You couldn't have hurt him much. Not at a distance, with a twenty-bore and a light load. He didn't fall down, did he?"

"No; he only ran harder."

"Then it's all right."

"But what am I to *do*?"

" 'Put thy sweet hand in mine and trust in me.' "

"Alan Campbell!"

"Well, isn't it the proper course?"

Kathryn sighed. She walked to the window, and looked down over the loch. Its waters were peaceful, a-gleam in sunshine.

"And that," she told him, after a pause, "isn't all."

"Not more ——!"

"No, no, no! Not more trouble of that kind, anyway. I got the letter this morning. Alan, I've been recalled."

"Recalled?"

"From my holiday. By the college. A.R.P. I also saw this morning's Scottish *Daily Express*. It looks as though the real bombing is going to begin."

The sunlight was as fair, the hills as golden and purple, as ever. Alan took a packet of cigarettes from the bedside table. He lit one and inhaled smoke. Though it made his head swim, he sat contemplating the loch and smoking steadily.

"So our holiday," he said, "is a kind of entr'acte."

"Yes," said Kathryn, without turning round. "Alan, *do* you love me?"

"You know I do."

"Then do we care?"

"No."

There was a silence.

"When have you got to go?" he asked presently.

"Tonight, I'm afraid. That's what the letter says."

"Then," he declared briskly, "we can't waste any more time. The sooner I get my own things packed, the better. I hope we can get adjoining sleepers on the train. We've done all we can do here anyway, which wasn't much to start with. The case, officially, is closed. All the same—I should have liked to see the real end of it, if there is an end."

"You may see the end of it yet," Kathryn told him, and turned round from the window.

"Meaning what?"

She wrinkled up her forehead, and her nervous manner was not entirely due to her apprehensions about the night before.

"You see," she went on, "Dr. Fell is here. When I told him I had to go back tonight, he said he had every reason to believe he would be going as well. I said, 'But what about you-know?' He said, 'You-know will, I think, take care of itself.' But he said it in a queer way that made me think there's something going on. Something—rather terrible. He didn't come back here until nearly dawn this morning. He wants to see you, by the way."

"I'll be dressed in half a tick. Where is everybody else this morning?"

"Colin's still asleep. Elspat, even Kirstie, are out. There's nobody here but you and me and Dr. Fell. Alan, it isn't hangover and it isn't Swan and it isn't nerves. But— I'm frightened. Please come downstairs as quick as you can."

He told himself, when he nicked his face in shaving, that this was due to the brew of the night before. He told himself that his own apprehensions were caused by an upset stomach and the misadventures of Swan.

Shira was intensely quiet. Only the sun entered. When you turned on a tap, or turned it off, ghostly clankings went down through the house and shivered away. And, as Alan went down to get his breakfast, he saw Dr. Fell in the sitting room.

Dr. Fell, in his old black alpaca suit and string tie, occupied the sofa. He was sitting in the warm, golden sunlight, the meerschaum pipe between his teeth, and his expression far away. He had the air of a man who meditates a dangerous business and is not quite sure of his course. The ridges of his waistcoat rose and fell with slow, gentle wheezings. His big mop of gray-streaked hair had fallen over one eye.

Alan and Kathryn shared buttered toast and more coffee. They did not speak much. Neither knew quite what to do. It was like the feeling of not knowing whether you had been summoned to the headmaster's study, or hadn't.

But the question was solved for them.

"Good morning!" called a voice.

They hurried out into the hall.

Alistair Duncan, in an almost summery and skittish-looking brown suit, was standing at the open front door. He wore a soft hat and carried a brief case. He raised his hand to the knocker of the open door, as though by way of illustration.

"There did not seen to be anybody about," he said. His voice, though meant to be pleasant, had a faint irritated undertone.

Alan glanced to the right. Through the open door of the sitting room he could see Dr. Fell stir, grunt, and lift his head as though roused out of sleep. Alan looked back to the tall, stoop-shouldered figure of the lawyer, framed against the shimmering loch outside.

"*May* I come in?" inquired Duncan politely.

"P-please do," stammered Kathryn.

"Thank you." Duncan stepped in gingerly, removing his hat. He went to the door of the sitting room, glanced in, and uttered an exclamation which might have been satisfaction or annoyance.

"Please come in here," rumbled Dr. Fell. "All of you, if you will. And close the door."

The usual odor as of damp oilcloth, of old wood and stone, was brought out by the sun in that stuffy room. Angus's photograph, still draped in crepe, faced them from the overmantel. Sun made tawdry the dark, bad daubs of the pictures in their gilt frames, and picked out worn places in the carpet.

"My dear sir," said the lawyer, putting down his hat and brief case on the table which held the Bible. He spoke the words as though he were beginning a letter.

"Sit down, please," said Dr. Fell.

A slight frown creased Duncan's high, semi-bald skull.

"In response to your telephone call," he replied, "here I am." He made a humorous gesture. "But may I point out, sir, that I am a busy man? I have been at this house, for one cause or another, nearly every day for the past week. And, grave as the issue has been, since it is now settled ——"

"It is not settled," said Dr. Fell.

"But ——!"

"Sit down, all of you," said Dr. Fell.

Blowing a film of ash off his pipe, he settled back, returned the pipe to his mouth, and drew at it. The ash settled down across his waistcoat, but he did not brush it off. He eyed them for a long time, and Alan's uneasiness had grown to something like a breath of fear.

"Gentlemen, and Miss Campbell," continued Dr. Fell, drawing a long sniff through his nose. "Yesterday afternoon, if you remember, I spoke of a million-to-one chance. I did not dare to hope for much from it. Still, it had come off in Angus's case and I hoped it might come off in Forbes's. It did."

He paused, and added in the same ordinary tone:

"I now have the instrument with which, in a sense, Alec Forbes was murdered."

The deathlike stillness of the room, while tobacco smoke curled up past starched lace curtains in the sunlight, lasted only a few seconds.

"Murdered?" the lawyer exploded.

"Exactly."

"You will pardon me if I suggest that ——"

"Sir," interrupted Dr. Fell, taking the pipe out of his mouth, "in your heart of hearts you know that Alec Forbes was murdered, just as you know that Angus Campbell committed suicide. Now don't you?"

Duncan took a quick look around him.

"It's quite all right," the doctor assured him. "We four are all alone here—as yet. I have seen to that. You are at liberty to speak freely."

"I have no intention of speaking, either freely or otherwise." Duncan's voice was curt. "Did you bring me all the way out here just to tell me that? Your suggestion is preposterous!"

Dr. Fell sighed.

"I wonder whether you will think it is so preposterous," he said, "if I tell you the proposal I mean to make."

"Proposal?"

"Bargain. Deal, if you like."

"There is no question of a bargain, my dear sir. You told me yourself that this is an open-and-shut case, a plain case. The police believe as much. I saw Mr. MacIntyre, the Procurator Fiscal, this morning."

"Yes. That is a part of my bargain."

Duncan was almost on the edge of losing his temper.

"Will you kindly tell me, Doctor, what it is you wish of me: if anything? And particularly where you got this wicked and indeed dangerous notion that Alec Forbes was murdered?"

Dr. Fell's expression was vacant.

"I got it first," he responded, puffing out his cheeks, "from a piece of blackout material—tar paper on a wooden frame—which should have been up at the window in Forbes's cottage, and yet wasn't.

"The blackout *had been* up at the window during the night, else the lantern light would have been seen by the Home Guard. And the lantern (if you remember the evidence) *had been* burning. Yet for some reason it was necessary to extinguish the lantern and take down the blackout from the window.

"Why? That was the problem. As was suggested to me at the time, why didn't the murderer simply leave the lantern burning, and leave the blackout in its place, when he made his exit? At first sight it seemed rather a formidable problem.

"The obvious line of attack was to say that the mur-

derer had to take down the blackout in order to make his
escape; and, once having made it, he couldn't put the
blackout back up again. That is a very suggestive line, if
you follow it up. Could he, for instance, somehow have got
through a steel-mesh grating, and somehow replace it
afterwards?"

Duncan snorted.

"The grating being nailed up on the inside?"

Dr. Fell nodded very gravely.

"Yes. Nailed up. So the murderer couldn't very well
have done *that,* could he?"

Duncan got to his feet.

"I am sorry, sir, that I cannot remain to listen to these
preposterous notions any longer. Doctor, you shock me.
The very idea that Forbes ———"

"Don't you want to hear what my proposal is?" suggested Dr. Fell. He paused. "It will be much to your
advantage." He paused again. "Very much to your
advantage."

In the act of taking his hat and brief case from the little
table, Duncan dropped his hands and straightened up. He
looked back at Dr. Fell. His face was white.

"God in heaven!" he whispered. "You do not suggest
—ah—that *I* am the murderer, do you?"

"Oh, no," replied Dr. Fell. "Tut, tut! Certainly not."

Alan breathed easier.

It was the same idea which had occurred to him, all the
more sinister for the overtones in Dr. Fell's voice. Duncan
ran a finger round inside his loose collar.

"I am glad," he said, with an attempt at humorous
dryness, "I am glad, at least to hear that. Now, come sir!
Let's have the cards on the table. What sort of proposition
have you which could possibly interest me?"

"One which concerns the welfare of your clients. In
short, the Campbell family." Again Dr. Fell leisurely blew
a film of ash off his pipe. "You see, I am in a position to
prove that Alec Forbes was murdered."

Duncan dropped hat and brief case on the table as
though they had burnt him.

"Prove it? How?"

"Because I have the instrument which was, in a sense, used to murder him."

"But Forbes was hanged with a dressing-gown cord!"

"Mr. Duncan, if you will study the best criminological authorities, you will find them agreed on one thing. Nothing is more difficult to determine than the question of whether a man has been hanged, or whether he has first been strangled and then hung up afterwards to simulate hanging. That is what happened to Forbes.

"Forbes was taken from behind and strangled. With what, I don't know. A necktie. Perhaps a scarf. Then those artistic trappings were all arranged by a murderer who knew his business well. If such things are done with care, the result cannot be told from a genuine suicide. This murderer made only one mistake, which was unavoidable. But it was fatal.

"Ask yourself again, with regard to that grated window ——"

Duncan stretched out his hands as though in supplication.

"But what is this mysterious 'evidence'? And who is this mysterious 'murderer'?" His eye grew sharp. "You know who it is?"

"Oh, yes," said Dr. Fell.

"You are not in a position," said the lawyer, rapping his knuckles on the table, "to prove Angus Campbell committed suicide."

"No. Yet if Forbes's death is proved to be murder, that surely invalidates the false confession left behind? A confession conveniently written on a typewriter, which could have been written by anybody and was actually written by the murderer. What will the police think then?"

"What are you suggesting to me, exactly?"

"Then you will hear my proposition?"

"I will hear anything," returned the lawyer, going across to a chair and sitting down with his big-knuckled hands clasped together, "if you give me some line of direction.

Who is this murderer?"

Dr. Fell eyed him.

"You have no idea?"

"None, I swear! And I—ah—still retain the right to disbelieve every word you say. *Who* is this murderer?"

"As a matter of fact," replied Dr. Fell, "I think the murderer is in the house now, and should be with us at any minute."

Kathryn glanced rather wildly at Alan.

It was very warm in the room. A late fly buzzed against one bright windowpane behind the starched curtains. In the stillness they could distinctly hear the noise of footsteps as someone walked along the hall toward the front.

"That should be our friend," continued Dr. Fell in the same unemotional tone. Then he raised his voice and shouted. *"We're in the sitting room! Come and join us!"*

The footsteps hesitated, turned and came toward the door of the room.

Duncan got to his feet, spasmodically. His hands were clasped together, and Alan could hear the knuckle joints crack as he pressed them.

Between the time they first heard the footsteps, and the time that the knob turned and the door opened, was perhaps five or six seconds. Alan has since computed it as the longest interval of his life. Every board in the room seemed to have a separate creak and crack; everything seemed alive and aware and insistent like the droning fly against the windowpane.

The door opened, and a certain person came in.

"That's the murderer," said Dr. Fell.

He was pointing to Mr. Walter Chapman, of the Hercules Insurance Company.

Chapter 20

EVERY DETAIL of Chapman's appearance was picked out by the sunlight. The short, broad figure clad in a dark blue suit. The fair hair, the fresh complexion, the curiously pale eyes. One hand held his bowler hat, the other was at his necktie, fingering it. He had moved his head to one side as though dodging.

"I beg your pardon?" he said in a somewhat shrill voice.

"I said, come in, Mr. Chapman," answered Dr. Fell. "Or should I say Mr. Campbell? Your real name is Campbell, isn't it?"

"What the devil are you talking about? I don't understand you."

"Two days ago," said Dr. Fell, "when I first set eyes on you, you were standing in much the same place as now. I was standing over by that window there (remember?), making an intense study of a full-face photograph of Angus Campbell.

"We had not been introduced. I lifted my eyes from studying the photograph; and I was confronted by such a startling, momentary family likeness that I said to you, *'Which Campbell are you?'*"

Alan remembered it.

In his imagination, the short, broad figure before him became the short, broad figure of Colin or Angus Campbell. The fair hair and washed-out eyes became (got it!) the fair hair and washed-out eyes of that photograph of Robert Campbell in the family album. All these things wavered and changed and were distorted like images in water, yet folded together to form a composite whole in the solid person before them.

"Does he remind you of anyone *now,* Mr. Duncan?" inquired Dr. Fell.

The lawyer weakly subsided into his chair. Or, rather, his long lean limbs seemed to collapse like a clothes horse as he groped for and found the arms of the chair.

"Rabbie Campbell," he said. It was not an exclamation, or a question, or any form of words associated with emotion; it was the statement of a fact. "You're Rabbie Campbell's son," he said.

"I must insist—" the alleged Chapman began, but Dr. Fell cut him short.

"The sudden juxtaposition of Angus's photograph and this man's face," pursued the doctor, "brought a suggestion which may have been overlooked by some of you. Let me refresh your memory on another point."

He looked at Alan and Kathryn.

"Elspat told you, I think, that Angus Campbell had an uncanny flair for spotting family resemblances; so that he could tell one of his own branch even if the person 'blacked his face and spoke with a strange tongue.' This same flair is shared, though in less degree, by Elspat herself."

This time Dr. Fell looked at Duncan.

"Therefore it seemed to me very curious and interesting that, as you yourself are reported to have said, Mr. 'Chapman' always kept out of Elspat's way and would never under any circumstances go near her. It seemed to me worth investigating.

"The Scottish police can't use the resources of Scotland Yard. But I, through my friend Superintendent Hadley, can. It took only a few hours to discover the truth about Mr. Walter Chapman, though the transatlantic telephone call (official) Hadley put through afterwards did not get me a reply until the early hours of this morning."

Taking a scribbled envelope from his pocket, Dr. Fell blinked at it, and then adjusted his eyeglasses to stare at Chapman.

"Your real name is Walter Chapman Campbell. You hold, or held, passport number 609348 on the Union of

South Africa. Eight years ago you came to England from Port Elizabeth, where your father, Robert Campbell, is still alive: though very ill and infirm. You dropped the Campbell part of your name because your father's name had unpleasant associations with the Hercules Insurance Company, for which you worked.

"Two months ago (as you yourself are reported to have said) you were moved from England to be head of one of the several branches of your firm in Glasgow.

"There, of course, Angus Campbell spotted you."

Walter Chapman moistened his lips.

On his face was printed a fixed, skeptical smile. Yet his eyes moved swiftly to Duncan, as though wondering how the lawyer took this, and back again.

"Don't be absurd," Chapman said.

"You deny these facts, sir?"

"Granting," said the other, whose collar seemed inordinately tight, "granting that for reasons of my own I used only a part of my name, what for God's sake am I supposed to have done?"

He pounced a little, a gesture which reminded the watchers of Colin.

"I could also bear to know, Dr. Fell, why you and two Army officers woke me up at my hotel in Dunoon in the middle of last night, merely to ask some tomfool questions about insurance. But let that go. I repeat: what for God's sake am I supposed to have done?"

"You assisted Angus Campbell in planning his suicide," replied Dr. Fell; "you attempted the murder of Colin Campbell, and you murdered Alec Forbes."

The color drained out of Chapman's face.

"Absurd."

"You were not acquainted with Alec Forbes?"

"Certainly not."

"You have never been near his cottage by the Falls of Coe?"

"Never."

Dr. Fell's eyes closed. "In that case, you won't mind if

I tell you what I think you did.

"As you said yourself, Angus came to see you at your office in Glasgow when he took out his final insurance policy. My belief is that he had seen you before. That he taxed you with being his brother's son; that you denied it, but were ultimately compelled to admit it.

"And this, of course, gave Angus the final triple security for his scheme. Angus left *nothing* to chance. He knew your father for a thorough bad hat; and he was a good enough judge of men to diagnose you as a thorough bad hat too. So, when he took out that final, rather unnecessary policy as an excuse to hang about with you, he explained to you exactly what he meant to do. You would come to investigate a curious death. If there were *any* slip-up, any at all, you could always cover this up and point out that the death was murder because you knew what had really happened.

"There was every inducement for you to help Angus. He could point out to you that you were only helping your own family. That, with himself dead, only a sixty-five-year-old Colin stood between an inheritance of nearly eighteen thousand pounds to your own father; and ultimately, of course, to you. He could appeal to your family loyalty, which was Angus's only blind fetish.

"But it was not a fetish with you, Mr. Chapman Campbell. For you suddenly saw how you could play your own game.

"With Angus dead, and Colin dead as well . . ."

Dr. Fell paused.

"You see," he added, turning to the others, "the attempted murder of Colin made it fairly certain that our friend here must be the guilty person. Don't you recall that *it was Mr. Chapman, and nobody else, who drove Colin to sleep in the tower?*"

Alistair Duncan got to his feet, but sat down again.

The room was hot, and a small bead of sweat appeared on Chapman's forehead.

"Think back, if you will, to two conversations. One

took place in the tower room on Monday evening, and has been reported to me. The other took place in this room on Tuesday afternoon, and I was here myself.

"Who was the first person to introduce the word 'supernatural' into this affair? That word which always acts on Colin as a matador's cape acts on a bull? It was Mr. Chapman, if you recall. In the tower on Monday evening he deliberately—even irrelevantly—dragged it into the conversation, when nobody had suggested any such thing before.

"Colin swore there was no ghost. So, of course, our ingenious friend had to give him a ghost. I asked before: what was the reason for the mummery of the phantom Highlander with the caved-in face, appearing in the tower room on Monday night? The answer is easy. It was to act as the final, goading spur on Colin Campbell.

"The Masquerade wasn't difficult to carry out. This tower here is an isolated part of the house. It has a ground-floor entrance to the outside court, so that an outsider can come and go at will. That entrance is usually open; and, even if it isn't, an ordinary padlock key will do the trick. With the assistance of a plaid, a bonnet, a little wax and paint, the ghost 'appeared' to Jock Fleming. If Jock hadn't been there, anybody else would have done as well.

"And then?

"Bright and early on Wednesday, Mr. Chapman was ready. The ghost story was flying. He came here and (don't you remember?) pushed poor Colin clear over the edge by his remarks on the subject of ghosts.

"What was the remark which made Colin go off the deep end? What was the remark which made Colin say, 'That's torn it,' and swear his oath to sleep in the tower? It was Mr. Chapman's shy, sly little series of observations ending, 'This is a funny country and a funny house; and I tell you *I* shouldn't care to spend a night up in that room.' "

In Alan's memory the scene took form again.

Chapman's expression now, too, was much the same

as it had been. But now there appeared behind it an edge of desperation.

"It was absolutely necessary," pursued Dr. Fell, "to get Colin to sleep in the tower. True, the artificial-ice trick could have been worked anywhere. But it couldn't have been worked anywhere by *Chapman*.

"He couldn't go prowling through this house. The thing had to be done in that isolated tower, with an outside entrance for him to come and go. Just before Colin roared good night and staggered up all those stairs, Chapman could plant the box containing the ice and slip away.

"Let me recapitulate. Up to this time, of course, Chapman couldn't for a second pretend he had any glimmering of knowledge as to how Angus might have died. He had to pretend to be as puzzled as anybody else. He had to keep saying he thought it must be suicide; and rather a neat piece of acting it was.

"Naturally, no mention of artificial ice must creep in *yet*. Not yet. Otherwise the gaff would be blown and he couldn't lure Colin by bogey threats into sleeping in the tower. So he kept on saying that Angus must deliberately have committed suicide, thrown himself out of the window for no cause at all—as our friend did insist in some detail, over and over—or, if there were any cause, it was something damnable in the line of horrors.

"This was his game *up to the time Colin was disposed of*. Then everything would change.

"Then the apparent truth would come out with a roar. Colin would be found dead of carbon-dioxide poisoning. The artificial ice would be remembered. If it wasn't, our ingenious friend was prepared to remember it himself. Smiting his forehead, he would say that of course this was murder; and of course the insurance must be paid; and where was that fiend Alec Forbes, who had undoubtedly done it all?

"Therefore it was necessary *instantly,* on the same night

when Colin had been disposed of, to dispose of Alec Forbes."

Dr. Fell's pipe had gone out. He put it in his pocket, hooked his thumbs in the pockets of his waistcoat, and surveyed Chapman with dispassionate appraisal.

Alistair Duncan swallowed once or twice, the Adam's apple moving in his long throat.

"Can you—can you prove all this?" the lawyer asked in a thin voice.

"I don't have to prove it," said Dr. Fell, "since I can prove the murder of Forbes. To be hanged by the neck until you are dead, and may God have mercy upon your soul, is just as effective for one murder as for two. Isn't it, Mr. Chapman?"

Chapman had backed away.

"I—I may have spoken to Forbes once or twice—" he began, hoarsely and incautiously.

"Spoken to him!" said Dr. Fell. "You struck up quite an acquaintance with him, didn't you? You even warned him to keep out of the way. Afterwards it was too late.

"Up to this time your whole scheme had been triple foolproof. For, d'ye see, Angus Campbell really *had* committed suicide. When murder came to be suspected, the one person they couldn't possibly suspect was you; because you weren't guilty. I am willing to bet that for the night of Angus's death you have an alibi which stands and shines before all men.

"But you committed a bad howler when you didn't stay to make sure Colin was really dead after falling from the tower window on Tuesday night. And you made a still worse howler when you climbed into your car afterwards and drove out to the Falls of Coe for your last interview with Alec Forbes. What is the license number of your car, Mr. Chapman?"

Chapman winked both eyes at him, those curious light eyes which were the most disturbing feature of his face.

"Eh?"

"What is the license number of your car? It is,"—he

consulted the back of the envelope—"MGM 1911, isn't it?"

"I—I don't know. Yes, I suppose it is."

"A car bearing the number MGM 1911 was seen parked by the side of the road opposite Forbes's cottage between the hours of two and three o'clock in the morning. It was seen by a member of the Home Guard who is willing to testify to this. You should have remembered, sir, that these lonely roads are no longer lonely. You should have remembered how they are patrolled late at night."

Alistair Duncan's face was whiter yet.

"And that's the sum of your evidence?" the lawyer demanded.

"Oh, no," said Dr. Fell. "That's the least of it."

Wrinkling up his nose, he contemplated a corner of the ceiling.

"We now come to the problem of Forbes's murder," he went on, "and how the murderer managed to leave behind him a room locked up on the inside. Mr. Duncan, do you know anything about geometry?"

"Geometry?"

"I hasten to say," explained Dr. Fell, "that I know little of what I was once compelled to learn, and wish to know less. It belongs to the limbo of school days, along with algebra and economics and other dismal things. Beyond being unable to forget that the square of the hypotenuse is equal to the sum of the square of the other two sides, I have happily been able to rid my mind of this gibberish.

"At the same time it might be of value (for once in its life) if you were to think of Forbes's cottage in its geo-metrical shape." He took a pencil from his pocket and drew a design in the air with it. "The cottage is a square, twelve feet by twelve feet. Imagine, in the middle of the wall facing you, the door. Imagine, in the middle of the wall to your right, the window.

"I stood in the cottage yesterday; and I racked my brains over that infernal, tantalizing window.

"*Why* had it been necessary to take down the blackout?

It could not have been, as I indicated to you some minutes ago, because the murderer had in some way managed to get his corporeal body through the grated window. This, as the geometricians are so fond of saying (rather ill-manneredly, it always seemed to me) was absurd.

"The only other explanation was that the window had to be used in some way. I had examined the steel-wire grating closely, if you remember?" Dr. Fell turned to Alan.

"I remember."

"In order to test its solidity, I put my finger through one of the openings in the mesh and shook it. Still no glimmer of intelligence penetrated the thick fog of wool and mist which beclouded me. I remained bogged and sunk until you,"—here he turned to Kathryn—"passed on a piece of information which even to a dullard like myself gave a prod and a hint."

"I did?" cried Kathryn.

"Yes. You said the proprietress of the Glencoe Hotel told you Forbes often came out there to fish."

Dr. Fell spread out his hands. His thunderous voice was apologetic.

"Of course, all the evidences were there. The hut, so to speak, reeked of fishiness. Forbes's angler's creel was there. His flies were there. His gum boots were there. Yet it was only then, only then, when the fact occurred to me that in all that cottage I had seen no sign of a fishing *rod*.

"No rod, for instance, such as this."

Impelling himself to his feet with the aid of his stick, Dr. Fell reached round to the back of the sofa. He produced a large suitcase, and opened it.

Inside lay, piecemeal, the disjointed sections of a fishing rod, black metal with a nickel-and-cork grip into which were cut the initials, 'A.M.F.' But no line was wound round the reel. Instead, to the metal eyelet on what would have been the end or tip of the joined rod, had been fastened tightly with wire a small fishing hook.

"A neat instrument," explained Dr. Fell.

"The murderer strangled Forbes, catching him from

behind. He then strung Forbes up with those artistic indi-
cations of suicide. He turned out the lamp and poured
away the remaining oil so that it should seem to have
burned itself out. He took down the blackout.

"Then the murderer, carrying this fishing rod, walked
out of the hut by the door. He closed the door, leaving the
knob of the bolt turned uppermost.

"He went round to the window. Pushing the rod through
the mesh of the grating—there was plenty of room for it,
since I myself could easily get my forefinger through those
meshes—he stretched out the rod in a *diagonal* line, from
the window to the door.

"With this hook fastened to the tip of the rod, he caught
the knob of the bolt, and pulled toward him. It was a
bright, *new* bolt (remember?) so that it would shine by
(remember?) the moonlight, and he could easily see it.
Thus, with the greatest ease and simplicity, he pulled the
bolt toward him and fastened the door."

Dr. Fell put the suitcase carefully down on the sofa.

"Of course he had to take the blackout down from the
window, and, you see, could not now replace it. Also, it
was vitally necessary to take the rod away with him. The
handle and reel wouldn't go through the window in any
case; and, if he were to pitch the other parts in, his game
would be given away to the first spectator who arrived and
saw them.

"He then left the premises. He was seen and identified,
on getting into his car ———"

Chapman let out a strangled cry.

"—by the same Home Guard who had first been curious
about that car. On the way back, he took the rod apart and
threw away its pieces at intervals into the bracken. It
seemed too much to hope for a recovery of the rod; but, at
the request of Inspector Donaldson of the Argyllshire
County Constabulary, a search was made by the local unit
of the Home Guard."

Dr. Fell looked at Chapman.

"They're covered with your fingerprints, those pieces,"

he said, "as you probably remember. When I visited you at your hotel in the middle of the night, with the purpose of getting your prints on a cigarette case, you were at the same time identified as the man seen driving away from Forbes's cottage just after the time of the murder. Do you know what'll happen to you, my friend? You'll hang."

Walter Chapman Campbell stood with his fingers still twisting his necktie. His expression was like that of a small boy caught in the jam cupboard.

His fingers moved up, and touched his neck, and he flinched. In that hot room the perspiration was moving down his cheeks after the fashion of side whiskers.

"You're bluffing," he said, first clearing his throat for a voice that would not be steady. "It's not true, any of it, and you're bluffing!"

"You know I'm not bluffing. Your crime, I admit, was worthy of the son of the cleverest member of this family. With Angus and Colin dead, and Forbes blamed for it, you could go back quietly to Port Elizabeth. Your father is very ill and infirm. He would not last long as heir to nearly eighteen thousand pounds. You could then claim it without ever coming to England or Scotland at all, or being seen by anyone.

"But you won't claim it now, my lad. Do you think you've got a dog's chance of escaping the rope?"

Walter Chapman Campbell's hands went to his face.

"I didn't mean any harm," he said. "My God, I didn't mean any harm!" His voice broke. "You're not going to give me up to the police, are you?"

"No," said Dr. Fell calmly. "Not if you sign the document I propose to dictate to you."

The other's hands flew away from his face, and he stared with foggy hope. Alistair Duncan intervened.

"What, sir, is the meaning of this?" he asked harshly.

Dr. Fell rapped his open hand on the arm of the sofa.

"The meaning and purpose of this," he returned, "is to let Elspat Campbell live out her years and die happily without the conviction that Angus's soul is burning in hell.

The purpose is to provide for Elspat and Colin to the end of their lives as Angus wanted them provided for. That is all.

"You will copy out this document"—Dr. Fell took several sheets of paper from his pocket—"or else write at my dictation, the following confession. You will say that you deliberately murdered Angus Campbell . . ."

"What?"

"That you tried to murder Colin, and that you murdered Alec Forbes. That, with the evidence I shall present, will satisfy the insurance companies and the money will be paid. No, I know you didn't kill Angus! But you're going to say you did; and you have every motive for having done so.

"I can't cover you up, even if I wanted to. And I don't want, or mean to. But this much I can do. I can withhold that confession from the police for forty-eight hours, in time for you to make a getaway. Ordinarily you would have to get an exit permit to leave the country. But you're close to Clydeside; and I think you could find an obliging skipper to take you aboard an outgoing ship. If you do that, rest assured that in these evil days they won't bring you back.

"Do that, and I'll give you the leeway. Refuse to do it, and my evidence goes to the police within the next half-hour. What do you say?"

The other stared back.

Terror, befuddlement, and uncertainty merged into suspicious skepticism.

"I don't believe you!" shrilled Chapman. "How do I know you wouldn't take the confession and hand me over to the police straight away?"

"Because, if I were foolish enough to do that, you could upset the whole apple cart by telling the truth about Angus's death. You could deprive those two of the money and tell Elspat exactly what her cherished Angus actually did. You could prevent me from achieving the very thing I'm trying to achieve. If you depend on me, remember that I depend on you."

Again Chapman fingered his necktie. Dr. Fell took out a large gold watch and consulted it.

"This," Alistair Duncan said out of a dry throat, "is the most completely illegal, fraudulent—"

"That's it," stormed Chapman. "You wouldn't dare let me get away anyway! It's a trick! If you have that evidence and held up the confession, they'd have you as accessory after the fact!"

"I think not," said Dr. Fell, politely. "If you consult Mr. Duncan there, he will inform you that in Scots law there is no such thing as an accessory after the fact.

Duncan opened his mouth, and shut it again.

"Rest assured," pursued Dr. Fell, "that every aspect of my fraudulent villainy has been considered. I further propose that the real truth shall be known to us in this room, and to nobody else. That here and now we swear an oath of secrecy which shall last to the end of our days. Is that acceptable to everyone?"

"It is to me!" cried Kathryn.

"And to me," agreed Alan.

Duncan was standing in the middle of the room, waving his hands. If, thought Alan, you could imagine any such thing as a sputtering which was not funny, not even ludicrous, but only anguished and almost deathlike, that was his expression.

"I ask you," he said, "I ask you, sir, before it is too late, to stop and consider what you propose! It goes beyond all bounds! Can I, as a reputable professional man, sanction or even listen to this?"

Dr. Fell remained unimpressed.

"I hope so," he answered calmly. "Because it is precisely what I mean to carry out. I hope you of all people, Mr. Duncan, won't upset the apple cart you have pushed for so long and kept steady with such evident pain. Can't you, as a Scotsman, be persuaded to be sensible? Must you learn practicality from an Englishman?"

Duncan moaned in his throat.

"Then," said Dr. Fell, "I take it that you have given up

these romantic ideas of legal justice, and will row in the same boat with us. The question of life or death now lies entirely with Mr. Walter Chapman Campbell. I am not going on with this offer all day, my friend. Well, what do you say? Will you confess to two murders, and get away? Or will you deny both, and hang for one?"

The other shut his eyes, and opened them again.

He looked round the room as though he were seeing it for the first time. He looked out of the windows at the shimmering waters of the loch; at all the domain which was slipping away from him; but at a house cleansed and at peace.

"I'll do it," he said.

The 9:15 train from Glasgow to Euston slid into Euston only four hours late, on a golden sunshiny morning which dimmed even the cavernous grime of the station.

The train settled in and stopped amid a sigh of steam. Doors banged. A porter, thrusting his head into a first-class sleeping compartment, was depressed by the sight of two of the most prim, respectable (and probably low-tipping) stuffed shirts he had ever beheld.

One was a young lady, stern of mouth and lofty of expression, who wore shell-rimmed spectacles severely. The other was a professorial-looking man with an even more lofty expression.

"Porter, ma'am? Porter, sir?"

The young lady broke off to eye him.

"*If* you please," she said. "It will surely be evident to you, *Dr.* Campbell, that the Earl of Danby's memorandum, addressed to the French king and endorsed, 'I approve of this; C.R.,' by the king himself, can have been inspired by no such patriotic considerations as your unfortunate Tory interpretation suggests."

"This 'ere shotgun don't belong to you, ma'am, does it? Or to you sir?"

The gentleman eyed him vaguely.

"Er—yes," he said. "We are removing the evidence out of range of the ballistics authorities."

"Sir?"

But the gentleman was not listening.

"If you will cast your mind back, madam, to the speech made by Danby in the Commons in December, 1680, I feel that certain considerations of reason contained therein must penetrate even the cloud of prejudice with which you appear to have surrounded yourself. For example . . ."

Laden with the luggage, the porter trudged dispiritedly along the platform after them. *Floreat scientia!* The wheel had swung round again.